MW00791923

ALSO BY RICHARD PAUL EVANS

The Mistletoe Collection

The Mistletoe Promise

The Mistletoe Inn

The Walk Series

The Walk

Miles to Go

The Road to Grace

A Step of Faith

Walking on Water

The Four Doors

A Winter Dream

Lost December

Promise Me

The Christmas List

Grace

The Gift

Finding Noel

The Sunflower

A Perfect Day

The Last Promise

The Christmas Box Miracle

The Carousel

The Looking Glass

The Locket

The Letter

Timepiece

The Christmas Box

For Children and Young Adults

The Dance

The Christmas Candle

The Spyglass

The Tower

The Light of Christmas

The Michael Vey Series

Michael Vey: The Prisoner of Cell 25

Michael Vey 2: Rise of the Elgen

Michael Vey 3: Battle of the Ampere

Michael Vey 4: Hunt for Jade Dragon

Michael Vey 5: Storm of Lightning

Michael Vey 6: Fall of Hades

RICHARD PAUL EVANS

The Mistletoe Secret

SIMON & SCHUSTER

NEW YORK LONDON TORONTO SYDNEY NEW DELHI

Simon & Schuster
1230 Avenue of the Americas
New York, NY 10020

This book is a work of fiction. Any references to historical events, real people, or real places are used fictitiously. Other names, characters, places, and events are products of the author's imagination, and any resemblance to actual events or places or persons, living or dead, is entirely coincidental.

First Simon & Schuster hardcover edition November 2016

Manufactured in the United States of America

1 3 5 7 9 10 8 6 4 2

Library of Congress Cataloging-in-Publication Data is available.

ISBN 978-1-5011-1981-1
ISBN 978-1-5011-1982-8 (ebook)

✦ To Trish Todd ✦

With gratitude for your boundless patience.

It's been a pleasure working with you.

PROLOGUE

Aria winced as she picked up a half-eaten rice-paper egg roll that someone had smashed into the table's crystal centerpiece. "Really? Would you do that at your own home?" she mumbled to herself, then dropped the roll into the tub she was busing the table with. The diner she worked at occasionally catered weddings, and in a town as small as Midway, Aria always knew someone at the wedding—usually the bride or groom, if not both. At tonight's celebration the bride, Charise, was her boss's niece.

The bride had looked beautiful in her lace-topped, ivory satin dress. Beautiful *and* happy. Aria scolded herself for wondering how long it would last.

She remembered her own wedding day and the beautiful

dress she'd had to sell three months ago to make rent after her Jeep's alternator went out. Even though it hadn't been much of a wedding, not even by a small town's standards, she had been happy then too. She had the pictures to prove it. But there had been cracks in the façade of nuptial bliss. Her groom, Wade, had been controlling and short-tempered and shouted at her just a half hour before the wedding ceremony, berating her for inviting someone he didn't like to the wedding. He had also drunk a lot and embarrassed the few people who actually showed up to the party. She remembered fearing that she'd made a mistake, a fear she quickly brushed away with thoughts of her alternative option—embarrassment, loneliness, and living with her mother.

All the same, her fear had been right. Just a few years after the ceremony, Wade left her stranded—alone and broke in a small, Swiss-style town out west, far from her home in Minnesota. And tonight she was picking up the mess of someone else's wedding before going home alone. She tried to ignore the painful inner voices that chided her. If she never made it home, would anyone really care? Would it be this way the rest of her life? And the biggest question of all: Is anyone else out there?

CHAPTER

One

Whether we admit it or not, most of us live our lives on autopilot. We wake at the same hour, go to the same place of work or worship, talk to the same people, eat at the same restaurants, even watch the same TV shows. I'm not criticizing this. Habit is stability and stability is vital to survival. There's a reason farmers don't change crops midseason. When wisdom does not require change, it is wisdom not to change.

But sometimes the evolving terrain of life requires us to evolve with it. When those times come, we usually find ourselves quivering on the precipice of change as long as we can, because no one wants to dive headlong into the ravine of uncertainty. No one. Only when the pain of being becomes too much do we close our eyes and leap.

This is the story of my jump—a time when I did one of the most bizarre things I've ever done: I hunted down a woman I didn't know, in a small town I'd never heard of, just because of something she posted on the Internet.

✦

I've heard it said that solitude is among the greatest of all suffering. It's true, I think. Humans don't do well alone. But it's not really solitude that's the problem—it's loneliness. The difference between solitude and loneliness is that one exists in the physical world, and the other exists in the heart. A person can be in solitude but not lonely, and vice versa. My job has taken me to some of the most crowded cities in the world and I've still seen and felt loneliness. I've seen it in the cold spaces between strangers jostling next to one another on the crowded sidewalks. I've heard it in a thousand rushed conversations. We have more access to humanity than ever before and less connection.

I'm not a stranger to loneliness. It was part of my childhood. There was loneliness between my mother and father. They never divorced. I think they stayed together because they didn't want to be alone, but they were terribly lonely. And terribly unhappy. By the time I was sixteen I promised myself that if I ever got married, my marriage would be different. Ah, the best-laid plans.

✦

My name is Alex Bartlett. Bartlett like the pear. If I had to pick a starting point for when my story began, it was this time last year, approaching the holidays.

I live and work in Daytona Beach, Florida, a town made famous by fast cars and smooth beaches. I have one of those unromantic jobs with a company you've never heard of, doing something you've never thought about and never would have if I didn't tell you about it. I work for a company called Traffix. We sell traffic management systems for transportation departments. Basically, the product I sell counts the vehicles on the freeway and then sends in traffic analyses. If you've ever seen one of those electric freeway signs that tell you how many minutes to the airport, that's probably my company's software doing the calculating. I don't design it. I just sell it.

My sales territory was in the US Northwest, which includes Northern California, Oregon, and Washington State. Since I live on the East Coast, that meant I traveled a lot for work, sometimes for stretches of weeks. I hated the loneliness of the road and being gone from home. My wife, Jill, hated my traveling too. But only at first. After a few years, she got used to it and took to creating a life without me. It seemed that every time I came home, reentry was more difficult. After five years she seemed indifferent to my traveling. I was lonely at home as well.

Believing that my absence was hurting our marriage, I took a pay cut and traveled less. But as soon as I started spending more time at home, I realized that things had changed more than I realized. At least Jill had. She was different. She seemed uninterested in us—or maybe just me. She had become secretive.

Then she started traveling with a group of women she met online. At least that's what she told me she was doing. One day I was helping out with the laundry while she was gone and I found a folded-up, handwritten note in her jeans.

My deer one,

Each day were apart from each other feels like years. Your so far away. Im sorry that I couldnt come with you this time. I cant bear the idea of loosing you. I cant wate until you return and we will feest again on each others love.

—Your Clark

A sick, paralyzing fear went through my body. My face flushed red and my hands began to tremble. The idiot couldn't even spell. But idiot or not he had my wife. When I had calmed down enough to speak I called Jill.

"Who's Clark?" I asked.

There was a long pause. "Clark? Why?"

"Tell me who he is."

"I have no idea what you're talking about."

"I found a note from him in your jeans."

She hesitated for a moment, then said, "Oh, right. He's Katherine's lover. She handed that note to me as we got off the Phoenix flight so her husband didn't find it. It's nothing. I mean, to Katherine it's something, she wanted me to hold on to it, but it has nothing to do with me."

I just sat there processing her excuse. The fact that Jill's name wasn't on the note left me little ground to dispute her claim, even though it seemed unlikely. "You're not cheating on me?"

"Why would I cheat on you?"

"But Katherine's cheating on her husband."

"Yes. And I can't say that I blame her. She's been going to divorce him for, like, two years, she's just waiting for the right time. He's got a bunch of real estate deals pending and she doesn't want to throw a divorce on top of that."

"Thoughtful of her," I said sarcastically.

"She's not doing it for him," she said, apparently missing my sarcasm. "If these sales go through, she'll make a boat-load in the divorce. Why would you think I was cheating on you?"

I wasn't sure how to answer. "You're gone a lot lately."

"You've been gone most of our marriage. I never assumed you were cheating."

I honestly didn't know if I should feel more foolish for doubting her or for believing her. I finally just breathed out slowly. "All right. Be safe. I miss you."

"I miss you too. 'Bye."

We were together only five days after she returned before I left town on business to Tacoma. A week later I came home to an empty house and a note on the kitchen table.

Dear Alex,

There is a season for all things and it is my season to spread my wings and fly. I can no longer be held inside this cage, gilded though it may be, like a sad, lonely bird. I cannot bear the thought of someday looking back with regret over what might have been.

It's not you, Alex, at least it hasn't been your intent to keep me so unhappy. You are a kind soul. It's me and the human spirit yearning to fly. I need to be free and freedom cannot be contained within the shackles of a loveless marriage. I wish you to find freedom and love as well.

Sincerely,
Jill

P.S. I took the money from our savings and 401k.

She needed to be "free?" She was already free to do whatever she wanted, wherever and whenever she wanted. It was painful not understanding, not knowing what she meant, other than not wanting to be attached to me.

A few weeks later, pictures surfaced online of my ex-wife with another man. She wasn't traveling with "just the girls" as she had claimed. I saw a picture of Clark with his arm around my wife. He looked like a cross between a young Tom Selleck and a mandrill monkey. I felt like such an idiot for missing her secrets and believing her lies. Especially for believing her lies. The lies hurt more than her betrayal. Anyone can have their head turned, but the lies were continual evidence that she didn't love me. She hadn't for a very long time. Maybe she never had.

I vowed that I would never let someone lie to me again.

Now that she was gone I was just as alone as when I had been married, only now it was official. Some of us, maybe most of us, are good at attracting what we claim we don't want. My life seemed doomed to loneliness.

CHAPTER

Two

It was the Friday evening before Thanksgiving and I was still at work. Half the office lights were off and, except for the janitorial staff, I hadn't seen anyone in the building for several hours. I didn't really need to work late, I just didn't have anywhere else to be and going home to an empty apartment was the last thing I wanted to do.

A little after eight, I heard footsteps shuffling toward me. I looked up to see Nate, one of my co-workers, leaning against his cane and holding out an unopened can of Red Bull. "Here, man. Just what every insomniac needs for dinner."

I took the can from him and popped its tab. "Thanks."

"How's it going?"

"It's going."

I had worked with Nate for about three and a half years in the sales department, and during that time he'd become more friend than co-worker. I'd always thought that Nate didn't look like a salesman. He was a scary-looking guy—"formidable," one of our managers once called him. He was as bald as a thumb, with a long blond beard that forked like a snake's tongue. His biceps and forearms, which were massive, were covered in tattoos. At one time he could bench-press more than four hundred fifty pounds—roughly two and a half of me.

Before coming to Traffix, Nate had been a Marine. If you asked him, he would tell you that he was still a Marine. Once a Marine, *always* a Marine. Between Operation Desert Shield and Desert Storm, Nate had seen lot of action and a lot of bad things. He still suffered from PTSD. One time his wife woke in the night to find Nate crawling around the room on his elbows and knees, dodging enemy fire.

He left the marines after surviving his second IED explosion, in which he'd lost all of his teeth, broken his back, and partially lost his sense of balance. Even broken up as he was, he was still the toughest person I'd ever met.

Nate had good stories, and by "good" I mean interesting to listen to, which he rarely shared and only with the few people he trusted. But when he did, they practically erupted out of him, as if they'd been building up pressure just waiting to burst out.

Once, about a year after he left the marines, Nate was at a gun expo and stopped at a vendor's booth to admire a hunting rifle. "This for deer?" he asked.

The proprietor looked at him with a condescending smile. "Of course. What's the matter, haven't you ever hunted before?"

Without flinching, Nate looked him in the eyes and said softly, "Not animals."

The man's smile disappeared.

✦

"What are you still doing here?" I asked.

"That's what I was going to ask you," Nate said. He pulled a chair out from the cubicle across from me and sat, resting his cane between his legs. "I just landed. I wanted to input the sale before I went home."

"Where have you been?"

"St. Louis. Finally closed it."

"Congrats."

"Thanks. That bonus check will be the down payment on my Christmas present to myself this year. My new truck. Unless Ashley takes it." He smiled slightly. "So what's your excuse?"

"No place else to be."

"Have you had dinner?"

"No."

He stood. "Let's get some man food. And by that I mean beer." As I closed out my computer Nate said, "I'm calling Dale to meet us."

Dale was another salesman at Traffix. His region was the mirror opposite of mine: East Coast, the New England area. He was shorter than me by at least six inches and looked a little like Michael Keaton when he wore his wire-rimmed glasses.

Dale was also the self-proclaimed, designated wisecracking comic relief that every man-pack requires. Really, the guy lived in a mental bounce house. Sometimes being around him seemed like more work than it was worth, but he was a good guy and always lightened things up.

I drove Nate to our usual haunt, The Surly Wench Pub & Café. We had been going to this place for years, even back when it had different management and a different name: The Pour House. The new name was more fitting for its new proprietor.

Dale was already seated at a table when we arrived. Being a weekend night, the pub was crowded and the noise level was only slightly lower than a chain saw demonstration. There were three mugs of beer in front of Dale, one of them a quarter down.

"Ahoy, me maties," Dale said in a pirate voice. "Join me in a grog."

"Why are you talking like that?" Nate asked, sitting down.

"Arrr, doncha know what day it be?"

"Day to talk like an idiot?"

"No, you filthy bilge rat. It be International Talk Like a Pirate Day."

Nate took a drink, then said, "There's no such thing."

"Aye, that's whar you'd be wrong, matie."

"Stop that," Nate said.

Dale turned to me. "What be going on, you landlubber? Nate said it be arrrr-gent."

"Nate closed St. Louis."

"Aye," Dale said, lifting his mug. "Thar be reason for a celebratin'!"

Nate pointed a finger at him. "If you keep talking like that, I swear I will rip out your tongue and strangle you with it."

Dale, who was something like half Nate's size or, at least,

muscle mass, cleared his throat. "All right," he said, resuming his normal voice. "As you wish."

"Thank you," Nate said. "And we're not here to celebrate my sale. We're here to talk about Alex's woman problem."

Dale set down his drink. "Argh. Tales of the filthy wench."

Nate pointed at him again and Dale lifted his hands in surrender. "All right, you and your steroidal biceps win." He turned back to me. "Nate's right, my man. You've got to get over her. It's been a year."

"Eleven months."

"Close enough," Nate said. "Really. It's time to stop grieving your marriage's corpse. It's time to just bite the bullet."

"I'd rather put one through my head."

Dale glanced at Nate. "That's not good."

Nate took a long drink of his beer and then leaned in close. "Let me ask you something. If Jill called you tonight and asked you to come back, would you?"

I thought for a moment, then said, "Yeah. I probably would."

He shook his head. "I was afraid of that."

"What's wrong with forgiveness?" I asked.

"To err is human, to forgive is divine. Neither is Marine Corps policy." He took a drink, then said, "Jill was sucking the life out of you long before she cheated on you. Why are you looking for happiness where you lost it?"

"We always look for things where we lost them. Keys, wallets, sunglasses."

"He's got a point," Dale said.

Nate frowned. "Just be grateful there aren't kids involved. She'd use them as human shields."

"She's not that bad."

"Since when is she not that bad?"

Nate was right. "So how does one 'bite the bullet'?"

"You burn the bridges, sink the boats. You cross the Rubicon."

Dale started in. "In non-Marine jargon, it means you leave the past behind and start living your future. It's time to find someone new. You're a good-looking guy, successful, smart—there's a million women out there who would love to hook up with you."

"They're pounding down my doors," I said.

"They would be if they knew you were available," Nate said. "It's like this: you don't stop someone in a parking lot to ask if their car's for sale unless it has a sign in the window. You need to put up the sign."

"You want me to wear a sign saying I'm single?"

"Figuratively," Nate said.

"He could get a T-shirt," Dale interjected. "Available."

Nate continued. "I could name at least a half dozen women at Traffix who would be interested."

"You think I should date someone at work?"

"Absolutely not. I'm just saying there're opportunities out there."

Just then our waitress, Corinne, brought over a tray of cheeseburger sliders, buffalo wings, and spinach artichoke dip with tortilla chips. "There you go, my darlings."

"Avast, me buxom beauty," Dale said. "Now give us a twirl and show us your aftside."

She shook her head. "What's wrong with him?"

"It's Talk Like a Pirate Day," I said.

"That must be why the kitchen's all talking like that." She turned to me. "Where have you been, dear?"

"Hiding," I said.

"Men usually come *here* to hide."

"Woman problems," Nate said.

"That's usually why they're hiding." She smiled at me. "Need another drink?"

"He could use a keg," Nate said.

"Keep 'em a-comin, ya wench," Dale said. "And don't go a-hornswoggling us on the bill."

Corinne shook her head, then looked back at me. "For the record, I'm available." She winked and walked back to the kitchen.

"There you have it," Nate said. "Opportunity."

"The hurt's still fresh," I said. "I'm not looking for *opportunity*."

"Don't you miss waking up to something soft and warm in bed?" Dale asked. "Be truthful, aren't you lonely?"

I took a slow drink, then nodded. "Yeah. Sometimes it feels like the flu."

Both men looked at me sympathetically.

"Your situation isn't going to change by itself," Nate said. "You've got to make the world change. If you're looking for something, where do you go?"

"Looking for what?"

"Anything. A new stereo system. A book."

"I'd probably look it up on the Internet."

"Bingo. That's where you start."

"You think I should try Internet dating?"

"At least in the beginning," Nate said.

"I've heard bad stories about Internet dating."

"All dating has bad stories. Big deal. So you have to sift through a few tares to get to the wheat."

"What's a tare?" Dale asked.

"It's a weed," Nate said. "Don't you ever read the Bible?"

Dale shook his head. "Not enough, apparently." He turned to me. "I know it doesn't sound fun, but sometimes you have to go through hell to get to heaven. Do you know Wally in engineering? The short guy with a bad haircut?"

"The guy with a big handlebar mustache that makes him look like a walrus?"

"That's the man," Dale said, touching his nose as if we were playing charades. "So, three years ago he was married to this demon shrew who was as bossy as she was lazy. He's working his butt off to pay bills, while she stays at home during the day shopping for junk jewelry on TV and eating chocolate, you know what I mean?" He didn't wait for me to answer.

"After their youngest kid starts school, the shrew makes friends with a group of younger students and starts staying up all night clubbing. Then she stops getting out of bed in the morning because she's too tired from staying up so late, so Wally starts getting up at five in the morning so he can make the kids' lunches and breakfasts, send them off to school, and go to work.

"But it doesn't end there. Her enlightened friends convince her that she's a domestic slave, so she claims herself 'emancipated' from Wally, which means she officially doesn't have to do anything other than cash his checks and spend his money.

"So every day after work the man comes home, makes dinner, does the dishes, puts the kids to bed, then goes to bed himself to start again the next day. I mean, it's an insane arrangement, but Wally's a timid, peaceful soul and he does this without complaint.

"This goes on for more than a year. Then one day the demon shrew tells him that he's boring and ugly and she wants a divorce. He pleads with her to stay because of the children, but she's not having it. So she drains their savings and takes off with her buddies and the guy she was secretly seeing."

"This sounds kind of familiar," I said.

"Too familiar," Nate said.

"So, the divorce goes through and it wreaks havoc on the kids. They start getting in fights and getting expelled from school, that kind of stuff. Still, Wally does his best to be both parents, since the ex never has time to see her kids anymore.

"Then, about three months after the divorce is final, Marco in engineering comes up to Wally and says, 'Aren't you divorced?' Wally says, 'Yeah, why do you ask?' Marco tells him that his wife's sister is coming up from Mexico and even though she doesn't speak much English, she's sweet and pretty and not married. He invites Wally on a double date.

"Wally asks, 'Why me?' Marco says, 'Why not you? You're a nice guy.' So Wally shows up at Marco's house and it turns out that his sister-in-law isn't just pretty, she's gorgeous. Like, *drop-dead* gorgeous. I mean, on a scale of one to ten she's pushing fifty, and here's Wally on a good hair day pushing four. Love must be blind because Martina, that's her name, is smitten. She barely speaks English, but they speak the language of love. They start dating.

"One night she asks if they can stay home. Martina makes Wally a real home-cooked Mexican meal, then afterward, she tells him to just relax in the living room. She brings him a cold drink and turns the TV on for him, then—get this—gets down on her knees and rubs his feet. He doesn't know how to handle it.

"Six months later, they get married. One day Martina comes to him crying. Wally asks her what's wrong. She says, 'My love, you are so handsome. I know you have many beautiful women who want you. I am afraid one will come and take you from me.'

"Wally says, 'No one is going to take me. No one thinks I'm handsome but you.' She says, 'You are humble too. I will never be able to hold you.'

"Karma," Dale said, leaning back in emphasis. "Sometimes the route to heaven goes through hell. Karma may pay slow, but she eventually covers the bill."

"Where did you hear this story?" I asked.

"Marco. Martina came down to bring Wally lunch and I asked him who the looker was."

Nate raised his glass to me. "Dale's right, man. Heaven awaits. You just need to apply yourself. It's like Stuart always says in sales conference, 'Nothings sells itself.'"

I took another drink and then said, "The Internet, huh?"

Dale nodded. "You can find whatever you want on the Internet."

"Give it a try," Nate said. "There's a dating site for everyone."

I thought for a moment, then said, "All right."

Nate looked at me seriously. "'All right,' you'll do it, or 'all right,' you've said your piece, now leave me alone?"

"The former," I said. "I'll try."

"Try not," Dale said in a pitched voice. "Do, or do not."

"You sound like Yoda."

"I was imitating him."

"I prefer the pirate."

"Aye, then. Make us proud, matie," Dale said. "Scuttle ye boats."

"Scuttle ye boats," Nate said.

"Scuttle ye boats," I repeated.

We all took a drink.

CHAPTER

Three

We stayed at the pub until a little after eleven, when Dale's wife, Michelle, called to see where he was. From Dale's end of the conversation we could tell she wasn't happy.

"You really left Michelle alone on a Friday night and didn't tell her where you were going?" Nate said as Dale hung up.

"Slipped my mind."

"Keep that up," Nate said, "and *you're* going to be Internet dating."

"No, she'll just give me the silent treatment for a few days, which is kind of like a staycation. That reminds me. The other day Michelle asked me to hand her the lip balm but I accidentally handed her the superglue instead. She's still not speaking to me."

I laughed.

"Good one, Dale," Nate said. "Good one."

I picked up the tab, gave Nate a lift back to his car, then drove home to my apartment. Even though it was past midnight, I turned on the television. I watched the last twenty minutes of *Citizen Kane*, then began surfing channels.

Just as I was about to turn off the television, an advertisement came on for a dating site—a video collage of happy, love-frenzied couples swooning over each other. It seemed to me like some kind of a sign. I took a deep breath and got up from the couch. "All right, fine. Let's do this."

I walked over to my computer and pulled up the dating site advertised on the commercial. The home page showed an attractive couple laughing, their faces touching, their eyes blissfully closed.

LONELINESS OR LOVE?

It's your choice with eDate.

As I looked at the page a pop-up box appeared.

Tell us, are you:

a) A man seeking a woman
b) A woman seeking a man
c) A man seeking a man
d) A woman seeking a woman
e) Other

Other? I clicked "a," then entered my zip code and country. The box disappeared and three words appeared:

Let's Go, Stud.

Interesting beginning. I wondered what it said to women.

I started answering questions. There were a lot of them. I hadn't realized that signing up for a dating site would be like taking an SAT exam, but the site advertised the proven power of its matching process, and if true love was at the end of it all, it was a small price to pay.

I clicked through the basic questions, answering them as quickly as possible. Gender, age, city, relationship status—single or divorced. One of the prompts asked me how many times I'd been married; the options started at zero and went all the way up to five-plus. *Who goes after people that have been married five-plus times?* I wondered. Probably other people who have been married five-plus times. They should get a frequent marriage card.

In the next segment, I was asked to rate my own personality traits on a scale of one to five. Was I warm? Clever? Sensitive? Generous? After a while I just started marking fours for everything until the website scolded me.

> Slow down, partner. We know you're excited, but you're answering too many questions the same. Take time to carefully consider and answer each question. Your future happiness is at stake.

So much at stake. I threw in some threes and fives, not necessarily because I thought it was more accurate, but rather just to please the software. After ten minutes of questions, I clicked FINISHED. The site congratulated me for not quitting, and then a graph popped up showing that I was only 10 percent done. "Ten percent?" I said to myself. This was going to take all night.

The third segment asked more questions along the personality line and I was asked to pick out adjectives that described me:

Content
Genuine
Vivacious
Wise
Bossy
Aggressive
Opinionated
Romantic

Are people actually honest on these sites? Do people actually choose people who admit to being bossy, aggressive, and opinionated? So far the site hadn't asked if I had a police record or if I'd ever been accused of a felony. Maybe that came later.

The questions continued. It was annoyingly long, sometimes asking the same question in a different way, presumably to trick liars into revealing themselves. There were a lot of questions I should have asked Jill before marrying her. But then, the Jill who divorced me wasn't the same person I'd married anyway. If you think about it, when you marry someone, you're just jumping into one part of a very long river, hoping the current takes you somewhere worthwhile.

Then again, maybe she would have just lied anyway; she was good at it.

After the fifth segment I was informed by the graph that I was only halfway done. It was half past one in the morning and I was tired of answering questions, but now I felt trapped, unwilling to throw away all my work. I reminded myself of how lonely I was and that I'd had a Red Bull along with my beers. There was no turning back.

The ninth segment asked me what I did for a living. I wrote *consultant,* which, in a matter of speaking, was true, but mostly just sounded better than saying I was a salesman. Still, it made me feel a little sneaky.

The next segment asked me to rate my looks, then post pictures of myself. I suppose that it's somewhat revealing that I didn't have any pictures that didn't have Jill in them. I'm not a "selfie" kind of guy, but I snapped a picture of myself and uploaded it.

By experience, I know that most women think I'm attractive, but I'm not vain and the selfie I took should have proved it, easily dropping me a few points on the *Hot or Not* scale. At least no one would accuse me of Photoshopping my profile pic. That was my professional slogan: underpromise, overdeliver.

When I finally reached the end of the survey I was asked which of the service's packages I wished to purchase. I got out my credit card and paid for ninety days of the gold package, the highest level possible.

Okay, I did it, I thought. *The trap is set.*

✦

Sometimes the most profound experiences of our lives start with an act so simple and careless that we hardly think about it—like tossing a small stone that causes a massive avalanche. I don't know what possessed me, maybe it was the beer or the hour, but, on a whim, I typed "lonely" into a search engine and scrolled through a few pages of mostly song lyrics before landing on a blog post with the title "Is Anyone Out There?"

I clicked on the link, which took me to a blog site with the initials LBH at the top. There was a silhouette of a woman, but her face was indistinguishable.

Is Anyone Out There?

Dear Universe,

I'm so lonely tonight it hurts. Is anyone out there? Can you hear me? I once heard it said that the Internet is like a dark hallway you shout down—you don't know if anyone is there.

So here's the existential question of the day. If you blog something and nobody reads it, did you make a sound?

Sigh.

—LBH

I looked at the navigation bar for a profile or an *about me* page but there wasn't one. Whoever this woman was, she wasn't particularly interested in being identified. Just initials. LBH.

I scrolled down and read the previous blog entries she had posted, reading from the most recent back to the beginning.

Dear Universe,

This morning I was walking in to work from my car and looked up to see a single orange balloon floating into the sky. I was late for work but something made me stop and watch it get smaller and smaller, until it disappeared into the clouds. I guess I felt like it needed a witness, someone to stand there and say *I saw you float away. I saw you disappear.* I wish someone would do that for me.

—LBH

Dear Universe,

Many great minds and people have addressed loneliness. In *East of Eden*, John Steinbeck wrote, "All great and precious things are lonely." Mother Teresa said, "The most terrible poverty is loneliness, and the feeling of being unloved." Norman Cousins wrote, "The eternal quest of the individual human being is to shatter his loneliness."

I don't know that I'm adding anything with these little blog posts, but the thought that someone might read them somehow makes me feel less alone. If you're reading this, Thank you. If you're not, don't tell me.

—LBH

Dear Universe,

Why do we consider loneliness to be so shameful? A recent study showed that we are not alone in our loneliness. A full 40 percent of adults described themselves as being lonely. Yet people go to great lengths to make it appear as if they are *not* lonely. I recently read an interview where a top loneliness researcher sat reading a copy of his own book in public (a self-help book with the word *lonely* in the title) and suddenly became very embarrassed. What if the people around him noticed the book and thought he was lonely? His thought surprised him. Why was it that he, someone who studied loneliness for a living and therefore *knows* how pervasive it is, was so afraid of being perceived as lonely?

I have a theory. Perhaps we're afraid our loneliness will make us appear less lovable, less attractive, and less worthy of connection, and therefore more lonely.

Ironically, I'm not alone in my loneliness. Maybe that's why I keep these posts anonymous. We want to be lovable. We don't want to be alone. So we hide our loneliness, and it makes us . . . well . . . lonely.

—LBH

Dear Universe,

Okay, here's something that concerns you, dear reader. Did you know that the amount of time you spend online is inversely related to your general state of happiness and connection? In other words, the more time you spend online, the more unhappy and isolated you feel. I know that doesn't put either of us in a very good position, seeing as we are both online right now. But have you ever taken the time to think about why we spend so much time online? Why the average adult checks their social media upward of seventeen times a day?

I think that, misguided as it is, we *are* trying to connect. It's just that we don't know how, and maybe we can't stop ourselves from trying in this way. I know that the answer to my loneliness won't be found on a computer screen. And yet here I am. Reaching out. I wish I knew if anyone was reading this.

—LBH

Dear Universe,

Tonight I'm trying something new. I heard a psychiatrist talking on the radio. She said that writing out our feelings can not only help us understand ourselves, but can help take the pain from us. So here I go with my own experiment. Starting tonight I will begin the task of chronicling the life of a lonely woman. A woman who desperately wants to love and to be loved. I don't know if anyone will ever read this except me and God, but I'm trusting the psychiatrist. At least for now. It's that or Prozac.

—LBH

Whoever this woman was, I was taken by her sheer vulnerability. Or maybe it was her honesty. *Is there a difference?* I bookmarked the blog and then got ready for bed, her words stuck in my head. *Is anyone out there? Can you hear me?* Her words were perfect. I wanted to write back, *I know what you mean.* Or maybe just, *I am. Where are you?*

That's what I was thinking when I finally fell asleep.

CHAPTER

The next day was Saturday and I slept in, waking a little past nine. I woke still thinking about the blog. I got out of bed and went right to my computer and pulled up the site. There was a new post.

Dear Universe,

Tonight I read an article where a reporter asked a scientist if he believed there was life on other planets. The scientist replied, "The only thing more frightening than the possibility of there being extraterrestrial life out there is the distinct possibility that there's not and we are alone in the universe."

I suppose that's exactly how I've felt most of my life.

—LBH

Tonight? I had been on the site at 2 a.m. Either she didn't sleep at night or she lived in a different time zone. Somewhere out west. Could it be in my sales region? Oregon? Washington? California?

As I sat there thinking, a notification popped up on my computer.

Alex,
We have some matches for you!

Below the words were pictures of six women. If I had wondered whether people fudged the truth on the questionnaire, I now had my answer. The women all looked ten to fifteen years older than me. One of them looked like my late aunt.

They had also all described themselves as athletic and fit, but I couldn't imagine any of them running more than a few yards without collapsing. Perhaps their definition of *athletic* was watching golf from their couch.

When I logged in to the dating site I found that all of the women had already messaged me. I wasn't attracted to any of them. In admitting this I felt a twinge of guilt. No one really wants to believe that physical appearances are such a big criteria—but they are. To both men *and* women. It's psychology. One study showed that attractive people got less jail time than unattractive people. These feelings start young. It's why Cinderella is pretty and her stepsisters are ugly, so we'll naturally pull for her. It's also why Prince Charming is always . . . well . . . charming.

I went back and reread my mysterious LBH.

CHAPTER

The next Monday, the twenty-first, I met up again with Nate and Dale at lunch. We all came in from different places. It was raining, and Nate was soaking wet. He didn't look too happy about it.

"It's raining," I said.

Nate glared at me. "You think?"

Dale said, "Sometimes, when it rains, I find my wife just standing by the window with a sad look on her face." He paused, then added, "It makes me think that maybe I should let her in."

I shook my head. "I have no idea why she stays with you."

"It's my sense of humor. Women love a sense of humor."

"That must be why she married a joke," Nate said.

"That was cruel," Dale said. "But speaking of jokes. Here." He dropped a bumper sticker in front of me. "I bought it in the Newark airport. It reminded me of you."

Dear Algebra,
Stop asking us to find your "X."
She's not coming back.

"Thank you," I said.

"Don't mention it. How goes the hunt?"

"I think people might lie on those dating sites."

Dale laughed. "*Everyone* lies on those sites. A friend of mine met someone online. He talked to her for several weeks before he finally flew out to meet her. When he got there, he didn't recognize her. The woman had chin hair and had put on more than ninety pounds since the photo she'd posted had been taken.

"When he asked her why she'd lied to him, she said, 'Would you have come if you knew what I really looked like?' Which would be like me saying to a client, 'Would you have bought our product if you knew it actually counted clouds instead of cars?' "

"That's reassuring."

"It's human nature," Nate said, "Everyone lies when it comes to describing themselves. Sometimes without even thinking about it."

"Then why did you send me there?"

"You were wallowing, man. You've got to start somewhere."

"Look at this," Dale said, holding up his iPhone. "This confirms my point. This article says that the vast majority of dating site users lie. Men are more likely to lie about their height, and women are more likely to lie about their weight. Both lie about their body type, with almost eighty percent saying they are athletic and fit—a number far exceeding the national average of athletic and fit bodies."

"That would be my experience," I said.

Dale continued. "It says that women are more likely to lie about their age, rounding down to the nearest five, while men lie about their job and income, generously giving themselves huge raises." Dale looked at me. "Did you lie?"

"I said I was a consultant instead of a salesman."

"That's not lying," Dale said. "That's selling."

"What's the difference? I asked.

"You should always round up," Nate said. "Like how did you rate your looks?"

"Eight."

"Snap!" Dale said. "Failure alert."

"See, that's your problem right there," Nate said. "In the real world, outside the Clooney-Pitt matrix, you're a high nine, pushing ten. If you sold our software the way you just tried to sell yourself, you'd be out of a job."

Dale nodded in agreement. "You're underselling, man. *Way* underselling. Those women are rounding up a five to an eight. You're rounding down a ten to an eight. Now there's a five-point gap."

"You're a salesman," Nate said. "You should ace this thing."

"It's not the pitch," I said, "it's the product."

"You know better than anyone that's not true," Dale said. "A good pitch can sell a bad product and a bad pitch won't sell jack."

"You need to rework your pitch," Nate said. "Pronto. Does the dating site let you revise your profile?"

"I'm not sure it's worth the effort."

"So the first day out fishing you threw some back. No big deal."

"Was there *anyone* of interest?" Dale asked.

"I found someone interesting. Just not on the site. She writes a blog."

"A blogger," Nate said.

"What does she look like?" Dale asked.

"I have no idea."

"What do you mean?"

"Just what I said. There wasn't a picture. Just kind of a silhouette."

"You mean she purposely shadowed her face."

"Yes."

There was a brief pause, then Dale said, "Now, there's a Texas-size red flag. Beautiful people always post their pictures."

"*Vain* people always post their pictures," I said.

Nate said, "Vain or not, I'm with Dale on this one."

"Look, she's beautiful, okay?"

"How do you know?" Nate asked.

"I read her blog."

They both looked at me like I was taking crazy pills. Finally Nate shook his head. "That's admirable, man. Really admirable. I'm just happy for you that looks don't matter. That's going to swing the opportunity door wide open."

"I didn't say that looks don't matter. They're just not *everything*. Jill was beautiful on the outside. This time I want someone I'm attracted to inside and out."

After a moment Nate leaned back in his chair, lacing his fingers behind his neck. "Well, like I said, don't worry about it. It's just the first week. Believe in the process."

"And my blogger?"

"You're a salesman. It's another lead. Doesn't matter where it came from."

Dale glanced down at his watch. "I've got to go. I've got to finish up the paperwork on the Newark sale before the holiday. *Ciao, ragazzi.*"

After he was gone Nate asked, "What are you doing for Thanksgiving?"

"I don't know. Probably watching football with a frozen turkey dinner."

"You're breaking my heart, man. Why don't you spend it with Ashley and me? You know the woman can cook, and I'm deep-frying a turkey. It's going to be epic."

"By *epic* do you mean disaster?"

"Eating a TV turkey dinner alone at Thanksgiving is a *disaster*."

"Is Ashley okay with it?"

"It was her idea. She was feeling sorry for you."

"Now I'm pitiable."

"Yeah, you are." He hit me on the shoulder. "This too shall pass."

"When?"

"I don't know. That's up to God."

"I meant, *when* is dinner?"

He grinned. "Oh. Three. I think. I'll get back to you on that. You ready to go back?"

"I'm going to finish my lunch," I said.

"Yeah, you talk too much," he said, standing. "See you at

HQ." He leaned against his cane and limped out into the rain.

✦

That night there were two more dating suggestions. One of them looked a lot like Jill. It took me a minute to realize that it was her. I was tempted to read her self-description but deleted it instead. I guess Clark hadn't worked out. It wasn't seeing her there that bothered me most, it was that she might have seen me there. Why did that feel so humiliating?

I clicked off the site and then over to LBH. I was happy to see that she had posted another blog entry.

Dear Universe,

Last night I came across yet another study about loneliness. You, being a sane person, might ask, "What kind of person does a study on loneliness?" I'll tell you. The same kind of person who spends her nights looking up those studies—a lonely person. And I'm starting to believe that there are more than a few of us.

This study showed that chronic loneliness impacts our bodies as negatively as smoking two packs of cigarettes a day. Not the same way, of course, just the life risk part. And there's more bad news. The article went on to say that lonely people had worse reactions to flu shots than non-lonelies (I think I just made up that word; my computer put a red squiggly line under it) and that loneliness depresses the immune system. In other words, if you're lonely, not even your body wants to be around you, so it tries to off itself.

Maybe that's why I feel like I'm coming down with something tonight. I wish I had someone to rub Vicks menthol on my chest and tuck me into bed. Actually, if I had someone to do that, they'd be in bed with me. Or bringing me hot honey and lemon tea. That would be heaven. But then, if I had someone who loved me like that, I wouldn't be lonely. Then I probably wouldn't be sick.

Sometimes I would still pretend I was.

—LBH

Whoever she was, I was dying to meet her.

CHAPTER

The next day Dale was out of town so I went out for sushi with just Nate.

"Any more leads?" Nate asked before popping a piece of spider roll into his mouth. I think he was more interested in my dating site experience than I was.

"A few. One of them was Jill."

"They tried to match you up with Jill?"

"Yes, which, for the record, makes me doubt the site's credibility."

"Small world, man. Or maybe it's not a mistake. Maybe Jill's subconsciously still in love with you and she's looking for someone like you."

"Yeah, right," I said, though some twisted part of me wanted to believe it.

"Any other females of interest?"

I shook my head. "Not really. One gal has seven children."

"Wow. I'm surprised that she was forthcoming about it. That's the kind of news you drop after the fourth date. Maybe fifth."

"So, she was being honest. She seemed nice."

"Seven kids? That's not nice you're sensing, it's desperation."

I broke open an edamame. "Yeah, that's a bit too much of a lifestyle change for me."

"What about your blog lady? LOL."

I shook my head. "It's *LBH.* She posted another blog entry."

"Did she leave any clues to her identity?"

"No. Just her initials."

"Good luck with that," he said. "Oh, I told Ashley that you're spending Thanksgiving with us. She was pleased."

"Thanks. I'm looking forward to it."

"And if my turkey doesn't work, at least you won't be alone."

That night I made myself a protein smoothie for dinner, watched an hour of television, and then, as had become my habit, I checked the blog. There was another post. Two, actually.

Dear Universe,

Tonight I was thinking about something my father said to me when I was a girl. My father was German; he had an accent and everything. One day he said to me, when the time comes for you to want a man, wait for the one who brings you edelweiss. I asked him what edelweiss was, and he said, it's a small white mountain flower from the old land. I asked him why, and he said, edelweiss grows very high up in the mountains in rocky terrain. It takes great faith and commitment and courage for a man to pick edelweiss and then bestow it on his love.

I've never forgotten that. I miss my father. He was such a good man. Where are the men like that? Where is my man with edelweiss?

—LBH

Again her words were beautiful. Was I a man who would bring his love edelweiss? I thought I was. I hoped I was. I read it over again before I started on the next post.

The second entry had been posted an hour before the other.

Dear Universe,

Great (I type sarcastically). I just discovered more science working against me. There was a study that showed that loneliness actually makes people colder. Not just *feel* colder, but actually *be* colder, like making skin temperature drop. It seems like a cruel irony that the coldest people have no one to warm up with.

It's so cold here. Tonight the snow keeps falling, covering everything beneath a silent, cold blanket. The mountains look so pretty painted white. The weatherman says that we might get several feet tonight. The world outside is abandoned. My world inside is abandoned.

I feel so cold tonight. I wish I had someone to hold me.

—LBH

I wish I had someone to hold me. I wished that I was holding LBH. Was I crazy to feel this way about someone I didn't know? I wanted to take her edelweiss.

Then I realized that she'd given me my first clue. *Mountains and snow*. I wondered if I could determine her location using a weather map. I tried. It was snowing in nineteen different states. At least I could mark off all the nonmountainous cities without snow, narrowing my search down to just a hundred million people. No problem.

"Come on, LBH," I said aloud. "Just give me a little more to go on."

CHAPTER Seven

Thanksgiving had never been kind to me. You hear stories of families getting together over the holidays only to wreak havoc on each other. That's pretty much my family's story. My memories of Thanksgiving, back when I was home and my grandparents were still alive, consisted of my parents volleying insults back and forth across the table until my mother threw something moist at my father and huffed away. My father would then storm out of the house to the nearest bar, leaving my grandparents and me sitting at the table in silence until my grandmother, who dealt with conflict by pretending it didn't exist, would ask me some benign question like "How's school going?"

I hated the day.

✦

I woke up not feeling well (psychosomatic?), so I slept in. When I couldn't sleep anymore, I watched a little of the Macy's parade and then, on a whim, checked the blog. There was something new.

Dear Universe,

I know I don't usually post twice a night, but I couldn't sleep. And I found more science. (You know how I love science.) A neuroscience magazine recently published a theory claiming that loneliness developed as a survival trait. The basic premise is this: to survive as a species, humans had to learn to band together—form communities to help each other thrive. This connection was so important to our survival that our brains developed a biomechanical function that caused us to feel pain (aka loneliness) whenever we found ourselves not connecting with others. Therefore, we experience loneliness the same way we experience other biological needs like tiredness or hunger—as something that drives us to action. So in theory, loneliness is *good* for the species. Good for the whole, bad for the one.

—LBH

I took a deep breath. *That's for sure.* I turned off my computer and got in the shower. I wondered what LBH was doing for Thanksgiving.

I arrived at Nate's house shortly before three. He opened the door before I rang the bell. "Alex, brother. Welcome." We man-hugged. The sound of Mitch Miller's Christmas music filled the home, along with the rich aromas of Thanksgiving baking.

"I hope you came hungry. Ashley has outdone herself."

"I was born hungry. And I'm prepared to abuse my stomach for Ashley's sake."

Nate slapped me on the back, which, incidentally, always hurt. "I like that. Always willing to take one for the team."

"How'd your turkey turn out?"

"Great," he said. "Just took it from the oven."

"I thought you were deep-frying the turkey."

"Yeah, Ashley vetoed that. She read about all these fools burning down their houses on Thanksgiving."

"I vetoed what?" Ashley said, emerging from the kitchen.

"Deep-fried turkey."

"Yeah, can you imagine?" She kissed me on the cheek. "Hi, Alex."

"Hi, gorgeous." Ashley was just about the opposite of Nate. As refined as she was beautiful, she was also petite, barely a hundred pounds. I was afraid that Nate would someday roll over in bed and crush her.

"It smells wonderful," I said to her.

"Thank you. When Nate asked if he could invite you, I changed the menu a little. He told me how much you love pecan pie. So I made you one."

"Will you marry me?"

Ashley shook her head. "No, one man's enough. But I will send you home with the leftover pie."

"At least there's a consolation prize," I said.

Ashley smiled, then said to Nate, "I'm just waiting for the rolls. We'll be eating in about ten minutes. Stay close."

He turned to me. "C'mon, buddy. Let's watch the Dolphins finish off Pittsburgh."

I followed Nate into his den, where the television was tuned to a Dolphins-Steelers game. It was the fourth quarter. The Dolphins led by a touchdown.

"How's your day?" Nate asked.

"It's been all right."

"Any online dating action?"

"You keep asking. You got a bet going on this?"

"Maybe."

"You and Dale bet on whether I'll find someone online?"

"No. We bet on whether or not you'll marry someone you met online."

"I'm speechless."

He was quiet for a moment and then said, "He gave me ten-to-one odds. I'd be a fool to pass that up."

"That's faith."

"For the record, I got a hundred on you that you will. Don't let me down."

✦

Ashley called for us a few minutes later. The three of us gathered around the dining room table, which held far more food than three people could eat. Even when one of them was the size of Nate.

"I'll say grace," Nate said. "We are grateful this day for our great country and our great flag and ask thy blessings upon those who are in harm's way, away from their families today, defending our freedoms. We are grateful for the abundance of our lives and especially, today, for this fine meal. We are grateful for friends, and ask you to bless lonely Alex to find a nice lady to soothe his loneliness. Maybe even his mystery blog lady. Amen."

I looked at him and shook my head. "Thanks."

"Don't mention it," he said. "I've got your back."

Ashley handed me a basket of rolls and asked, "Who's this mystery blog lady?"

"Alex has been stalking a woman on the Internet," Nate said.

"Really?"

"It's not as interesting as Nate makes it sound," I replied.

"It never is," Ashley said. "Which is good, because it sounds really creepy."

"Thanks for making me sound creepy," I said to Nate. "As well as pitiable."

"Those are not mutually exclusive traits."

"So what's the story behind this Internet stalking?" Ashley asked. "That's one thing about Nate's tales: they may be crazy, but there's always some basis in truth. It may be just one percent, but it's always there."

"That's because it's beyond me to conjure something up out of thin air," Nate said. "I simply have no imagination."

"I didn't say that," she said. "So who is this mystery lady, and what does my husband have to do with her?"

"Nate talked me into signing up for an Internet dating service. While I was online, I came across a woman's blog that caught my attention."

"A famous blogger?"

"No. Her site seems pretty small."

"Have you contacted her?"

"I would, except she doesn't post any contact information."

"Which means she doesn't *want* to be contacted." Ashley turned to Nate. "You really sent him to an Internet dating site?"

"Why wouldn't I?"

"You know why not. After what I went through."

"This sounds like a story," I said.

She looked at me, shaking her head. "You don't know the half of it."

Nate shook his head. "You're going to tell him about the eye doctor."

"The *eye* doctor?" I said.

She nodded. "About two months before I met Nate, I met a guy online who was an optometrist. He wasn't especially handsome, but he was a professional and he seemed nice enough. Besides, he was local, so we planned a date.

"At dinner he told me which eyeglass store he worked at; coincidentally, I had been there just a few weeks earlier. I told him that when I was there I had seen some really cute sunglasses I wished I'd bought.

"After dinner he said, 'I'm a manager at the store. If you're serious about those glasses, I can get you anything at cost—less than half price.'

"I really wanted the glasses and I thought that sounded pretty good, so we went to the eye store. I should've realized that something was wrong when we went in through the back door and he told me to be quiet and not look into the security cameras. I asked him why, but he just mumbled something about company protocol, then said, 'Don't worry about it,' which is when I should have started worrying.

"We got in the store and he took me to the showcase with all their glasses, then he stepped into a back room. Neither of us was aware that we'd set off the silent alarm. So after I found the glasses I went to find him, and he's in one of the examining rooms, sitting in a chair, totally naked.

"I'm planning my escape when someone shouts, 'Freeze! Put your hands up.' It's the police, and they're pointing guns at us. I'm totally freaked out, because I think I'm either going to be shot or going to prison, and this nut I'm with is totally naked.

"They took us aside, and after I stopped crying and explained the situation, they had a good laugh and let me go. One of the officers drove me home. My date was a different matter. They told him to put his clothes on, then they handcuffed him and took him away. As they were walking him out of the store, he shouted to me, 'Call me.'" She looked at Nate. "That's why you shouldn't have suggested Internet dating."

I grinned. "Yeah, Nate didn't share any of that with me."

"It wasn't relevant," Nate said. "The chances of Alex running into another naked eye doctor are next to nil."

✦

After dinner, Nate and I did the dishes while Ashley spoke on the phone with her mother in Oklahoma. Then all three of us went into the den to eat pie and talk. After a half hour Ashley excused herself to take a nap. Ten minutes later Nate left me to join her. I got another piece of pecan pie and then drove home. Another Thanksgiving bites the dust.

CHAPTER

Eight

The weekend after Thanksgiving was basically a blur. The achiness I had felt Thanksgiving morning wasn't just a passing thing; somehow I had caught a cold, so I spent the next day wiped out, staying mostly in bed or a steaming shower. Jill used to make fun of my "man-colds" as she called them, but she jests at sniffles who never felt a man-cold.

Not that I was missing anything by staying inside—at least nothing that I didn't want to miss. During my early years of marriage, Jill would drag me out of bed while it was still dark for Black Friday shopping. More surprising is that I let her. I hated every minute of it. The event was probably where the differences in our personalities were most keenly revealed. Jill thrived in the crush of holiday shopping chaos, soaking in the sounds, deals, and assault and battery, while I saw the experience more as a consumer's version of Pamplona's running of the bulls, dodging people, trying not to be gored by shopping carts.

After three years of dutifully following her around, I finally admitted to not enjoying the excursion. To my surprise, she admitted to really wanting to shop with her girlfriends instead of me, both of us doing what we didn't want to do because we thought it was what the other wanted—

sort of a twisted "Gift of the Magi" thing. From then on, she shopped while I slept. Problem solved.

✦

This year, other than Nate and Dale, I had no one to shop for. As pathetic as it made me feel, and in spite of what Jill had done, I missed her. I wondered if she was out shopping. Of course she was. She had our 401k.

Even though I was sick, I toyed with the idea of going out alone, for tradition's sake, but I couldn't bring myself to do it—not because of my cold so much as my heart. It's an irony that nothing makes you feel more lonely than crowds of people you are not connected to.

I had pretty much written off another wasted holiday until later that night when I went online. That's when LBH wrote something that changed everything.

Dear Universe,

Another Thanksgiving alone. Why do you think it is that we feel our loneliness most keenly during the holidays? I have much to be thankful for. And, in spite of my loneliness, I am thankful. I'm healthy. I'm not rich but I have a roof over my head. I hope all my writing about loneliness doesn't make me seem ungrateful. Sometimes I feel like a whiner. I write not to complain, but for the therapy of it all.

Tomorrow everyone will head out en masse to the stores. Here, many will head to the larger towns. Everywhere there will be crowds, which is why I'll stay in. It's strange to me that I feel most lonely in crowds. Ironic I suppose.

Every September, at a park near my home, this little town holds a Swiss Days festival. As I look out my window at all the people coming and going in their groups, I wonder where they all come from. Humans need to belong. Humans have always needed tribes. Today we find tribes in family or clubs or religion. What happens when we fall out of them? I suppose, in prehistoric times, it was fatal to be cast out of a tribe, to be exiled or excommunicated from the group, away from the people we love and need. Exile from the tribe is a form of execution.

—LBH

Swiss Days? What were Swiss Days? Finally she'd given me something I could go on. I typed "Swiss Days" into Google and three results came up—three different cities: Berne, Indiana; Midway, Utah; and Santa Clara, Utah. I had never heard of any of these places.

I began searching online for information on the three towns. They were all small, with populations of around four thousand people—about 5 percent the size of Daytona Beach. This was good. The fewer people to sift through the better.

Berne, Indiana, is a town thirty-five miles south of Fort Wayne, settled in 1852 by Mennonite immigrants who came from Switzerland and named their new home after Switzerland's capital city. From the pictures online, it didn't look much like the original Berne.

Santa Clara, Utah, is a southern Utah town near the Arizona border and in the late nineteenth century was largely inhabited by converted Mormon immigrants from Switzerland. It was a desert town and looked mostly flat, though there were distant mountains visible in some images of the city I found.

Of the three towns, Midway looked the most like Switzerland in geography and architecture. It was a lush, hilly area discovered by fur trappers and later settled by Mormon Swiss immigrants. Many of its present-day buildings, including what I assumed was the town hall, were designed after Swiss architectural styles. It was also known for its abundance of natural hot springs.

According to a previous blog entry, the town LBH lived in had mountains and a lot of snow. While all three locales had mountains or hills, only two received any significant amount of snowfall, Midway and Berne. Berne averaged twenty-seven inches of snow a year, and Midway got more than a hundred. Though Santa Clara was also in Utah, it was nearly three hundred miles south of Midway and averaged less than three inches of snow a year. LBH had written that she was expecting several feet of snow in one night, which disqualified Santa Clara and was improbable for Berne, though it was still a possibility.

Then I looked up the dates of each of the towns' Swiss Days festivals to see which ones were held in September. Berne held their event near the end of July. Santa Clara and Midway held their events in September. Only one of the towns met all the criteria. LBH lived in Midway, Utah.

Wherever the devil that was.

CHAPTER

Since my clients were government bureaucrats, the end of the year was always a manic time for sales as city, county, and state officials scrambled to spend their annual budgets lest they find them reduced by their state legislatures the next fiscal year. This trend usually continued at a feverish pace until the end of the second week of December, which was when everything shut down as abruptly as if someone had turned off a faucet. This was why the Traffix management always held our company party on the evening of the second Saturday of December. It's also why nothing got done after that.

Even though our official company break began on December 22, for all intents and purposes, we were closed for business the last half of the month. This was the first year that I wasn't looking forward to all that time off. If Thanksgiving was any indication, it wasn't going to be much of a holiday. Still, it had to be better than the previous December. That's when Jill had left me.

LBH posted blog entries on the Friday, Saturday, and Sunday after Thanksgiving.

Dear Universe,

I took a quiz on loneliness last night. I was doing one of my late-night Internet searches and I found a quiz from a psychology magazine titled "How Lonely Are You?" Even though I already knew the answer, I went through the whole quiz, answering things like "How often do you feel that you have no one to talk to?" and "How often do you feel overwhelmed by your loneliness?" I answered OFTEN to every question, except one: "How often do you find yourself waiting for someone to call or write?" That one I responded to with NEVER. There's no one out there who thinks about me enough to call or write. I guess it comes as no surprise that the quiz categorized me as "Extremely Lonely." I didn't need a quiz to tell me that.

—LBH

Dear Universe,

My last few posts have been pretty heavy so I wanted to lighten the mood by posting some jokes about loneliness:

Question: Why didn't the skeleton go to the dance?

Answer: He had no body to go with.

Terrible, I know. Not even worthy of being on a bubblegum wrapper. How about this one?

There was a man who desperately wanted to be alone, so he built himself a house on top of a mountain. One day there was knock on the door. When he went to answer it, there was no one there but a snail.

The man, angry that his solitude had been disturbed, picked up the snail and threw it as far as he could.

One year later there was another knock on the door and the man opened it to see the snail again. "What did you do that for?" the snail asked.

For the record, I would have let the snail in.

—LBH

Dear Universe,

There's a famous painting by Edward Hopper called *Nighthawks*. It's a very iconic image. You've probably seen it. The painting is of a downtown diner at night, something I especially relate to. Through the windows you see a man and a woman sitting on one side of the counter, a second man sitting across from them, and a third working behind the bar.

That painting has always struck me as being intensely lonely. Maybe it's because as the viewer you are put in the position of being on the outside, looking in. But even the people on the inside look lonely. When asked about it, Hopper said, "Unconsciously, probably, I was painting the loneliness of a large city."

Unfortunately, large cities don't have a monopoly on loneliness. It can be found in small towns as well. Loneliness can be found everywhere there are people.

That last sentence seems horribly ironic.

—LBH

✦

Monday morning I flew out to Seattle to meet with the city's Traffic Engineering Department, and then, two days later, continued on to Portland to meet with the Oregon Department of Transportation. My meetings went well, though my Seattle clients decided to push back implementation of our product until the new year, something that would shift some of my year-end bonus to next year. I didn't care. I might be lonely, but I was doing well financially, at least.

On my way home from Portland I changed planes in Salt Lake City. I had a window seat and I looked out the window as we prepared to land. Salt Lake City and its surrounding suburbs were white as a bedsheet. It was as if someone had taken a giant can of white spray frost to it. The Rocky Mountains encircling the city were always majestic, but in winter they rose like great heaping banks of snow pushed to the side.

As I sat there looking out over the mountains, I couldn't help but think how close I was to LBH. Midway was just east of the range, about thirty miles. I might have seen the town from the air and not known it. She was down there somewhere. LBH had been silent since Thanksgiving weekend. I wondered why she hadn't been blogging. I realized I was worried about her. Strange that I was worried about someone I didn't know.

I arrived back home Thursday night. Daytona Beach was warm compared to where I'd been the last week, but people still wore coats.

Before going to bed I turned on my computer and pulled up the LBH blog, hoping but not expecting that she'd written something. She had.

Dear Universe,

This is my last entry. If you've been following my ramblings, let me take this moment to say good-bye. I hoped that blogging would help ease my loneliness, but it hasn't. Nothing has. I am so weary of hurting all the time. I think it's time go home. In my heart, home is not a place. It's a person. It's my father. I miss my father. I miss him every day. I want to see him again. I want to tell him to his face that I am sorry for what I've done.

I plan to stay here until Christmas. For the sake of the season. That's what I'm telling myself. Maybe I'm still hoping that something might change. Hope springs eternal.

I'll leave on New Year's Eve. May you, dear wanderer, find what I couldn't.

—LBH

Her last entry. There was a deep melancholy to her message, deeper than anything she'd posted before. There was a finality to it. My heart ached. I didn't know this woman, yet my heart was breaking for her. I felt loss. I suppose, in a way, I did know her. I knew her because I knew her pain. I knew her because she'd shared her vulnerability and honesty. In that way I'd known her better than someone I'd shared a bed with. I wanted to know her better because of her honesty. And now I knew that if I didn't find her before New Year's, I never would.

CHAPTER

The next morning I called Nate. He answered the phone with, "Dude, when'd you get back?"

"Last night. Do you have time for lunch?"

"Yes, sir. I always have time for food."

"Is Dale around?"

"Yes, but he's working from home today. I'll give him a call. What's up?"

"I found her."

"You found who?"

"LBH."

"Your blogger woman," he said. "You spoke with her?"

"I'll tell you about it at lunch."

✦

Two hours later we met up at a steak house not far from the office. Dale was there. As soon as we sat down he said, "So, don't leave us hanging. What's she like?"

"I don't know," I said.

"But you said that you found her," Nate said.

"I know where she lives. In one of her posts she mentioned something called Swiss Days."

Nate's brow furrowed. "She's in Switzerland?"

"No. She's in a small town in Utah called Midway. Every year they have a Swiss Days celebration."

Nate sat back, his expression changing from concern to disappointment. "That can't be the only Swiss Days in the world. There's probably hundreds of them."

"No, there are only three Swiss Days festivals in America, one in Indiana, the other two in Utah. And only one of those matches the date and weather she wrote about."

"Impressive, Sherlock," Dale said.

Nate still didn't look convinced. "So you know the town she lives in. That's a long stretch from knowing who she is. How many people live in this Midway?"

"A little over four thousand people."

"That's not bad," Dale said.

"That's still a lot of people," Nate said.

"Not once you break it down," I said. I took out a piece of paper I'd written some numbers on. "Listen. According to the last census, there were 2,074 females in Midway. Utah has the youngest population in the US, so thirty-six percent are nineteen or under, that leaves one thousand, three hundred twenty-eight possibilities. Finding one of them with the initials LBH can't be that difficult."

"If this sales thing doesn't work out, you could find work as a private investigator," Dale said.

"I just hope she's not catfishing," Nate said.

I looked at him. "What's catfishing?"

"Internet dweebs who pretend they're someone they're not."

"Why would she do that?"

Nate shrugged. "Lots of reasons. Boredom. Thrill of the hunt. Revenge. Insanity."

"He's right," Dale said. "There are stories all over the Internet. There was a British woman who convinced a half dozen women that she was a man named Sebastian. She was courting them all at the same time. One of the women figured it out when her Internet lover posted a picture of 'his' favorite perfume, not realizing that her own image was reflected in the bottle." Dale looked me in the eyes. "In other words, LBH might be a bored, twenty-two-year-old manboy."

"It doesn't make sense," I said. "If she were really trying to 'catfish,' why would she keep her identity hidden?"

"You're right," Nate said. "It would be like running a classified ad in the paper and not leaving a phone number."

"Exactly," I said. "What would be the point?"

"You know," Dale said, "I don't think that finding her will be the most difficult part."

"What do you mean?"

"I mean once you find her, what are you going to say? Excuse me, I found you on the Internet and I tracked you down in Utah. You're going to freak her out. Big-time. If she doesn't deny it's her, she'll probably call the police."

I hadn't thought it through that far. "You're right," I finally said. "I guess I'll jump off that bridge when I reach it."

"So what now?" Nate asked.

I looked at them for a moment, then said, "I guess I'm going to Utah."

CHAPTER *Eleven*

That night was our company party. It was held in downtown Daytona Beach at Bratten's Cove, a swanky seafood restaurant overlooking the ocean. There were a little more than fifty employees there, most with their spouses or partners. I intentionally arrived late. I hated going alone and I didn't want to arrive before Dale or Nate. I did anyway.

I got a glass of merlot, then sat down with a dish of cocktail sauce and a cold plate of peel-and-eat shrimp. I had sat there alone for a half hour when Dale and his wife arrived. Michelle, a stunner, was the best evidence of Dale's sales expertise.

"Hey, how's my favorite wallflower?" Dale said.

"If it isn't Beauty and the Beast," I replied.

"Don't call my wife a beast," Dale said. Michelle just rolled her eyes.

"How does he keep you?" I asked.

"I guess he's a good salesman," she said, hugging me. "How are you, Alex?"

"Hanging in there."

"Dale says you met someone on the Internet?"

"There are no secrets."

"I'm happy for you. She's from Utah?"

"Yes."

"I used to ski in Utah in my college days. Mostly Deer Valley and Park City. Sometimes Alta. It's really beautiful. You won't believe the mountains out there. They're incredible."

"She lives near Park City," I said.

Michelle's smile grew. "That's really great. You're going to love it. Does 'she' have a name?"

"I'm sure she does," I said. "I just don't know it."

Michelle looked at me and then at Dale with an amused grin. "I can't tell if he's kidding."

Dale shook his head. "He's not. It's complicated."

Michelle hesitated for a moment, as if still trying to figure things out, then said, "Well, I hope things work out."

"Thank you. Me too."

Dale saluted. "We're going to get something to eat. When are you leaving?"

"Tomorrow."

"Good luck, buddy. Keep in touch."

"Will do."

They wandered off to the food table with all the other couples.

✦

The evening just got more depressing. Technically, the party was great. The food was great. Everyone looked great. Everyone seemed to be having a good time. I just kept drinking and peeling shrimp. I was finally about to leave when Nate walked up to me.

"Dale said I'd find you here."

I looked up at him. "Where have you been?"

He groaned as he sat down next to me. "Just as we were walking out of the house, Ashley's sister called. She got in a big fight with her husband and was crying buckets. Ashley was on the phone with her for an hour. I finally had to drag her out to the car."

"Where is she?"

"She's still in the car talking to her."

"I'm sorry."

"Hold on, I'm going to get a drink." He returned a minute later holding a short glass. "So, I'm glad we're alone. I wanted to talk to you."

"About what?"

"I'm worried. Are you really going to Utah to find that woman?"

"Yes."

He frowned. "Is now really the best time?"

"It's the perfect time. I don't have any appointments until January."

"I mean . . . emotionally. You know how it is, the holidays can make you kind of . . ."

"What? Crazy?"

"Yes," he said, owning up to his concern. "Being alone during the holidays can make you crazy. I looked up LBH on the Internet. It's code for *Let's be honest*. Think about it. Isn't that what you liked about the blog entries—her honesty? What if those aren't even her real initials?"

I had considered the possibility but had always pushed it from my mind. "Then I'm screwed."

"Exactly. So why not wait?"

I took another drink, then said, "Because she posted her last entry. She wrote that she's going home, wherever that is, and she's leaving on New Year's Eve. If I don't find her before New Year's, I'll never find her."

Nate continued to look at me grimly.

"I take it you don't approve."

"No, I don't. You don't know her name, you don't know anything about this woman."

"I know." I took a breath. "Look, it's hard to explain, but it's like there's this voice inside telling me that I've got to do this. Maybe it's desperation. Maybe it's just crazy, but it's there. I feel it."

"You're right," Nate said. "It *is* crazy. It's a lunatic affair."

"So what if it is? Look at me. I'm all alone drinking while everyone else is having a good time. I've been doing *predictable* and *sane* for my whole life, and where has it gotten me? I'm thirty-two, divorced, lonely, living in an apartment I hate, working the same job for the last decade, and watching Netflix alone every night before going to bed. Maybe it's time I tried something crazy."

Nate didn't answer.

"Haven't you ever just had a feeling deep in your heart that you needed to do something, even if you didn't know why? Even if it seemed a little *crazy*?"

He was quiet for a moment, then said, "Yes. I have."

"So do I ignore it? Do I pretend it's not there?"

Again he didn't answer.

"Have you forgotten what it was like before Ashley?"

Nate shook his head. "No. I remember." His mouth rose in a sad smile, then he reached over and patted me on the shoulder. "Do what you need to do, brother. Good luck."

"Thanks."

"When do you fly out?"

"Tomorrow around noon."

"Where do you land?"

"Salt Lake City. I've got a rental car. Midway's only an hour's drive from the airport."

"Are there any decent hotels?"

"I'm staying at a little place called the Blue Boar Inn. If it's half as nice as it sounds on the Internet, I will be very happy."

He smiled. "I hope the same is true of LBH."

CHAPTER

Twelve

My flight landed at Salt Lake City International Airport around half past four. Even though I'd been through it just days before, it seemed different. It was the first time I'd landed there as a final destination.

The airport was decorated for the holidays with tinsel snowflakes pinned to the walls and hanging from the tile ceiling by wire.

As I stepped outside the terminal the cold hit me like a slap. It rarely gets below seventy degrees in Daytona Beach, so I didn't have much (actually any) experience with nostril-freezing cold—which is exactly what the cold did. It froze the inside of my nose as it turned each breath into a visible cloud.

I had brought the warmest coat I owned, a sheepskin-lined leather aviator jacket, but against this kind of a cold it was about as much protection as Bubble Wrap on a demolition derby car. Just dragging my bag across the terminal road to the car rental center was enough to convince me that I would probably be investing in a parka. How did people live in such cold weather? *Why* would they?

Truthfully, I felt a little wimpy as I looked over and saw, on the curb near the passenger pickup, two teenagers wearing nothing but shorts and T-shirts. For the record, one of them was shaking and both were hugging themselves, so at least they were not oblivious to the cold. I guess coats aren't cool but hypothermia is.

The man at the car rental booth asked if I was going to one of the ski resorts.

"No. Midway."

"Same thing," he said. "You're just next to Park City. You should have four-wheel drive for the snow."

"Is there a lot of snow?"

He smiled. "Yeah."

He upgraded me to a Ford Explorer and within ten minutes I was on my way to Midway.

Following my GPS, I drove the I-215 freeway south to I-80 east toward the mountains until I reached the mouth of the canyon. The guy at the car rental wasn't kidding about snow. Snow-covered rock walls rose more than a hundred feet above me on both sides of the freeway. It was beautiful but made me feel anxious and claustrophobic. The traffic was somewhat heavy, not just because of the weather conditions, but because it was six o'clock and I had hit the tail end of rush hour.

I passed the sign for the Park City and Deer Valley ski resorts, then took exit 146 for US-40 toward Heber/Vernal. No mention of Midway. Fortunately, the man at the rental car place had also told me that Heber and Midway were sister cities and even many of the locals didn't know where one ended and the other began. About ten miles after the exit, a sign directed me west toward Midway and I turned off the highway.

Midway was more rural than I had imagined, and both sides of the two-lane road were lined with snow-covered trees, pastures, and red, rustic, snowcapped barns. It looked like something out of a Grandma Moses painting.

I crossed a bridge over a small river and followed the road west past a roundabout with a miniature bell tower in the center, then farther west past a development of Swiss-style chalets, until the road ended in a *T*. On the side of the road there was a round wooden post with blue metal signs that pointed south to several resorts and one that pointed north, with the words *The Blue Boar Inn*.

I turned right. The narrow road wound between more open fields for a hundred yards until it curved west again leading up to a large Swiss chalet. On the wall of a second-story balcony, overhanging the flags of America, Switzerland, France, and Germany, was the inn's logo—a blue, tusked boar painted above a flourish of olive leaves. In Gothic lettering it read:

THE BLUE BOAR INN

On the front corner of the property was a large bronze statue of a boar. Both sides of the road were lined in thick, ice-crusted snowbanks nearly four feet tall.

The inn's cobblestone driveway had been cleared and I drove up to the front door beneath a brook stone façade overhang with a massive Alpine clock. I got my bag out of the backseat and walked up the stairs.

There was a large Christmas wreath on the arched front

door, encircling a door knocker, a boar's head made of dark, rustic metal.

I pulled open the door and walked inside, stepping onto the parquet floor of an elaborately decorated lobby. The room smelled of cinnamon and apple, and a dozen or so poinsettias lined the tile floor.

The dining room was directly ahead of me, a luxurious, red velvet curtain pulled back to one side of the room as if revealing the opening of a show. On the far side was a large, intricately decorated Christmas tree.

The inn was every bit as luxurious as the webpage had described it to be. More so. I thought of Nate's words, hoping that I would be as impressed with LBH as I was with the inn.

I was admiring a picture of a boar set in a frame made of deer antlers, when someone said, "That etching is from the seventeen hundreds."

I turned back to see a petite Asian woman standing at the counter, smiling at me. "Are you Mr. Bartlett?"

"Yes. How did you know?"

"You're the last of our guests to check in. Welcome to the Blue Boar Inn."

"Thank you," I said, walking up to the reception counter. "This place is beautiful."

"Thank *you* for appreciating the work we've put into it. The owners have gone to extraordinary lengths to make this inn special. I'm afraid much of it is missed." She glanced down at her computer screen and said, "We have you registered for the William Shakespeare Room."

"That's right."

"I have you down for nine days, departing the following Tuesday morning, the twenty-second, is that correct?"

"Yes, ma'am. If I need to extend my stay a little longer, would that be a possibility?"

"You think you might be staying longer?"

"I'm not sure, but it's possible. I don't know exactly how long I'll be in town. I'm a little bit in limbo."

She looked back down at her computer screen. "As of right now your room is open until Christmas, but if we start to fill up I'll let you know." She set a guest form on the ledge between us. "If you'll just sign here."

She handed me a pen and I signed the form.

"Your room is on the second floor. I'll lead you up." She retrieved a key from a wall cubbyhole and walked out of the back room, joining me in the lobby.

Bag in hand, I followed her up a circular staircase. The lower half of the staircase walls and banister were stained and polished, dark wood beneath an oxblood-red plastered wall. The lighting fixtures on the wall were electric candle-shaped bulbs mounted to small deer antlers.

The second-floor landing had a hallway on one side with the other open to the dining room below. My room was at the top of the stairway across from the inn's library.

The antique wooden door had an inset hand-carved wood panel of a hare, hung by its feet. Above the door was painted, in delicate calligraphy:

William Shakespeare

"The Shakespeare is one of my favorite rooms," she said as I read the words above the door. She unlocked the door with the heavy key and pushed it open. "After you."

I stepped into the room. It was large with a tiled, European fireplace in the center. The south wall was mostly paned windows, and in the center of the room was a large, four-poster bed. The floor was covered by a black wool carpet.

"Do you like to read, Mr. Bartlett?"

"Yes."

"Just across the hall is our library. And right here, in keeping with the room's name, is our collection of Shakespeare. All of our rooms are named for authors—Shakespeare, Austen, Dickens, Thoreau, Brontë, Chaucer—the classical writers." She smiled at me. "If all is well, I'll leave you to your room. Breakfast is served between six and ten. We are well known for our breakfasts, which are complimentary for our guests. And there's always something to snack on in the dining room. Right now, there's some lemon-blueberry bread you may help yourself to."

"Is there somewhere close you would recommend for dinner?"

"Our own restaurant, of course. We're very proud of it." She smiled again. "You won't need to make reservations, just come on down. It's open tonight until ten."

"Thank you," I said.

"I hope you have a good stay, Mr. Bartlett. My name is Lita. If there's anything I, or my staff, can do to make your visit more pleasant, just let us know."

She handed me my room key. It had a large circular pewter key chain with the inn's embossed crest. "The door doesn't lock by itself so you'll need to use the key. If you leave the inn, feel free to leave your key at the front desk. That way, you won't have to lug it around and we'll know when your room is vacant for service."

"Thank you."

"Thank you for staying with us." She stopped at the doorway. "If you don't mind me asking, what brings you to Midway?"

"I'm looking for someone."

She looked at me with a quizzical expression. "Well, they shouldn't be too hard to find. Midway's not that big a town. Good night."

"Good night," I said.

After she left, I locked the door and looked around the room. The bed was king-size and at least three feet off the ground, resting on a dark oak wooden frame. On the adjacent wall was a tall crested armoire of cherry and birch veneer, elaborately carved in Old English designs.

I opened the armoire's bottom drawer and emptied the whole of my suitcase into it, with the exception of my shirts, which I hung in the upper section.

I slipped off my shoes, then climbed up onto the bed. Without pulling down the covers, I lay back on the padded duvet cover. The concierge's parting words came back to me. *They shouldn't be too hard to find.*

I hoped she was right.

CHAPTER

Thirteen

About an hour later my hunger exceeded my tiredness, so I washed up and headed back downstairs.

The dining room wasn't crowded. There were only three tables of couples, but it sounded like more, as they were all talking and laughing, happy to be in each other's company. Pachelbel's *Canon in D* played lightly from the room's sound system.

I was again greeted by Lita. "Hello, Mr. Bartlett. Would you like to join us for dinner?"

"Yes, thank you."

"Follow me, please." She seated me at a small table for two near the front of the restaurant, away from the other guests. "Is this acceptable?"

"Perfectly."

She smiled at me, then handed me a sheet of white paper and a heavy leather menu. "Someone will be right out to take your order."

As she walked away, I looked down at the paper she'd given me. It contained information on the room's antiques.

The dining area consisted of two rooms, and the walls

were painted a distinct green, a shade between fern and dark olive drab. The interior room was a darker hue than the outer and both were abundantly decorated with paintings and antiques.

On the north wall was a carved wooden crest of the Habsburg dynasty. Crossbows were mounted on either side of it. According to my paper, they had all seen battle.

The rooms were lit by three chandeliers made of varying sizes and types of antlers. I was in a world very different from the Spanish-infused setting of Florida.

A young, wholesome-looking woman with short blond hair brought me a cloth-covered bread basket. "Our bread is baked on the premises," she said, folding back the fabric to reveal two kinds of bread. She was obviously a young local and was earnestly trying to appear as sophisticated as possible. "Sourdough and wheat. May I get you something to drink?"

"Do you have a wine list?"

"Yes, sir. I'll bring it right out."

She returned with the list and I looked through their selection, then back over my menu. I ordered the chicken scaloppine with a glass of chardonnay. Then I returned to my inspection of the room, trying not to look as alone as I was, which reminded me of what LBH had written about how embarrassed we are to appear lonely.

Just fifteen minutes later my waitress brought out my soup, a butternut squash bisque. This was followed by the chicken scaloppine with baked spaetzle and asparagus spears. For dessert I had cheesecake. Everything was delicious.

When my waitress brought me my bill, she asked, "Are you staying in the inn?"

"Yes."

"Which room shall I bill this to?"

"The Shakespeare."

My response seemed to please her. "I love that room. But they're all nice. If you get a chance, you should have someone show you around. Our pub in back is especially amazing."

"I didn't know there was a pub."

"It's called Truffle Hollow," she said. "It's small, but pretty cool."

I charged the bill to my room and decided to take a walk around the inn. I followed a hallway back to the pub. Mounted along the wall were two large display cases with hundreds of collector pins from the 2002 Winter Olympics. I paused to look at them, but there were too many to devote much attention to them.

As I made my way back to the lobby, passing through the hall near the kitchen, I came to two paintings. Both were set in either kitchens or restaurants, which was appropriate for their location, and the first, to me, was especially haunting—a portrait of a waitress in an apron standing before a table. It was titled *Ester*. There was something about the look in the woman's eyes that I was drawn to. Something honest. Strong, yet vulnerable.

According to a gold plate on the wall, the artist's name

was Pino. I didn't know anything about him and I vowed to look him up.

It felt late, especially since I was still on Eastern Standard Time, so I went up to my room and got ready for bed. I wondered what tomorrow would bring.

CHAPTER *Fourteen*

When I woke the next morning, the window blinds were glowing. I rolled over onto my back, feeling the soft mattress contour with my body. Maybe it was the elevation or the fresh air, but I hadn't slept that well in a long time.

I climbed out of bed and lifted one of the blinds. It was bright and blue outside, subfreezing, and droplets of water had condensed inside my window. *Beautiful*, I thought. *Just beautiful.* I was glad that LBH lived in such a beautiful setting. It seemed fitting.

I showered and dressed, then went downstairs to the dining room. There was music playing, though it was contemporary, not the holiday music that had played the evening before.

There were about four other groups dining, and I seated myself at a table set for two. A waiter soon came out holding a wooden menu, the cover engraved with the inn's trademark boar.

I ordered the buttermilk griddle cakes with fruit, and less than ten minutes later the waiter returned with my meal. I had just started to eat when four elderly women and one man walked into the dining room. The man, who was gray-haired and large of tooth and nose, glanced at me, then left the women and walked up to my table.

"Are you alone, sir?" he asked.

"Yes."

He smiled broadly. "My name is Herr Niederhauser. But you may call me Ray. I am the innkeeper." He stated this with only slightly subdued pride.

"It's a pleasure to meet you. Are you German?"

"Only in spirit. But I speak Deutsch. In my youth I lived in Germany for a few years. Would you mind if I joined you?"

"Not at all. Please."

He pulled out the chair across from me and sat. Then he raised his finger at the waiter, who made a beeline to our table. "Yes, Ray."

"Gary, may I please have a coffee with ham and eggs? And I'll need utensils."

"Of course."

The waiter hurried to the kitchen.

"How is your meal?" Ray asked.

"I just started eating. But good so far."

"If you're here for Sunday brunch, you must try the Scotch eggs. Nothing like them in the world. Are you staying at the inn?"

"Yes, sir."

"What room?"

"The Shakespeare Room."

"Ah. Lovely room. One of my favorites. And how are your accommodations?"

"Everything is wonderful," I said.

"Very good, very good. Wonderful is our goal. We do our best to pay special attention to detail."

"So you're the innkeeper," I said.

"Yes, sir."

"How long have you been with the inn?"

"Almost eighteen years now, ever since the Warnocks purchased the property. Mrs. Warnock is my wife's cousin. We were dining with them in Park City when Mr. Warnock mentioned this property he had seen in the local real estate papers. We finished our dinners and drove to Midway that very evening. If my memory serves me, the Warnocks purchased the inn the next day.

"Of course, it didn't look like this back then. It used to be called the Huckleberry Inn. Mr. Warnock didn't want to tell his hunting buddies that he owned an inn called the Huckleberry, so he changed the name to the Blue Boar after an old pub in Oxford, England—which not coincidentally was mentioned in the legends and ballads of Robin Hood. There's a framed picture of a woodcut in your room showing Robin Hood and the Tinker sitting in front of the Blue Boar Inn."

"I saw that," I said.

"Our boar logo," he said, motioning to it on my key chain, "came from a three-hundred-year-old woodcut Mr. Warnock found in his travels."

"So the inn's English, not Swiss?"

"It's European. I would call the inn's design more Alpine than Swiss," he said. "The Warnocks remodeled the inn and we've been busy ever since. Of course, things really took off after Utah hosted the Winter Olympics in 2002. The Olympics were a special time." Again, a large smile crossed his face. "Among our guests we had the IOC members from Russia and Norway. The Russians didn't speak English, but they spoke *Deutsch*, as do I, so we communicated quite well."

"How did they find the inn?" I asked.

"I found them. I went over to Soldier Hollow, where they were building part of the Olympic venue, and invited them over for breakfast. It's easy to become friends over good food."

He suddenly laughed. "Ah, but when they came back over for the games, things really got interesting. The Russians arrived with a truckful of luggage—more than two dozen cases. They dropped them off by the front door and said, 'We'll be back to figure out what to do with them.' A half hour later a truck from the Utah National Guard arrived. The driver said he had a delivery for the Russian IOC delegation. Then the soldiers pulled back the tarp covering the truck and there were twenty-two cases of vodka. 'Where would you like them?' he asked."

Ray laughed jovially and slapped the table. "What a time, what a time. If you get a chance, you'll have to look at my Olympic pin collection. It's in the hallway on the way to Truffle Hollow. I have one thousand, one hundred and eighty pins."

"I saw it last night," I said. "It's impressive."

"I would hope so. It cost me a few groceries to collect them all."

"What did you do before you came to manage the inn?"

"I was a peddler," he said. "I sold high-end skiwear. And what about you?"

"I'm a peddler too. I sell technology."

"Ah. I was never so smart."

"I don't believe you," I said.

"It takes more heart than brains to be an innkeeper. It's the Golden Rule. Give them the hospitality that you would like for yourself."

"That sounds pretty intelligent to me."

The waiter returned with Ray's ham and eggs. Ray cut into the ham steak, took a bite, then asked, "Where are you from?"

"Daytona Beach, Florida."

"Racing capital of the world."

"Have you been there? Or are you a racing fan?"

"Neither. I once had someone stay here from Daytona Beach. I have a good memory that way. I looked the city up on the Internet. It's beautiful."

After I'd finished eating, Ray said, "If you have a minute, I'll show you around."

"I'd like that," I said.

We both stood, and he led me over to the west wall of the interior dining room. "These paintings once hung in a very famous Paris restaurant. They were painted in 1852 by Jean-Maxime Claude. The building went through the war, and the only reason these paintings weren't looted was because they were set into the walls." He stepped closer. "Now, notice the cabbage in this painting. Originally, this dining room was painted brown, but Mrs. Warnock didn't like the brown walls, so she matched the two greens in this cabbage and painted the dining room after them." He grinned. "I told you, there is much special attention here."

He led me down the hallway, past his Olympic pin collection, to the Truffle Hollow pub.

"The truffle is the boar's mainstay, so it was natural that we named the pub after it," Ray said as we walked inside. "This wooden sign outside the door is a replica of one the Warnocks found in England. Come sit."

There were about a dozen identical tables in all, and I sat down at one in the center of the room. Ray picked up a few nuts from a small dish of pistachios on the table and began to crack them open.

"Let me tell you about this room. The bar here was originally a travel trunk from the 1600s. You can see the locks on it."

The case was about four feet high and twice that long.

"How would someone carry a case that large?" I asked.

"Servants, no doubt. But she's beautiful, isn't she? The floor in here is made of southern pine imported from a World War I airplane hangar in North Carolina. And these tables all came from a bar in Austria. They've been together for more than one hundred and fifty years. But this table is especially valuable. Look here." He tapped the outer edge of the table. There was a brass plaque that read *Ray's Place.*

"Not bad," I said.

"I will live in infamy." He pointed up to the lamp above the bar. One half of it was a wooden carving of a woman's upper body, the other half were deer antlers. "This lamp is from the sixteenth century. The style is called *Lusterweibchen*."

He grinned. "It means 'lustful wench.' There's one just like it upstairs in the library."

"I saw it," I said.

"Then you've seen the library. Beautiful, is it not?"

"Every room I've seen in the inn is beautiful," I replied.

He stood. "Well, I'd better get back to work."

"Thanks for the tour," I said.

"You're very welcome."

As we headed back to the lobby, we walked down the hall with the two paintings I'd admired the night before. "I love these paintings," I said.

He stopped in front of them. "Both of these are by Pino. Are you familiar with Pino?"

"I had never heard of him until yesterday. But I was planning to look him up."

"Interesting man. Pino Daeni was an Italian artist who came to America and did book covers. He was one of the highest-paid cover illustrators in the world. He did many of Danielle Steel's book covers.

"Near the end of his career he grew weary of the publishers' deadlines and turned his attention to fine art, such as these. These two paintings are from his kitchen collections."

"Are they prints?" I asked.

He hesitated for just a moment, then said, "Between us, never to be shared, no. They are originals. We do not want people to know this because of their value." He turned back to the wall. "There is an especially interesting story behind these two paintings. Many years ago, a friend of the inn's owner had purchased a box of assorted wallpaper at a garage sale. She had them in her basement for nearly ten years when her daughter began rummaging through them. When she unraveled one of the rolls of wallpaper she found these two paintings rolled up inside of them."

"You hear stories like that," I said. "It's never happened to me."

"Don't give up yet. There is a lot of hidden treasure in this world," he replied. "Much of it human."

I nodded. "I agree with you. In a way, that's what brought me here."

"What do you mean?"

"I'm looking for someone."

"Someone?"

"A woman."

"Aren't we all," he said. "Let me tell you, you could do worse than Midway. There aren't many available women, but the ones I know are the salt of the earth."

"I'm looking for a specific woman."

He looked at me with intrigue. "Oh? Perhaps I could help you in your quest. What is her name?"

"That's the problem. I don't know her name."

He grinned. "That will definitely complicate things."

"All I know are her initials. LBH."

He rubbed his chin. "Very interesting. And how did you come to know this LBH?"

"I would say that I met her on the Internet, except we haven't really met. She writes a blog, and I just kind of fell for her." I thought he might think me crazy, but instead he looked at me as if with newfound admiration.

"My friend, I already thought you were an interesting fellow, but I was low in my estimation. You are a true romantic. I will do anything I can to help you find this woman. Where will you begin?"

"She wrote that she lived close to where the Swiss Days festival is held."

"That's the community center, the large Alpine building on Main Street. There's a park behind it."

"I was hoping to find some kind of registry of residents' names. Does Midway have a city hall?"

"Yes, the city offices are near the community center. I'll write the address down for you. Neither is far from here." He smiled. "It's a small town, nothing in Midway is far from here." He retrieved a colorful tourist map of Midway and penciled out the route to the city offices. As he handed it to me he said, "Just tell them Herr Niederhauser sent you."

"Thank you."

"My pleasure. May you find your woman."

CHAPTER *Fifteen*

Our tour had taken more than an hour. It was nearly noon when I walked out of the inn. The cold air was exhilarating. My breath clouded in front of me, billowing like a tailpipe.

As I walked to my car I was again astounded by the beauty and serenity of my snow-covered surroundings. Across the street from the inn was a golf course, covered with a large, crystalline blanket, sparkling with the high sun.

I got into my car, the cold vinyl stiff against my weight. I turned the heater on high, then looked down at my map. The route to the Midway city offices seemed simple enough.

Initially I mistakenly pulled up to the Midway community center. The building looked like a city hall. It was large and had the traditional Swiss-Alpine decoration with gingerbread eaves and a large clock. The door was locked and it was dark inside. It must have been noon because, as I walked back to my car, the clock began to ring. Then Swiss music with yodelers began playing. I looked up to see wooden figurines in Swiss lederhosen dancing around, like a massive cuckoo clock. I watched until the clock completed its show, then got back into my car and, consulting Ray's map again, drove to the city offices.

✦

The city office building looked a little like a church, with a gabled roof and a large clock tower in the middle of the structure. A man was walking down the sidewalk in front of the building with what looked like a fertilizer or seed spreader. He was twisting the handle and something was flying out.

I parked my car and got out. "Getting an early start on fertilizing the lawn?"

He looked at me like I was an idiot. "It's rock salt. I'm salting. So you don't slip and fall and sue the city."

"You're onto me," I said.

He just walked on.

The sidewalk forked when it reached the building. On a sign in the middle of the fork was an arrow pointing left, to *City Recorder*, the other pointed right, to *Mayor*.

I walked to the recorder's office. Hanging on the doorknob was a sign, *Will Return At* . . . with a little clock dial turned to four o'clock.

I retraced my steps to the other side of the building. I stomped the snow off my feet on the mat outside. As I opened the door I was greeted by a rush of warm air. At a desk near the middle of the room a fortysomething woman with bright red hair glanced up at me from a Mary Higgins Clark novel.

"Good afternoon," she said, looking a little annoyed that I had disturbed her reading. "May I help you?"

"Yes, I need some help locating someone. I was wondering if you could help me."

She set down her book. "Locating who?"

I suddenly felt the awkwardness of my task. "She's someone who lives in Midway. She's a blogger."

The woman just looked at me. "Does she have a name?"

"Her initials are LBH."

"You don't know this person's name?"

"No. I was hoping you'd have some kind of a list of residents."

"No," she said flatly.

"Is there someone else who could help me? Is your boss here?"

Her eyes narrowed. "I'm the *mayor*."

"I'm sorry."

Having worked with city officials for the last decade, I deduced that I had just killed any chance for governmental assistance. To my surprise she said, "Perhaps you should talk to our city treasurer and recorder."

"Thank you. How would I reach them?"

"*Them* are the same person. Just a moment." She rooted around her desk for a moment, then walked over to me holding a business card. "Brad isn't in right now. You should be able to find him at home."

I took the card. "It's okay to go to his home?"

"Yes," she said, as if she were talking to a three-year-old. "That's why I gave you his home address."

"Right. Thank you."

"Please shut the door on the way out. It's cold."

✦

I'm sure that I was as glad to leave the mayor's office as she was to see the back of me. I got in my car and input the address into my phone's GPS system. To my dismay, it couldn't find the address. After a few more minutes of trying, I walked back into the mayor's office.

"Back so soon," she said snarkily.

"Sorry. Could you help me find this address? My phone's GPS can't find it."

"Come here."

I walked over to her desk and she took out a piece of paper and started drawing lines on it. "This is Main Street. We are here. Go down a quarter mile to Holstein Way and turn left. Brad's the third or fourth house on the left. It's a two-story chalet-looking thing, but everything here's a chalet-looking thing, so just look for the gargantuan RV, one of those Death Star–size Winnebagos." She handed me the paper. "You can't miss it. Unless you don't know what a Winnebago is."

"Thank you."

"What's your name, anyway?"

"Alex Bartlett."

"Like the pear?"

"Yes."

"Where are you from, Mr. Bartlett?"

"Daytona Beach, Florida."

She lifted her phone and took a picture of me.

"You wanted my picture?" I said.

"You came all this way to find someone you don't know. I can only hope your motives are not homicidal. If they are, I now have your picture. That should, at least, give you pause."

For a moment I just looked at her. "I wasn't planning on killing anyone while I'm in town. Have a nice day."

It wasn't hard to find the recorder-treasurer's house. The home was, as the mayor had informed me, constructed in the Alpine style, with the characteristic wood shutters with tulips cut into them. On the front of the house there was both an American and a Swiss flag. And there was the Winnebago. I could see why the mayor had used the RV as a landmark—the thing was massive.

I parked my car in his driveway because the snowbank in front of the house was nearly as tall as my car and protruded well out into the street.

After I rang the doorbell, it took a few minutes before someone answered, a woman in her midforties, wearing a sweat suit, leg warmers, and a headband, like a 1980s aerobics throwback. Or a Richard Simmons impersonator. She was red-faced and slightly huffing and I assumed that I had just interrupted her Jane Fonda workout.

"May I help you?" she asked.

"I'm looking for Brad Wilcox."

"Brad's in the shower."

She just stood there. I wasn't sure what I was supposed to do with that. I finally said, "I'll come back."

"What is the nature of your visit? Is this governmental?"

"You could say that."

"Come inside. He's not one to leave a constituent out in the cold."

"Thank you."

I stepped inside the house and she quickly shut the door behind me. "Wipe your feet or take your shoes off."

"I'll take them off," I said, slipping the loafers from my feet.

"You can sit on the sofa there. Would you like a hot cider?"

"Thank you, no."

"All right. He shouldn't be more than an hour."

An hour?

She walked downstairs and a moment later I heard music start up. Eighties music: Wham!, Dire Straits, Supertramp, Duran Duran, Tears for Fears, a-ha.

After about half an hour the music stopped. Still, no one came up or out.

About ten minutes after the music stopped, a man, bald and wearing a robe, walked out into the kitchen. He opened the fridge, took out a glass bottle of milk (when was the last time I'd seen a glass bottle of milk?), drank from it, then turned around. He was startled to see me.

"Who are you?"

I stood. "My name is Alex Bartlett."

"Bartlett. Like the pear?"

"Yes."

"You related to the Bartletts in Lehi?"

"Where?"

"Lehi. Traverse Mountain area."

"Uh, no. I'm not from here. Are you Brad Wilcox?"

"You should know that. You're in my home."

"Your wife told me to wait here for you."

"My sister," he said. "I'm not married." He put the milk back into the fridge, then came to the edge of the room where I was sitting and asked, "What can I do for you?"

"I'm looking for someone."

"Are you a private investigator or a bounty hunter?"

"Neither. It's personal."

"Who are you looking for?"

"I don't know her name. Just her initials."

Just then his sister walked up the stairs and into the kitchen. She had large patches of sweat under her arms.

"You forgot to get more milk," Brad said to her.

"Chill, man. I haven't been to the store yet. I had to exercise. And this guy came to the door."

He turned back to me. "You're looking for someone but you don't know their name?"

"No, sir."

"What is the nature of your manhunt?"

"I've been following her blog."

"Her what?"

"He said *blog*," his sister said. "It's when people write on the Internet."

"Why can't you get her name from the Internet?"

"She only put her initials."

"What initials?"

"LBH."

He squeezed his chin. "Lima Bravo Hotel. Doesn't ring any bells. Did said female write something offensive?"

"No, sir. Actually, the opposite."

"You're a fan of this Internet blog?"

"You might say so."

"Then you're one of those stalkers."

"No."

"You're not stalking her?"

"No, I'm just . . . I want to meet her."

They both just looked at me. Then Brad said, "It would not be prudent for me to be a party to any such affair. We do not have records available to the public."

"You don't have any records?"

"I didn't say that. I said we don't have records *available to the public*. I have billing records for utilities and water but I am not at liberty to share that data with John Q. Public, i.e., you. So, unless there's something else I can help you with, I'll see you to the door."

"No," I said. "That would be it. Thank you."

I walked back to the door, slipped my shoes back on, and then walked out to my car. *These Midway people are interesting*.

On Main Street I found a grocery store, where I bought some bottled water and a premade turkey salad. I ate in my car, then drove back to the inn. I lay down on my bed fully intending to think about my next step, but fell asleep instead. I woke around eight and went downstairs for dinner. There were only two other tables occupied in the dining room.

Lita walked up to me holding a menu. "Would you like dinner, Mr. Bartlett?"

"Yes. Thank you."

She led me to a quiet section of the dining room and handed me the menu. "Have a nice dinner."

A moment later a waiter came out. "What will it be tonight?"

"I'd like the escargots to begin."

"Very good. And for your main course?"

"I'll have the salmon."

"Seared salmon with artichoke and squash. What will you have to drink?"

"A glass of your pinot noir, please."

"A very good choice." He took my menu and walked away.

There was a local newspaper on a side chair and I picked it up. On the front page was a picture of the mayor talking about the importance of tourism and attracting Park City visitors. All I could think of was how she thought I'd come to kill someone.

My escargots came five minutes later along with my wine.

I had just started to eat when someone said, "Snails; nothing like snails with a fine glass of burgundy." I looked up to see Ray walking into the dining room.

"You're working late," I said.

"Not working, Mr. Bartlett. I came back for my glasses and stopped in Truffle Hollow for a drink. May I join you?"

"Please. Would you like some escargots?"

"I love escargots, but not after Scotch." He pulled the chair out across from me and looked at my glass. "What are you drinking?"

"Pinot noir."

"A complicated grape. What did you order for dinner?"

"The salmon."

"You chose well," he said, lightly nodding. "So how was your day, Mr. Bartlett? *Fruitful?*"

I think he meant the comment as some kind of pun on my name. "No. The city wasn't much help."

"You went to the city offices?"

"Yes. I followed your map."

"And they weren't helpful? Surprising." His bushy eyebrows fell. "You didn't run into Jan, did you?"

"Is she the mayor?"

"Jan's the mayor."

"Yes, I met her."

He grimaced. "I'm sorry."

"She wasn't much help."

"No. I don't imagine she would be. I hope you didn't use my name. I ran against her for mayor some years ago. She still holds a grudge. You probably should have gone to Brad Wilcox. He's the city recorder. He'll have all the names."

"I went to Mr. Wilcox's house."

"And he didn't help you?"

"No. He just said he wasn't at liberty to share public records."

"I guess I can understand that. He probably thought you were a serial killer."

"No, that was the mayor. Wilcox thought I was a crazed stalker."

Ray grinned. "Well, it's not like anyone in town is private. I mean, pretty much everyone's listed in the local phone book."

I looked at him blankly. "Midway has a phone book?"

"Of course. Doesn't every city have a phone book?"

I felt stupid for not having thought of that. "A phone book would be helpful."

"I'm sure we've got a few extra lying around. Would you like me to find you one?"

"Yes, please."

Ray walked up to the front counter. He returned carrying a small directory printed on newsprint. "Here you go, sir.

I should have just given you that to begin with. Probably would have saved you some humiliation."

I took the book from him and examined the cover.

The Park City / Heber Valley phone book
Comprising Summit & Wasatch Counties

The directory was about the size of a trade paperback novel. I thumbed through it, then set it down. "This is just what I need. Thank you."

"My pleasure. I have one question for you."

"Yes?"

"I'm assuming you're going to come up with a list of possible residents to visit. So, when you visit these people, what are you going to say to them?"

Dale's dilemma. "I'm not sure."

"Well, you might find that you need to be a little sneaky. If you tell them that you're trying to find someone from the Internet, they might close up. Especially if she's the *one.* You know what I mean?"

"What do you mean by 'sneaky'?"

"Well, maybe you tell them that you're with the US Census."

"They'd believe that?"

"I would think so. I would."

I thought a moment. "I don't know. I think I'd rather be straightforward."

"I'm not telling you how to conduct your hunt," he said, pushing back his chair, "just giving some advice. Good luck finding your woman. I'd better get on home to my own before she puts out a missing-persons report. Is there anything else I can do for you?"

"There's one thing," I said. "Please don't take this wrong, the food here is delicious but a bit . . ."

"You would like a recommendation of somewhere to eat besides the inn."

"If you wouldn't mind."

"Of course I wouldn't mind. We've got the usual fast food haunts, which I would *not* recommend. I would recommend the Mistletoe Diner. It's just off Main Street, only a few blocks from the Midway community center, near the city offices. You probably drove past it this afternoon."

"Food's good?"

"Food's excellent."

"Thanks. I'll give it a try."

"Oh, and if Thelma makes pie, eat it." Ray stood and walked out of the room.

Just a minute after he left my waiter brought out my meal. "Here you are, sir. *Bon appétit.*"

After dinner I carried the phone book up to my room. I sat on my bed and began thumbing through its pages. The first two-thirds of the book were yellow-paged business listings. I turned to the white pages and leafed through it until I found where *H* began. There were six pages of last names that began with the letter *H*.

I took a pen from the nightstand and began going down

the pages. There were two columns on each side, with about a hundred listings in each column. There were only a few names with the middle name or initial of *B*, but I didn't want to rule out the rest.

Many of the listings were men or residents of Park City, which disqualified them. By the time I was done, I was left with a list of eighteen names.

Hall, Leslie B.
Hanks, Linda
Harding, Linda
Harman, Lindsey
Hardy, Liz
Harkness, Lori
Heger, Laurie
Henrie, Lillian
Heughs, Layla
Hewitt, Lisa
Hickman, Leah
Higham, Louise
Hill, Lorraine
Hitesman, Laurel
Holbrook, Lilly
Howard, Lydia
Howell, Lisa
Hoyt, LaDawn

I was making progress. At least I had a list. Tomorrow morning I would start my search at the top, with Leslie Hall.

CHAPTER

Sixteen

Breakfast the next morning was eggs Blackstone. The difference between eggs Blackstone and eggs Benedict is the former is made with bacon instead of ham. It was delicious, as were the apple fritter pancakes. I expected to run into Ray in the dining room but he never came by.

After breakfast I went for a brisk two-mile walk along the road next to the golf course, then came back to my room and showered. There was a text from Nate. As usual, he was succinct.

How goes it?

I texted back.

The hunt has just begun. I've narrowed LBH down to 18 leads.

He texted back.

Seek and destroy.

After I had dressed, I sat down and looked at my list again. I wasn't sure how long it would take to visit eighteen people, but unless LBH was, coincidentally, the last name on my list, I wouldn't need to visit them all.

I grabbed Ray's map and walked out to my car with the list. My windshield was iced over, so I brushed the snow off with my arm, then, using a credit card, attempted to scrape off the ice. A man in the parking lot next to me was also scraping the snow from his SUV. He watched me with amusement. After a moment he approached.

"Don't you have a scraper?" he asked.

"No."

"Stand aside." He scraped, then brushed the snow off my windows. After he finished he said, "You're going to need to pick up a scraper."

"Thanks. Do you know where I can find one?"

"Anywhere. Grocery stores, gas stations."

I thanked him again and he walked back to his car. I got inside and started my car. As I waited for it to heat up, I looked at the first name on my list. Leslie B. Hall. 1219 Montreux Circle.

"All right, Leslie. Let's see if you're the one."

I typed her address into my phone's GPS. This time it came up with a location. The house was about a half mile from the Swiss Center, but if Swiss Days attracted thousands of people, it was conceivable that people would still be parking out that far. Leslie could be the one.

✦

Leslie Hall's house was modest and set back from the street. The front walkway hadn't yet been shoveled. There was a snow-covered refurbished John Deere tractor in the driveway with a *For Sale* sign taped to its engine.

I had not prepared for the snow. Wearing just loafers, I trudged through shin-deep snow up the walk and cautiously climbed the stairs to a wooden porch, which creaked a bit beneath me. I pushed the doorbell but didn't hear anything, so I knocked. Just seconds later a well-fed man holding a can of Budweiser opened the door.

"What can I do you for?" the man asked.

"Sorry to bother you, but I'm looking for Leslie Hall."

He looked at me narrowly then said, "Well, you found me."

"You're Leslie?"

"That's what it says on my driver's license. Who you expecting?"

"Sorry. I must have the wrong address."

"You were expecting a woman, weren't you? I know. I get it all the time."

"You're right. My mistake."

His eyes narrowed. "You one of them bounty hunters?"

"Me? No."

"Salesman?"

"No. Well, I mean, I am, but that's not why I'm here. I'm just looking for someone I met on the Internet."

The corners of his mouth rose in a knowing smile. "Ah, yeah. I get it. She blew you off, huh? Gave you a bad address, wrong name?"

I nodded, deciding it would be easier to go with his theory than my real story. "Wouldn't be the first time."

"I know how you feel, buddy. Happens to me *all* the time.

I meet a hot babe at a bar, she gives me her address, I drive to it, blammo, it's a freakin' landfill or a church parking lot, you know what I mean? Happens all the time. Women are ruthless."

"They can be. You have a good day."

"You too. I didn't catch your name."

"Alex."

"Alex, Leslie. Guess you know that already."

"Yeah, thanks, Leslie. Sorry to bother you."

"No worries."

As I walked away he shouted after me, "Hey, there's a Jazz game on tonight if you're not busy. Playin' the Trailblazers. Cold brew, game, could be fun."

I turned back. "Thank you. But I have work to do."

"She really broke your heart, didn't she? I tell you, nothing eases woman pain like a little bromanship."

"Thanks. I'll think about it."

"Game starts at seven. I'll put some brats on."

"I'll think about it. Thanks."

I heard the home's door shut behind me as I walked back to my car.

Interesting people.

CHAPTER

Seventeen

The next name on my list was Linda Hanks. Her house was only a few blocks from where the Swiss Days festivities were held, so it could potentially be the place. The real LBH. And I'd never met a man named Linda.

The house, a one-level bungalow with a small front yard, was covered in olive-green wood paneling with an orange door and orange trim around the windows. Pink plastic flamingos stood breast-high in the snow. A white Subaru wagon was parked in the driveway.

I parked in the street, near the mailbox, and walked up the concrete driveway to the shoveled sidewalk that led to the front door.

I rang the doorbell and the door opened almost immediately, catching me off guard. An attractive blond woman stood in the threshold. "That was fast. I just barely hung up with your office. Come in, please. It's in the kitchen."

"Excuse me?" I said.

"Hurry, it's getting all over."

She turned her back to me and rushed toward the dining area. I hesitated for a moment, then followed. The kitchen's linoleum floor was covered with water and I could hear running water over the sound of the grinding of a garbage disposal.

"I don't know what happened. I just turned on the disposal and just a few seconds later water started shooting all over. I shut the cupboard door but it keeps coming out." She looked as distressed as she sounded, so much so that I didn't have the heart to tell her that I wasn't the plumber. At any rate, what better chance to discover LBH? She certainly fit the criteria.

"Just a minute," I said, crouching down in front of the sink. I took off my coat, then opened the cupboard door, catching a splash of water in my face. I saw the problem right away. The black plastic pipe connected to the disposal had slipped off.

"Could you turn the disposal off, please?"

"Yes, sorry." She reached over the counter and turned off a switch. The grinding stopped.

I lifted the pipe and slipped it back over the disposal and the water stopped spraying. I pushed it in as tight as I could but still needed to adjust the clamp. "Do you have a flathead screwdriver?"

"I . . ." Her brow fell. "Didn't you bring tools?"

"I don't want to let go of this. May I use yours?"

"What kind of screwdriver?"

"The kind with a flat end."

"Just a minute." She returned with three different sizes of screwdrivers. I took the largest of the three, loosened the clamp, then slid the hose clamp over the outer pipe and tightened it until the pipe indented under its pressure. I climbed out from under the sink and handed her back the screwdriver. She had calmed, and I was finally able to get a good look at her. She was maybe a few years older than me, pretty, with thick blond hair pulled back in a ponytail. She wore skinny jeans and a red sweater.

"That should hold."

"Thank you," she said. "Now I just have to mop this up. You'd think that after being single for three years I'd know something about plumbing."

"I really don't know that much myself," I said. "Just enough to get by."

She gave me a peculiar look. "I thought you had to pass a test or something to be a plumber."

It took me a moment to process her confusion. "Right. Of course. You know what they say, the more you know, the more you know you don't know."

She looked even more confused but said, "How much do I owe you?"

The question caught me off guard. "I'll send you a bill."

"Okay. How much was it? So I can plan on it."

"Ten dollars," I said.

"Just ten dollars? Your receptionist said the house call was a minimum fifty dollars."

"That's the normal price, but I was driving by the neighborhood, so no problem. If you could just write down your name for me, I'll have the office take care of this."

"Oh," she said. "That explains why you didn't have any tools."

"Right. And that's also why I don't have an invoice. My apologies."

"No problem."

She retrieved a pad and pen, then wrote in a distinctly feminine scrawl:

Linda Hanks

"Is that your full legal name?" I asked.

"No, sorry." I watched as she wrote her name again.

Linda Wells Hanks

I looked at it with disappointment. "Is that your maiden name? Wells?"

"Yes. I still use my ex's last name. Actually, my middle name is Michelle."

I folded up the paper. "Thank you."

"No, thank you. I feel guilty only paying you ten dollars. I really should pay you back somehow. Would it be inappropriate for me to invite you to dinner?" I noticed that she furtively glanced at my bare ring finger. "I mean, if you're available."

I hesitated for a moment, then said, "Of course. That would be nice."

"What are you doing tomorrow night?"

"I should be free."

"Wonderful. Seven o'clock?"

"I'll have to check my schedule, but I'll give you a call."

"Sure." She wrote down her phone number and followed me to the door. She watched me walk to my car, then waved as I drove away.

Just halfway down the block I passed a truck wrapped with a picture of a drain and the words *Linton Plumbing* written on the side. I thought of driving back and intercepting him, but I wasn't sure what I'd say, so I just kept on. Dinner plans with Linda probably weren't going to work out.

CHAPTER *Eighteen*

Two down, sixteen to go. I looked at my list. The next name was also a Linda. Linda Harding. I glanced down at my phone to check the time. It was a little past two and I had a text message from my boss. There had been a problem with my client in Oakland, and even though the next home on my list was just three blocks away, I decided to go back to the inn to take care of it.

It was past four before I went back out. I drove directly to the house, a small, white brick rambler. The roof was covered in snow and icicles, some reaching all the way to the ground to form columns. The only color was from the pale-blue front door and the red alarm-system signs poking up through the snow like crocuses.

There was an opened bag of ice melt next to the front door and blue pebbles of snowmelt (I now knew what it was) were scattered about, crunching beneath my feet.

I rang the doorbell and a chime went off inside. A moment later I heard the scuffle of something across the floor, then there was the slide of a chain lock followed by a dead bolt. The door slowly opened.

The woman in the doorway looked to be at least in her late eighties, with gray-white hair. She was leaning against a walker. "May I help you?"

"I'm sorry," I said. "I must have the wrong address."

"What address were you looking for?"

I wasn't sure how to reply. "Actually, this one."

"Well, who are you looking for? I know about everyone in this city. I've been here my whole life."

"Linda Harding?"

"That's me. I'm Linda."

"Yes," I said, still not sure where to go with this. "Actually, the Linda I was looking for was supposed to be a bit . . . younger."

"I'm sorry, I can't oblige you there. I would if I could. I am the only Linda Harding in Midway. Perhaps I could be of assistance. You can tell me more over some hot cocoa. Please come inside."

"No, I've taken enough of your time."

"Time is all I have," she said. "At least what's left of it. And, truthfully, I'm a bit lonely today. I'm sure a fine-looking man like you doesn't know what that feels like, but please, come in. I insist."

She looked at me with such eagerness that I couldn't refuse. Especially someone lonely. "Sure, I have a few minutes," I finally said.

She clapped her hands with delight. "Wonderful."

I stepped inside. The home's interior was outdated but immaculate and smelled of menthol and lavender. The floor was carpeted in vibrant blue shag and the walls were baby-blue with bright white gold leaf on the wainscoting.

All around the house were pictures—framed photographs of families and youth, presumably her children and grandchildren.

"When you rang I was about to put some popovers in the oven. I love a good popover, don't you? Especially with a little marmalade. Now I have someone to share them with. Just shut the door behind you." She lightly waddled as she pushed her walker to her kitchen. "Have a seat at the table while I make us some cocoa. I like mine extra chocolaty—how about you?"

"However you make it is fine," I said.

"Fine, fine." She was gone for nearly ten minutes while I sat there looking over her dining room. There were more photographs—some, I presumed, of my hostess in her youth.

She came back without her walker, hunched over and carrying two steaming mugs. "It's a little hot." She set them both down on the table and sat down across from me. "I haven't seen you before. Are you new to Midway?"

"I'm not from here. I'm from Florida."

"Oh, yes. I went to Florida once. My parents took me when I was a little girl. I saw the Okefenokee swamp. Never forgot that. Those alligators were something. They were feeding them chickens. No alligators in Utah. Maybe in the Hogle Zoo, but not running around. It's too cold. I guess the cold's good for something."

"It's definitely cold."

"Don't let that be a deterrent to moving here, if that's your inclination. The weather may be cold but the people are warm. Most of them, anyway. Here in Midway, we like to look after each other. The boy across the street comes and shovels and salts my driveway whenever it snows . . ."

For the next sixty minutes Linda espoused the virtues

of life in Heber and Midway while teaching me the towns' 156-year history. She told me that Midway was renamed from "Mound City," after the relocation of an Indian tribe forced the building of a fort midway between the towns of Heber and Mound City, hence Midway.

There was just one break from the conversation, when the timer on the oven sounded and Linda brought out a tray of hot popovers, orange marmalade, and raw honey.

She finally came back to the purpose of my visit. "Now, this other Linda Harding you're looking for, could it be that you have the wrong Midway? You know, there are at least a dozen cities named Midway in this country, including the famous Midway Island, which marked a turning point in World War II. My great-uncle Kirby was in the Navy. He was stationed at Midway—not this Midway, the island in the Pacific, Midway—when the war began. That's where the Japanese—"

Realizing that we were potentially entering another hour-long lecture, I quickly stood. "Ms. Harding?"

"Linda, please, Alex. Call me Linda. Why are you standing? Do you need to use the washroom?"

"No, but I think you may be right. I might be in the wrong city, and I'd better get right on this while there's still time. Thank you so much for the cocoa and popovers and your company."

"The cocoa and popovers were certainly no trouble, and I'm always so glad for company. As a matter of fact, I'm just about to start making dinner. Would you like to stay? You have to eat."

"Thank you so much, but I have other commitments I need to attend to. And thank you so much for setting me straight. I'll see myself to the door."

I headed to the front door with Linda still talking behind me. "I would love to have you for dinner. It's no trouble."

When I opened the door it was already dark outside, the curtain of evening accented by a softly falling snow. "Thank you, but I'd really better get on my way."

"Come back soon," she said. "Tomorrow I'm baking my cinnamon pull-aparts."

✦

As peculiar as my first day of visits had been, outside of the two city bureaucrats, everyone I'd met so far had wanted to spend more time with me. I had come away with three dinner invitations. *What if the world's best-kept secret was that the whole world was lonely?*

I was able to clear some of the snow off my windshield with the wipers but had to use my hands for the rest, leaving them wet and cold. On Main Street I found a convenience store. There was a box of snow brush/scrapers near the front door and I bought the largest size they had.

In spite of Mrs. Harding's popovers, I was hungry, so I decided to find the restaurant that Ray had told me about. The Mistletoe Diner.

CHAPTER

Nineteen

I drove cautiously, my wipers flailing wildly against the increasingly steady snowfall as I looked for the diner. I had the car's defroster on full, which had cleared patches of windshield about the size of two large pizzas but not all of it, which is partially why I drove past the diner twice before finally finding it, a block and a half east of the Midway community center.

Unlike most of the other establishments on the street, the diner didn't look Swiss. It also didn't have much going on by way of signage. The *Mistletoe Diner* on the neon sign above the front door didn't light—only a sprig of green mistletoe that moved back and forth, looking more like a feather duster than holiday-themed foliage.

The diner was built adjacent to the road and was long and narrow, with a curtained window at each booth along the front of the building. The windows glowed invitingly.

I parked my car, then walked inside. Hanging directly above the waiting area was a sprig of dusty mistletoe that looked a few decades old. Christmas music was softly playing. *Bing Crosby*. I wondered if, considering the diner's name, there was always Christmas music playing.

"Someone will be right with you," an older woman said

as she walked past me to a table. She was wearing a white apron over a black shirt with the sleeves rolled up. She said to a younger woman on the far end of the front counter, "Ari, will you help the gentleman?"

"Of course." The waitress had been facing away from me and she turned, wiping her hands on her apron. "Hi. Welcome to the Mistletoe Diner."

The young woman was dressed the same as the other waitress, with a white apron and black blouse, except her blouse was short-sleeved, exposing the pale, smooth flesh of her arms. Her dark-brown hair softly cradled her face. She had lush lips and full, high, defined cheeks that almost seemed to crowd her dark eyes.

The truth is, most of the time when we meet someone it barely registers a memory—you know, those times when someone tells us their name and we forget it before we even use it. Then there are times that some force, invisible as magnetic waves, creates an immediate pull and connection. The latter describes the first moment I saw *her*. She was attractive, which in itself implies some form of magnetism, but it was more than that. If she was beautiful, she also looked, like the diner, a little worn down and frayed around the edges. Peculiarly, there was something familiar about her.

I was so busy taking her in that it almost startled me when she spoke.

"Dinner for one?" she asked softly, grabbing a menu from the front counter.

"Yes. It's just me." *Why was I always embarrassed to say that?*

"Would you like a table or a booth?"

"Booth," I said, adding, "I'm a recluse."

She gently smiled and it was warm and pretty. "The isolation booth it is."

I followed her to the back corner of the diner. "Here you are. Seclusion."

"Thank you." I sat and she handed me a menu.

"My name is Aria. Can I get you something to drink?"

"That's a pretty name," I said.

She lightly smiled and pulled back a strand of hair from her face. "Thank you. I had nothing to do with choosing it. Would you like something to drink?"

"Do you have lemonade?"

"Yes. We have Minute Maid. I can put some strawberry or blackberry syrup in it if you like."

"Strawberry, please."

"One strawberry lemonade. I'll give you a minute to look over the menu."

I watched her walk back to the kitchen, then opened my menu. The food selection was typical of a diner: chicken-fried steak, mashed potatoes, that sort of thing. I was still perusing the menu when she returned carrying my drink and a basket of bread. "Here you are, your drink and some bread. Did you have time to decide on what you'd like?"

"I'm still undecided. What do you like?"

She leaned comfortably against the opposite vinyl backrest. "I usually order the chicken pot pie."

I set down my menu. "That sounds good. I'll have that."

"We're out of it tonight." When I looked at her blankly she said, "You asked me what I like, not what we have."

I smiled. "Fair enough. What do you like that you *have*?"

"I would recommend the meat loaf. Or the sage-roasted chicken. They're both good."

"And you're sure that you have both?"

She grinned slightly. "I'm pretty sure we do. And I also recommend the split pea soup, if you like split pea soup. If you don't, then don't order it."

"I'll have the meat loaf and a cup of the soup."

"The meat loaf comes with mashed potatoes with mushroom gravy and corn or mixed vegetables."

"What kind of vegetables?"

She thought. "It's mostly corn too."

I laughed again. "I'll have that."

"All right, that'll be just a few minutes. Would you like your soup first?"

"Yes."

"Oh, and enjoy the bread. I baked it this morning."

She disappeared back into the kitchen. I tasted my lemonade, then stirred in the strawberry syrup that had settled to the bottom of the glass. As I sipped my drink I panned the dining room.

Some modern diners try to mimic traditional old-time diners with faux vintage Coke signs, vinyl bar chairs, and neon clocks, accessories now more likely to be made in China than Toledo, Ohio. But the accessories surrounding me were old and authentic, as if the place were caught in a time warp. And the other patrons seemed as eclectic as the diner itself: truck drivers, old folks out for pie, tourists.

Aria returned carrying my soup steaming in a porcelain

bowl on a matching plate. "Here you are. The soup du jour. Be careful, it's hot."

"That was fast."

"It doesn't take long to ladle soup into a bowl." She set the bowl down in front of me. "I'll be back with the rest of your meal in a few minutes."

I tried the soup and was pleased to find that it was as good as anything I'd had in my travels. Per Aria's suggestion, I took a piece of thick white bread, buttered it, and took a bite. It was good as well. I broke some pieces of the bread into the bowl and began to eat.

I had just finished the soup when Aria returned carrying my meal and a fresh lemonade, even though I had drunk less than half of what I had.

"Here you are. How was the soup?" She looked at my empty bowl. "It must not be terrible."

"I could probably force down another bowl."

"I think you'll like this as well." She set down a platter with meat loaf and a generous helping of mashed potatoes covered with brown gravy. That's when I noticed the small diamond on her ring finger. Peculiarly, it bothered me.

"Can I get you anything else?"

"No. Thank you."

"Just wave if you need anything." She walked across the room to a new booth of diners.

She moved gracefully. She was in a small-town diner, but she was not without poise. I suspected that she could have been in one of the finest restaurants in Europe and won the crowd. I wondered if she was from the town or a transplant.

I ate slowly, in no particular hurry to be anywhere. I tried not to stare at her. I saw her glancing over at me several times, though I'm sure she was just doing her job. As I was finishing she came over to check on me.

"How's your dinner?"

"I'm glad you recommended the meat loaf."

"Comfort food," she said. "Perfect for a cold winter night."

I desperately scrambled for something to keep the conversation going. "I sounded a little weird telling you that I'm a recluse. I'm not, like, Howard Hughes."

"A lot of people don't like company when they eat. I used to have a dog who wouldn't eat if you looked at him."

"You just compared me to your dog."

She smiled again, and it was beautiful. "At least he was a *cute* dog."

I laughed. *Was she flirting?*

"It surprises me that most of the truck drivers want to be alone. You would think that being on the road all the time would make them want company, but I think it does the opposite. Most of them shun it. At least when they come here."

"I think I understand," I said. "I travel a lot for work. It seems that the more I travel, the more I just want to stay inside my hotel room and order room service. It happens."

She thought a moment, then said, "Maybe we get out of the habit of being around people faster than we think." She took a deep breath and smiled. "That got deep, fast."

I put out my hand. "By the way, my name is Alex."

"Hi, Alex. What brings you to Midway?"

"How do you know I'm not from Midway?"

She cocked her head. "Because if you were, I would have already known you."

"I'm from Daytona Beach, Florida."

"The beach. It's been so long since I've seen beach. And sand. And warmth. They say there's four seasons in Utah. Almost winter, winter, still winter, and road construction."

"There's a lot of snow out there."

She looked out the window. "It's still coming down."

I shook my head. "It's relentless. Are the roads safe?"

She unsuccessfully hid her amusement. "Is it your first time in snow?"

"It's my first time driving in snow."

"Just don't drive too fast. We're supposed to get a lot more snow this week. We get, like, a hundred inches a year. How long are you here?"

"I'm not sure. About a week."

"What is it that you do?"

"I sell software that counts cars."

"Why would someone want to do that?"

"For a lot of reasons. Traffic control. Safety."

She nodded. "Government stuff."

"Exactly."

"Where are you staying?"

"At the Blue Boar Inn."

"The Blue Boar is really nice," she said. "I've never stayed there, but I've had dinner there. It's a lot fancier than the diner."

"The innkeeper there recommended your diner."

"Ray," she said. "He's sweet. He comes here every Thursday for pie. On Thursdays Thelma makes pecan pie just for him. Speaking of which, would you like some pie? Tonight we have Thelma's caramel apple pie."

"Ray warned me not to pass on any pie," I said. "So yes, please."

"Would you like cheese with that?"

"Cheese with pie?"

"You know what they say, apple pie without the cheese is like a kiss without a squeeze."

"I've never heard that."

"Maybe it's a small-town thing. Being from Florida, you're probably more of a Key lime pie kind of guy, anyway."

"I love Key lime pie."

"Why wouldn't you?" She glanced over at the counter, where a man was looking at us. I couldn't tell for sure but it looked like he was glowering at me.

"I need to check on my other tables, then I'll get your pie. I'll hurry."

As she walked away I was again struck by how familiar she looked. *Where did I know her from?*

Five minutes later she returned with the pie. It was lattice-topped and the crust was lightly browned and encrusted with sugar.

"It's a work of art," I said.

"Thelma is to pie what Michelangelo was to sculpture," she said. "And here's your check."

I looked it over. "May I add something to my bill? I'd like to take some pie back to Ray. To thank him for the recommendation."

"I'll get the pie. Don't worry about it. Just tell him Aria says hi."

"Thank you."

She went over and poured coffee to a man at a booth, then disappeared into the kitchen while I ate my pie. Thelma was indeed a pie-making genius.

When Aria returned I gave her my credit card. She took care of the bill and brought me my receipt. I left her a large tip. "It was nice meeting you, Alex," she said. "I hope you'll come back in before you leave town."

"I'm sure I will. Pecan pie is my favorite."

"Thursday," she said. "She makes it on Thursday."

As I walked out to my car I didn't mind the cold. I started up the car, turned on its heater, grabbed my new snow scraper, and cleaned the snow off the windshield. In spite of making little progress with LBH, I felt happy. I don't think it was because of the pie.

CHAPTER *Twenty*

The next morning at breakfast Ray stopped by my table. "Good morning, my friend. How goes the hunt?"

"It goes," I said. "I'm glad you're here. I have something for you."

"You do?" he said, sitting down.

I handed him the Styrofoam box with the piece of pie. He opened it and smiled. "Oh, yes. Thelma's caramel apple pie. Food of the gods."

"I had the kitchen refrigerate it overnight."

"Did you have some for yourself?"

"Yes."

"Then you know Thelma's genius. You should try Thelma's pecan," he said. "That's worth writing home about." He grabbed a fork from another table and began to eat. Then he looked up at me. "So you found the diner."

"It was as good as you said. And the pie's courtesy of Aria."

A pleasant look came across his face. "Better yet, you found *Aria*." He put a special emphasis on her name. "If I were younger . . ."

"So you like Aria?"

"*Like? Adulate* or *worship* are better words. Did she say anything about me?"

"She sent the pie and said to say hi."

"That's it?"

"She also called you 'sweet.'"

He frowned. "Sweet. Like a puppy. That's the problem with age. You're cute, not sexy."

"It's just as well," I said, hiding my amusement. "You're married."

"Yes, I am. Very, very married."

"As is she."

He took another bite of pie then looked up. "No, Aria's not married."

"She had a ring."

"I know. That's truck driver repellent. She *was* married. When she first came to Midway. But that was a long time ago."

"She's not from Midway?"

"No, she's a transplant. She came here about six years ago. She and her husband, Wayne, Wade, Walt, something with a *W*, started a coffee shop, but it didn't make it. He left, she stayed. That pretty much sums it up."

"She's been alone since?"

"Yes, it's a wonder. Beautiful girl like that. Beautiful inside and out. One of those rare women who are beautiful but don't know it." He thought a moment then said, "I think Polish girls are like that. The whole country." He looked up at me. "Not like the Midway men leave her alone. They don't. The problem is, the young ones are all married, and the guys . . . well, we're not really in the running, are we?"

"I'm sure you would be if you weren't already taken."

"Now you're being unctuous."

I grinned. "Where is she from?"

"Minnesota, I think." He took another bite of pie. "Yes, Minnesota. She doesn't talk much about her life before Midway." He leaned back and his voice softened. "I worry about her, though. I worry about her a lot."

"Why is that?"

"She has eyes of sadness. Deep, deep sadness. It's pretty, in a way—vulnerability can be pretty. But hers . . ." He sighed. "Every year the light in her eyes is a little less bright. I wonder if someday the candle will just flicker and go out." He took a deep breath. "Loneliness gets to you. You know what I mean?"

His words filled me with sadness. "I do."

We briefly languished in the moment, then Ray took another bite of pie and said, "Well, onward, right? Did you make use of the phone book I gave you?"

"Yes. I made a list of all the LHs in the area. I came up with eighteen possible candidates."

"Do you have the list with you?"

"Yes." I pulled the list from my pocket, unfolded it, and handed it to him. He smoothed it out against the table, looked at it for a moment, then took out a pen.

"Okay, the first name here on your list, Leslie Hall, is not a woman."

"That would have been good to know yesterday."

He looked up at me. "You went and visited old Les?"

"Old Les? Yes."

Ray smiled. "How did that go?"

"Awkward. But he did invite me over for brats and a basketball game."

"His wife left him last year. Took their two kids and ran off with a lawyer from Salt Lake City." He looked back down at my list. "Don't know about the second name here. But Linda Hanks, she's older. Probably wouldn't know how to turn the computer on, but sweet as divinity."

"Yes, I met her. Had a long talk." I sat back. "Those three were pretty much my day yesterday. I should have shown you this first. Would you mind going through the rest of it?"

"I would not mind." He ran his pen down the list, occasionally stopping to cross someone out.

~~Hall, Leslie B.~~
~~Hanks, Linda~~
~~Harding, Linda~~
Harman, Lindsey
Hardy, Liz
Harkness, Lori
Heger, Laurie
~~Henrie, Lillian~~
~~Heughs, Layla~~
Hewitt, Lisa
~~Hickman, Leah~~
Higham, Louise
Hill, Lorraine
~~Hitesman, Laurel~~
~~Holbrook, Lilly~~
Howard, Lydia

Howell, Lisa
Hoyt, LaDawn

"You can take Layla Heughs, Leah Hickman, Lilly Holbrook, and Lillian Henrie off your list. Layla and Leah are in their eighties. Lilly and Lillian are in their nineties. In fact, Lilly might have passed last month." He thought for a moment then said, "Yes, she passed.

"Laurel Hitesman is hot and heavy on the golf pro over at the Homestead Resort and has a boyfriend in Connecticut, so I don't think she's your lonely woman."

I wondered how he knew so much about these people, but didn't ask.

"I think LaDawn's in her fifties. She's still a possibility. She's a checker over at Ridley's, the grocery store off Main Street. She's well preserved. She does a lot of yoga and stuff."

"That leaves just ten people," I said.

He handed me back the list. "Ten people out of an entire city. That's not bad. You could do that in a couple more days."

"Then I best get at it."

"Yes, you best," he said. He closed the container around his pie and stood. "I hope you don't mind if I take this with me."

"Of course not."

He started to turn, then stopped and looked back at me. "And Alex?"

"Yes, sir."

"When you see Aria again, thank her for the pie."

"What makes you think I'll see her again?"

He slightly leaned forward. "You noticed that she had a ring." He winked at me, then turned and walked away. After he was gone I laughed to myself. *Smart man*.

After I finished breakfast, I went upstairs to gather my things, then went back out into the cold to find LBH.

CHAPTER

Twenty-one

It didn't take me long to find my first stop. Lindsey Harman. Her redbrick house, with its white gingerbread trim under the eaves, was picturesque, looking more like one of the Swiss-themed stores along Midway's Main Street than a private residence. In keeping with the season, it was strung with red and white Christmas lights matching the Swiss-themed elements as well as bestowing a festive holiday feel to the façade.

The house was close enough to the fairgrounds that LBH would have definitely seen a lot of festival attendees. There was a *For Sale* sign in front, which would also make sense, since she was planning on moving back home.

I walked up to the front door. There was no doorbell, so I knocked. Nothing. I knocked again. After a few minutes without any response, I walked around the side of the house and knocked on a side door. Still no answer.

I walked back to my car and made a notation on my list to return later on. Then I drove on to find the next candidate, Liz Hardy.

This next house was only a few blocks from the first but not nearly as nice. It was dated and looked to be made of old, handmade bricks—the large kind with thick mortar between them. Its snow-laden shake roof peaked in the middle of the house, above the front door, which was beneath a small second-floor balcony with a door opening out of it. There were white shutters and finials over the windows.

The door opened slowly. "Yes?" The man was slightly shorter than me and a few years older. He wore a sweater and thick-rimmed glasses.

"Hi. My name is Alex, I'm looking for Liz Hardy."

"You are?" he said with a condescending tone. "You're looking for Liz."

His response baffled me. "Yes, sir."

"And how do you know *Elizabeth*?"

"From the Internet."

"Is that so?"

"Yes, sir. I've been following her blog."

He just continued to gaze at me with the same peculiar expression, then he said, "All right. Just a minute. I'll get her."

He walked back into the house, returning a moment later carrying a bright copper urn. "Here she is. What would you like to say to her?"

I stood there looking at him. "She's where?"

"Here," he said, holding out the urn. "She's in here."

I couldn't decide which was worse, that he was joking or that he wasn't. Either way, it was time to leave.

"Sorry for your loss," I said. I turned and walked quickly back to my car, almost slipping on a patch of ice. *Interesting people*.

CHAPTER
Twenty-two

The fact that the next house had at least a dozen *No Trespassing* and *No Solicitation* signs and the welcome mat said *GO AWAY* should have been clues enough to stay away. Whoever lived here clearly wasn't fond of visitors.

I rang the doorbell and a moment later the door opened just a few inches. I could see the eclipsed face of a gaunt, angry woman.

"Why are you on my property?"

"I . . . are you Ms. Harkness?"

"Who are you?"

"I'm with . . . the census. I'm just verifying that you are the occupant of this home."

"You're not with the census."

"I just need to verify your record and I'll be gone. Does your middle name start with a *B*?"

"Show me your identification. Census workers are required to wear identification."

"If you could just . . ."

"You're a fraud!" she screamed. "Show me your ID or I'm calling the police."

"I'm not showing it to you."

"Then I'm calling the police, you pervert. The police

chief is a friend of mine, you can tell your story to him." She lifted her phone and pushed a button.

"Look, I'm just . . ."

I could hear the phone ringing on the other end.

"Really? You have the police on speed dial?"

Just then she lifted a bottle of Mace. "Let's see how you like this."

I turned and ran across the snow, catching a whiff of the Mace she sprayed after me.

"Yeah, you better run, you sick perv! I'm taking a picture of your license plate." She ran out after me holding the Mace in one hand and her phone in the other. I hit the gas and gunned my car out of there.

If she was LBH, there was a good reason she was lonely.

CHAPTER

Twenty-three

After the day's failed visits I was ready to take a break for lunch. It wasn't all failure. At least my list was smaller. I didn't know whether or not Aria worked during the day, but I decided to drop by anyway. The truth was, I'd thought about her all day. The odd thing was, it made me feel sort of guilty—as if I was cheating on LBH.

As I walked into the diner, I saw Aria standing at the front counter ringing up a ticket for a stooped, elderly customer. She glanced over at me and smiled. She looked a little different, less tired, perhaps the difference between the beginning of a shift and the end of one.

As she handed the old man back his change he said, "I'm standing under mistletoe, do I get my kiss?"

"Of course, George. You always get your kiss." Aria walked around the counter and pecked the old man on the cheek. As the man turned toward me I saw the extent of his nearly toothless smile, which was so large I thought it might crack his face in two.

Aria turned to me. "Back already."

I was pleased that she remembered me. "It was the pie."

"The apple pie or the chicken pot pie you didn't get?"

"Both."

"Darn. And I was hoping it was me."

This was flirting, right?

She glanced behind her. "Would you like to sit in the same place?"

"Sure."

"It's . . . Alex?"

She either had a photographic memory or I had made an impression on her. I hoped for the latter. "That's right. And you're Aria."

"Still me." She grabbed a menu. "Follow me, please."

I followed her back to the same booth where I'd sat the day before and sat down. She handed me the menu.

"So, today, we do have our chicken pot pie."

"Then that's what I'll have."

"And, I should warn you, there's just one piece of Thelma's huckleberry pie left. If you think that might be in your future, I can set it aside."

"Set it aside," I said.

"You won't be disappointed." I wondered if I would ever meet Thelma—the pie goddess.

"Strawberry lemonade?"

Maybe she did have a photographic memory. "Just a plain lemonade today."

"Lemonade it is. I'll be right back."

The diner was not as full as it had been at night, but Aria seemed to be running the floor by herself. As I watched her (I couldn't keep my eyes off of her), I thought about what Ray had said about her eyes of sadness. I could see what he meant. At first I had mistaken them for fatigue, but beneath her constant greetings, I could see something restrained. Something hurt. Like a spiritual fracture.

Aria brought out a lemonade, setting it in front of me. "There you are. So how's your car counting going?"

I gave her a slight grin. "It's interesting."

"Is interesting good or bad?"

"Just not quite how I expected it to go. That's the thing about traffic—you can't always predict how things will work out."

"Does that mean you'll have to stay longer than you expected?"

I liked the question. "It's likely."

She smiled. "I'll be right back."

As a salesman, I prided myself on my ability to read body language, but with this woman I felt illiterate. I really couldn't read whether she was interested in me or she was just the world's greatest waitress. Maybe both were true.

Or, then, maybe I was just an idiot misreading her kindness for flirtation. I'm told that happens a lot with men. I once had a female colleague tell me that she'd stopped smiling at men.

"Why would you do that?" I had asked.

"Because half of them are so hard up that if a decent-looking woman gives them any attention, they mistake it for a come-on."

Was that me?

About ten minutes later Aria walked back to my table, carrying my meal. "There you go, Thelma's famous chicken pot pie. I hope it's worth the wait. Can I get you anything else?"

"I'm good for now."

"I'll be back to check on you in a minute."

Not surprisingly, it was excellent. I hadn't realized that Thelma had her magical hands in the chicken pot pie too.

When Aria came back I was ready for her.

"How's the pie?"

"Worth the wait."

"Good. Let me know if I can get you anything else."

She was about to leave when I took the leap. "I wanted to ask you, in the event that I do have to stay longer, is there anything to do in Midway?"

"There's a lot to do here," she said. "Not a lot compared to, say, New York or Paris, or even Florida, but there are things worth seeing."

"What kind of things?"

"Have you seen the ice castle?"

"What's that?"

"It's a castle made entirely of ice. The artist made it using something like twenty million pounds of ice. It has tunnels and caverns and archways of solid ice. Then he puts lights inside it. It looks like something out of a fairy tale. People come from all over the country to see it."

"You just walk through it?"

"Yes. I mean, there's a fee. It's like ten dollars."

"Do many people go?"

"The paper said that more than a quarter million people go through it each year. It's almost getting to where you need a reservation."

"What happens when the weather gets warm?"

An amused smile crossed her face. "It melts."

I laughed. "Maybe I'll go see it tonight. How late is it open?"

"I think they close up around ten. But one of the managers is a diner here. He said that if I wanted to go later he would let me in the back way. I'm sure he wouldn't mind. Just ask for Craig."

"Why don't you come with me?"

She didn't reply and I suddenly thought that I really had read her wrong. *How could I have been so obtuse?* I hadn't even planned on asking her right then, the words had just kind of leapt out of my mouth. Now they were hanging awkwardly in the air between us. I wished I could call them back but it was too late. There was nowhere to go but forward. "Would you like to come with me?"

Suddenly her look of surprise gave way to a pleasant smile. "Yes. I'd like that."

Now I was the surprised one. It took me a moment to recover. "What time do you get off work?"

"Usually around ten. But I'll ask Valerie if she can close for me. If she can, I could leave around nine thirty." She glanced around, then said, "I'll let you know before you go. I better take care of my other tables." She walked off.

We didn't talk much after that, even when she brought me the huckleberry pie. When I walked up to the counter to pay, Aria came up to check me out. "Sorry, I got busy. Valerie says she can close."

"Great," I said, handing her my credit card. After she ran it I said, "So I'll see you at nine thirty."

"Nine thirty," she repeated. I turned to go when she said, "Alex."

"Yes?"

"It's ice. And it's night. Do you have another coat?"

I looked down at my jacket then back at her. "No. Just this."

"You should probably get a real one."

"This isn't a real coat?"

"It's ice," she said again. "And it's night." With a smile, she returned to the floor.

✦

She was right, of course. With the exception of my time at the inn, even with my car's heater blasting, I'd pretty much been cold since I arrived in Utah. Like, chilled-to-the-bone cold. I planned on spending the first week back in Florida just thawing out.

I called the inn to see where I could find a coat. Lita told me that I'd have to go to Park City, which was only about twenty minutes from Midway.

I found an L.L. Bean outlet store near the Park City off-ramp where I picked out a rust-colored down parka with a hood and faux fur trim. I also bought a pair of their least expensive boots. Even being an outlet store, it wasn't cheap, especially considering that I'd probably never wear either item again.

I went back to the inn to relax for a while, then left around a quarter after nine. When I drove up to the front of the diner, Aria was standing outside, her hands deep in her coat pockets. She walked up to my car, looked inside to make sure it was me, then climbed in.

"I think my fingers are frozen," she said.

"Why didn't you wait inside?" I asked.

"It's okay. I didn't want you to have to come in."

I looked at her quizzically. "Why?"

"I just didn't."

I turned the heat all the way up and pointed the dash vents toward her. She rubbed her hands together in front of the closest vent. "Thank you."

"You're welcome."

She looked at me and remarked, "You got a new coat."

"A *real* coat," I said. "A parka. Just like you told me to."

She smiled. "You'll be glad. It gets so cold at night."

"Which is why you really should have waited inside. What if I'd been in a wreck and didn't come?"

She grinned. "Then the next morning I would be found frozen on the front porch like the Little Match Girl."

"Exactly." I put the car into gear. "So, speaking of freezing, where do we find this ice castle?"

"Just head east." She pointed. "You'll drive about a quarter mile until you see a sign that says Soldier Hollow. Then turn right again. You can't miss it. There will be a lot of cars."

"Hopefully all leaving," I said.

"That's the plan," she said. "To have the castle to ourselves."

✦

The ice castle was even more spectacular than I had expected. We arrived around ten o'clock to a throng of cars and people exiting the field. Following Aria's instructions, I pulled my car up around the back of the exhibit. Someone in a yellow reflective vest came over to stop us, but Aria just waved to him and he smiled and let us through.

As we made our way to the back entrance, Aria told me a little of the history behind the ice castle. The artist or, more aptly, the architect behind the castle was a Utah man named Brent Christensen. His ice creations began one cold winter eight years earlier, when he made them in his backyard for his daughter.

What started out of amusement turned into an obsession that had him pushing the limits of ice creation, trying new things with the medium, and soon building larger and larger structures.

Then he convinced a Midway resort to pay him to build a massive ice exhibit—not as big as the castle we were walking around but larger than anything that he, or anyone else, had built before. The public response was phenomenal and inspired Christensen to build full-size ice castles in different locations around the world. Since then, millions of people had toured his ice constructions in Utah as well as elsewhere, including New York and Edmonton, Canada.

During the daylight hours the ice castle is a striking, glacial blue, but at night it is even more spectacular, lit up by thousands of LED lights embedded in the ice.

It took Aria and me forty-five minutes to move through the structure. Still, as beautiful as our setting was, it wasn't the castle that commanded my attention. Aria was far more beautiful than anything that could be created of crystal and light. Near the end of our tour the lights all went off, leaving us alone in the dark, the ice caverns and walls lit only by moonlight.

"I don't think they know we're still in here," Aria said.

"Now I'm especially glad I got a 'real' coat," I said. "Since we'll probably end up spending the night."

To my surprise, she looked a little nervous. "Do you know how to get out?"

"This way," I said.

"Wait." She took my hand. Her fingers were slim and delicate and her hand felt soft and warm in mine. When we were finally out of the castle I was reluctant to give her hand up.

As we walked back to my car she said, "It's not Daytona Beach, but what did you think?"

"I loved it," I said. "And I guarantee that there will never be one in Daytona Beach."

"That's okay," she said. "No one will ever go surfing in Midway. I'm glad you liked it."

It was late and I wasn't sure what was to come next, only that I didn't want the night to end. "Do you want to get a drink or something?"

"I don't drink."

"I meant a hot chocolate."

"Oh." She smiled. "I don't think anything's open."

"The inn is," I said. "We could go there."

She looked a little hesitant.

"If you don't want to . . ."

"I do, I just . . ."

I suddenly understood her reticence. "We'll stay in the dining room."

She nodded. "Okay. Sorry. I'm just a little old-fashioned that way."

"And I'm a gentleman that way."

She smiled. "A gentleman. I almost forgot what those look like."

✦

As we turned onto the road before the inn, Aria said, "Do you know anything about that statue of the boar?"

"No, but it seemed a little familiar."

"It's a casting of a statue in Florence, Italy. There are replicas of it around the world, including the Butchart Gardens in Victoria, British Columbia. But what's really cool is that the statue can be seen in the movie *Hannibal* and two of the Harry Potter movies."

I looked at her in wonder. "How do you know all this?"

"Ray," she said. "He talks a lot. About the inn."

I grinned. "I hadn't noticed."

I parked the car on the cobbled driveway and led her in. A woman I didn't recognize was standing at the front desk. The dining room was empty, though the lights were still on.

"Is anyone in the kitchen?" I asked.

"No, sir. They've gone home for the night."

"I'd like to make some hot chocolate."

"There's a coffeemaker with a tray of tea and cocoa on the counter in the back of the small dining room."

"Thank you." I grabbed a napkin and a few butter cookies from the tray near the stairway, then Aria and I walked back to a table near a window in the smaller dining area.

I held her chair for her, then walked over to the counter and made two cups of hot cocoa. I brought them over and set both cups on the table.

"It's nice to be on the other side of that," she said.

"Of what?"

"Being served."

I smiled. "Be careful, I think it's too hot."

"It smells good."

"The package said it's mint chocolate." I sat down across from her.

"What time do you have to be at work in the morning?" she asked.

"I'm flexible. How about you?"

"Early," she said.

"Do you work every day?"

"Almost. I'm working a lot more lately because of the holidays."

"Extra Christmas money?"

"No. I mean, yes, I can always use the money, but mostly because the other waitresses have a lot of family things. So I pick up their shifts just to help out."

"That's noble of you."

"I don't know about noble but it works out. It's not like I have much going on. And, added bonus, people tip more during the holidays." She took a sip of her cocoa, then quickly withdrew. "That is hot."

"Sorry." I walked out into the hall and returned with a couple cubes of ice. "May I?"

She nodded and I dropped one of the cubes into her cup, the other in mine. "That should help."

"Thank you."

"Remember that woman who sued McDonald's for millions of dollars because her coffee burned her?" I said.

"Yes. Could I sue you for millions because the cocoa's too hot?"

"Sorry, I don't have millions."

"Me neither."

"So tell me about your name. There's got to be a story behind it."

"It came from my father. He was a musician. He played the violin, second chair for the Minnesota Orchestra."

"So he was good."

"He was very good." She looked at me. "He told me that he named me Aria because an aria is an expressive melody and that's how he wanted me to live life, not as the background beat, not the repetitive harmony, but to create my own song.

"The strange thing is that if you look the word up, it says the meaning has changed through time. Today, an aria is usually a self-contained piece for one voice. That pretty much describes my life." She stirred her cocoa again, then took another small sip. "That's better." After a pause and another sip, she said, "Do you think that our name actually affects who we are in life?"

"There's a name for that theory, you know. It's called nominative determinism."

"That's a little scary that you know that."

"Then I'll really scare you. The famous psychoanalyst Carl Jung said that there's a 'grotesque coincidence between a man's name and his peculiarities' . . . or something like that."

"I'm not scared, I'm impressed," she said.

"I just read a business book about that very thing. It pointed out a study on names and concluded that because people tend to gravitate to things that are familiar, we are attracted to things that are similar to our names. One of the examples the study gave was the extraordinarily high number of dentists named Dennis."

"Is that true?"

"It was in the book. The book actually had some funny examples. Such as a famous psychiatrist named Angst."

She laughed. "That's not true."

"And there's a meteorologist named Blizzard, a gynecologist named Dr. Ovary, and my personal favorite was a union leader named Raymond Strike."

She laughed again. "You're making this up."

"I wish I was that clever," I said. "Then, of course, you have the famous English poet William Wordsworth."

"You've made your point. We are what we are named. And I'm an Aria."

"What does that make me?"

"Alex?" she said. "I've no idea."

I took a long drink of my cocoa. "You mentioned Minnesota. Is that where you're from?"

"Wayzata, Minnesota. It's near Lake Minnetonka."

"Is there snow?"

"Lots and lots of snow."

"That's why it doesn't bother you."

"Yes, I'm used to it. I suppose *acclimated* is the word. The snow *and* the cold. Minnesota is colder than Utah." She shook her head. "In more ways than one."

I wasn't sure how to read her last comment. "How did you end up in Midway?"

She lightly groaned as if the question were painful. "I came here with my husband. My *ex*-husband."

"Ray told me that you had a coffee shop."

"*Had* is right. It was pretty short-lived."

"How did you end up in Midway?"

"Shortly after we got married, my husband's cousin called and said that he was starting a coffee shop in Utah and asked him to come and be a partner in it. He couldn't afford to pay salaries, so we were going to earn sweat equity." She shook her head. "How stupid is that, a coffee shop in Midway, Utah?"

"What's wrong with that?"

"Almost three-quarters of the people in Midway are Mormons. They don't drink coffee."

"Like selling bicycles to fish."

"Exactly."

"Then why Utah?"

"He overthought it. He read some book about how Starbucks was founded and decided that he was going to be the next big thing. He thought he was smarter than everyone else. He started looking for cities with the least competition. He never considered that there was a reason there were fewer coffee shops here. I have to admit that the name of the place was pretty good though. *Brewed Awakening*."

I laughed. "And it was."

"Literally."

"So what happened to the Brewed Awakening?"

"After things started going bad, his cousin blamed it on my husband and said we owed him ten thousand dollars. They got in a big fight. They were punching, throwing coffee cups at each other. One of the customers called the police. They were both arrested. I had to post bail to get my husband out of jail.

"After that, Wade—that's my ex's name—never went back to the coffee shop. For about six months he mostly just slept or watched television or played video games. I was already working full-time at the diner but I had to start taking extra shifts to pay bills.

"Then, one day, Wade had this idea that was going to make us rich. He was going to rent snowmobiles to tourists. I should have been more wary, but the truth was I was just so happy that he was going to do something. He was so excited. I believed in him.

"He needed a hundred thousand dollars to get his business going, something, of course, we didn't have. He found this guy who raised capital. His name was Chad something. Maybe Brown. Wade had met him at the coffee shop.

"Chad said he could get us the money, we just needed to come up with ten percent, up front. Chad looked the part. I mean, he was kind of weird-looking, like, his eyes were close together, like a spider, but he dressed in designer clothes, wore expensive sunglasses, drove a Mercedes, all the trappings, you know?"

I nodded. "I know the type."

"So he took us to a nice restaurant. Actually, here. Chad told us, 'If you want to *live* big, you have to *dream* big.' Then he said that the reason most businesses fail wasn't because they weren't a good idea, but because of undercapitalization. So we should go for at least a quarter million. If we gave him just ten percent up front, he'd get us the money. I said, 'We don't have that kind of money.' He said, 'No problem—just take out a loan, and you can pay it back with the money I raise.' The next day we took a loan out for twenty-five thousand dollars and gave it to Chad."

"You never saw Chad again."

"No. About a month later I never saw my husband again either. He just kind of faded away. Last I heard, he was in Minneapolis selling tires." She took a deep breath. "Unfortunately, my signature was on the loan. I'm still paying on it. I will be for years."

"I'm sorry."

"You live and learn, right?"

"Sometimes we do," I said softly.

Aria said, "Tell me about you."

I took a deep breath. "Me. I've lived in Daytona Beach for most of my life, except for a year at the University of North Florida in Jacksonville, where I mostly learned that college wasn't really for me. It was, for better or worse, where I met my wife. We were married for six years but divorced about a year ago."

"What happened?"

"I don't know. I mean, I thought I did. At first I thought it was because I traveled too much. And maybe that was it in the beginning, but in the end she had someone else."

"I'm sorry."

"Yeah. Me too. I wanted it to work."

"Do you have friends?"

"A few. My best friend is Nate. He works with me. But he's nothing like me."

"In what way?"

"He's tough. Like, Kevlar tough."

She asked, "Who's Kevlar?"

I smiled. "Sorry. Kevlar's what they make bulletproof vests from."

"Oh."

"This story explains him perfectly. Before Nate joined the marines he was delivering pizza. One night a guy walks up to him, pulls out a gun, and says, 'Give me all your money.' Nate looked at the gun, then at the guy, and said, 'Really? You brought a .38 to rob me? That's just going to make me mad.' And he turned and walked away. He said he kept waiting for the guy to shoot him in the back but he never did."

"He's tough or crazy?"

"Sometimes it's a fine line," I said.

She laughed. Then she yawned.

"You're tired," I said. "It's late."

"I'm sorry. I worked a double shift today. I was into work at five."

"Then I'd better get you home."

As we walked out the back of the diner we passed the Pino painting. Suddenly I stopped. "Wait a second."

"What?"

"Stand right here, next to this painting."

She looked at me like I was crazy but did as I asked.

"That's why," I said.

"That's why what?"

"Ever since I met you, I've been wondering why you looked so familiar. Look"—I motioned to the picture—"it looks just like you."

She looked at the painting for a moment. "I can kind of see that. And she's got the waitress thing going."

"Not *kind of*," I said. "She looks *exactly* like you. You could have modeled for the picture."

"I'm not as pretty as she is."

"Prettier," I said. "Even prettier." I glanced at her and she was looking at me gratefully. "All right," I said. "Let's get you home before you pass out from exhaustion."

I drove her back to the diner, pulling up next to her car behind the restaurant, an older-model Jeep Wrangler, covered with about a foot of snow.

She sighed when she saw it. "I'm buried."

"No worries," I said. "I just got this." I lifted my new snow brush-scraper. "I'm practically local. Just one minute." I left my car running as I brushed the snow off her Jeep, leaving huge mounds of snow on the ground around her car. After I finished I came back to my car and got in.

"Thank you," she said.

"My pleasure."

She smiled sweetly. "Pleasure? Really? You hate the cold." She took my wet, cold hands and looked at them. "Don't you have gloves?"

"I have cycling gloves," I said. "In Florida."

She began rubbing my hands. Then she lifted them to her mouth and blew on them with her warm breath. After a few times she said, "I think I've saved them."

"Thank you."

"Thank *you*. I had a really nice evening."

"Me too," I said. "Do you work tomorrow?"

"Yes. Another double."

"Then I'll see you tomorrow at dinner."

"I'd like that," she said. She looked at me a little nervously and then said, "Do you want to do something after work?"

"I would, but won't you be too tired?"

"I'm sure I will be," she said. "But, do you want to do something?"

"Yes. What would you like to do? Besides sleep."

She thought for a moment, then said, "I'll surprise you. Good night." She leaned over and kissed me on the cheek, then opened her door. She got out, stopped, and then turned back. "Do you know how long it's been since a man pulled out a chair for me or scraped the snow from my car?"

"No idea," I said.

"Yeah. Me neither." She closed the door and walked to her car. I waited for her to pull out before leaving myself. As I drove back to the inn, I realized that I was gradually losing interest in my hunt for LBH.

CHAPTER

Twenty-four

The next morning I hoped to see Ray at breakfast, but didn't. I wanted to talk to him about Aria. As I was about to leave the dining room, Lita walked through.

"Good morning, Mr. Bartlett. How is everything with your stay?"

"Everything's great," I said. "Where's Ray this morning?"

"He's visiting his grandchildren in Salt Lake. He'll be back tomorrow. Have a good day." She scurried off to help someone standing at the front counter.

I went up to my room and got ready for the day. I had at least three visits planned: Laurie Heger, Lisa Hewitt, and Louise Higham.

✦

The first place I visited, the Laurie Heger residence, was an apartment about three miles east of the community center—a stretch, as far as festivalgoers walking by were concerned. Also, her window faced the opposite direction of the park. I couldn't imagine people walking by in crowds past her apartment during the festival. Americans don't walk that far.

We just don't. If it's more than five minutes, we drive. Europeans will walk that far, but going to a Swiss festival doesn't make people Swiss.

I knocked, but no one answered. I crossed her off my list anyway.

✦

My second stop was Lisa Hewitt. Unlike the previous prospect, Lisa lived only a half mile from the community center. There was a young woman in the driveway brushing snow off her car as I pulled up in front of the house. She watched me park, then, as I got out, she threw her brush inside her car and walked up to me. She looked to be in her late twenties. "Hi," she said brightly.

"Hi, I'm looking for Lisa Hewitt."

"That's me."

She seemed so forthright, I followed suit. "My name is Alex. I'm not from Midway. I'm just trying to find someone. She's a blogger from around here."

"Cool. What does she blog about?"

I had to think before I answered. I didn't want to say "loneliness," again revealing my aversion to the word. "Reflections on life, that sort of thing."

"Cool," she repeated. "How can I help?"

"I was wondering if it was you."

She laughed. "No way. I hate writing. In college it took me, like, an hour to write a paragraph for English."

"So you're not a blogger."

"No. I follow a few, though. Have you read Allie Brosh? She's hilarious."

"Is she the one with the funny, bizarre drawing of a fish-like thing?"

"Yeah, that's her! That's cool you know who she is." She took a step back, motioning to her running car. "Well, I better get to work. Good luck finding your bloggess." She turned and walked back to her car. I waved at her as she drove away.

That was easy, I thought. Another lead bites the list.

✦

My next stop, Louise Higham, lived about four blocks northwest of the diner. Her house was run-down and in need of a paint job.

The doorbell had a piece of silver-gray duct tape across it, so I knocked. A moment later I heard steps, then an extremely large, middle-aged woman in a nightgown answered. She looked anxious.

"May I help you?"

"Hi. I'm looking for Louise Higham."

Awkwardly, she didn't say anything.

"Are you Louise?"

"No, sir. Louise lives in the apartment downstairs. It's around back."

I looked over to the side of the house to see if there was

some kind of walkway. If there was one, it was covered in snow. "Is there a separate entrance?"

"Yes. It's over there. You'll have to open the gate."

"Do you know if she's home?"

She strained her head out the door to look at the carport. "That's her car there, so I suppose she is. No guarantee she'll answer."

"All right. Thank you."

"Please don't let the dog out."

She shut the door without saying good-bye. I walked around the side of the house to a tall wooden-plank fence and unlatched the gate. Immediately there was barking. I pushed open the gate just a few inches to look inside, mostly to see what kind of a dog it was. There was a medium-size, honey-colored collie standing on the covered back patio, her coat and belly white with snow. She continued barking but didn't leave the dry concrete.

The backyard was completely covered in snow. I put my shoulder against the gate to push it open just enough to squeeze through, then stepped into the snow. The dog was running around on the patio, barking like crazy.

"Come on, girl," I said, slightly stooping and putting out my arms. The dog came to me, her tail wagging as she bounded through the thick snow like a gazelle. She jumped up on me with snow-covered paws. I crouched down and scratched her for a while. After a few minutes, I stood, and the dog followed me over to the side of the house, where a vinyl awning jutted out over a concrete stairwell.

"Stay," I said. She obeyed.

I clutched the cold metal handrail and walked carefully down the icy stairs. If it weren't for the awning, the stairs would have looked like a mountain slope. It seemed like no one had been in or out of the place for a while. The landing was crowded with three full plastic garbage sacks, one partially opened, with trash—mostly beer cans and booze bottles—spilling out.

There was no doorbell, so I knocked on the door. It was a few minutes before the door opened to a red-faced, inebriated woman. She wore no makeup and her hair was matted to one side. Her blouse was unbuttoned, exposing her bra. The house stank like cats or some collection of animals.

"What do you want?" Her words were slurred.

"I'm looking for Louise Higham."

"What do you want?"

In her condition there was no reason not to speak plainly. "I'm looking for a blogger."

"A what?"

"A blogger." She just looked at me, so I added, "Someone who blogs."

"I don't dance."

There was really no need to explain. "Okay. Thank you."

She shut the door.

I petted the dog once more before leaving the yard, and I remembered to shut the gate.

CHAPTER Twenty-five

After checking my list, I decided to go back to the Swiss home I had visited the day before—the one that was for sale.

This time there was a car parked out front. I walked in through the gate and was immediately greeted by a stout, redheaded woman. "Hello!"

"Are you Lindsey Harman?" I asked.

"No, Ms. Harman's already moved out. I'm Gloria, with Keller Williams Real Estate. Would you like to see the house?"

"No, I actually came to see Lindsey. I was interested in talking to her about her blog."

"I didn't know she had a blog."

"When do you expect her back?"

"I don't. She already moved to St. George with her boyfriend."

"Oh," I said, gleaning in one sentence all I needed to know about Lindsey Harman. "All right. Thanks for your help."

"Don't mention it. When I talk to her can I tell her anything?"

I turned back. "Sure. Just tell her to keep up the good work."

✦

Just four names left. Actually, this wasn't really a good sign. Sometimes in my travels, while waiting at airport luggage carousels, I would guess how many bags it would take before mine appeared. What I learned is that if my bag didn't come before the last ten, chances were great that it wouldn't make it at all, and I'd have to go stand in the lost baggage line with all the other tormented people. What were the odds that LBH was among the last four leads? Or was fate just teasing me?

✦

Even though I was near the Mistletoe Diner, I didn't want to wear out my welcome with Aria, so I drove past it two blocks to a local burger stand and got a chicken sandwich, fries, and Coke. When I got back to the inn I checked my phone messages. Satisfied that there wasn't anything that was going to cost me my job, I rolled over and fell asleep. Other than that haze of a month when Jill had left me, I don't remember ever taking so many naps in my life. Maybe it was the altitude. Or maybe I was just finally catching up on two-million-plus miles of travel.

I drove to the diner around seven. The parking lot wasn't particularly crowded but the restaurant was. Ridiculously crowded. Every table and booth was taken and there were at least two dozen people standing around the *Please Wait to Be Seated* sign.

Aria, who was bouncing from booth to table, didn't see me until she came to the front to seat the next guests. She smiled at me wearily. "I'm so sorry, we're slammed. If you don't mind, just take that seat at the counter."

"Thanks."

I started to walk when a man standing next to me said angrily, "Excuse me, Miss. We were here first."

Aria didn't flinch. "I'm sorry, he has reservations. Do you have reservations?"

The man just looked at her blankly.

"I'll be with you shortly."

"You've done that before," I said to her when we had taken a few steps.

"More than once."

I took the last seat at the counter. It was a few minutes before Aria got back to me. She brought me a plain lemonade. "I'm so sorry. This is crazy."

"What's going on?"

"There's a crèche convention going on at the community center. They came here on a bus, so they all walked here."

"What's a crèche convention?"

"They're for people who collect nativity scenes. You know, a crèche . . ."

I shrugged. I had never heard the word.

She took a deep breath. "Anyway, about tonight . . ."

My heart fell. Considering her circumstances, I figured she was going to cancel. I wouldn't blame her.

". . . I'll probably be a half hour later. Do you still want to go?"

"Of course. Are you sure you're up to it?"

"Absolutely."

"Excellent," I said. "I'll be here."

✦

Not surprisingly, we didn't talk much, even though she smiled at me in passing. After I finished eating, I waved to her and she came up to me. She was out of breath. "How was everything?"

"Thelma's in good form."

"Thelma's always in good form." She took a deep breath. "So, I forgot to tell you something about tonight. Wear a swimsuit."

"We're going swimming?"

"Sort of. And wear a robe or something or you'll freeze." She smiled. "See you at eleven thirty."

Wear a robe?

Instead of going directly back to my room, I decided to explore a little and drove east to downtown Heber. The town of Heber is larger than Midway and a four-lane highway runs through the center of it. Both sides of the road are crowded with businesses and restaurants.

In addition to the commercial section's decorations and light-strewn trees, the street was decorated for the season with large strands of tinsel crisscrossing the road at intersections. Oversize lighted plastic candy canes were fastened to the streetlamps that lined the highway. It pleased me to see it. Christmas Americana.

I stopped in a grocery store to buy some sundries—

deodorant, shaving cream, and razors—then drove back to the inn.

At a quarter past eleven I put on my swimsuit, donned the thick terry-cloth robe from the inn, and put my shoes back on. I thought of wearing my parka over the robe but decided I'd rather die of exposure than look that stupid. I walked downstairs and handed my key to Claudia at the front desk. "I'll be back in a couple hours."

"You're going out in a robe?"

"I'll bring it back," I said.

"That wasn't my concern," she said, raising her eyebrows. "It's subfreezing. Keep warm."

"No guarantees," I said. I pushed open the door and the brisk, chill air hit me in the face like a slap. I walked out to my car and got inside. I could feel the cold of the vinyl seat through my robe. *It's freaking Antarctica*, I thought. My windshield was frosted inside and out so I started the car, turned on the front and rear defrosters, and sat for nearly ten minutes while the heater cleared up the windshields. Once I could see, I drove to the diner.

I arrived to see Aria's white Jeep idling at the far end of the parking lot, evidenced by a cloud of smoke and steam billowing out of its tailpipe. As I pulled in next to her, Aria stepped out of her car. She didn't have a robe but wore a long peacoat with her bare legs exposed at the bottom. On her otherwise bare feet, she was wearing only flip-flops.

"Aren't you cold?" I asked, climbing out of my car.

"Freezing," she said, smiling. "The trick is not minding the pain."

I grinned. "Sorry I'm late. My windshield was frozen."

"No worries," she said. "Nice robe."

"Thanks. It's from the inn."

"I know. It has a pig head on it."

"So, couldn't we have just changed into our suits wherever we're going?"

She cocked her head. "We could have, but I don't know you that well. Come on, get in. I'll drive."

I climbed into the passenger seat of her Jeep. I noticed that the back side window was broken and covered with a black plastic garbage sack duct-taped to the window frame. The heater was blowing loudly in compensation.

"Sorry, my car's a mess. I haven't had time to clean it."

"How did your window break?" I asked.

"Some kids threw a snowball at it."

"Recently?"

"Last year."

She pulled out onto Main Street, which, not surprisingly, was deserted. We drove about a half mile west, then pulled off onto a dark side road still partially covered with snow. The road looked like it led up into the mountains and I couldn't see any sign of a building or any place to swim.

We continued past a grove of bare trees that opened into a large, snow-covered meadow. "In the summer this is all covered with sunflowers," she said. "It's beautiful. I love sunflowers."

"Me too," I said. What actually came to mind was the time I gave Jill a bouquet of sunflowers for her twenty-eighth birthday. She asked me why I had given her weeds.

"Just down this road is where we used to cut our Christmas trees," Aria said.

"You can cut your own?"

"Yes. You need a permit, but it's easy to get, and the trees are just right here."

"I've always wanted to do that," I said.

"Then why don't you?"

"There's not a lot of Christmas trees in Daytona Beach."

"No, but at least you could find a starfish for the star on top."

About two hundred yards from where we had turned off we came to another grove of trees. Aria pulled to the side of the road and turned off the Jeep. It sputtered once like a mechanical death-rattle, then died. "We're here."

I looked around at the snow-covered landscape. The crystalline white sea of snow reflected a bright moon. "Where are we?"

"The hot pot," she said. She grabbed a towel from the backseat, opened her door, and stepped out. A moment later I followed, stepping out onto the tundra-like road. The cold air bit my exposed legs, and the only noise I could hear was the Jeep's hot engine ticking and Aria's footsteps as she crunched through the crusted snow in her flip-flops. The snow came nearly to the bottom of her coat.

She was walking toward a mound about sixty steps from the Jeep. At the top, there was a crater where the snow was melted, revealing porous-looking lumps of rocks. Heat rose from the hot water, turning to steam in the cold air, almost as thick as smoke from a bonfire.

The hot spring was surrounded by a wire fence excessively posted with *No Trespassing* signs, something I was keenly aware of after my visit to the crazy Mace woman.

Aria twisted the wire off the fence and pulled it back as if she had done it a hundred times before.

I looked around. "Is this legal?"

"That depends on what you mean by *legal*," she said.

"Will someone arrest us?"

"No. It's a small town."

I nodded. "Okay, no problem."

"The owner might shoot us for trespassing. But you like taking risks, don't you?" She stepped inside the wire cage, set down the towel, then took off her coat, folding it carefully over a rock. She was wearing a black bikini that showed off her beautifully curved body. She covered up well in her work smock, because honestly, she was even more beautiful than I had noticed or imagined.

I think she must have noticed my attention and she smiled. "Well? Are you coming? Or are you afraid of . . . *trespassing?*"

The way she looked, I would have eaten my way through the fence, No Trespassing signs and all. "I'm coming."

I followed her over the rocks. The top of the hot pot had the rough, layered texture of an oyster's shell. As I neared the rim, Aria took off her flip-flops and carefully picked her way down the rock to a small outcropping that jutted out about three feet below the rim. She smiled at me, then stepped off into the water. She came up with a loud sigh. "Come in. It feels so good."

I looked down into the steaming crater. The dark pool looked bottomless and had an acrid sulfur smell. "I'll be right there."

I took off my robe and lay it over a rock next to Aria's coat. Then, sitting on my robe, I removed my shoes and put them next to her flip-flops. I walked over to the crater's rim.

"Is this where you get in?"

"Uh-huh."

As I started lowering myself down the ledge I slipped, throwing myself into the middle of the pot. I came up, sputtering.

"Nice entrance," she said, her voice slightly echoing in the cavernous rock. "You didn't have to do that to impress me."

"As long as you're impressed."

The water was hot but not uncomfortable. I swam over to her. She was holding on to a narrow ledge of rock. Six feet off to her side was a homemade rope ladder. It must have been there for a while, as it was white with mineral deposits.

"This is so healing for your body," she said. "It's perfect after a long day on your feet."

"What kind of rock is this?"

"Limestone. This crater was formed by the minerals in this water. Actually, it has a name. Tufa. I remember that because it reminds me of tofu. The name, not its taste."

"It probably tastes better than tofu," I said, adding, "I hate tofu." I swam over to the ladder and rested on it. "So, do many people know about this place?"

"Locals. But they don't come here."

"Because they'll get shot?"

She smiled. "Maybe." After a moment she said, "Actually, the man who owns this land is a customer of mine. I serve him ham and runny eggs on wheat toast every morning. He told me that I can come up here anytime."

"So the shooting part . . ."

"I was just teasing."

"Teasing or testing?"

"Pick one." She swam over next to me. "Still cold?"

"No. How hot is the water?"

"Most of the hot pots in Midway are considered warm springs instead of hot springs. This one is ninety-eight degrees, a little below body temperature." She floated closer to me. "Turn around."

"How come?"

"You ask too many questions. Trust me."

"All right." I turned away from her.

"Now hold on to the ladder."

I clutched the ladder and leaned into it, my forehead resting on one of the rungs. Aria put her hand on the back of my neck and began to rub it. The water had a slick, gel-like consistency that made her hand glide easily over my flesh.

"How does that feel?"

I softly groaned with pleasure.

"So you like it."

"Yes, ma'am."

"I'm not a ma'am."

After another minute of her massage I turned back and looked into her eyes.

"I don't know what we're doing, but I haven't been this happy for a very long time."

"Me too," she said.

"And I think you just might be the most beautiful woman in the world."

She smiled. "I think you're beautiful too." She moved in a little closer, her eyes locked on mine. "Very."

"I have a question about your job," I said.

"That's what you're thinking about right now?"

"It's relevant. Do your customers always try to kiss you under the mistletoe?"

"How is that relevant?"

"You ask too many questions," I said.

Her smile widened a little, then she said, "Only the wrong customers."

"What would happen if I tried?"

"I don't know. Why don't you find out?"

For a moment we just looked into each other's eyes. Then I began to lean forward. She leaned forward too, until our lips met, lightly at first, then exploding into full passion.

I had one arm hooked through the ladder and reached out with the other and put it around her narrow waist, pulling her into me. She put both arms around me. The softness of her body and lips was the most exquisite thing I'd felt for a very long time.

I don't know how long we'd been kissing when someone shouted, "What are you doing in there?"

We looked up to see an old man in a fringed leather

rancher jacket and a cowboy hat standing above the rim of the crater. He was holding a shotgun.

Aria swam out away from me toward the center of the pool. "Cal, it's me. Aria."

The man bent down a little and squinted. "Aria?"

"Yes, it's me."

He still didn't look happy. He lowered his gun. "Sorry. Didn't know it was you. Earl Belnap called and said I had some hippies in my pot."

Hippies in his pot?

He looked at me and his eyes flashed. "Who's the boy?"

"This is Alex. He's a friend of mine."

"Nice to meet you, sir," I said.

He ignored me. "Sure you don't need me to shoot him?"

I couldn't tell if he was serious. He might have been. Aria stifled a laugh. "No. Not this time. I'll let you know if that changes."

"All right," he said still looking a bit miffed. "Don't drown or nothin'."

"Thanks, Cal. Love you."

"Yeah," he drawled. He slowly picked his way back down the crater, mumbling and swinging his shotgun like a baton.

Aria turned back to me. "You thought you were going to get shot, didn't you?"

"Maybe."

"So, was it worth it?"

"Was what worth it?"

"Getting shot just to kiss me."

I reached out for her. "Definitely."

A large smile crossed her face and she swam back to me, pushing her body up against mine. "Where were we?"

I put my arms back around her and we went back to kissing.

CHAPTER

Twenty-six

After a half hour she said, "We can go back to my place."

"You're not too tired?"

"I think I just got my second wind."

We got out of the spring, the water on our bodies steaming in the freezing air. Fortunately, Aria had guessed that I would not think of bringing a towel and had brought two. She handed me one, and I quickly dried off and put on my robe. We slipped our shoes back on, then walked down to her Jeep.

"You drive," she said.

"Where am I going?"

"I'll show you," she said. "Just go back toward the diner."

I did a three-point turnaround and headed back to town, following Aria's directions about a quarter mile past the diner to a small duplex just behind a gas station on Main.

"This is where you live?"

"Uh-huh. Cheap rent."

"You're close to the diner."

"Yes. I usually just walk to work, unless it's icy or I'm working late." She unlocked the door and we went inside. The apartment was simple but tidy, with a few chairs and a simple black sofa behind a rectangular wooden coffee table.

On one side of the room, next to the wall, was a computer table with an older-model PC.

There was a framed quote on the wall.

NOT ALL THOSE WHO
WANDER ARE LOST.

"I like that," I said.

"I thought of getting a tattoo of it," Aria replied.

"Why didn't you?"

She smiled. "I didn't want a tattoo." She walked out of the room, returning a minute later wearing sweats. "Would you like some herbal tea?"

"Yes, please."

"I have peppermint and chamomile."

"Chamomile will put me to sleep."

"Peppermint it is."

She boiled water in a kettle, then brought two cups out to the coffee table. After she sat I tried the tea, then said, "I have a question. I hope it's not too personal."

"Yes?"

"After Wade left, why didn't you go back to Minnesota?"

She looked down for a moment, then said, "It wasn't much of an option."

"Why is that?"

"My mother's there." I could see the emotion this confession brought.

"You don't get along with your mother?"

"No." She took a sip of her tea, then set down her cup.

"My mother was emotionally ill. She had been diagnosed as schizophrenic, but she wouldn't get help and she wouldn't take her medications.

"When I was seven she started telling everyone that my father was sexually abusing me—my schoolteachers, the neighbors, our pastor. Eventually the police came and arrested him.

"My mother was always telling me that men were bad. She made me tell the police that my father was abusing me, even though he wasn't." She shook her head. "She was sick. My father was a good man. Even with what she did, he tried to help her. He tried to protect me from her.

"Then she filed for divorce and a restraining order. I don't know how she got the restraining order. The laws in this country are against fathers. They assume they're guilty until proven innocent. But it was my testimony . . ." She teared up. "I betrayed the one person who was protecting me."

The thought that she had falsely accused him made me sick, but it wasn't her fault. It was her mother's. "You weren't old enough to know better."

She wiped a tear from her cheek. "He wasn't found guilty. But he left. After that my mother only got worse. She didn't have him to torment, so she turned her crazy elsewhere.

"She believed that the government was spying on us. She told me that any red lights in the house meant that the CIA, the FBI, and a secret organization she couldn't reveal were tracking our movements. Every night we would have to go around the house in the dark and unplug everything with a light—the microwave, clocks, everything. She said that they could shoot lasers through the lights that would control our minds.

"She had also read that the government had added chemicals to jet fuel so the tracks you see in the sky behind jets was really poison flying down on us to brainwash us."

"When did you begin to see through it?"

"My first boyfriend helped me. I was fourteen, he was seventeen. He would laugh when I'd tell him things my mother said. He wasn't the first person to tell me my mother was crazy, but he was the first I believed.

"Then something happened that really opened my eyes. At the time I was doing all of the cooking. One evening after dinner I heard her on the phone calling poison control. She told them that she had been poisoned.

"Then she ran to the store and bought these charcoal pills and started swallowing them. She must have taken too many of them because she started throwing up all over until she passed out. I called 911. The paramedics came, and they rushed her to emergency.

"When she came to, she told the doctors that I had poisoned her. The doctors knew she wasn't well. They had a psychiatrist visit her. Afterward he took me aside and told me that my mother was schizophrenic and a borderline personality." She took a deep breath. "The thing is, when crazy is normal, normal is crazy. I had to rebuild my entire world."

"Do you have siblings?"

"No. I was an only child, thank God. She would have

messed them up too. What I had was a string of boyfriends. But my mother's crazy seeped into that as well. In a way, I was trying to match the paradigm my mother had programmed into me that men were bad, so I looked for bad men, the wild, mean ones. I think, in some wacked-out way, I was still trying to make my mother's crazy right so I could make sense of the world." She looked at me. "You think I'm crazy now, don't you?"

"No. I think you're resilient."

"Thank you," she said. "So I moved in with Wade when I was sixteen and we got married the day I turned eighteen. We were married on my birthday. Six months later, his cousin offered him a job in Midway, Utah, and here I am."

"Here you are," I said.

"And here you are," she said, touching my arm. She took a deep breath. "Yesterday you asked me why I was waiting outside at the diner."

"Yes."

"Wade and I lived a few miles north of here. We only had one car, so he would drive me to and from work. He used to get raging mad at me if I wasn't outside waiting for him after my shift. Sometimes he'd be almost an hour late picking me up. I'd be nearly frozen." She slowly shook her head. "He was an angry man."

"I'm sorry," I said.

"I'm glad he left town."

I squeezed her hand. "How about your father now? Do you ever talk to him?"

She looked down for a moment. "Almost every day." When she looked back up her eyes were moist. She said, "So I've told you all my secrets. Now you need to tell me one."

"What would you like to know?"

"I'd like to know, Mr. Bartlett, what you are really doing in Midway."

"You don't believe that I'm here for work?"

She slowly shook her head. "No, we have two traffic signals. We don't need software for that."

"I should have known you were smarter than that."

"The truth is, I was willing to give you the benefit of the doubt, except I've had two customers tell me that there's a stranger in town who looks just like you, making random visits to women."

"Wow."

"Like I've said, it's a very small town."

"Fair enough. But now I'm the one who's going to sound crazy. I hope you're still willing to give me the benefit of the doubt."

"Try me."

I clasped my hands together. "Here goes. I came here to find someone."

"You're a bounty hunter?"

I grinned. "No. It's someone I met on the Internet. Actually, that's not quite true. We've never actually met." I looked up into her eyes. "This is going to sound really crazy. I mean, it's the craziest thing I've ever done."

"I know crazy," she said.

"This person, this woman, she wrote a blog that really spoke to me."

"What kind of blog?"

"She writes about loneliness and love. It was so honest and vulnerable . . . after all the lies in my marriage, to hear someone speak so honestly . . . I decided I had to meet her. But she didn't leave any information on her website except her initials."

"You came all the way to Midway to find someone with only their initials?"

"I know, crazy, right? I mean, if it was New York, I wouldn't have tried. But, like you said, Midway's a small town."

"What are her initials?"

"LBH."

Aria was quiet for a moment. I could see her thinking.

"Do you know anyone with those initials?" I asked.

She shook her head. "No. Mrs. Harding. But she's eighty years old."

"Yeah, I found that out."

"She's one of the customers who told me about you."

"She could talk like no one I've ever met," I said.

Aria smiled. "She's lonely. And she's very sweet. She's the only one who comes into the diner and brings us food." She looked into my eyes. "So how do you even know this LBH is in Midway?"

"For a long time I didn't. Then, in one of her blog entries she wrote about Swiss Days. I looked up Swiss Days on the Internet and Midway, Utah, was the only place that celebrated it at the time she wrote about. So I came out to see if I could find her."

"And when you find her, what will you do?"

"I don't know." I took her hand. "Things aren't the way I thought they'd be. I didn't plan on meeting you."

She smiled coyly. "That wasn't in my script either. So, will you keep on looking?"

"I don't know. Part of me feels like I need closure with this woman."

"And the other part of you?"

I leaned into her and we kissed.

✦

We talked and kissed until Aria couldn't keep her eyes open and asked what time it was. "Almost three," I whispered.

She lightly groaned. "I have to be at work in three hours."

"I'm sorry," I said.

She smiled dreamily. "I'm not." I kissed her good night.

"I better let you sleep tomorrow," I said.

"I don't want to sleep."

"You need sleep. Do you work on Saturday?"

"No."

"Good. We'll go cut down a Christmas tree," I said.

"Why would I want to cut down a Christmas tree?"

"Because it's almost Christmas. And I may never get another chance."

"Whatever you say," she said. "As long as I get to be with you."

✦

I got back to the inn about half past three. In spite of the hour, I didn't fall right to sleep. I didn't want to sleep. I wanted to relive the night in my memory. I just wanted to be with her. So why did I feel like I needed to keep looking for LBH?

CHAPTER

Twenty-seven

I didn't wake the next morning until after ten. I pulled on the same clothes I'd worn the day before and walked down to the dining room. I sat in my usual place and ordered griddle cakes with a side of sausage.

I was almost done eating when Ray walked into the room. In spite of the cold he was wearing long shorts with knee-high socks and thick leather walking boots. He looked very German. He also had a brown leather satchel slung over his arm.

He smiled when he saw me. "Mr. Bartlett," he said. "Just the man I'm looking for." He walked over and sat down at my table. He shrugged off the satchel, put it on the table next to him, then looked into my eyes. "I'm glad you are here, my friend. I need to talk to you."

He leaned closer and, in a more serious tone, said, "You know, the longer I live, the more I believe in heaven ordinant—the Shakespearean edict that 'there's a divinity that shapes our ends, rough-hew them how we will.'" He leaned back and his voice relaxed. "So, did you find your LBH?"

I wiped my mouth with my napkin. "Not yet."

I was about to tell him that I was considering aborting my

search when he said, "I didn't think so. Let me tell you why. I have a story to tell you.

"Nine years ago I was at an art showing in Park City when a man asked me for some help. He was trying to get his elderly grandmother in a wheelchair down a set of stairs. I don't know where the ramp was, but the stairs only had five steps, so I offered my assistance.

"We're just about down the last step when *pop!* something gives in my back. I ruptured a disk, L5-S1. It pinched off my sciatic nerve, so I've got no feeling in my left leg. Hurt like the devil. Two surgeries and a diskectomy later, I can walk without a cane. It's like they say, 'no good deed goes unpunished.'" He leaned forward until he was uncomfortably close. "You're probably wondering why I'm sharing this story."

"It crossed my mind," I said.

"My back's been sore ever since. So once a month I treat myself to a massage. There's a wonderful, beautiful young lady in Midway with nothing short of magical hands. So the day before yesterday I was getting my monthly massage when it occurred to me that this young lady is not on your list, but she should be.

"Her name is Lynette Hurt. Granted, it's a bit of an unfortunate name for that profession, or maybe it's ideal, I don't know. She lives in Heber, which is why you didn't have her on your list, but her parlor, or studio, whatever they call them these days, is only a few blocks from the park. She gets a lot of business during Swiss Days."

"How old is she?"

"About your age. Maybe a few years younger."

"And she's single?"

"She's been single and alone for a while now. Her husband was killed in a tractor accident just on the other side of the Homestead. What a tragic day that was for the community."

"And her family?"

"She never had any children and his family moved away after their son's death, so she's very much alone. And lonely. She told me. I don't know if she blogs, but I know she's very active on the social media, Facebook and such." He pointed a sausage finger at me. "I think Lynette's your woman. She's a sweet one. Lonely. Contemplative. Pretty, in a natural way, you know, not one to wear a lot of makeup. Doesn't need it. Soft eyes. Soft-spoken . . ."

"Does she have a middle name?"

"I honestly don't know. But I do know that her maiden name was German. Bucher. It means beech tree or something like that."

"Her father was German," I said. "LBH mentioned that in one of her posts."

Ray nodded. "Yes, Lynette Bucher Hurt."

I looked at him. "Her initials are LBH."

"Yes, sir." He reached over and patted me on the shoulder. "I knew that wouldn't be lost on you. I'll have Claudia schedule you an appointment for her next available opening."

"Thank you," I said.

He then took something from his satchel. "Here, I brought

something for you." He handed me a small cluster of dried flowers bundled together with twine. "It's edelweiss. It's an important symbol to the Swiss. Edelweiss grows high in the mountains on rocky soil, so if a young man wanted to impress a young lady, he would bring her edelweiss. She might not marry him, but it would certainly get her attention. I thought it might come in handy."

"It's very strange that you would bring this to me." I looked him in the eyes. "In one of the blog entries LBH wrote that her father told her to wait for a man to bring her edelweiss."

Ray smiled. "There you go. Just as I was saying. Divinity."

My breakfast with Ray had left me feeling a little confused. *Had I really found LBH?* I realized that there was a part of me that had actually doubted that I would ever find her. And, in consequence of my budding relationship with Aria, there was now a part of me that didn't want to find her.

Still, I had to see this through. I had to know. The fact that the woman was a masseuse was convenient. I could casually talk to her about her life without creeping her out or making her suspicious. I don't know if it was divinity, as Ray claimed, but it couldn't have worked out better.

After breakfast I went back up to get ready for the day. I was shaving when my room phone rang. I wiped the shaving cream off my face and answered.

"Mr. Bartlett, it's Claudia at the front desk. I just wanted to let you know that I was able to get you a one-hour massage appointment with Ms. Hurt at two o'clock this afternoon."

"Thank you."

As I hung up the phone, I realized that after all the miles and all I'd been through, I might actually be meeting LBH. So why was it that I couldn't stop thinking of Aria?

CHAPTER

Twenty-eight

Before I left the inn, Claudia handed me the address of the massage studio. It was just three doors north of Main Street, in a small, single-story house. I passed the diner on the way there and I couldn't help but look for Aria. I didn't see her. I parked in the street, then walked up to the front door. A plastic sign read:

Awaken Massage by Lynette
Swedish • Shiatsu • Hot Stone • Deep Tissue • Reflexology
9 a.m. – 6 p.m. / Mon – Fri / Walk-ins welcome

I stepped inside. The home's front room had been converted into a lounge area with a modern, bright red sofa behind a glass coffee table covered with magazines on massage therapy, health, and holistic healing. The space had a comforting ambience.

I examined the room carefully, looking for clues. On a counter in the corner of the room was a scented candle whose fragrance filled the room with a pleasant pineapple-citrus smell. Next to the counter was a cabinet with a glass front. I walked over to inspect what was inside. There were small, amber apothecary bottles filled with different types of essential oils: lavender, frankincense, lemon, and at least a dozen others.

I sat down on the couch to wait. My anticipation was growing, teased by a sign hanging from the door in front of me:

Massage in Progress
Please be quiet,
I will be right with you.
—LBH

There it was. LBH. I checked my watch. I was early for my appointment. I had just started reading an article on the benefits of cupping therapy when the hallway door opened. I looked up to see an attractive young woman with short blond hair step out. She had wide, fleshy cheeks and soft blue eyes. Even though her maiden name was German, I thought she was more Swedish-looking. She was wearing a short-sleeved, dark blue smock.

There was something very surreal about finally seeing her.

"Mr. Bartlett?"

I stood. "Yes."

She smiled. "No, please, sit. My client is getting dressed. She's elderly, so it takes her a little longer. I'll be right back to get you. Please relax and make yourself comfortable."

"Thank you," I said.

She disappeared back through the door. About five minutes later an older woman came walking out from the hallway. She was a little bent, with silver hair that was slightly mussed from her massage. She was speaking to Lynette. "I'll be out of town next week, and it's the holiday, so I won't need my usual appointment. But I'll be back the next."

"Where are you going?"

"Up north," she said. "Logan. McKenzie—that's Barry's second daughter—is marrying one of those Logan boys. On Christmas Eve, no less. I don't know what she's thinking."

Lynette walked out behind her, smiling. "Well, travel safe. And don't forget to do your stretches. Fifteen minutes a night."

"You sound just like my daughter. She keeps trying to get me to go to one of those yoga classes."

"You should try it. I've seen it do wonders."

The old woman rooted through her purse for a moment, lifted out a hundred-dollar bill, and handed it to Lynette. "Thank you, dear. It's the best hour of my week. And keep the extra. Christmas is coming."

"You don't need to do that."

"You deserve it. Have a merry Christmas."

The women hugged and the elderly woman left, furtively glancing at me. There was a brief pause, as if in deference to the woman's departure, then Lynette walked up to me, extending her hand.

"Hi, I'm Lynette."

I stood and took her hand. "I'm Alex."

"Thank you for your patience, Alex. Come on back."

As I followed her I said, "Thank you for getting me in on such short notice."

"You're welcome. I always try to accommodate the local resorts. They're my bread and butter."

She led me to an open door at the end of the corridor. Inside the room was a wide massage table covered with beige cotton sheets. The room was dimmed and light, Asian-sounding flute music was playing against a background ambience of nature sounds.

"Go ahead and get undressed to your comfort level, then slide under the sheet with your face down. I'll go wash my hands and I'll be right back."

She shut the door. I took off all my clothes, folded them in the corner, then climbed onto the warm table, pulling the sheet over my back. I rested my head in the cradle. I wondered if Lynette's hands would feel as good as Aria's. My thoughts were interrupted by a light knock on the door.

"May I come in?"

"Yes."

I could hear the door open as she stepped inside. She dimmed the lights a little more, shut the door, and walked over next to me, gently putting her hand on the middle of my back. "Have you had a massage before?"

"Many."

"Good. Do you have a preference today? Deep tissue, relaxation, hot stones . . ."

"Just relaxation," I said.

"Are there any places you would like me to pay special attention?"

My heart. "My scalp," I said. "And my feet."

"Whatever you like." She poured oil onto her hands, rubbed them together, and then lightly pulled the sheet down to my lower back. "Just let me know if the pressure is too much." She ran her hand up my spine and began rubbing the oil into my back. Her hands were soft yet strong.

She had worked my back for a few minutes when I asked, "Have you been doing this long?"

"Almost six years," she said. "You're staying at the Blue Boar?"

"Yes."

"It's a beautiful inn. Have you stayed there before?"

"No. This is my first time in Midway. Actually, in Utah."

"What do you think of it?"

"I think it's cold."

She laughed. "Where are you from, California?"

"Florida."

"The other side." She pressed on a tender spot beneath my right shoulder blade and I recoiled a little. "Sorry, you've got a knot here. Let me work it out."

Neither of us spoke as she rubbed the area.

"Do you have a lot of stress in your life?"

"The usual," I said.

She kept rubbing until the tension was gone.

"You're good," I said. "Do you get a lot of business here?"

"I keep busy. I do a lot of work for the resorts, Zermatt and the Homestead. In the fall there's a festival here called Swiss Days. I'm pretty much nonstop those days and for several weeks after.

"There's a parking lot on the other side of this block, so there's constant traffic and I get a lot of walk-ins. Sometimes I wonder where all those people come from."

I recognized those words from her blog.

"There's also a lot of new development going on around here. It's not Park City with the celebrities and all that, but there's still a lot of new money coming into the city. It makes the locals kind of crazy, these new people moving in with their own ideas. Some of these families have been here since the Mormon pioneers."

"How long have you lived here?"

"I moved here eight years ago, but my husband's family goes way back to the pioneers." She paused. "Take a deep breath, then slowly breathe out."

I did as she said.

"What brings you to Midway?"

I hesitated. "Business."

"What kind of business are you in?"

"I'm an assassin."

She was quiet for a moment, then said, "Do you get health benefits with that?"

We both laughed. I liked this woman.

After a half hour Lynette had me roll over onto my back. I looked into her face and she smiled. She had a kind smile. I could imagine her writing the kinds of blog entries that had brought me three thousand miles west.

"Do you do much on the Internet?" I asked.

"I try. I have a Facebook page and an Instagram account. Nothing big, a few hundred people, but for a town this size, that's not bad. I also have a blog, but that's just for personal things."

"I'd like to read it."

She looked uncomfortable. "It's kind of embarrassing. It's just my thoughts. I write for self-therapy. I'd hate to actually meet someone who read it." She took a deep breath. "How do you feel?"

"I feel great," I said. "You have a very nice touch."

"Thank you."

I closed my eyes and let her finish her work in silence. I'd found LBH. Now what?

CHAPTER

Twenty-nine

As Lynette worked my scalp, I thought over my next move. I was confused. This is what I'd come three thousand miles for. I should have been wildly excited, not wildly conflicted. LBH was exactly what I hoped she'd be: kind, sincere, beautiful. But my heart was somewhere else. It was like going to a car dealership to purchase the car you've done all the research on and then your head gets turned by a model you've never even heard of. I don't mean to sound that shallow, comparing these women to cars, but you get my point.

Still, as I'd told Nate, I had felt powerfully inspired to find LBH, and now I had. I supposed that I owed it to the universe at least to see where it went from here.

✦

Twenty minutes later Lynette ran her hands down the length of my body then gently set a hand on my knee. "That's our session, Alex. How do you feel?"

"Like a new man," I said.

"Good. I'm going to step out so you can dress. Would you like some water?"

"Please."

"I'll be right outside the door," she said. After she left the room, I just lay there in the darkness, taking deep breaths. The next move was mine. I sat up and dressed, then walked out into the hallway. Lynette was standing near the door, holding a plastic cup of water. "There you go," she said, handing me the cup.

I took a drink. "Thank you."

"Remember to drink a lot of water. There was a lot of tension built up in your neck and shoulders that I worked out, and you want to flush the toxins out of your system."

I followed her out to the lobby. I was glad that there was no one waiting. I gave her a credit card and signed on an extra twenty-dollar tip.

"Do you leave town soon?" she asked.

"Next week," I said. "I was going to leave on the twenty-second, but I might stay a little longer."

She grinned. "More people to kill?"

"So many hits, so little time."

"Well, if you ever come back into town, be sure to stop by. Unless you're coming on business. Then I've moved."

I laughed.

She grabbed a business card. "Here. In case you find yourself back in Midway."

I looked over the card, which basically had the same information as the front door, with the addition of her cell phone number. I realized that our time was at an end and I needed to act now.

"I don't know if this is appropriate or not, it's kind of spontaneous, but would you like to go to dinner with me tonight?"

She looked as surprised at my invitation as I was. "I've never gone out with a client . . ."

"There's a first time for everything, right?"

She thought for a moment then smiled. "Yes. I'd like that. What time?"

"What's good for you?"

She looked at the clock on the wall. "It's almost two-thirty. I need to get a few things done at home. Say seven?"

"Seven would be great. I don't know a lot of restaurants in town, but the one at the Blue Boar is nice."

"The Blue Boar is very nice. Shall I meet you there?"

"Or I can pick you up," I said. "If you're okay with that."

"Thank you. Let me write my home address on the card."

I handed her the card and she scrawled something on the back and returned it to me. "Thank you. I'll see you at seven."

Sometime during my massage it had started snowing again. I brushed off my car, then headed back to the inn. As I drove down Main Street, I glanced at the diner. This time I thought I saw Aria inside and it made my stomach ache a little. I wanted to see her.

When I got to my room I called Nate and then Dale, but neither answered. I checked my emails, then pulled up LBH's blog. Not surprisingly, there was nothing new. One by one I reread her previous posts. They felt different now that I could put a face to them.

At six thirty I went downstairs. The dining room was the most crowded I'd seen it since I'd arrived. I'd gotten used to just walking in at my convenience and forgotten that the restaurant was open to the public and I might need reservations, especially on a Friday night a week before Christmas. Claudia was still at the front desk.

"How was your massage?" she asked.

"Perfect. In fact, I'm taking Lynette to dinner tonight."

She smiled. "That did go well."

"I was planning on bringing her here for dinner, but it looks like you're already full. Do you have any openings?"

"We always have openings for our inn guests," she said. "There's a private party here tonight, but we can seat you in Truffle Hollow, if that's okay."

"That would be fine. Thank you."

Lynette lived on the north side of Midway in an older, fairly large home, a long, white, stucco-walled rambler. The street in front of her home was lined with trees, and as I pulled into her driveway I could see a horse stall and corral in her backyard. There was also a picturesque red barn about fifty yards behind the house. The home was decorated for the holidays with colorful lights outlining its frame. There was also a large, snow-shrouded plastic Nativity scene in the center of the yard. The bulbs of the four electric porch lights had been replaced with red and green bulbs for the season.

I rang the doorbell and Lynette promptly answered. She was wearing a form-fitting burgundy sequin dress with a wide gold belt that accentuated the narrow curvature of her waist. She looked stunning.

"Hi, come in," she said.

"Thank you." I stepped inside. The front room was also decorated for the season. There was an upright piano in the center of the room with plaster figurines of Christmas carolers arranged on the top. The fireplace had pink angel hair stretched along its mantel. Above the fireplace was a Thomas Kinkade print of a snow-covered gazebo next to an icy pond.

To the right of the fireplace was a tall, white-frosted Christmas tree hung with metallic blue baubles and white lights.

"Did you have any trouble finding me?" Lynette asked.

I almost burst out laughing. In light of what I'd been through in the last week, the question was funny. "Not at all," I said.

"Good. I'll just get my coat."

She returned wearing a full-length black wool coat that fell to her ankles.

"You look very nice," I said.

"I was thinking the same thing about you."

I opened the car door for her. As I climbed in she said, "This is a rental?"

"Yes."

"Is it good in the snow?"

"It's good, I'm not."

She smiled. "I'm excited about dinner. It's been at least two years since I've eaten at the Blue Boar."

"When I came down from my room tonight I was afraid that we might not be able to get a table because there was a private party. But since I'm a guest, they won't refuse me."

"You're telling me that you have friends in high places?"

"I think you're the one with friends in high places. One call from you to Ray and he would have served us dinner himself."

"He's a sweet guy."

"He is. But, just so you know, he hates it when pretty women call him that."

✦

The restaurant was crowded but we had the pub to ourselves. For an appetizer I ordered the fondue for two, followed by the French onion gratinée and the filet mignon with crab-and-spinach-stuffed portobello and béarnaise sauce. Lynette ordered the Blue Boar salad and the duck breast with sour cherry purée.

After we'd been served our entrées I said, "I hope this

isn't inappropriate, but Ray told me your husband passed away."

She nodded. "About seven years ago."

"I'm sorry."

"Thank you."

"So, tell me about yourself."

She wiped her mouth with a napkin. "I don't know the last time someone said that to me. In a small town, it's like everyone already knows everything about you. Or thinks they do." She shook her head. "I'm the pretty young widow, you know. The one every wife pities and fears."

"Fears?"

"I've actually seen them grab their husbands as I passed them on the sidewalk."

"I'm sorry. It's been seven years?"

"Seven long years." She sighed. "You know, you think you know what your life's going to look like, so you make these big plans, thinking you have some right to expect them. But it's like writing in the sand on the beach. The waves come up onto the shore and erase them and you're back to where you started."

I loved the poetry of her explanation. It reminded me of her blog posts.

"What about you? Have you ever been married?"

"Yes. But I'm divorced." I looked at her. "I hate saying that. It's like announcing failure. I never thought I'd be divorced. It just wasn't in my game plan."

"Did your parents divorce?"

"No, they stayed together. For better or worse. Mostly worse. They probably should have divorced."

"What happened with your marriage?"

"I thought she was unhappy because I was gone too much. So I changed my schedule. I took a pay cut to spend more time with her. But she really didn't want that. That's when she left."

"You took a pay cut to be with her? That's really sweet." She grinned in prelude to her next question. "So what do you do when you're not assassinating?"

"Something much less exciting. I sell traffic systems to city and state governments."

"And that's why you're here?"

My answer barely made sense. "Sure."

"How much longer will you be here?"

"Three days."

"Not long," she said. She took a drink, then looked into my eyes. "I'm driving to Salt Lake City tomorrow. Have you ever been there?"

"Just the airport."

"Would you like to come with me?"

The offer surprised me. I wasn't sure how to respond. Aria and I had planned on spending the day together. Lynette must have noticed my hesitation because she quickly said, "I'm sorry, I'm not usually so forward, but Saturday's my only day off and I'm leaving town Sunday evening. I'd like to get to know you better."

I wasn't sure what to do. Finally I said, "I'll make it work. I'd like to get to know you better too."

✦

The rest of the night was pleasant. We talked a lot about Florida, not because I wanted to, but because Lynette did. She had never been to the East Coast. Truthfully, I wanted to tell her about my visits in Midway, but I couldn't figure out any context I could do that in without telling her everything. She was peaceful and I enjoyed every minute being with her. But I still couldn't keep my mind off of Aria.

After dinner I drove Lynette home, then called Aria to change our plans. She didn't answer her phone. Considering her schedule, I'm sure she'd already been asleep for several hours. I didn't want to break our date by voice mail, so I just hung up, planning to call in the morning.

I hoped she'd understand.

CHAPTER
Thirty

The next morning I woke late because the alarm on my phone didn't go off. I had forgotten to charge it and it had gone dead in the night, which also meant I couldn't call Aria. I plugged it in, then went downstairs to meet Lynette, who had come to join me for breakfast. She was dressed in a form-fitting dark-green sweater with black leggings. She looked beautiful.

As we were eating, Ray walked up to us. "Well, well, now. What a lovely sight." He looked at Lynette. "Hello, my dear."

Lynette stood and the two of them hugged. After she'd sat down, Ray said, "Allow me to vouch for this man. It's been a sheer delight getting to know him."

She smiled at me. "That's good to know."

"Thank you," I said to Ray. "Likewise."

"So what are you kids planning on doing today?"

"We're driving to Salt Lake," Lynette said. "I'm going to show him around."

"That sounds wonderful. Be safe." He winked at me. "Divinity."

✦

The drive to Salt Lake City was pleasant, with natural conversation. Maybe it came from her being a masseuse, or perhaps it was the reason she had become one, but she was easy to talk to. There was no judgment. No hurdles.

When we reached downtown, Lynette directed me to a place called City Creek, an outdoor mall that was festively decorated for the season. Not surprisingly, the mall was crowded.

After wandering around the stores for an hour she said, "Could you excuse me a moment? I need to pick something up."

"Should I go with you?"

"No," she said, smiling. "I'll meet you back here in . . . forty minutes?"

"Sure."

She quickly walked off. I wondered why she didn't want me to go with her. I couldn't imagine she was purchasing something for me.

I found a bench and sat down. I had been people-watching for a few minutes when I spotted a Tiffany jewelry store about fifty yards from me, and I walked to it.

As I wandered around, looking inside their glass showcases, a particular piece caught my eye. It was a quarter-size, white gold pendant in the shape of a star with yellow gems inside.

A saleswoman walked up to me. "May I help you?"

"Could you tell me about that piece? The star one . . ."

"Of course." She reached inside the case and lifted the pendant from its dark blue felt display. "This piece is called the noble star. The emblem itself is made of white gold. The gems are canary diamond chips."

"Canary diamonds?"

"Yellow diamonds," she said. "They're chips, so they're not faceted."

I looked at the price. It was almost fifteen hundred dollars.

"Would you like to handle it?"

"Yes."

She gingerly handed it to me. "It's really a unique pendant," she said. "I've never seen anything like it."

Neither had I. Chalk it up to my recent insanity, but for some reason I had to buy it. I wasn't even sure who I was buying it for. I assumed it was for LBH. But the truth was, it was Aria who kept coming to mind.

Lynette was waiting for me as I walked back. She was now carrying several large shopping bags. I should have known that the robin's-egg-blue Tiffany sack would catch her attention.

"You bought something at Tiffany?"

I glanced down at the small sack. "Yes. For a friend."

She didn't say anything.

✦

Afterward we drove to the Grand America Hotel. We had lunch at the elegant Garden Café, then followed their holiday "window stroll," a tour of the hotel's Christmas-themed windows, culminating in a life-size gingerbread house that allegedly had taken thirteen hundred pounds of flour, three hundred pounds of sugar, and fifteen hundred eggs to make.

All day long I waited for the right time to tell Lynette that I'd been reading her blog and why I had really come to Utah, but the right time never came. We concluded our day with dinner at a restaurant that overlooked the impressively illuminated Temple Square. Afterward we went to see the grounds.

The air was cold but not as brisk as in Midway. As we walked, Lynette moved close to me, and I could tell that she wanted to hold hands. I took her hand, though, for some reason, it felt a little unnatural.

She was quiet. We both were. It had been a nice day. A pleasant day. But something felt wrong. Maybe that it was nice and pleasant and nothing but that was exactly what was wrong. I had expected something more from meeting LBH—something magical and passionate. Instead the day felt like a pleasant outing with a good friend. Or a sister.

Lynette didn't say much until we were nearly to the mouth of the canyon.

"Thank you for today. It was really nice."

"It was my pleasure. Thank you for the invitation."

She looked over at me. "I wish you weren't leaving town so soon."

"Me too," I said.

The silence boomed. I wasn't sure what to say. Then she said, "Would you like to come over for lunch tomorrow?"

"I thought you were leaving town."

"Tomorrow night. But if you already have other plans . . ."

I didn't have plans. At least not yet. "No, that sounds nice. What time should I come?"

"Two?"

"Two it is."

Even though I was missing Aria, I had to go. It was my last chance to tell her why I was really there. It was my last chance to confront LBH.

When I got back to my room I picked up my phone, afraid of what I'd find. There were six voice-mail messages—one from Nate, one from Dale, the other four from Aria. I felt a sharp stab of guilt.

I listened to Nate's and Dale's messages first just to get them out of the way. Nate was characteristically succinct.

It's Nate, call me back.

Dale wasn't so succinct.

Hey, dude, it's Dale, returning your call. Don't know what you need. Maybe you got married. If it was just a butt call, this never happened. Call me anyway.

I selected the first of Aria's messages. Her voice started out bright and happy and fell with each succeeding call.

9:17 - *Hi, Alex. It's Aria. I saw that you called last night, sorry I went to bed the second I got home. I was so tired. So, I was just checking to see if we're still on for today. I missed seeing you yesterday. . . . Looking forward to seeing you.*

9:56 - *Hi, it's me again. Aria. I don't know if you got my last message. Please call when you get a chance. Let me know what's going on.*

12:16 - *Hi, it's Aria. I don't know what's going on. If I did something to offend you, I'm sorry. Please call me.*

On her last message her voice was soft and painful. Vulnerable.

4:36 - *Hi. I don't know if you're trying to say good-bye without talking to me. I guess you are, right? My heart hurts. I really liked being with you. I don't know what I did, or if you just realized that you didn't want to be with me. . . . Anyway, I know you'll be leaving soon and I just wanted to tell you that it was nice getting to know you. I wish you well.*

Her voice rang off with sadness. My heart ached. I immediately called her back but she didn't answer. Her phone must have been turned off or maybe I was blocked, because it wouldn't even allow me to leave a message. How stupid could I be?

CHAPTER

Thirty-one

I didn't sleep well. I had dreams about Aria. I felt like I had dozens of them, but I only remembered one. It was disturbing. Lynette was putting a black bag over Aria's head. Before she did, Aria looked up at me. Her eyes turned to stone.

I didn't know if Aria was working or not, and I didn't want to wake her if she wasn't, so I waited until nine to call her. She didn't answer. I called again. And again.

Then Lynette texted me to ask me how I liked my steak.

I texted back.

Medium well. I'll see you soon.

Finally I called Nate. He didn't answer, and I figured he was probably at church, so I called Dale. He answered on the second ring.

"Hey, man. When did you get back?"

"I'm not. I'm still in Utah."

"Still in Utah? Can't find her?"

"No, I found her. But I've got a problem."

"She's *married*. She's a *he*. She's *ugleeeee . . .*"

"Stop," I said. "No, it's . . . I came out here for one woman and I found two."

Dale was quiet for just a moment, then burst out laughing.

"Stop laughing," I said. "Not everything's a joke."

"I'm sorry, man. I'm not laughing at you, I'm laughing with the universe. I think it's great."

"It's not *great*. It's a problem."

"You fell in love with two women in, like, a week?"

"No. I fell in love with Lynette months ago. But there's another woman . . . It's like . . ." I didn't know how to describe Aria.

"Speechless. I love it. Wait, I've got the answer. You're in Utah; they do that *Big Love* thing out there. Bring them both back."

"Stop it," I said.

"Look, lighten up, man. You sound like you have an actual problem, like third-world debt or world hunger. Your problem is a good problem. What's better than having two potential clients competing for your sale? You just take the highest bidder. And in this case, by *highest bidder* I mean the largest bra size."

"I'm hanging up."

"I can't wait to meet her."

I hung up. I sat there for a minute, then went to the counter and retrieved the dried edelweiss that Ray had given me. I looked around for something to put it in. The only thing I could find, besides the room's laundry bag, was the Tiffany bag. I took the pendant out and hid it inside my suitcase, then put the edelweiss in the bag.

I know, in hindsight, I should have known better. It was a man-dumb thing.

✦

On the drive over to Lynette's my mind was going faster than the car, which wasn't surprising, since the roads were like tundra and I had to drive as slow as a Miami retiree to keep from going into a ditch.

The same worry played over and over in my mind. *How will she respond once she knows the truth about why I'm here?*

When I got to the house I rang the doorbell. Lynette greeted me with a hug. "I'm so glad to see you again."

"Me too."

She looked down at the Tiffany bag but said nothing about it. "Come in; everything's ready."

I followed her into the dining room. The food was already on the table. "Let's eat," she said.

Everything was delicious, and we didn't talk much. After a few minutes, she said, "You're quiet today."

I looked up and smiled. "It's a good sign. I'm always quiet when there's good food."

"Thank you."

The truth was, my mind was still shuffling through the deck of possible outcomes I was about to face. How would she respond to my stalking her? How would she respond to the edelweiss? Was it as big a deal as she'd said in her blog? What if it was too big a deal? What if she took it as a proposal? Was it one? I began to question the wisdom of giving her the flower. Still, she'd already seen the bag. I was committed.

"So, where are you off to tonight?" I asked, trying to fill the silence.

"I'm going to a soul restoration camp in Star, Idaho," she said.

"Soul restoration?"

She nodded. "It's part of a community of women I belong to called Brave Girls Club."

"Are you brave?" I asked.

"I try to be."

When we'd finished our meal she brought over a chocolate Bundt cake and started cutting it. "You're going to have to take the rest back to the inn with you. It won't be good when I get back."

"I'll share it with Ray," I said.

"He'll be happy." She handed me a plate, then looked at me with a serene smile. It was time.

"I have something for you," I said. I lifted the Tiffany bag. Her face lit with excitement. Then I took out the edelweiss and handed it to her. She looked down at my gift, then back at me. Her expression had changed from happiness to confusion. Or maybe disappointment.

"Thank you," she finally said.

Her response wasn't what I expected. "It's edelweiss."

She hesitated a moment and then said, "It's pretty."

"It's pretty?"

She laughed. "Yes, it's pretty." A moment later she added, "Is something wrong with that?"

"No. I just expected . . . more." (Looking back, I'm sure she was thinking the same.)

"I'm sorry. I like it. I especially like that you brought me a flower."

I looked at her quizzically. "Didn't your father once tell you something special about edelweiss?"

"My father? No. How do you know my father?"

"Is your father German?"

"My father's French. Bucher is a French surname."

I just gazed at her for a moment, then said, "Did you know that being lonely actually drops your body temperature?"

Now she looked at me as if I'd just lost my mind. Maybe I had. "Why did you just ask me that?"

"You're not her," I said.

"I'm not who?"

"You're not the one I came here for."

She looked upset. "I don't understand. You came here looking for someone?"

I stood. "I'm so sorry. I've made a very big mistake."

CHAPTER *Thirty-two*

On the way from Lynette's house I called Aria again, but there was still no answer. I drove across town to the diner and hurried inside. The restaurant wasn't crowded, just four tables of customers, but I couldn't see Aria anywhere.

The older waitress, Valerie, had glanced over at me as I walked in, but she didn't seem to be in much of a hurry to help me. She finished talking to some diners, then casually walked over to me. "What can I do for you?" Her voice was hard.

"Is Aria here?"

"No, she's not."

"Did she work today?"

"No, she didn't."

"Do you know where she is?"

"Why would I know that?"

Talking to her was like pulling thistles with bare hands. Finally I said, "All right. When you see her, please tell her I came by."

She didn't speak for a moment, and then she said, "I don't think I will."

"Excuse me?"

"I don't think I will. Let me tell you something about Aria.

She's one of the sweetest people I've ever known. She's like a delicate piece of porcelain, precious but fragile. But a big-city man like you doesn't care about things like that. She was supposed to be working today, but she called in sick last night. I don't remember the last time she called in sick. It's been years. I could tell she'd been crying. I pressed her, and she told me that you had stood her up.

"Maybe it's okay to treat women like that where you come from, but here it's not." Her eyes squinted until they were almost closed, and she jabbed at me with her finger. "So you listen well, big city. If you're going to contact her again, and I hope you don't, but if you do, you better be good to her. Aria's got a lot of big men with little brains who would like nothing more than to earn a few brownie points by defending her honor—if you catch my drift."

"I catch your drift," I said. "And no, I don't believe in treating women that way. Things happened that were out of my control. I'm trying to find her to apologize."

"Yeah, well, you do that. And you watch your back. We small towns have our ways."

In one sentence she had gone from *Steel Magnolias* to *Deliverance*.

✦

I drove directly to Aria's house. Her Jeep was parked in front, but the house lights were out. I walked up and pounded on the door. "Aria."

She didn't answer. I tried calling her on the phone

again, but my call still didn't go through. I pounded again. "Aria!"

After several minutes of pounding I heard footsteps inside. The door opened slowly, slightly, the security chain still attached. Aria looked at me through the crack. "What do you want?"

"I am so sorry. I tried to call you. I called you Friday night. I tried to call you as soon as I got your messages."

She didn't say anything.

"Can we talk?"

"No."

"May I explain?"

She looked at me for a moment, then said, "You have one minute."

"Out here?"

"Where were you Saturday?"

"I'm so sorry. I had to finish the search. That's why I came here. I thought I found her."

"And did you?"

"I thought I did. But it wasn't her. I made a mistake."

"And if she had been LBH, you never would have come back?"

"I would have come back. I couldn't stop thinking of you. I promise. Please give me another chance. I want to be with you. I still want to get that Christmas tree with you."

"Saturday was my only day off."

"Then we'll go after your shift."

"You leave tomorrow."

"I'll extend my stay."

She just looked at me angrily. Then she said, "Why would you do that?"

Her words stung. For a moment I was speechless. I couldn't believe how quickly I had messed up something so beautiful. Finally I said, "I'm sorry. I thought you might want me to." I took a deep breath. "I'm really sorry. More than you'll ever know. I think you're really wonderful and brave. I loved getting to know you. I was hoping to get to know you even better." I took another deep breath. "I'll leave you alone." I turned and began to walk away.

As I stepped off the porch, Aria shouted, "Did you get a permit?"

I turned back. "What?"

"You need a permit to cut down a tree."

"No."

"Get one. Tomorrow." She shut the door.

"Okay," I said to the closed door. "I'll get a permit."

CHAPTER Thirty-three

As soon as I got back to the inn, I stopped at the front desk to extend my stay. The Shakespeare Room wasn't available on the twenty-sixth, so they moved me to the Jane Austen Room. I didn't care.

I walked up the stairs to my room and went right to bed. Frankly, I felt like I'd messed up more lives in this little town in the last week than I had in the last decade in Daytona Beach. I felt awful about leaving Lynette like that. She deserved better. Maybe someday I'd explain it to her, though I doubted she'd ever speak to me again. At least she was on her way to a Brave Girls soul retreat or whatever it was called. I'm sure those women would have a lot to say about me and my Tiffany bag of dried edelweiss.

Still, she had played an important role in my journey. I realized that I no longer cared about finding LBH. I was just grateful that Aria had given me a second chance.

✦

The next morning I spent nearly forty minutes changing my flights home. Then I dressed and went downstairs to eat a light breakfast of oatmeal with milk, brown sugar, and walnuts, then headed off to get my tree-cutting permit. To my dismay, Ray had told me that I'd have to go back to the mayor's office.

I considered myself fortunate that he didn't ask me about Lynette. I wouldn't have even known where to start. I felt bad that he had personally vouched for me. I hoped I hadn't jeopardized their relationship. Or at least his monthly massages.

As I walked into the city office, the mayor remembered me.

"You're back."

"I'd like a permit to cut a Christmas tree. Am I at the right place?"

"You would like permission to kill one of our trees."

"Yes, ma'am. Mayor."

"And you still haven't killed any of my constituency?"

"Not that I'm aware of."

She eyed me for a moment more, then said, "I will grant you a permit." She bent over and scribbled on a form. Then she looked up and said, "That will be ten dollars."

I gave her cash and she handed me the permit, a receipt, and a paper with the rules of tree cutting.

"Have a nice day," I said.

"You too, Mr. Pear."

I didn't know if she was mocking me or if she had just confused me with one of the murder suspects in the board game Clue.

With my permit in hand, I drove into Heber for Christmas tree decorations. The only place I could find Christmas paraphernalia was a grocery store called, appropriately, The Store, and an Ace Hardware.

At The Store, I bought several boxes of colored lights, baubles, and tinsel. I also bought a package of mistletoe, hoping it might come in handy as a tension breaker. Or, worst case, to replace the prehistoric sprig of mistletoe hanging in the front of the diner.

Drew, the guy at the hardware store, took a proactive role in helping me prepare for my tree-cutting outing. He either sensed that I needed help or, more likely, since I was the only one in the store, he needed the sales. He never left my side.

Drew sold me a festive red-and-green metal tree stand, fifty feet of nylon rope to tie the tree to my car with, and a very expensive handsaw to cut the tree, as well as work gloves to handle the very expensive handsaw. He also tried to sell me a tarp to protect my car from the tree, but that's where I drew the line.

Sometimes it takes a salesman to appreciate a good salesman. Drew was a good salesman. Our *free* tree was getting expensive.

By the time I finished my purchases, it was a little past noon. As I drove over to the diner to see Aria, I was pretty anxious. I had no idea how she was going to respond. It wasn't like we had had much of a talk through the crack in the door. I never even really saw all of her face—at least not all of it at the same time. Yes, I had apologized, but I didn't know to what extent she had accepted it. I hoped that she hadn't changed her mind. I wouldn't blame her if she had, but I hoped.

I walked into the diner to the Carpenters' "I'll Be Home for Christmas" playing on the jukebox. To my dismay, Valerie was standing at the front counter. When she saw me, her expression abruptly changed from a smile to a scowl.

"Hi, Valerie."

She glared at me, then said in a low grumble, "I'll tell her you're here."

She walked around to the kitchen, and a moment later Aria walked out. She looked at me with an expression that was difficult to read. Noticeably, she didn't hug me. But, in fairness, she didn't slap me either.

"Hi," I said.

"Hi," she echoed.

I swayed nervously on the balls of my feet. "I got our permit. And decorations. And baubles and lights and tinsel. And a saw. And gloves. And a rope . . ."

To my relief she smiled. "I have a saw."

"I can take mine back," I said. "It was expensive."

"Thank you. Would you like some lunch?"

"I . . ."

"Say yes."

"Yes. I'd love some lunch."

"Your booth's open. Seat yourself; I'll be right over."

I grabbed a menu, walked over to the booth, and sat down. Aria came over a few minutes later.

"How's your day?" I asked.

"Better than yesterday. Thank you for coming over last night. I was really hurt."

"I'm so very, very sorry."

"I know. You were sweet last night. And cute."

"As long as you know I was sorry."

"I do. And I understand. Now, what can I get you to eat?"

I ordered a Reuben sandwich and a bowl of vegetable beef soup. At the risk of offending Thelma, I passed on peach pie. Before leaving, I asked Aria what time she was off.

"I was supposed to work until nine, but Valerie said she'd work late for me. So I'm off at three."

I was surprised to hear this; maybe even a little suspicious. "Valerie offered to work for you so you could go out with me?"

"Yes. You should thank her."

"I'll pass on that," I said. "Valerie's not really a fan."

"Of course she is. She's just teasing you."

"No. She's not. She scares me a little."

Aria smiled. "Valerie scares you?"

"A little."

"Well, she bought your lunch for you."

I looked at my food, then back at her. "Are you sure she didn't poison it?"

"She never touched it."

"She's a very complex woman," I said. "I'll be back at three." I got up to leave, then said, "Aria, do something for me."

"What's that?"

"Wait for me *inside* the diner."

She smiled, kissed me on the cheek, and then walked away. I looked over, and Valerie again glared at me. Then she pointed. She was very complex.

I returned to the diner a little before three. Aria was standing outside, but only because she saw me pull into the parking lot. She had changed from her waitress outfit and was wearing a parka, high boots, and a red Santa Claus cap.

"Ready for this?" she asked as she climbed into my car.

"You know," I said, "this is a bucket-list moment for me. I've wanted to cut down my own Christmas tree since I was a kid. It just always looked like so much fun on those coffee commercials."

She smiled. "I'm glad."

"Where do we go?"

"We're headed back over by the hot pot. Do you remember how to get there?"

"I might need some help."

I drove the route we had followed before, though she had to show me where the turnoff was. We continued about a half mile past the hot pot, which was easy to see with the steam rising off it. I kind of expected to see Cal watching us with binoculars. Or his shotgun.

"Is this all your rancher's property?" I asked.

"This part is, but where we're going isn't. Otherwise we wouldn't have needed a permit."

"Why don't we just take one of his trees?"

"He never offered."

We drove on, snaking our way back and forth to the top of the mountain, which, incidentally, Aria referred to as a *hill*, not a mountain. The depth of the snow around us increased as we climbed in altitude, but the road was clear. Finally she said, "This is the place."

I parked on the side of the snowbanked road and we got out. We had forgotten to go back to Aria's to get her saw, so I had to unwrap my new one, rendering it unreturnable. At least I had a souvenir to commemorate the day.

The top of the mountain—actually, the whole mountain—was covered with trees, though most of them were much larger than we could use. It took us almost a half hour wading through knee-high snow to find the right one.

There were rules to this tree-cutting business. We could only take subalpine fir trees—*Abies lasiocarpa*—that were twenty feet high or shorter. I had no idea what a subalpine fir was—actually, I didn't know the difference between a fir and a spruce—but the paper said that we could recognize the tree by its needles, which were blunt and tended to turn upward. Fortunately, Aria didn't need the paper to find the right kind of tree; she knew exactly what we were looking for.

We picked out a tree about seven feet high, well shaped, with only one bare spot, which Aria said she would turn toward the wall.

I kicked the snow from the base of the tree, then took my saw to its trunk. I tried to make sawing through it look easy. *It wasn't easy.* Aria patiently watched as I sawed and sawed and sawed my way through the base. She clapped when the tree finally fell. I dragged our subalpine fir back to the car, leaving a hundred-yard-long furrow in the virgin snow.

We tied the tree to the roof of my Ford with my fifty feet of nylon rope and drove back to Aria's, where we untied it and carried it to her front porch. I didn't need to brush any snow off the tree, as the drive back had done that for us.

While I carried the tree in, Aria set up the stand in the corner of her front room. It took several tries to get the tree into the stand, but I eventually did, with the bare spot facing the wall, and we clamped it in place. The tree fit nicely in the corner, and we sat on the floor to admire it. Then I got the decorations from my car and we strung the lighting first, and then, one by one, the baubles.

As Aria went through the sack of decorations, she lifted out the package of mistletoe. "What's this for?"

I looked at her innocently, then shrugged. "It's a secret."

"A mistletoe secret." She opened the package and put the sprig in her hair. Then she took my hand and pulled me over to the couch. We didn't finish the tree for several hours after that.

CHAPTER

Thirty-four

"I know what we should do tomorrow," Aria said, rolling off me. The room was dark, lit only by the colorful flashing lights of the Christmas tree.

"More of this," I said.

"No. I mean, yes, of course, but we can't do this *all* day."

"You have all day?"

"I got tomorrow off."

"You said you had to work."

"I can work any day. But how often do I get you?"

I went to kiss her again, but, still smiling, she pushed me away. "Hold on. So, about tomorrow. As long as you're in Utah, I think we should go skiing."

"Snow skiing?"

She rolled her eyes. "No, waterskiing."

"I've never skied before. Not a lot of opportunity in central Florida."

"So?"

"You'll teach me?"

"No. But I'll enroll you in a class and come with you to laugh."

"I can't wait."

"It's a date," she said.

✦

The next morning I picked Aria up at eight o'clock. We stopped by the diner for coffee, biscuits, and eggs, then headed off to Deer Valley Resort, which was a bit more expensive than Park City but less crowded.

I took a two-hour lesson with a bunch of kids (except for a teenager from Jamaica, I was the only one older than seven), then we went up on the slopes. I didn't look cool, but I only fell twice on the beginner hills and, at the end of the day, went down an intermediate hill with Aria without killing myself. She made it look pretty easy, and I assumed that she was an expert.

By four o'clock we were exhausted—at least I was—and we returned my skis, then I treated her to dinner at the lodge.

After we had ordered I asked, "Have you ever skied the black diamond?"

She nodded. "Yes, but I don't like working that hard."

"So you do this a lot?"

"Rarely."

"Why's that?"

She looked at me as if she was surprised I didn't know. "I'm a girl of limited means."

At that moment I remembered the Tiffany pendant I'd bought in Salt Lake City. "May I give you something for Christmas?" I asked.

She smiled. "Yes. If I can give you something."

"Fair enough."

"I know what I want," she said. "If you can afford it."

"Try me."

"I want to spend Christmas with you."

After dinner we drove back to Midway. We went back to her house for coffee and ended up on the couch in front of the tree. Aria was quiet for a little while, then set down her coffee. "May I ask you something?"

"Of course."

"You said you're done looking for LBH. And you had made a mistake."

"Yes."

"What happened?"

"Do you really want to know?"

She nodded.

"Okay," I said. "Do you know someone named Lynette Hurt?"

"Yes, she's a massage therapist over by the community center. I went to her a while back when I hurt my shoulder." She thought a moment, then said, "Lynette Hurt. Lynette *Bucher* Hurt. LBH. You thought it was her."

"Yes. And Ray thought it was her. He was the one who told me about her. When I went to see her I found out that she was leaving town, so it was my only chance to really check her out."

Aria cocked her head. "Check her out?"

"In a manner of speaking," I said.

"She *is* pretty," Aria said.

"I didn't notice."

"Yeah, right." Aria took another sip of coffee and then said, "So how did you know it wasn't her?"

"I gave her edelweiss."

To my surprise, Aria's expression abruptly changed. She was quiet for a moment, then she said, "You gave her edelweiss?"

"Yeah. But it meant nothing to her. Edelweiss was an important thing to the real LBH."

Suddenly Aria's eyes welled up with tears.

"Why are you crying?" I asked softly. When she didn't answer, I said, "I'm sorry, it didn't mean anything to me. I just had to know if it was her . . ."

Tears began to fall down Aria's cheeks. Suddenly it was as if a curtain had been pulled back from my mind. I understood. "You're LBH."

Aria just looked at me. She looked afraid.

"Aria."

Nothing.

"Aria, who is LBH?"

"I don't know."

"Aria, tell me."

"I don't know!" she shouted.

I could feel my face turning red. "What are you hiding from me? Who is LBH?"

"She's someone you said you cared about."

"Aria!"

She looked at me, then shouted, "Lonely Broken Heart, okay? Are you happy?"

I stood. Something she said had flipped some subconscious trigger. I felt my skin turn hot. I felt something crashing inside me, like the moment I found the note from Clark in Jill's pants.

"You've been lying to me. You knew I was looking for you. You knew this whole time."

"I didn't know this whole time. I didn't know until you told me you were looking for LBH. I was already in love with you."

"You said you didn't know who she was."

"You asked me if I knew anyone with those initials. I didn't. I told you the truth."

"That's not the truth. You knew what I was really asking. You knew, and you deceived me. Just like Jill. You're no different than Jill." I put my hand on my forehead and walked to the side of the room. I felt like a madman. I *was* a madman. It was as if my brain had been hijacked by my deepest fears.

"I've spent the last five years listening to lies and secrets. All I wanted from you was honesty. I fell in love with LBH because she was honest. And you gave me more lies."

"Please don't make me pay for what your wife did. What was I supposed to do?"

I spun around. "You were supposed to tell me the truth! Was that asking too much?"

Aria began sobbing. "I wanted to. But I was afraid. I was afraid I might lose you."

"For telling the truth? It's not the truth—it's the lies that get you into trouble. Just like when you lied to the police about your father!"

I regretted the words even before they came out of my mouth. Aria froze. It was as if I'd slugged her. I suppose I had done worse than that. For a moment she couldn't talk. She couldn't even breathe. Then she fell forward to her knees, holding her sides and shaking. Without looking at me, she said, "Please leave. Please leave me. Please don't ever come back."

✦

I felt sick. I wished I could take the words back, but it was too late. I had said too much. Strikes two and three, and I was out. I looked at her for a moment, then turned and walked out the door. *What had I done?*

CHAPTER

Thirty-five

It was the twenty-third of December, the busiest travel day of the season and second-busiest travel day of the year. Trying to get back home was a nightmare. I first tried to book a flight to Daytona Beach, but came up with nothing. Then Florida. Then I looked for *anything* out of Utah. Every seat out of Salt Lake International was full with confirmed oversales. I should have known better. I couldn't have picked a worse time for my world to collapse.

✦

Fate may have kept me in Utah, but I didn't have to stay in Midway. I couldn't stay in Midway. It was as if the air in the city had dissipated. The proximity to Aria was killing me. Early the next morning I found a hotel vacancy near the airport and booked a room. By nine I carried my bag downstairs to check out. Ray was in the dining room, visiting with some guests, when he noticed me standing at the front desk with my suitcase. He immediately jumped up and rushed to me, his face bent with distress.

"Alex, are you leaving us?"

"Yes, sir."

"I thought you were staying until after Christmas. I hoped to share some more time with you."

"I had planned on it. But . . . something came up."

He carefully studied my countenance, his face mirroring the pain and sadness in mine. "I'm sorry you didn't find what you were looking for."

"No," I said. "The problem is, I did."

He put his hand on my shoulder. "No, my friend. You most certainly did not find what you were looking for."

I looked back into his eyes for a moment, then said, "Thanks for everything. It was a pleasure getting to know you."

"I've grown rather fond of you, young man. I hope to see you again."

Then he turned and walked back to the dining room.

I went back to the front counter. Lita smiled at me sadly. "We're sorry to see you go, Mr. Bartlett. I hope you've had a memorable visit."

"Most definitely memorable," I said. I handed her my key. "Thanks for everything."

"Merry Christmas. It's been a pleasure having you with us."

"Thank you, Lita. The same to you."

I couldn't leave the small town fast enough. When I reached Salt Lake I checked in at the hotel, then drove to the airport to return my rental car. I was glad I was dropping off, not picking up. The lines at the rental car service were obscene. Actually, the lines everywhere were obscene, the mobs uniting for the holiday. Once again, I was going against the traffic.

CHAPTER

Thirty-six

I ended up taking a taxi back to my hotel even though it was only a mile from the airport. It wasn't the distance, it was the traffic. Airport grounds aren't really designed for pedestrians. My cabdriver was already in a sour mood, made more so by my minimal fare. I left him a twenty-dollar tip to stop his grumbling.

In the ninety minutes I'd been gone, the hotel's population had grown considerably, and the lobby was crowded. Ironically, it was there, in the crush of the crowd, that my mistress Loneliness finally caught up with me again. Maybe she had always been with me and I'd just been too distracted by my quest to notice her soft footsteps or to hear her familiar whisperings, but I heard them now. *"Don't worry that you have no one, Alex; I'm here for you. You'll always have me. I'll never leave you . . ."*

Where do all these tribes come from? I thought. Then I realized that I had regurgitated a line from LBH. Funny thing; in my mind I continued to keep separate the two beings—Aria and LBH—as if my heart still hadn't reconciled that they were one. I suppose it was emotionally safer that way.

I retrieved my bag from the bell stand and went up to my room. I checked on flights again. There was no direct flight to Daytona Beach, but there was a flight the next morning at 8:17 to Atlanta and, after a four-hour layover, another flight to Jacksonville—an hour and a half from Daytona. I didn't care what the cab ride cost. I just wanted to be home.

✦

When I was in second grade, a girl brought a robin's egg she'd found in her yard for show and tell. Our teacher had put a sign next to it saying DO NOT TOUCH. I was just seven years old, so, of course, I had to touch it. To my horror, it broke. I looked around to see if anyone had seen what I'd done, and then I quickly crept back to my desk where no one could connect me with the broken egg. Right now was no different. I just wanted to be far away from the mess I'd made in Utah.

CHAPTER *Thirty-seven*

I woke the next morning at six. I suppose it was telling that I had set two wake-up calls, my phone's alarm clock and the alarm clock in the room. I wasn't taking any chances on missing my flight. Nothing short of a terrorist attack was going to keep me in Utah.

After I'd boarded the plane I checked my phone. To be honest, there was a small part of me that hoped Aria had called. It was good she hadn't. I wasn't ready for it. Even after we screw up, it's amazing the lengths our psyches will go to protect our egos. *She lied*, it screamed at me. *You did the right thing. When you pick up one end of the stick, you pick up the other. In the end, it would finish with a lie, just like it did before. Just like it did when you tried to pretend lies don't matter. Just like it did with Jill.*

As I looked at my phone I noticed that someone had left a message. It had a Daytona Beach area code, but I didn't recognize the number. I pushed Play.

Alex, it's Jill. I'm probably the last person you expected to hear from, but I just wanted to wish you a Merry Christmas. I came by a little earlier, but it didn't look like you were home. Or maybe you were home and were hiding from me. I wouldn't blame you. But it is the season, right? If you'll let me know when you'll be there, I'll come by again. I have something for you. A little Christmas gift. [Pause] Okay, well, take care. 'Bye.

What did she want? I turned off my phone. I didn't want to talk to anyone. With my Diamond Medallion status I was almost always upgraded to first class or, at the least, coach comfort, but not this time. For the four hours of the flight to Atlanta, I didn't even have a decent coach seat. I sat in the middle seat between two overfed men and directly behind a crying baby. I was certain it was just the universe's way of punishing me for what I'd done.

When we finally reached Atlanta I camped out in the Crown Room. Still, the wait seemed interminable. I never turned on my phone. I still didn't want to talk to anyone. I didn't want anyone to know that I was back.

I was upgraded to first class on my flight to Jacksonville, which was no big deal, since the flight was less than an hour, and then I waited forty minutes for my bag and another thirty minutes for a cab.

The driver played Christmas music in the car for the entire ninety-minute ride. It already seemed strange to look out the window and not see snow.

With the two-hour time change, I arrived home past midnight. I paid the driver, then started into my apartment when he yelled, "Hey!"

I turned back.

"Merry Christmas."

"Yeah," I said. *Freaking Merry Christmas.*

I now understood why suicides go up during the holidays.

CHAPTER

Thirty-eight

I woke the next day about noon. Christmas Day. I lay in bed with the blinds down for more than an hour. The world outside my bed offered me nothing. It was weird being back—surreal, like I'd just woken from a dream. Actually, a nightmare.

I didn't care that it was Christmas. The more tragic commemoration was that it was almost the anniversary of my divorce. It had gone through on the twenty-seventh of December. I wondered if that had something to do with why Jill had called.

I felt like my chest had been run over by a semi. Not just my chest—my whole body. My back and neck ached. Even my feet ached. How can depression make your feet ache?

I was in so much pain that I went for a bottle of Jack Daniel's, but I put it back, not out of wisdom or temperance but out of self-hate. *How dare I run from what I brought on myself? I deserve to hurt*. Though outwardly I still blamed her, my inner self knew the truth. Ray had told me she was a flickering flame about to go out. What had Valerie called her? *A precious, fragile thing*. I had blown out a candle. I had broken a precious, fragile thing. I deserved to pay for what I had done. I didn't know how I could.

✦

I stayed in bed for the next two days. I kept my phone off, as if it would release me from liability that way. I didn't shower. My beard began to grow. I was a mess.

It was late Sunday night, two days after Christmas, when Nate knocked on my door. I didn't know it was Nate; I just knew someone was pounding on my door with the force of a battering ram. Actually, he was hitting my door with the business end of his cane. Then I heard him shout, "Open up, man. I know you're home."

I wondered how he knew that, as there was no outward sign of life. When I wasn't sleeping I had been watching all five seasons of *Breaking Bad*. I was ready to run off to New Mexico and open a meth lab. I opened the door.

"So you are alive," he said. He looked me over. "I think."

"I'm not in a mood to talk," I said.

"I can see that. That's why we're going to." He walked into my house and into my TV room, where he sat down on my couch. I followed him and settled into a recliner across from him.

"When did you get back?"

I sighed heavily. "Christmas Eve."

He looked at me incredulously. "And you didn't call? What's going on? Dale told me that you found her."

"I thought I had."

"So you didn't find her."

"No, I did."

"You're talking in circles, man."

"While I was looking, I fell in love with a woman. Aria . . ."

"That's her name? Aria?"

"Yeah."

"Pretty name," he said.

I didn't want to hear that. "It turned out that Aria was really LBH."

"You accidentally ran into the woman you were looking for?"

"Yes."

"That's incredible."

"It's not incredible. She knew I was looking for her and she played me."

Nate looked at me unsympathetically. "Played you? What does that mean?"

"She *lied* to me. She pretended to be someone she wasn't."

"Who did she pretend to be?"

"Not LBH."

"And, so, now you're upset with her?"

"Of course I am."

He thought for a moment, then said, "And you told her up front exactly what you were up to?"

"No. It would have freaked her out."

He looked at me as if I were dumb. "Have you considered that maybe that's how *she* felt?"

I didn't answer. He leaned forward. "Look, man. This was your crazy idea, not hers. You got to read her blog posts and get to know her intimately before you even met. Didn't she have the right to get to know you, in a safe place too?"

Again I didn't answer him.

"Honestly, man. What was she supposed to do?"

I blew up. "She was supposed to be honest."

Nate didn't even flinch. I suppose, compared to mortar fire and IEDs, my tirade wasn't much. "Under normal circumstances, you'd be right," he said calmly. "But these weren't normal circumstances, were they? You flew to Utah to track down someone you didn't know without telling them what you were doing. You said it yourself—that's crazy stuff. And crazy people do crazy stuff. She would have been a fool to tell you who she was." He leaned forward. "Be honest, here. Are you fighting her or are you fighting Jill? Because she's not Jill, and she deserves a fresh slate, just like you do. The past is a lesson, not a sentence. Let it go."

"I don't get why you're taking her side. You don't even know her."

He looked at me with an amused grin. "You think I'm taking her side?" When I didn't answer he said, "You're right, I don't know her. I couldn't pick her out of a police lineup. I'm not doing this for someone I don't know, I'm doing this for you."

"Why do you think you know what's right for me?"

"Because I remember what you said before you left. You told me that you knew deep in your heart you had to find her. You knew."

I looked down for a moment, then said, "I was wrong. The inspiration was wrong. It was just hopeful thinking. I wanted to believe something good was out there."

Nate just looked at me quietly, and then said, "Did I ever tell you about how I got so broken up?"

"You ran over an IED."

"Yeah," he said. "I did. Twice. You think that's unlucky?"

"I'd say so."

"You're wrong. I'm the luckiest man alive. The second time I hit the mine was my fifty-ninth mission. I had just landed up in Sulaymaniyah, near the Kurdish region.

"When we hit dirt I was ordered to report immediately to the CO for action. The CO there had a reputation for being a belligerent SOB. He always made it a point to rip some unlucky guy a new one before each mission, just to keep everyone else on their toes.

"As I ran to the CO's tent I had this overwhelming urge to stop in the worship tent. Every camp has a worship tent. It has icons and religious stuff. The thing is, I had never even been in a worship tent. I wasn't religious. I thought religion was nothing more than a crutch, and Marines don't need crutches. We put people in them. Or graves.

"Trust me, I had no delusion that there was some good-time afterlife party waiting for me. My sergeant in basic drilled it into us. He said, 'You're all going to hell. Get used to it. The only comfort is, you've already been there, so it's no big deal.' After some of the things I'd done, I was pretty damn certain I wasn't on God's friends and family plan.

"But here I am walking to the worship tent. I thought, *This is insane*, but the feeling was unlike anything I'd felt before.

"I went inside and I didn't even know what to do, so I did

what I thought I should do. I knelt down and started to pray. I didn't know how to, so I just started talking.

"Next thing I know, I check my watch. I'd been there for almost thirty minutes. *Thirty minutes*. The CO was going to rip off my head and shove it down my throat.

"I jumped up to go, but as I went to leave I saw this little metal cross lying on a table—it was a Celtic cross. I didn't know what it was called at the time, I just knew it was a cross with a circle in the middle. The same voice that sent me to the tent said to me, 'Take it.'

"I thought, *I can't take it. It belongs to the tent.* The voice said again, 'Take it.'

"I resisted. *This is crazy*, I told myself. *I'm talking to myself.* I went to leave the tent when that voice inside said, 'Don't leave without it.' You could say it was my subconscious, but I swear that whatever I was hearing had an authority my own thoughts never had. It felt like an order. So I grabbed the cross, shoved it into my pocket, and walked out.

"Just as I feared, when I hit the CO's tent he was waiting for me. He ripped me up one side and down the other in front of the whole squad. He said I'd held up the war for forty minutes and he was going to take it out of my flesh when I got back. Then he sent us off.

"Two hours later, we're coming to this little village when we hit an IED. Our Humvee was blown to pieces. When I came to, I was lying on my back bleeding from a hundred places. My back was broken. My hip was torn wide open.

My buddies were also blown up. One of them was next to me, shaking.

"The enemy was firing missiles and machine guns at us from a nearby building. I couldn't move. I knew it was over. As I lay there waiting to die, I suddenly felt the cross burning in my pocket. I reached down for it. It was covered with blood. I held it to my chest, waiting to be overrun by our enemy.

"Then out of the corner of my eye I saw a cloud of dust coming toward us. I wasn't sure what it was I saw, but I knew it couldn't be good. Suddenly it started firing. But not at us. It was an M1 Abrams, a US tank. It parked itself between us and harm's way, then proceeded to take out the whole of the enemy.

"I just lay there listening to the battle, tears rolling down my cheeks, not because I was in pain but because I knew this was impossible. We had no backup. There was no cavalry in the area. That tank came out of nowhere to save our lives.

"After the firing stopped, a man kneeled down next to me. He looked me over, then lifted the cross I was holding. He said, 'What do you know?' Tank commanders name their tanks and paint those names on their gun barrels. The name of the tank was the Celtic Cross. It had a picture of the exact same cross I was carrying painted on it.

"I found out later that the tank had been separated from its command and was speeding back toward HQ when the crew heard the explosion from us hitting the IED. If I hadn't stopped at the tent and we had left when we had been commanded to, it wouldn't have been there. We all would have been killed."

Nate leaned forward. His eyes were wet. "My point is, you heard *the voice*. It told you to go find that woman. So go get her."

I raked my hair back with my hand. "It's too late, man," I said. "I screwed up. Big-time."

To my surprise, Nate smiled. "No, you're not powerful enough to override fate. So go back and finish what you started."

"She's leaving the day after tomorrow."

"Leaving to where?"

"I don't know."

"Then you better hurry."

CHAPTER

Thirty-nine

With Christmas over, flights were wide open. I booked one for the next day and flew out of DAB at one thirty, then changed planes in Atlanta. The whole time I worried about Aria, but I didn't call her. I didn't dare. Chances were she'd shut me down before I even got there. But to fly all the way back to Utah, well, that had to mean something.

✦

I arrived in Salt Lake City a little after 6:00 p.m. It was snowing again. Of course it was. I got a rental car and drove directly to Aria's house.

The lights were off, and her car was gone. I looked inside her house. There was still furniture. That meant she hadn't left, right?

My next stop was the diner. I ran inside, only to be greeted by Valerie.

"Is Aria here?"

Valerie just looked at me contemptuously.

"Is she here?" I repeated.

"No."

"Do you know where she is?"

"Why would I know that?"

"Because you're friends."

"Which is why I wouldn't tell you if I did know." Her jaw tightened, and she thrust a finger at me. "I warned you about her. I warned you to leave her alone. And what did you do? You went for her throat."

"I don't have time for this. Just tell me, when's her next shift?"

She chuckled cynically. "Boy, you are some special kind of stupid. She has no more shifts. She quit. After all these years, she just quit. I don't know what you did to her, but you broke her."

My mind reeled. "Do you know if she's left town?"

"Where'd you get the idea she's leaving town?"

"She wrote that she was going back to live with her father."

Valerie's face contorted, and her eyes narrowed into angry slits. "Just when I thought I couldn't hate you more, you say something like that."

"Like what?"

She shook her head with disgust. "*Live* with her father, you say. If you really knew her, you'd know that her father took his life when she was a little girl."

I was dumbstruck.

"You stay away from her, and you stay out of here. You're not welcome. I promise, the next time I see you, there'll be hell to pay." She turned and walked away.

✦

Valerie's news had left me speechless. The words of Aria's blog came back to me. What LBH—what Aria—had written about going to her father suddenly made sense—horrible, tragic sense. It was all right there in front of me; I just didn't see it. She never wrote that she was going back to Minnesota, she said she was going *home*. Minnesota wasn't home.

And she had never written that she was going there to *live* with her father. She'd written that she was going to *be* with him.

When she said that she was leaving "this place" to "be with her father," she'd been talking about taking her life all along. The candle had finally gone out. What if she'd already left?

CHAPTER

Forty

I sped back to Aria's house as fast as I could, fishtailing as I turned the corner at her street. I jumped out of my car, ran up onto her porch, and pounded on her door. "Aria, open up! Aria!"

I stepped back and kicked the door, praying beneath my breath the whole time, *Please be okay. Please, God, let her be okay. Please.*

"Aria!"

I spotted a shovel at the far end of her porch and went over and grabbed it. I was about to put it through the window when I heard something behind me. I turned around. Aria was standing on the sidewalk looking at me.

"What are you doing with my shovel?"

I froze. "You're still here."

"What are you doing here?"

I ran down to her. "I came back for you. I was wrong. And I'm sorry. With all of my heart, I'm sorry. Please, forgive me. Please. I love you."

She looked at me for a moment, then walked up onto the porch, examined her door where I had kicked it, and unlocked and opened it. She stepped inside, then turned back.

"Are you coming?" She disappeared inside.

I hurried up the stairs after her. As I came around the door, she put her arms around me. Then she pushed her lips against mine.

"What?"

"Just kiss me."

When we finally parted I said, "How can you forgive me?"

There were tears in her eyes. There were tears in both of our eyes.

"I knew you would come back."

"How did you know?"

"Sit down." We sat next to each other on the couch. She wiped her cheeks, then looked up at me. "That day, when my father told me about the edelweiss, about finding a man who brings you edelweiss, he also said, 'But remember, Aria, people make mistakes. Even a man who will find the edelweiss for you may fall. He may climb wrong peaks where nothing grows. But if his love is strong, he'll find his way back to you. If he truly loves you, he'll pick the edelweiss.'" She looked intently into my eyes. "It was you. You climbed the mountain. You came all this way with nothing more than faith and courage. You climbed the wrong places; you even fell. But in the end you came back."

For a moment I was speechless. Then I said, "But I didn't bring you edelweiss."

She looked at me, and a large, beautiful smile crossed her lips. "I am the edelweiss."

EPILOGUE

Six months later Aria and I were married on the beach just a few miles from my apartment. We had a ceremony in Midway as well. At the Blue Boar Inn, of course. Neither Nate nor Dale made it to that one, so, fittingly, Ray was my best man.

Nate and Dale are still arguing over whether Nate lost the bet and owes Dale a thousand dollars. If it were the other way around, Dale would have paid up. Not because he's more ethical—he's just a lot smaller.

On our wedding night I gave Aria the pendant. I hadn't known why it was so important to the universe that I buy it until I showed it to her. She examined it and looked up with a big smile. "Do you know what this is?"

"The woman at Tiffany called it the Noble Star."

She smiled. "That's another name for edelweiss."

We live in Florida now, but we still keep a foot in Midway, Utah. We go back for Swiss Days. I even ran into Lynette once. It was awkward.

We bought a small winter home just a mile from the Blue

Boar. A *winter* home. Imagine that. Aria said the cold was good for me. How she talked me into that I'll never know. I am getting pretty good at skiing, though.

Dale's brother is a partner in a large Miami law firm. They tracked down Wade, Aria's ex, and had the bulk of the loan assigned to him. I paid off the rest.

I finally met Thelma, the pie goddess. She didn't look anything like I expected. With a name like Thelma I assumed she was an old, seasoned grandmother making pies before butter came in cubes. The truth was, she was a year younger than me. Of course, we didn't have wedding cake for our Midway ceremony, we had pie. Ray took home all the leftover pecan.

Believe it or not, Valerie and I are now friends. Of course we are. We have much in common. We both love the same woman. Enough to fight for her. We both also like the Eagles. The band, not the team. There's nothing profound about that, but it's something.

I've thought a lot about Aria's and my conversations at the time of my quest. I remember our first talk at the inn about the meaning of her name. I've found that there are other meanings. Aria is a form of the Greek name Arianna, which means 'very holy.' Fitting, I think. But my favorite definition is the Italian, where aria means 'air.' That is what she is to me. She is what I breathe. Maybe our names really do make us who we are.

The day of our wedding, Aria posted one last blog entry. She showed it to me.

Dear Universe,

Thank you for everything. I'm doing just fine.

—LBH (Loved By Him)

Like I said in the beginning, this was the story of my jump. Sure, there were a few rough spots on the way down, but I wouldn't change a thing. We fear jumping because we fear falling. We fear being broken. But still, jump we must, because it's only in jumping that we'll ever find someone to catch us.

✦ THE MISTLETOE INN ✦ RECIPE CONTEST WINNER

from Cathy Austin

HOMEMADE CHOCOLATE PEANUT BUTTER FUDGE

This was my grandmother's recipe. I use a four-quart Dutch oven.

4 cups white sugar
1 cup canned evaporated milk
1 cup water
4 tablespoons cocoa
2 tablespoons light corn syrup
A pinch of salt
2 tablespoons butter, plus extra for the pan
3 heaping tablespoons peanut butter

In the Dutch oven, stir together the sugar, milk, water, cocoa, corn syrup, and salt. Cook over medium heat (do not turn heat up), stirring occasionally until it comes to a boil. Once it comes to a boil, continue cooking but DO

NOT stir again. Even though you will think you need to, it's important that once it boils you do not stir. Continue cooking until it reaches soft ball stage on a candy thermometer (235°F) or until a small amount dropped in cold water forms a soft ball. Remove from heat and add the butter and peanut butter. Using a wooden spoon, stir vigorously until the fudge loses its gloss and holds its shape when dropped. Pour it into a buttered 9x13-inch pan and let it cool. Once it's cool and has firmed up, cut it into squares and taste the goodness of homemade fudge.

90

ALSO BY RICHARD PAUL EVANS

The Four Doors:
A Guide to Joy, Freedom, and a Meaningful Life
A Winter Dream
Lost December
Promise Me
The Christmas List
Grace
The Gift
Finding Noel
The Sunflower
A Perfect Day
The Last Promise
The Christmas Box Miracle
The Carousel
The Looking Glass
The Locket
The Letter
Timepiece
The Christmas Box

The Walk Series

The Walk
Miles to Go
The Road to Grace
A Step of Faith
Walking on Water

For Children and Young Adults

The Dance

The Christmas Candle

The Spyglass

The Tower

The Light of Christmas

Michael Vey: The Prisoner of Cell 25

Michael Vey 2: Rise of the Elgen

Michael Vey 3: Battle of the Ampere

Michael Vey 4: Hunt for Jade Dragon

RICHARD PAUL EVANS

The Mistletoe Promise

SIMON & SCHUSTER

NEW YORK LONDON TORONTO SYDNEY NEW DELHI

Simon & Schuster
1230 Avenue of the Americas
New York, NY 10020

This book is a work of fiction. Any references to historical events, real people, or real places are used fictitiously. Other names, characters, places, and events are products of the author's imagination, and any resemblance to actual events or places or persons, living or dead, is entirely coincidental.

First Simon & Schuster hardcover edition November 2014

SIMON & SCHUSTER and colophon are registered trademarks of Simon & Schuster, Inc.

For information about special discounts for bulk purchases, please contact Simon & Schuster Special Sales at 1-866-506-1949 or business@simonandschuster.com.

The Simon & Schuster Speakers Bureau can bring authors to your live event. For more information or to book an event, contact the Simon & Schuster Speakers Bureau at 1-866-248-3049 or visit our website at www.simonspeakers.com.

Jacket design by Jackie Seow
Jacket photograph by Angela Butler/Moment Select/Getty Images

Manufactured in the United States of America

5 7 9 10 8 6 4

Library of Congress Cataloging-in-Publication Data
Evans, Richard Paul.
The mistletoe promise / Richard Paul Evans. —
First Simon & Schuster hardcover edition.
pages ; cm
1. Christmas stories. I. Title.
PS3555.V259M57 2014
813'.54—dc23 2014034377

ISBN 978-1-4767-2820-9
ISBN 978-1-4767-2823-0 (ebook)

To Gypsy da Silva

Elise is a derivation of Elishaeva,
a Hebrew name meaning God's promise.

The Mistletoe Promise

PROLOGUE

If you could erase just one day from your life, would you know the day? For some, a specific date comes to mind, one that lives in personal infamy. It may be the day you lost someone you love. Or it might be the time you did something you regret, a mistake you wish you could fix. It may be a combination of both.

I am one of those people who would know the day. There is one day that has brought me unspeakable pain, and the effects of that day continue to cover and erode my world like rust. I suspect that someday the rust will eat through the joists and posts of my life and I will topple, literally as well as figuratively.

I have punished myself for my mistake more times than I can remember. Each day I wake up in the court of conscience to be judged guilty and unworthy. In this sorry realm I am the judge, prosecutor, and jury, and, without defense, I accept the verdict and the sentence, a lifetime of regret and guilt to be administered by myself.

I'm not the only one who has punished me for what I've done. Not by a long shot. The world has weighed in on my failure as well. Some people I know, more I don't. And there are those who have learned to use my mistake against me—to punish or control me. My ex-husband was an expert on wielding my mistake against me, and for too long I offered up no defense.

Then one day a man came along who was willing to plead my case. Not so ironically, he was an attorney. And, for the first time since that black day, I felt joy without the need to squash it. I met him around the holidays just a little more than a year ago. And that too is a day I'll never forget.

CHAPTER *One*

I'm not ready for another Christmas. I haven't been since 2007.

Elise Dutton's Diary

NOVEMBER 1, 2012

I hated the change; the commercial changing of the seasons was more obvious than nature's. It was November first, the day after Halloween, when orange and black gives way to red and green. I didn't always hate the change; I once looked forward to it. But that seemed like a lifetime ago.

I watched as the maintenance staff of the office building where I worked transformed the food court. A large, synthetic Christmas tree was dragged out to the middle of the room, strung with white lights, and draped in blue and silver tinsel. Giant corrugated-styrene snowflakes were brought out of storage and hung from the ceiling, just as they had been every year for as long as I'd worked in downtown Salt Lake City.

I was watching the transformation when I noticed him staring at me. *Him*—the stranger who would change everything. I didn't know his name, but I had seen him before. I'd probably seen him a hundred times before, as we ate pretty much every day in the same food court: I near the Cafe Rio with my sweet pork salad and he, fifty yards away, over by the Japanese food emporium eating something with chopsticks. *Why was he looking at me?*

He was handsome. Not in your Photoshopped Abercrombie & Fitch catalog way—women weren't necessarily stopping midsentence when he walked into a room—but he certainly did catch their attention. He was about six feet tall, trim, narrow-hipped, athletically built. He was always dressed impeccably—in an expensive, custom-tailored suit, with a crisp white shirt and a silk tie.

I guessed he was a lawyer and, from his accoutrements, one who made good money. I, on the other hand, worked as a hotel and venue coordinator at a midlevel travel wholesaler booking educational trips for high school students. The company I worked for was called the International Consortium of Education, but we all just called it by its acronym, ICE, which was appropriate as I felt pretty frozen in my job. I guess that was true of most of my life.

The lawyer and I had had eye contact before. It was two or three weeks back when I had stepped on an elevator that he was already on. The button for the seventh floor was lit, which was further evidence that he was a lawyer, since the top two floors of the tower were occupied by law firms.

He had smiled at me, and I'd given him an obligatory return smile. I remember his gaze had lingered on me a little longer than I'd expected, long enough to make me feel self-conscious. He'd looked at me as if he knew me, or wanted to say something, then he'd turned away. I thought he had stolen a glance at my bare ring finger, though later I decided that it had just been my imagination. I had gotten off the elevator on the third floor with another woman, who sighed, "He was gorgeous." I had nodded in agreement.

After that, the lawyer and I had run into each other dozens of times, each time offering the same obligatory smiles. But today he was staring at me. Then he got up and started across the room toward me, a violation of our unspoken relational agreement.

At first I thought he was walking toward me, then I thought he wasn't, which made me feel stupid, like when someone waves at you in a crowd and you're not sure who they are, but you wave back before realizing that they were waving at someone behind you. But then there he was, this gorgeous man, standing five feet in front of me, staring at me with my mouth full of salad.

"Hi," he said.

"Hi," I returned, swallowing insufficiently chewed lettuce.

"Do you mind if I join you?"

I hesitated. "No, it's okay."

As he sat down he reached across the table. "My name is Nicholas. Nicholas Derr. You can call me Nick."

"Hi, Nicholas," I said, subtly refusing his offer of titular intimacy. "I'm Elise."

"Elise," he echoed. "That's a pretty name."

"Thank you."

"Want to see something funny?"

Before I could answer, he unfolded a piece of paper from

his coat pocket, then set it on the table in front of me. "A colleague of mine just showed these to me."

I know a guy who's addicted to brake fluid. He says he can stop anytime.

I didn't like my beard at first. Then it grew on me.

He pointed to the last one. "This is my favorite."

I stayed up all night to see where the sun went. Then it dawned on me.

"Is that what you do at work?" I asked.

"Pretty much. That and computer solitaire," he said, folding the paper back into his pocket. "How about you?"

"Candy Crush."

"I mean, where do you work?"

"On the third floor of the tower. It's a travel company."

"What's it called?"

"I.C.E."

"Ice?"

"It stands for International Consortium of Education."

"What kind of travel do you do?"

"We arrange educational tours for high school students to historic sites, like Colonial Williamsburg or Philadelphia or New York. Teachers sign up their classes."

"I wouldn't think there was a lot of travel on a teacher's salary."

"That's the point," I said. "If they get enough of their students signed up, they come along free as chaperones."

"Ah, it's a racket."

"Basically. Let me guess, you're a lawyer."

"How could you tell?"

"You look like one. What's your firm?"

"Derr, Nelson and McKay."

"That's a mouthful," I said. "Speaking of which, do you mind if I finish eating before my salad gets cold?"

He cocked his head. "Isn't salad supposed to be cold?"

"Not the meat. It's sweet pork."

"No, please eat." He leaned back a little while I ate, surveying the room. "Looks like the holiday assault force has landed. I wish they would take a break this year. The holidays depress me."

"Why is that?"

"Because it's lonely just watching others celebrate."

It was exactly how I felt. "I know what you mean."

"I thought you might."

"Why do you say that?"

"I just noticed that you usually eat alone."

I immediately went on the defensive. "It's only because my workmates and I take different lunchtimes to watch the phones."

He frowned. "I didn't mean to offend you. I'm just saying that I've noticed we've both spent a lot of time down here alone."

"I didn't notice," I lied.

He looked into my eyes. "So you're probably wondering what I want."

"It's crossed my mind."

"It's taken me a few days to get up the courage to come over here and talk to you, which is saying something, since I'm not afraid of much." He hesitated for a moment, as if gathering his thoughts. "The first time I saw you I thought, *Why is such a beautiful woman sitting there alone?* Then I saw you the next day, and the next day . . ."

"Your point?" I said.

"My point is, I'm tired of being alone during the holidays. I'm tired of walking through holiday crowds of humanity feeling like a social leper." He looked into my eyes. "Are you?"

"Am I what?"

"Tired of being alone during the holidays."

I shook my head. "No, I'm good."

He looked surprised. "Really?"

"Really."

He looked surprised *and* a little deflated. "Oh," he said, looking down as if thinking. Then he looked back up at me and forced a smile. "Good, then. That's good for you. I'm glad you're happy." He stood. "Well, Elise, it was a pleasure to finally meet you. I'm sorry to bother you. Enjoy your salad and have a nice holiday." He turned to leave.

"Wait a second," I said. "Where are you going?"

"Back to work."

"Why did you come over here?"

"It's not important."

"It was important enough for you to cross the food court."

"It *was* important. Now it's moot."

"Moot?" I said. "Sit down. Tell me what's moot."

He looked at me for a moment, then sat back down. "I just thought that maybe you felt the same way about the holidays as I do, but since you're *good,* you clearly don't. So what I was going to say is now moot."

I looked at him a moment, then said, "I might have exaggerated my contentment. So what were you going to say that is now moot?"

"I had a proposition to make."

"Right here in the food court?"

"We could go to my office if you prefer."

"No, here in public is good."

"I'll cut to the chase. Socially, this is a busy time of year for me. And, like I said, I'm tired of being alone during the holidays, going to all my company and client dinners and parties alone, enduring everyone's sympathy and answering everyone's questions about why a successful, nice-looking attorney is still single. And, for the sake of argument, we'll say that you're also tired of doing the holidays solo."

"Go on," I said.

"As one who would rather light a candle than curse the darkness, I say that we do something about it. What I'm proposing is a mutually beneficial holiday arrangement. For the next eight weeks we are, for all intents and purposes, a couple."

I looked at him blankly. "Are you kidding me?"

"Think about it," he said. "It's the perfect solution. We don't know each other, so there's no deep stuff, no pain, no bickering. The only commitment is to be good to each other and to be good company."

"And being good company means ending up back at your place?"

"No, I'm proposing a purely platonic relationship. Maybe we publicly hold hands now and then to sell the facade, but that's the extent of our physicality."

I shook my head skeptically. "Men can't have platonic relationships."

"In real life, you're probably right. But this isn't real life. It's fiction. And it's just until Christmas."

"How do I know you're not a serial killer?"

He laughed. "You don't. You could ask my ex, but no one's found the body."

"What?"

"Just kidding. I've never been married."

"You're serious about this?"

He nodded. "Completely."

"I think you're crazy."

"Maybe. Or maybe I'm a genius and everyone will be doing this in the future."

I slowly shook my head, not sure of what to think of the proposal or the proposer.

"Look, I know it's unconventional, but oftentimes the best solutions are. Will you at least consider it?"

I looked at him for a moment, then said, "All right. I'll think about it. No guarantees. Probably not."

"Fair enough," he said, standing. "I'm leaving town to-night, but I'll be back Monday."

"That will give me some time to think about it," I said.

"I eagerly await your response."

"Don't be too eager," I said.

"It's been a pleasure, Elise." He smiled as he turned and walked away.

CHAPTER

Often what we see clearest in others
is what we most avoid seeing in ourselves.

Elise Dutton's Diary

The encounter left me a little dazed. I didn't tell anyone about it. Actually, I didn't really have anyone to tell. The person at work I spent the most time with was my colleague Zoey, and I definitely wouldn't be telling her. You don't know Zoey, but you do. Every company, every school in the world has a Zoey—the kind of girl who attracts male attention like a porch light attracts moths. She was naturally beautiful, skinny without starving or Zumba, born with a body that designers design for. She even looked good without makeup, which I knew for a fact since she usually spent the first hour at work applying it.

Even worse than being beautiful was that she knew it. A few months after I started at ICE, before I really even knew her, she offered to give me some makeup, which sounded like her saying that I could be pretty if I tried. I think what hurt the most about her offer was that, whether she meant to convey that message or not, it was true. I didn't take care of myself. After Dan, my ex-husband, divorced me, I just sort of let things slide. Not completely, but enough to change. I put on a little weight, and stopped spending time at the mirror or buying clothes. I guess I was treating myself the way I felt—undesirable.

At the opposite extreme, Zoey was in her prime with a perpetually full roster of men, with someone always up to bat and someone always on deck, ready to fill in when she tired of the current player. She was the one our company's airline and hotel reps, mostly balding, middle-aged men, would plan their office visits around. I worked a trade show with her once, and the whole time men circled our booth like vultures over carrion. Zoey ate it up. Why wouldn't she?

What I had said to the lawyer about eating alone at lunch was true, mostly. One of us was supposed to watch the phones, but that's what voice mail is for, right? The real reason I hated to eat lunch with Zoey was because all I ended up doing was politely listening to her myriad stories of affairs and conquests while I sat there feeling frumpy and old. It's easy to hate the game when you're losing.

CHAPTER *Three*

I can't believe that I'm actually considering this man's proposal. Am I crazy, desperate or just really lonely? Probably all of the above.

Elise Dutton's Diary

That weekend, all I could think about was the proposition. *Who was this guy and what did he want? What was his motive?* I suppose, on a deeper level, the bigger question (considering how lonely I was) was *Why was I even questioning his motive?* Why couldn't he be exactly what he claimed to be? Was that really so hard to accept?

My father used to say, "If it ain't broke, don't fix it—but if it's already broke, it don't matter what you do." My life was definitely broken. So why not? Really, what did I have to lose? I even asked myself, *What would Zoey do?* I knew what she'd do. She'd say, "You only live once, girl," and she'd buckle up for the ride. I suppose that my mind was probably somewhere in Zoeyland when I decided to say yes.

The next Monday, Nicholas arrived in the food court about a half hour after I'd started eating.

"Hi, Elise," he said. "How's your salad?"

"Good."

"How was your weekend?"

"The usual," I said, even though it was definitely anything but.

He sat down across from me. "Did you come to a decision?"

"Right to the point," I said. I set down my plastic fork. "So, hypothetically, let's say that I said yes. What would this arrangement look like?"

He smiled. "First, we write up a contract."

"Why, you don't trust me?"

"Contracts are not always so much a matter of trust as they are a matter of understanding. This way we'll be more likely to meet each other's expectations."

I should have had one of those before my marriage, I thought.

He leaned in closer. "Let me tell you what I had in mind. I'll pay for all meals, transportation, and admissions. We'll have lunch together when possible and, in addition to the social functions, I'll take you to dinner or some holiday-themed event at least once a week, and I'll send you something, a gift, each weekday up until the end of the contract. Then, at midnight on Christmas Eve, the agreement terminates and we go back to our lonely, pathetic lives."

"If I agree, how do we start?"

"We'll begin by going through each other's calendars and determining what events we can attend. It's two-sided, of course. If you'd like, I'll attend your events as well."

I thought a moment more, then, with his eyes locked onto mine, said, "All right."

"All right, let's do it?" he asked.

I nodded. "Yes. Let's do it."

"Are you sure?"

"Why not? Lunch every day?"

"When possible. At least every workday. We're two days in on that now. It hasn't been too painful, has it?"

"It's definitely been interesting. I don't know about you sending me things."

"Why?"

I shrugged. "I don't know."

"You'll get used to it."

"Do I have to send you things too?"

"No. I expect nothing but the pleasure of your company."

I took a deep breath. "Okay. Get me a contract."

"Great," he said, standing. "I'll see you tomorrow."

"You're not having lunch?"

"No. I have a deposition in an hour that I still need to prepare for. I just came down to see you."

Something about the way he said that pleased me. "All right, I'll see you tomorrow."

"Thank you, Elise. I don't think you'll regret it."

A minute later, a food court worker said to me, "You have a cute husband."

"He's not my husband," I said. "He's . . ." I paused. "He's my boyfriend."

"Lucky you," she said.

CHAPTER

I'm not sure what I've gotten myself into with this contract, but I'm still looking for the fine print.

Elise Dutton's Diary

The next day Nicholas walked into the food court carrying a leather Coach briefcase. I was sitting at my usual table, waiting for him. He smiled when he saw me. "Shall we eat at Cafe Rio?" he asked.

"Sure," I said.

We walked together up to the restaurant's counter. "I've never eaten here before," he said. "What's good?"

"The sweet pork salad is pretty much my mainstay," I said.

"Two sweet pork salads," Nicholas said to the woman who was rolling out tortillas.

"Pinto beans or black beans?" she asked.

Nicholas deferred to me. "I didn't realize there would be a quiz. I'll let you take over."

"Pinto beans," I said. "With the house dressing. Cheese, no pico."

"I'll have the same," he said.

"Drink?"

"The sugar-free lemonade," I said.

"One sugar-free lemonade and a Coke," Nicholas said.

He paid for our meals, then, while I got our drinks, he carried our tray over to a table.

"This is pretty good," he said. "I can see why you have it every day."

"It may be the most delicious salad ever made," I replied.

After we had eaten for a few minutes, he reached into his briefcase and brought out some documents. "Here you go," he said, holding out the papers. "The contract."

"This looks so *official*."

"It's what I do," he said.

I looked it over.

MISTLETOE CONTRACT

"Why mistletoe?"

"You know how, at Christmastime, people show affection under mistletoe to people they're not necessarily affectionate with?"

"That's clever," I said. "Can we change the word *contract*? It sounds too . . . formal."

"What would you prefer?"

I thought a moment. "How about *promise*?"

"Done," he said, striking a line through the word *contract* and penning in the rest. "The Mistletoe Promise."

I looked over the agreement.

MISTLETOE ~~CONTRACT~~ PROMISE

This service agreement is made effective as of November 6th by and between

Elise Dutton (Lessor) and Nicholas Derr (Lessee).

"How did you know my last name?"

"I'm a lawyer," he said, which didn't really answer my question.

1. DESCRIPTION OF SERVICES. Lessor will exert due effort to provide to Lessee the following services (collectively, the "Services"):

a. Lunch together each weekday as individual schedules permit.

b. At least one evening activity per week through duration of contract.

c. Best effort to demonstrate a caring relationship.

I couldn't help but think how every relationship would benefit from such an agreement.

2. PAYMENT. In consideration of Lessor's services, Lessee agrees to pay for all dinners, joint activities, admission fees, travel expenses, etc., for the duration of Contract.

"Travel expenses?" I asked.

"Gas money," he said. "Mostly."

If Lessee fails to pay for the Services when due, Lessor has the option to treat such failure to pay as a material breach of this Contract, and may cancel this Contract but not seek legal redress.

3. TERM. This agreement will terminate automatically on December 24, 2012, at 11:59:59 P.M.

4. LANGUAGE. Lessor and Lessee shall, for the duration of this agreement, refer to each other as *boyfriend* or *girlfriend* or by any term of endearment including, but not limited to, *sweetie, sweetheart, love, dear, babe, beautiful, cupcake,* and any term found acceptable by both parties.

I looked at him incredulously. "Really? *Cupcake?*"

"I wasn't planning on using *cupcake*."

"Then why did you put it in the contract?"

"In case you were. It's just an example," he said. "Granted a poor one. But I don't know your preferences."

"I would rather not be called after any food or animal. Actually, avoid any noun."

"Consider all nouns, especially *cupcake,* stricken from my vocabulary. Does that include *honey?*"

I thought about it. "I guess *honey* is okay. It's gone mainstream."

"*Honey,* okay," he said to himself.

I went back to the contract.

5. PLATONIC NATURE OF ARRANGEMENT. This agreement does not constitute, imply, or encourage, directly or indirectly, a physical relationship, other

than what would be considered expected and appropriate public physical contact.

"What does that mean? *Expected* physical contact."

"Nothing exciting," he said. "Hand-holding in public, that sort of thing." When I didn't respond he added, "Things real couples do. For instance, we might hold hands at a company party, at least when walking into the party, but we wouldn't be holding hands when we are alone, since that obviously wouldn't be necessary to convince others."

"I get it," I said.

6. CONFIDENTIALITY. Lessor and her agents will not at any time or in any manner, either directly or indirectly, divulge, disclose, or communicate in any manner, any information that is proprietary to this agreement and agrees to protect such information and treat it as strictly confidential. This provision will continue to be effective until the termination of this Contract.

7. BREACH OF CONTRACT. If any of the above stipulations are not met, Contract will be considered null and void. No recourse is available.

ADDENDUMS

1. No deep, probing personal questions.
2. No drama.

"Talk to me about these addendums."

"The first is self-explanatory. We do not ask each other any deep, probing personal questions. It's irrelevant to our objective and will only cause problems. Do you really want me asking deep personal questions about your life and past?"

I tried to hide the effect the question had on me. "Nope, I'm good."

"Exactly. This relationship should be so shallow there's no possibility of drowning."

"Agreed," I said. "And the second?"

"No drama. Life's too short."

"Agreed."

"Then all that's left is your signature."

I looked at the signatory line. He had already signed the contract. "Why do I feel like I'm signing away my soul?"

"It's not an eternity. Just forty-nine days."

I breathed out. "All right. Do you have a pen?"

"I'm a lawyer. That's like asking me if I have a lung."

"As opposed to a heart," I said.

"Another fan of lawyers," he said. He extracted a pen from his coat pocket. It was a nice one—a Montblanc. I knew this only because my ex judged a man by the pen he carried. I took the pen from Nicholas and signed the document.

"There are two copies," he said. "One for your own files. Please sign both."

"Now you're really sounding like a lawyer."

"I am one."

"So you keep reminding me." I folded the contract in half and put it in my purse.

When I'd finished eating my salad I said, "I better get back to work."

"I'll walk you to the elevator," he said. As we waited for the elevator he said, "Don't forget to bring your calendar tomorrow so we can work out our schedule."

"I'll be ready."

As the elevator door opened he leaned forward and kissed my cheek. "Have a good day, dear."

"Thanks for lunch," I said. "*Cupcake.*"

He smiled. "This is going to be fun."

CHAPTER

Bad memories can attach themselves like barnacles to the hulls of our lives. And, like barnacles, they have a disproportionately large amount of drag.

Elise Dutton's Diary

Zoey screamed. Cathy, our company bookkeeper, and I rushed out of our offices to see a florist deliveryman standing in the middle of the office holding a massive bouquet of yellow roses. It was one of the largest bouquets I'd ever seen, the kind people were more likely to send to the dead than the living. Of course the man was drooling over Zoey.

"They're gorgeous," Cathy said. "Who are they from?"

"I don't know," Zoey said. "Probably Paul. Or Quentin. Could even be Brody. So many men, so many possibilities."

I rolled my eyes at her theatrics.

"Where would you like them?" the man asked.

"Oh, just set them there," Zoey said, motioning to her desk. "It practically takes up my whole desk."

"And if I could have you sign right here." He handed Zoey an electronic clipboard. Her expression abruptly changed. "They're not for me." She looked up at me. "They're for you."

"Elise?" Cathy said, not masking her surprise.

Just then Mark, our boss, walked into the room.

"Those are pretty . . . massive," he said, looking at Zoey. "Who now?"

"They're not for me," Zoey said. "They're for Elise."

He looked at me. "Someone's got a fever for you."

I walked over to my flowers. There was a small, unsealed envelope attached to the vase. I extracted the card.

Dear Elise,
Happy Day 1. I hope the
flowers brighten your day.
-Nick

"Who are they from?" Cathy asked.

I looked back up at them. "What?"

"Who gave them to you?"

"Just . . . a guy."

"What guy?" Zoey asked.

"My *boyfriend*." The word came out awkwardly.

They both looked at me with expressions of bewilderment.

"You have a boyfriend?" Zoey asked.

"It's new," I said. I lifted the heavy vase and carried it to my office. *Thank you, thank you, thank you,* I thought. I couldn't wait to thank Nicholas.

Flowers are complicated. The last time I had received flowers from a man was a nightmare. I was in the hospital and I'd just come out of intensive care after almost dying from a burst appendix, but the pain I remember most wasn't caused by the operation. It was caused by my husband. But I'll share more of that later.

I debated over whether or not I should take the flowers home, but finally decided to leave them at the office. I told myself that they were so big I doubted I could get them into my apartment without damaging them. But really I think I left them in the office in defiance of my co-workers' incredulity. Driving home, all I could think about was that it had been the best day I'd had in a long time.

The next morning at work I was making copies of a travel itinerary for a group of high school students from Boise, Idaho, when I heard Zoey greet someone.

"I have a delivery for Elise Dutton," a man said.

I walked out of my office. "That would be me."

"Here you go," the man said, handing me a box.

"What is it?" Zoey asked.

"I don't know," I said. "It's wrapped." I opened the box and smiled. "Oh. Chocolate cordials." I wondered how he knew that I loved them. There was a card.

Happy Day 2, Elise. So far so good?
-Nick

"What are cordials?" Zoey asked.

"Chocolate-covered cherries," I said.

"Why don't they just call them chocolate-covered cherries?"

"Because they're cordials," I replied. I took one out and popped it into my mouth. It was delicious. "Want one?"

"Sure." She looked a little injured as she walked over to me. "Tell me more about this guy."

Even though it was the first time she'd ever asked me about my personal life, I didn't want to share. "He's really just more of a friend," I said.

"Guys don't send chocolates and massive flower bouquets just to be friends. There's always an agenda. What's the lowdown?"

"His name is Nicholas."

"What does he do?"

"He's a lawyer on the seventh floor."

"Nicholas what?"

"Derr."

She puzzled a moment then said, "As in Derr, Nelson and McKay? You're dating one of the partners?"

"We're just . . ." The truth was, I didn't know whether or not he was a partner, but Zoey's incredulity made me angry. "Yes. Of course."

"Oh," she said. "Well done."

"Don't look so surprised," I said.

"It's just that you've never showed much interest in dating."

"Maybe I just hadn't met the right man," I replied.

"Nicholas is the right man?"

"Maybe." This was already more fun than I'd thought it would be. "I've decided to at least give him until Christmas."

"You're giving *him* until Christmas?"

"I think that's enough time to see if I like him."

She looked almost stunned. "Okay," she said. She started to turn away, then said, "Oh, could you trade me lunchtimes today? I met this guy last night and he's coming to meet me."

"I'm sorry," I said. "I'm meeting Nicholas."

You have no idea how good it felt saying no. It was the first time I'd ever turned her down. It was the first time I'd had a reason to.

A little after noon I went to the food court. Nicholas wasn't there yet, so I ordered my usual salad and sat down at my usual table. Nicholas showed up about ten minutes later.

"I'm sorry I'm late," he said, looking stressed. "Long-winded client, antitrust stuff. Too dull to discuss."

"It's okay," I said.

He sat down across from me. "How's your day?"

"Good," I said. "Thank you for the flowers. They're beautiful."

"Like you."

I smiled a little. "And the chocolates."

"Do you like chocolate?"

"All women like chocolate. It's like female catnip."

He grinned. "I hoped as much."

"You don't need to spend so much, you know."

"I know," he said simply.

"Are you going to get something to eat?"

"No, I'm sorry. I know we were going to go through our schedules today, but my morning fell apart and I have to get back to that meeting. I just didn't want to leave you hanging down here alone."

"It's okay, I'm used to it."

"You shouldn't be," he said. "Is tomorrow okay?"

"Same time, same place."

"Thanks. I'll see you tomorrow. Bye, Elise."

"Bye."

He got up and walked away.

Maybe it was a small thing, but the fact that in spite of his busy schedule Nicholas had come down to meet me meant even more than the flowers and chocolates.

Back when I was still married, my husband, Dan, invited me to lunch, then forgot about it. I waited alone for almost an hour before calling him.

"Sorry, I forgot," he said. "I got distracted."

"Am I that forgettable?" I asked.

"Don't talk to me about *forgetting*," he said.

That shut me up. I hung up the phone, then broke down crying.

✦

I finished my lunch and went back to work.

CHAPTER

The lawyer and I made our plans for the next seven weeks. It looks like fun. Which is probably what the last Hindenburg passenger thought as he boarded the blimp.

Elise Dutton's Diary

The next morning I was booking rooms at a New York hotel when Zoey walked in carrying a silver box from Nordstrom and set it on my desk.

"It's from the lawyer," she whispered. Then she just stood there, waiting for me to finish the call. As soon as I hung up she said, "Open it." She looked even more eager to see what was inside the box than I was. I opened the card first.

Day 3. It's been a cold winter,
Elise. I thought this might help.
-Nick

"So what did Lover Boy send today?" Zoey asked, sounding incredibly jealous. I'd be lying if I said that I didn't enjoy it.

"Let's find out," I said. I untied the ribbon, then lifted the lid. Inside was a piece of light tan cloth. I lifted it out.

"It's a scarf," I said. "It's soft."

Zoey touched it. "It's cashmere." She instinctively went for the label. "Pashmina from Bottega Veneta." She looked up at me. "You realize that's like six hundred dollars."

I tried not to look impressed. "Really?"

"This guy's made of money. What does he drive?"

"I don't know."

"How do you not know?"

"I haven't been out with him yet."

"Amazing," she said, shaking her head as she walked out of my office.

I wore the scarf to lunch. Nicholas was waiting for me near Cafe Rio. He stood, smiling, as I approached. "I see you got it," he said, looking at the scarf.

"What did I say about spending so much?"

"You told me I didn't have to, which I already knew."

"I feel uncomfortable."

"Why?"

"I don't know."

"Then don't worry about it. I don't expect reciprocity, so you don't need to worry about anything. Just enjoy it." He looked into my eyes. "Or at least let me enjoy it, okay?"

"Okay. Thank you. It's beautiful."

"It's cashmere," he said.

"I know. Zoey told me. She's insanely jealous."

"Is a jealous Zoey a good or bad thing?"

"That depends on who you ask."

"I'm asking you."

"Definitely a good thing."

He smiled. "What are we eating today? Cafe Rio again?"

"Of course."

"I should have just ordered for you. Before this is over I'm going to expand your culinary horizons. Save our place and I'll be right back. Sweet pork salad, pinto beans, house dressing."

"And a diet lemonade."

"Of course."

Not wanting to get food on my scarf, I folded it up and stowed it in my purse. Nicholas returned a few minutes later carrying a tray. "One salad with lots of sugar, and a lemonade sans sugar."

"Thank you."

He sat down.

"What did you get?" I asked, examining his meal.

"I thought I'd try the chiles rellenos with some of this rice." He took a bite, then asked, "Who is this Zoey person?"

"She's just someone I work with." A peculiar feeling swept through me. I didn't want him to know who Zoey was. I didn't want him to meet her. I didn't want her to take him. "She's, like, beautiful."

"Like you," he said.

"No, she's *really* beautiful."

His expression immediately changed. He almost looked angry. "As opposed to what?"

"As opposed to me."

He leaned back for a moment, then said, "How long have you been this way?"

"What way?"

"Self-deprecating."

Suddenly, to my surprise, tears began to well up in my eyes. I didn't answer. I was too embarrassed.

He didn't back off. "What makes you think you're not beautiful?"

"I'm not blind," I said. "I can look in a mirror."

"You have a flawed mirror," he replied. His voice softened. "Elise, anyone can open a book. Not everyone can appreciate the beauty of the writing. I want you to stop berating yourself."

"It's just . . ." I wiped my eyes with a napkin. "Around my office I'm not the one who gets the flowers."

"Funny," he said. "I could have sworn you told me that you just got some."

What was this man doing to me? "Can we just eat?"

"I want to add something to our contract. For the length of our agreement you will believe that you are beautiful."

"You can't just change a belief."

"People do it all the time," he said. "Besides, it's contractual. You don't have a choice. You'd be amazed at what people accomplish under contract."

"I don't know if I can do that."

"Then at least believe that I believe you're beautiful."

I sat there fighting back tears. "Can we please change the subject?"

"Will you agree to do this one thing for me?"

Finally I nodded.

"All right. Now we can eat."

We ate for a few minutes until he said, "I'm going to run out of time, so we'd better start planning our season." He reached into his briefcase and brought out some papers.

"I had my secretary print out copies of my calendar for the next two months. We can use it to plan."

He handed me two pages, and I quickly looked through the calendar. Not surprisingly, he had a lot more going on than I did. I didn't need a secretary to schedule my life. I didn't even need a notebook.

"You have two work parties," I noted.

"Yes, I'm sorry if that's excessive. There's an office party for the entire firm, then there's the partners' party."

"Gee, I wonder which one is nicer," I said.

"Actually, they're both nice," he said. "The company party is at La Caille."

"Really?" La Caille was an expensive French restaurant in the foothills of the Wasatch Mountains. "That's nice."

"You've been there?"

"It's been a few years. Actually, I was there for a wedding. It's a bit above my pay grade. Where's the partners' party, the Grand America?"

"The partners' party is at one of our founders' homes."

I went back to the beginning of the calendar. The first event Nicholas had marked was the evening of November ninth. Tomorrow night.

"What's this Hale Centre event?" I asked.

"That's the Hale Centre Theatre's production of *A Christmas Carol*. I've heard it's great, I've just never wanted to go alone." He looked at me. "I know it's sudden. If you have other plans . . ."

"No, it's okay," I said. "I'm not busy."

He looked pleased.

I moved down the calendar. "What about the following weekend? You marked an event on the sixteenth."

"There's nothing scheduled, but is there something you would like to do? We could go to the symphony, ballet, Walmart . . ."

"Let me think about it," I said. I moved my finger to the next week on the calendar. "The next week is Thanksgiving."

"Thanksgiving is early this year. Do you have plans?"

"I usually spend it with Dan's family."

"Who's Dan?"

"My ex."

He looked at me quizzically. "Really?"

"I know, it's weird. But I'm still close to his parents. The way they see it, their son divorced me but they didn't. I think they like me more than they like him."

"How does your ex feel about it?"

"He's strangely good with it. In a twisted way I think it makes him feel like he has a harem."

"That's creepy."

"That would describe him."

"You don't have a better alternative? Family?"

"There's no one close. My parents have both passed away. I have a sister in Minneapolis. She invites me to her house every year, but it's too expensive to fly there for a day."

"You don't get frequent-flier miles with the travel agency?" he asked. Then he answered his own question. "I guess you couldn't use them on Thanksgiving anyway. It's a blackout period."

"I don't get them. I don't travel with the groups. We have

people who do that. I just do the logistics, like booking hotels and admissions at some of the venues."

He nodded as he took this all in. "So, back to Thanksgiving at your ex's family. I assume Dan and company wouldn't like me joining them. Disrupt the harem and all that."

"No, that might be awkward."

"Then would you be willing to join me?"

"With your family?"

"No, in that department we're in the same boat. I celebrate Thanksgiving with the family of one of the attorneys I work with."

"What's their name?"

"The Hitesmans," he said. "Scott Hitesman. Real nice family."

I wrote the name down on the calendar.

"Scott joined the firm about the same time I did. We were working over a Thanksgiving weekend on a big case, and he invited me to join them. I've been with them ever since."

"Will they be okay if I come?"

Nicholas laughed. "No, they'll be *ecstatic*. Sharon is always trying to get me to invite someone."

"Then it's a date. Will I need to bring anything?"

"I usually just pick up some pies from Marie Callender's."

"I can make pie," I said. "I like baking. I make a pumpkin pie that's to die for. And a pecan pie that's a least worth getting sick for."

He grimaced.

"That didn't come out right," I said.

"I love pecan pie. You've got a deal."

"How many people will there be?"

"About seven, including us."

"How many pies?"

"I usually bring four. An apple, cherry, pumpkin, and mincemeat."

"Does anyone still eat mincemeat?"

"Grandma Hitesman does. She's ninety-six. When she dies, the industry will crumble."

I laughed. "Maybe you could pick that one up."

"I could do that."

We both looked back down at the calendar.

"The next week is our firm's Christmas party," Nicholas said. "Saturday, December first."

"The one at La Caille?" I asked.

He nodded.

"That's the week of my work party too," I said. "It's that Wednesday."

"Can you do both?"

"Absolutely. But I should warn you, it's not going to be La Caille. It's not even going to be Burger King, for that matter."

"I don't care," he said.

"You have no idea how nice it will be to go with someone this year. Ever since I divorced, I've been the odd one out."

"I think I have an idea," he said. "That's why we're doing this."

The next week there were two days marked on the calendar. December sixth and seventh. "What are these?"

His expression fell. "It's nothing," he said in a way that made me sure that it was. "It's just . . . something I do." He quickly moved on. "The next week, on the fourteenth, is the partners' party. Then the week after that I have to fly to New York City to meet with one of our clients, so we won't get together that week." He looked up at me. "Unless you come to New York with me."

I couldn't tell if he was serious. "I'm afraid that would be out of my budget."

"Travel expenses are in the contract."

I looked at him. "You're serious." To tell the truth, the idea of going to New York at Christmas thrilled me. "Let's see how things go."

"That's wise," he replied.

"Then there's nothing until Christmas Eve?"

"What are your plans for Christmas Eve?" he asked.

I was embarrassed to tell him that I hadn't anything planned. "Nothing. Yet."

"How about we have dinner?"

"That would be nice. Where?"

"I don't know, we can decide that later. We have seven weeks."

"And then we're done," I said.

He slowly nodded. "Exactly. The agreement is fulfilled, the contract is terminated." He slid his calendar into his briefcase, then stood. "I better get back. I'll see you tomorrow at lunch, then tomorrow evening for the play."

"Thank you for lunch," I said. I held up the calendar. "And for all this."

"It's my pleasure. I'm looking forward to it."

"Me too."

He looked into my eyes and said, "Elise."

"Yes?"

"No more complaints about gifts. It's been a long time since I've had anyone to give to, and I'm having a lot of fun. Don't ruin it for me. Okay?"

I nodded and smiled. "If you insist."

His serious expression gave way to a smile. "I insist. Have a good day."

As he started to go I said, "Nicholas."

He turned back. "Yes?"

"What kind of car do you drive?"

He looked puzzled. "Why?"

"Zoey wanted to know."

He grinned mischievously. "Tell her it's a very expensive one." He blew me a kiss and walked off. As he disappeared from sight, I took out my scarf and put it around my neck. It had been a long time since I had felt that warm.

CHAPTER

Seven

Why is it that we so easily confide secrets to strangers
that we so carefully hide from ourselves?

Elise Dutton's Diary

I once read that the secret to happiness is having something to do, something to look forward to, and someone to love. It must be true even if the love is contractual. The next morning was the first time in a long time that I woke happy. I followed my usual routine of shower, hair, health shake, then, looking at myself in the mirror, I took extra time for my makeup. I used to be good at makeup, but that was before I stopped caring. You don't take care of things you don't value.

I was a few minutes late to work, but, considering all the late evenings and unpaid overtime I'd pulled over the years, I wasn't worried.

"You're late," Zoey said as I walked into the office. She was applying mascara.

"I know," I said simply.

Around ten o'clock we were having staff meeting when the bell on our door rang. "I'll get it," Zoey said, standing. She was always the first to offer. She hated meetings.

Five minutes later, when Zoey hadn't returned, Mark said, "Elise, would you please remind Zoey that we're in the middle of a staff meeting?"

"Sure," I said. I walked out into the front lobby. Zoey was just standing there in a room filled with flowers. "The man's smitten," she said, shaking her head in disbelief. "It took two deliverymen to bring them all in."

There were twelve dozen roses, half white, half red. If Nicholas was making a point about sending me whatever he wanted, he'd succeeded. A minute later Cathy walked out. "Holy florist. We're going to have to start charging this guy rent." She looked at me. "What are you going to do with all those?"

"I have no idea," I said.

"The delivery people said they'd be back to take them to your apartment," Zoey said. "Here's the card that came with them."

I unsealed the envelope.

Day 4. Next time you complain that
I'm spending too much I'm doubling it.
Looking forward to tonight.
-Nicholas

I smiled.

"What did he say?" Zoey asked.

"He's looking forward to our date tonight."

"Where are you going?"

"We're going to watch a play. *A Christmas Carol.*"

"That sounds . . . fun." I knew that a play wouldn't be her idea of a good time. She looked at me for a moment, then said, "You know what the problem with all this is?"

I looked at her. "No. What?"

"No one can keep this up forever. Someday it's going to stop. And then it's going to suck."

"It's most certainly going to stop," I said. "The trick is to enjoy the ride while it lasts."

Zoey looked at me with surprise. "When did you get this attitude?" Then she looked closer at me. "Are you wearing eyeliner?"

When I arrived in the food court, Nicholas was already there, sitting at our usual table. He must have been early; he had already bought our food. He smiled when he saw me. "I took the liberty of ordering the usual."

"Thank you," I said, sitting down. I took a bite of my salad. He wore a funny expression, and I guessed that he was waiting for me to comment on the flowers. I decided to play dumb.

Finally he said, "So did you get anything today?"

I looked at him blankly. "Anything? Like what?"

"A special delivery?"

"Hmm, I said. "A special delivery. Oh, you mean like a hundred and forty-four roses?"

He grinned. "That wasn't too *excessive,* was it?"

"No. Just right. And once the delivery people return to get them, my apartment will look like a funeral parlor."

He laughed. "We're still on for tonight?"

"Yes."

"The play starts at seven, so I'll pick you up around six-thirty?"

"Okay," I said.

"Then, if you're not too tired, we'll get some dinner after."

"Sounds nice."

"Anything in particular?"

"No. Surprise me." Just going out to dinner was surprise enough.

It was snowing when I got home from work. As usual, my apartment was a mess, so I picked up the place or, at least, organized the chaos—throwing my clothes in a hamper and loading the dishwasher. I was about to freshen up for the play when the doorbell rang. *He better not be early,* I thought. He wasn't. It was the florist. "I've got your flowers," the man said.

I looked around my tiny apartment. "Bring them in."

"Where do you want them?"

"Wherever they'll fit," I replied.

My apartment was on the second floor of the building, and it took the man fifteen minutes to bring all the roses in from his truck. By the time he finished, it was twenty-five after. I quickly changed into some more comfortable jeans and a sweater, brushed back my hair, then went to put on some perfume but couldn't find any. *Girl, you've got to get back with it.*

I remembered that I had an unopened bottle of perfume

in the bottom of my closet—a gift from the girls at the office for my birthday last spring. I tore open the package and was spraying it on when the doorbell rang. I looked at myself one more time in the mirror, then hurried out past the garden of flowers, grabbing my coat on the way.

I opened the door. Nicholas was standing there holding a bouquet of yellow gerbera daisies. I almost laughed when I saw them. "You're kidding, right?"

"I wasn't sure what else to bring you," he said.

"Let me find something to put these in. Come on in."

He laughed when he saw the flowers splayed out over my front room. "You almost need a machete to get through here."

"Almost," I said.

I couldn't find a vase (other than the ones in my front room), so I filled a pitcher with water and arranged the flowers in it. When I came back out Nicholas was examining a picture on my wall of me with my sister.

"Is this your sister?" he asked.

"Yes."

"What's her name?"

"Cosette."

"As in *Les Misérables*?"

"Yes. My father liked the book. Shall we go?"

"Sure," he said. Then added, "You look nice."

"Thank you. So do you." He was dressed casually in a dark green knit sweater that was a little wet on the shoulders from falling snow. "I don't think I've ever seen you out of a suit."

"It's rare, but I do dress down on occasion."

I took his hand as we walked down the stairs. His car was parked out front, a white BMW sedan. He held the door open for me as I got in. The interior was immaculate and smelled like cinnamon. The seats and doors were two-toned leather, embossed like a football. He shut the door, then went around and climbed in.

"You have a nice car."

"Thank you. I just got it a few months ago. The dealer said it's good in snow. I hope he's right. I turned your seat warmer on. If it's too hot you can adjust it."

"Thanks."

He started the car. The heater and the windshield wipers came on simultaneously, along with a Michael Bublé Christmas album. "Is this music okay?"

"I love Bublé," I said.

"Then Bublé you will have."

"It smells good in here," I said.

"*You* smell good. What is it? Lovely?"

"How in the world did you know that?"

"My paralegal wears it." He pulled a U-turn, then drove out of my complex. "Thanks again for going to this with me. I've wanted to do this for a while."

"It's my pleasure," I said. "I told Cathy where we were going, and she said she loves it. Her family goes every year."

"Who's Cathy?"

"Sorry, she's our bookkeeper."

"Are all of your friends from work?"

I frowned, embarrassed by the question. "Yes."

He glanced over. "It happens. All my friends are lawyers. Except you."

Something about how he had said that made me glad. "Tell me about this play," I said.

"Hale Centre Theatre. They've been doing this for a long time. I'm kind of a sap when it comes to Christmas. I watch *A Christmas Carol* on TV at least twice every holiday season. My favorite television version is the one with George C. Scott."

"Me too," I said. "I mean, that's my favorite version too."

The Hale Centre Theatre was located on the west side of the valley, about fifteen minutes from my apartment. The place was crowded. We picked up our tickets at Will Call, then Nicholas asked, "Would you like a drink or a snack?"

I glanced over at the concession stand. "Maybe some popcorn."

"Okay. Wait, it's not popcorn, it's kettle corn."

"What's the difference?"

"You'll like it," he said. "It has sugar."

"How do you know I like sugar?"

"You eat it on your salad," he said.

We got a small box of kettle corn and climbed the stairs to the theater's entrance. The theater was in the round, and, not surprisingly, we had good seats, though in a theater that small I'm not sure there were any bad ones.

After we had sat down I ate some kettle corn and said, "Picking up our tickets at Will Call reminded me of something dumb I did."

"Tell me."

"When I first started at ICE, Mark, he's the owner, sent me over to Modern Display to pick up some plastic display holders for a convention we were doing. He said to get them from Will Call. When I got there I went up to the sales counter and asked for Mr. Call. There were two men there, and they both looked at me with funny expressions. One asked the other, 'Do you know a Call here?' He said, 'No.' Then he said to me, 'I'm sorry, there's no Mr. Call here. Do you know his first name?' I said, 'I think it's William or Will. My boss just said to pick it up from Will Call.' They laughed for about five minutes before someone told me why."

Nicholas laughed. "I did that exact same thing once."

"Really?"

"No, I'm not that dumb."

I threw a piece of kettle corn at him.

"So here's some trivia for you," he said. "Did you know that the original name that Dickens gave his book was much longer? Its real title is *A Christmas Carol in Prose: Being a Ghost Story of Christmas*. A carol is a song or a hymn, so the abbreviated title doesn't really make sense."

"I've never thought of that," I said.

"It's a much more influential book than most people realize. In a way, Dickens invented Christmas."

"I'm pretty sure Christmas existed before Dickens was born."

"True, but before *A Christmas Carol*, Easter was the biggest Christian celebration. December twenty-fifth was no more consequential than Memorial Day. In fact, the colony of Massachusetts had a law on the books prohibiting the celebration of the holiday. Christmas was considered a pagan celebration, and observing Christmas might cost you a night in the stocks."

"Why is that?"

"Mostly the timing, I suspect. The reason we celebrate Christmas on the twenty-fifth has nothing to do with Christ's birth. In fact, we have no idea when Christ was born. The twenty-fifth was designated as Jesus's birthday by Pope Julius I, in order to attract new Roman members to the church because they were already celebrating the day in honor of the pagan god of agriculture. Which is why Christmas not so coincidentally takes place near the winter solstice."

"I had no idea," I said.

"Also interesting is that historically, Dickens and Friedrich Engels were contemporaries. They were both in Manchester, England, at the same time and they were equally repulsed by the workers' living conditions."

"Who is Friedrich Engels?"

"He was Karl Marx's inspiration for the *Communist Manifesto.* The early nineteenth century was a dark time for the workingman. The majority of the children born to working-class parents died before the age of five. So while Engels wrote about a political revolution, Dickens was writing about a different kind of revolution—a revolution of the heart. He was writing about the things he wrote about in his other books, the welfare of children and the need for social charity."

"How do you know all this?"

"I'm a lawyer," he said, which again made no sense to me.

"What does that have to do with—"

"Shh," he said, laying his finger across his lips. "The play is starting."

As the lights came up at the end of the first half, just before Scrooge meets the Ghost of Christmas Yet to Come, I excused myself to go to the ladies' room. When I returned Nicholas was standing near our seats, talking to a beautiful young woman. She looked to be in her late twenties, with big brown eyes and coffee brown hair that fell past her shoulders.

"Elise, this is Ashley," Nicholas said. "We used to work together."

She smiled at me. "I was Nick's legal secretary. It's nice to meet you."

"It's nice to meet you," I echoed. I took Nicholas's hand, which she noticed.

"Where's Hazel tonight?" Nicholas asked.

"With Grandma," she said. "Kory and I needed a night out. Looks like you did too." She turned to me. "Nick's the best boss I've ever had, but an insatiable workaholic. I'm glad to see someone got him out of the office for a change."

"This is the first time I've seen him without a tie," I said.

"I can believe that. I'm pretty sure that he sleeps with one on." She turned back to Nicholas. "It's good to see you. You take care." She leaned forward, and they hugged. Then she walked around to a section directly across the theater from ours.

"How long did she work for you?" I asked.

"Three, almost four years. A year ago she quit to have a baby."

"She likes you."

"We worked well together," he said simply.

We sat back in our seats as the lights dimmed and the second half began. Near the end of the performance I heard a sniffle. I furtively glanced over at Nicholas as he wiped his eyes with a crumpled Kleenex.

After the show the cast came out to the lobby to shake hands with the audience. We thanked them for the performance before walking out into the cold night air.

"That was really good," I said.

"I'm glad I finally got to see it."

"It affected you."

He nodded. "It's about redemption and hope." He looked me in the eyes. "Hope that we can be better than our mistakes."

His words struck me to the core. It was as if he knew me intimately. It took me a moment to respond. "Thank you for taking me."

"You're welcome," he said. When we got back to his car he asked, "Are you hungry?"

"Famished."

"Do you like Thai food?"

"I've never had it. But I'd like to try it."

"Good. I know a place."

The restaurant was less than ten minutes from the theater. A young Thai woman seated us in a vacant corner of the restaurant and handed us menus. I looked mine over. "I have no idea what to order."

"How about I order a few dishes and we'll share?"

I set down my menu. "Perfect."

When our waitress came, Nicholas ordered a bunch of things I couldn't even pronounce, then said, "You'll love it." Then added, "Maybe."

A few minutes later the waitress set two bowls of white soup on the table in front of us. "What's this?" I asked.

"Coconut milk soup."

Our waitress returned with a large bowl of noodles, two platters of curry dishes, and a large bowl of sticky rice.

I dished up my plate with a little of everything. I liked it all, which wasn't too surprising, since everything was sweet.

In the middle of our dinner Nicholas asked, "Have you lived in Salt Lake your whole life?"

"No. I was born in Arizona. I lived there until I was fourteen."

"Where in Arizona?"

"Chino Valley. Near Prescott. Do you know Arizona?"

"A little," he replied. "I've spent some time there. What brought you to Utah?"

"My father."

"Work?"

"No. It's more complicated than that."

"How so?"

I hesitated. "My father was an interesting man."

"By *interesting* do you mean, a 'fascinating individual' or a 'living hell'?"

I laughed. "More of the latter," I said. Nicholas continued looking at me in anticipation. "Are you sure you really want to hear this?"

"I love to hear people's histories," he said. "*Especially* the interesting ones."

"All right," I said. "My father was fanatical. Actually, that's putting it mildly. He thought the world was going to hell, and since the 'lunatic' Californians were buying up all the land around us, he sold our farm and moved us to a little town in Utah of ninety-six people. We made it an even hundred."

"What town?"

"You've never heard of it."

"Try me."

"Montezuma Creek."

"You're right," he said. "Why there?"

"Because it was about as far from civilization as you could get. And, don't laugh, because there was only one road into town and he could blow it up when the Russians invaded."

"Really?"

"It's true," I said. "He had a whole shed of dynamite and black powder." I shook my head. "The biggest thing that ever happened in Montezuma Creek was when the Harlem Globetrotters came through town. I don't know what brought them to such a small town. I guess they weren't that big anymore, but the whole town showed up. I think the whole county showed up."

"What did your father do in Montezuma Creek? To provide?"

"We had greenhouses. Big ones. We mostly grew tomatoes. We sold them to Safeway."

"How did you end up in Salt Lake?"

"I just got out as fast as I could."

"Didn't like the small-town life?"

"I didn't like my father," I said softly. "He talked constantly about the end of days and the world being evil and corrupt, but the truth is, *he* was evil and corrupt. And violent and cruel. I lived in constant fear of him. I remember I was at our town's little grocery store when a man I'd never met said to me, 'I feel sorry for you.' When I asked why, he said, 'That you have that father. He is one awful man.'

"My father was always trying to prove that he was in control. Once I told him I was excited because we were going to have a dance lesson at school, so he made me stay home that day for no reason. Some days he would keep us home from school just to prove that the government couldn't tell him what to do.

"He would rant that the police were just the henchmen of an Orwellian government conspiracy, and anytime one tried to pull him over, he'd try to outrun them. It was a perverse game with him. Sometimes he'd get away, sometimes they'd catch him, and they'd drag him out of the car and handcuff him, which only proved his point that the police were brutal. He lost his license, but that was irrelevant to him. He didn't see that the government had any right to tell a person whether they could drive or not.

"I remember watching him being handcuffed and arrested, and I was afraid they were going to take me to jail too. I grew up terrified of police. Police and snakes."

"Snakes?" Nicholas said.

I nodded. "My father used to think it was funny to chase me around the house with live rattlesnakes. I remember him holding one on a stick and it trying to strike at me." I looked down. "I have a terrible phobia of snakes. I can't even see a picture of one without being paralyzed with fear."

"That's abuse," Nicholas said.

I nodded. "He was all about abuse. Only he didn't see it that way. He saw us as property, and, if something is yours, you can do what you want to it. Property doesn't have needs. Property only exists to suit to *your* needs.

"One time we had a problem with our truck. He said it was the carburetor, so he made my sister lie on the engine under the hood and pour gasoline into the carburetor while we drove. What kind of father puts his kid under the hood of a moving vehicle?"

"A deranged one," Nicholas said. "What were his parents like?"

"That's the strange part. My grandparents were sweet people. They used to apologize to me about him. Once my grandmother said, 'We don't know what happened to him, dear.'

"He considered reading for entertainment a waste of time. Once he found me in my room reading a Mary Higgins Clark book and he was furious. He called me lazy and said that if I had time to waste, he'd find something for me to do. He made me go out and move the entire woodpile from one side of the house to the other. It took me four hours. And I was terrified the whole time, because snakes hid in the woodpile. Twice I found rattlesnakes when bringing in firewood."

Nicholas looked sad. "I'm so sorry."

"Thanks," I said. "More than anything, I just wanted to be loved. In a small town like that, there aren't a lot of romantic options. Once I told my father that a boy walked me home from school, and my father beat me and sent me to my room for the night. He called me a tramp. I believed him. I felt so guilty about it."

"You couldn't see that you'd done nothing wrong?"

I shook my head. "The thing is, when you grow up with crazy, you don't know what sane is. You might suspect that there's something better, but until you see reality, it's impossible to comprehend.

"A year after I was married I caught my father with another woman. They were kissing. He lied about it at first, but when he saw that I didn't believe him, he admitted that he was having an affair and told me not to tell my mother."

"Did you?"

"No. But not because he said not to. My mother was kind of a doormat. It would have done nothing but humiliate her. She found out later on her own. It's the only time I ever saw her yell at him. But she still didn't leave him. He had alienated all of her family, so she really had no place to go.

"By the time I turned eighteen I couldn't take it anymore. I left high school and got a job more than three hundred miles away, at Bryce Canyon Lodge as a waitress. It was a good gig. They paid almost nothing, a dollar six an hour, but there was free food and lodging, and we got to keep all our tips. We just had to work two meals a day. The people at the lodge were really nice, and I made a lot of money in tips. Enough to pay for my first year of college.

"Every now and then celebrities would come through. I met Robert Redford once. He was really nice. He told me that I smelled like lilacs. I met people from all over. That's when I knew that I wanted to travel and see the world. But I think it was probably more that I wanted to get as far away from Montezuma Creek as I could. I wanted to get as far away from my father as I could." I forced a smile. "I didn't get too far, I guess. I carried a lot of it with me."

"It's hard to leave some things behind," Nicholas said. "So how did you turn out so lovely?"

I just looked at him. Suddenly my eyes welled up with tears. He reached over and took my hand. When I could speak I said, "Thank you."

"Is your father still alive?"

"No. He died of cancer. Both of my parents did. They both grew up near the Nevada Proving Ground, where the government tested nuclear weapons. For dates they used to go out and watch them detonate atom bombs. Crazy, huh? They didn't know better."

Nicholas just shook his head. "He was a downwinder."

"You're familiar with that?"

"Intimately. Our firm handled a massive lawsuit against the federal government involving downwinders."

"Well, I'm sure my father was part of it." I sighed. "I remember going back and seeing him before he died. He was so frail and weak. I thought, *Is this really the man who filled me with such terror, who towered over my past?* He was nothing. His meanness drained out. He was like a snake without venom. He was nothing but a hollow shell."

Nicholas looked at me, then said, "They that see thee shall narrowly look upon thee, and consider thee, saying, Is this the man that made the earth to tremble, that did shake kingdoms? Isaiah 14:16."

"You read the Bible," I said.

"At times," he replied. "So you went to college in Salt Lake?"

"No. I went to Snow College. My best friend from Montezuma Creek asked if I wanted to be her roommate, so I took her up on it."

"Snow College," he said. "Isn't that in Manti?"

"It's the town next to it," I said. "Ephraim. The one with all the turkey farms. Sometimes turkey dander would settle over the school. I was horribly allergic to it."

"To turkey dander?" he asked.

I nodded. "That's where I met my ex-husband, Dan." I paused. "Dan. Dan-der. I never made that connection before."

Nicholas laughed. "Dander. I like that."

"Dan was from Salt Lake. He was doing his general ed at Snow because it was cheaper than the University of Utah. He was ambitious back then. He promised to show me the world. Then he left college to sell water purifiers. Dan wasn't very nice, but that's what I was used to. The truth was, he was my way out. A counselor once told me that Dan was my 'vehicle of emancipation.' I think she was right. I followed Dan to Salt Lake, and we got married. We were married for eight years before he divorced me."

"Why did he divorce you?"

I looked at Nicholas and said, "Wasn't there a clause in our contract about deep and probing questions?"

"You're right. I crossed the line."

"Well, technically, we crossed the line about ten minutes ago," I said. "It's okay. Dan divorced me because he was cheating on me with my best friend."

"Your college roommate?"

"Yes. He's now married to her."

"Remarkable," Nicholas said. "What was your divorce settlement like?"

"Not good. It's not like Dan had much money, but I didn't get anything."

"Sounds like you had a poor attorney."

"No, he had a poor client."

"Why?"

I looked down. "Some people are born thinking they're pretty important. Some aren't."

Nicholas nodded slowly as if he understood.

I took a deep breath. "So now that I've spilled all my secrets, let's talk about you."

"That's a nonstarter," he said.

"Really? After I just shared my entire life history, you're holding out on me?"

"I'm only saving you from boredom."

"I think there are some answers that might interest me."

"Such as?"

"To begin with, why aren't you married?"

He looked at me for a moment, then said, "Isn't that why I asked for this contract? So I didn't have to answer that question?"

"I still want to know."

He looked at me thoughtfully and after a moment said, "A lot of people aren't married. A lot of people are married who shouldn't be."

"You're evading the question."

"It's complicated," he said.

"Is that all I get?"

"For now," he said.

"Then tell me about your childhood."

He frowned. "It's nowhere near as exciting as yours. I was born and raised in the Sugar House area. My parents were quiet, conservative Mormons. I went to church until I was sixteen, until . . ." He stopped and a shadow fell over his face. "Until things changed."

"What happened?"

"Just things," he said. "My dark ages. It took me a few years, but I pulled myself out. From then on it was all school and work. I finished college and took the LSAT. I got accepted to Stanford Law School on a scholarship, graduated at the top of my class, then came back to Utah to practice law."

"You started working at the firm you're at now?"

He hesitated before answering. "No, I worked at the prosecutor's office. I kept beating them in court, so they made me an offer."

"That must be nice," I said.

"What must be nice?"

"To be wanted like that."

He suddenly went quiet. Then he said, "I'm sorry. That whole conversation got pretty heavy. I just wanted to get to know you better."

"Well, you know it all now."

"Do I?"

I didn't answer. After a moment of silence he picked up the check. "Let's get you home."

It was cold in the restaurant's parking lot, and our breath froze in front of us. The cars were all covered with a thin veneer of freshly fallen snow. He started his car, turned on the heater and window defroster, then got out and scraped the windows. When he got back in, his hands were wet and red with the cold. He rubbed them together.

"Let me see them," I said.

He looked at me curiously, then held them out. I cupped them in my hands and breathed on them.

He smiled. "Thank you."

We didn't say much on the way home. I suppose I felt talked out. But the silence wasn't uncomfortable. When we pulled up in front of my apartment he said, "Thanks again for going with me."

"It was fun," I replied. "I'm sorry I talked so much."

"I enjoyed learning about you."

"Well, I kind of threw up on you. I guess it's been a while since I've had anyone ask me about myself."

"I'm glad it was me," he said.

I smiled at him, then said, "Me too. Have a good weekend."

"You too. I'll see you Monday."

I got out of the car and walked up the snow-covered sidewalk to my apartment stairs, leaving footprints as I went. Nicholas waited until I reached the door. I turned back and waved. He waved back then drove away.

Not surprisingly, my apartment smelled like roses. I went into my bedroom and undressed, turned out the light, then lay back on my bed.

"Who are you, Nicholas?" I said into the darkness. "And what are you doing with me?"

CHAPTER

Eight

People talk of life's storms as if they are universal experiences. But they're not. Some people hear thunder while others touch lightning.

Elise Dutton's Diary

THREE YEARS EARLIER

I couldn't sleep because of the pain. At first I thought it was an upset stomach. Then, as the pain increased, an ulcer. An ulcer made sense. I was a worrier. I'd worried my whole life.

While my husband, Dan, slept, I downed a bottle of Pepto-Bismol, which did nothing to relieve my agony. Finally, at four in the morning, I woke Dan, and he reluctantly drove me to St. Mark's Hospital emergency room. It wasn't an ulcer, it was appendicitis. And my appendix had burst. I was rushed into surgery and spent the next two days in intensive care being fed massive doses of antibiotics to attack the infection that had set in. On the third day I had shown enough progress that they moved me out of the ICU.

Dan came to see me that afternoon bearing a bouquet of spring flowers. It was only the second time I had seen him since I was admitted, and, in spite of his absence, I was glad to see him. We had talked for only about a half hour when he said he had to get back to work. Dan was working as a telemarketer and managed a phone solicitation office. After he left I was just lying there looking at the flowers when one of my nurses walked in. Keti was a Tongan woman as wide as she was tall.

"Oh, aren't you lucky," she said. "Somebody loves you."

I smiled. "Aren't they beautiful? They're from my husband."

"You hang on to him, honey. I can't tell you the last time my husband brought me flowers." She looked up at me. "Oh wait, I don't have a husband." She walked to my side. "How are you feeling?"

"It hurts where they made the incision."

"That's usual. An appendectomy is like a cesarean, except you don't get a baby for it."

"I feel a little warm."

"Warm? Like a fever?"

"Yes."

She sidled up to my bed. "I was just about to check your temperature." She rubbed an electronic thermometer across my forehead and frowned. "You have a temperature. A hundred and two point four. I don't like that."

"What does that mean?"

"Maybe a little infection." She checked my chart. "You're already on a pretty high dosage of antibiotics, but let me see if the doctor wants to up your dose a little."

"Thank you."

As she scribbled on her clipboard, I heard the vibration of a cell phone. We both looked around to see where it was coming from, then Keti discovered an iPhone lying next to the flowers. "Is this yours?"

"No. It's probably my husband's. He must have left it." I reached out my hand for it. "I'll text his office and let them know I have it."

"How sweet," Keti said looking at the screen. "Amore. Is that what he calls you?"

"Amore?" I looked at her blankly. "No . . ."

She handed me the phone. "It's right here."

Amore Mia

Text Message

Amore? My love? Who's calling my husband Amore? No, that's not how it works. Who is my husband calling Amore Mia? I pressed the notification.

Amore Mia

Are you on your way?

October 11, 2009 1:04 PM

I started reading backward through the thread of messages.

Amore Mia

Your so good

October 11, 2009 12:55 PM

Dan the Man

Not now. After she is back home. Feeling better

October 11, 2009 12:54 PM

Amore Mia

:(When are you going to tell her?

October 11, 2009 12:52 PM

Dan the Man

She's doing okay. Made it through the hard time

October 11, 2009 12:51 PM

Amore Mia

After. Pretty please? You'll be glad! ;-) How is Elise?

October 11, 2009 12:49 PM

Dan the Man

:) On way to hospital see Elise. I love you

October 11, 2009 12:45 PM

Amore Mia

Just had the sweetest dream of you.

I miss you. Can you come over?

October 11, 2009 12:42 PM

Amore Mia

Ditto. Ditto. Ditto. Please. Please. Please!!!!!!!!!!!!!!!!!!!!!!!!

October 11, 2009 10:07 AM

Dan the Man

Floating. Last night was unbelievable.

We need a rerun ASAP!!!!!!!!!!!!!

October 11, 2009 9:42 AM

Amore Mia

How is my dreamboy today?

October 11, 2009 9:39 AM

There were more. Many more. I couldn't read them because my eyes were filled with tears.

"Honey?" Keti said.

I looked up at her. "My husband is cheating on me."

"I'm sorry."

Just then Dan walked back into the room. "Hi, babe, I forgot my phone."

I looked at him, shaking, unable to speak.

"Why are you crying?" He looked at Keti. "Is she in pain?"

"I would think so," Keti said, her eyes narrow with anger.

"Can you get her something for it?"

"Not for this pain."

He looked at her quizzically, then back over at me. "Honey . . ."

"Who is she?" I said.

"I'll check on your antibiotic," Keti said, making her way toward the door. It sounded ridiculous, like telling someone in a hurricane that you would be back to wash their windows. She brushed by Dan on the way out.

"Who?" he asked, his eyes stupidly wide.

"Who is Amore Mia?"

He stepped toward me. "I don't know what you're talking about."

I held up his phone. "Who is Amore Mia?"

"Elise . . ."

"If you have something to tell me, tell me now."

"It's nothing. She's nothing."

"I read the texts. Don't lie to me."

For a moment we looked at each other, then he breathed out slowly, as if he'd resigned himself. "Okay, so you caught me. I'm having an affair."

"Who is she?"

He looked even more uncomfortable.

"Do I know her?"

"Kayla," he said.

The only Kayla I knew was my best, and only, friend and the thought that she would cheat with my husband was so far beyond possibility that I couldn't process it. "Kayla who?"

"Kayla," he said again but with more emphasis.

"My Kayla?"

"Yeah."

My pain doubled. When I could speak I asked, "How long has this been going on?"

"I don't know."

"How long?"

"A while."

I broke down crying again. He stepped forward and put his hand on my arm. "Elise."

I pulled away. "Don't touch me."

"Elise," he said in the condescending register he used when he thought I was being overly dramatic.

"Go away," I said. "Go to your . . . *amore*."

"I'm not leaving," he said.

"Get out of here!" I shouted.

Just then Keti walked back into the room. She must have heard our conversation because she looked angry. "You need to leave," she said, pointing a sausage finger at Dan.

"She's my wife," Dan said. "I don't need to go anywhere."

Her voice rose. "She's *my* patient and this is *my* house, and if she wants you to leave, you leave." She walked to a button on the wall. "Or should I call security?"

He glared at her, then looked back at me. "It's your fault, Elise. You're the one who ruined our lives. You have no one to blame but yourself." He turned and walked away. Two days later I was still in the hospital when Dan filed for divorce.

CHAPTER *Nine*

Today I overheard Zoey and Cathy talking about Nicholas.
It's not what they said about him that hurts.
It's what they were implying about me.

Elise Dutton's Diary

Mondays were always the hardest days at ICE. Invariably there would be some crisis that had occurred over the weekend: lost luggage, a canceled flight, a broken-down bus, or any of the thousand things that can go wrong when traveling with groups. That doesn't even include the things our students did. Like the time three of the boys were arrested in New York for dumping soda on people on the sidewalk below the hotel.

This Monday was no different. It began with our usual staff meeting and Mark ranting about a phone call he'd received over the weekend from a parent whose daughter claimed she had gotten pregnant on one of our trips. The mother had concluded that it was all our fault. I had to contact the teacher who had chaperoned the excursion and tell her what had happened. She already knew. The mother had already gone after her as well, threatening her with a lawsuit and assorted calumny.

I had just hung up the phone with the teacher when Zoey brought in a package and set it on my desk. All she said was "Here."

Happy for the distraction, I unwrapped the paper, then

opened the box. Inside was a beautiful, ornate hand mirror. It was oval-shaped with a twisted handle. The frame was tarnished silver that looked almost pewter. I opened the note.

Elise, Happy Day 7

Thank you for an enlightening weekend. I've sent you a new mirror. Hopefully it works better than the one you've been using.

-Nick

P.S. This is an 1807 antique. The metal is silver. The woman at the antique shop said the best way to clean it is with a cup of white vinegar, a Tbsp of baking soda, and a pinch of salt.

"So what did you get today?" Zoey asked.

I held up the mirror. "A hand mirror. It's an antique."

"It's pretty," she said simply, then left my office.

About a half hour later I went out to use the bathroom and was in one of the stalls when Zoey and Cathy came in together. It was soon obvious that they didn't know I was there.

"So what do you think of all this?" Zoey asked.

"All what?" Cathy replied.

"Elise's sugar daddy."

"Good for her," Cathy said. "She needed something. Have you met the guy?"

"No. But I'm not looking forward to it. You know what

they say, the amount of money a guy spends on a woman is in inverse ratio to his looks. He's probably some fat, bald guy with ear hair."

"At least he's rich," Cathy said.

"Rich doesn't make a man hot," Zoey said.

"No, but it can hide a lot of ugly," Cathy said, laughing.

I was furious. I was about to say something I would no doubt regret, but I calmed myself down. I waited until they left before going back to the office. When I got to my desk I looked up Nicholas's law firm's number and dialed. A professional voice answered. "Derr, Nelson and McKay."

"Hi. I'm calling for Nicholas Derr."

"Just a moment please."

The music on hold was Rachmaninoff, which I knew only because I was an Eric Carmen fan. A half minute later a young female voice answered, "Nicholas Derr's office. This is Sabrina speaking. How may I help you?"

"Hi, Sabrina. I'm calling for Nicholas."

"Mr. Derr is in a meeting right now, may I tell him who's calling?"

"It's not important. This is Elise."

There was hardly a pause. "Elise Dutton?"

I was surprised that she knew who I was. "Yes."

"Just a moment, please."

I was on hold for less than ten seconds before Nicholas answered. "Elise."

"Nicholas, I'm sorry to bother you."

"I'm pleased you called, unless you called to cancel lunch,

in which case, I'm pleased to hear your voice, but not that you called."

I smiled. "No, I'm not calling to cancel. I just wanted to see if you would do something for me."

"Name it."

"Would you mind coming to my office today to get me for lunch?"

"I would love to."

"I'm in office 322."

"I know."

Of course he did.

"Thank you for the mirror," I said. "It's pretty."

"Like you," he replied. "I'll see you at twelve-thirty. Bye."

I hung up the phone. "Fat and bald with ear hair," I said.

Then I realized what I had done. He was going to meet perfect Zoey.

Nicholas was punctual. I heard Zoey greeting him with her come-hither voice. "Hi. May I help you?"

I waited inside my office, listening to the exchange. "I'm here for Elise," he said.

"May I tell her who's calling?"

"Nicholas," he said.

Long pause. "You're Nicholas?"

"You must be Zoey."

"Yes. I am." I had never heard her sound so awkward.

"It's a pleasure meeting you," he said.

"I've heard a lot about you," Zoey said.

"I'm glad to hear that," he said. "I assumed that I was just one of Elise's many men."

Zoey said nothing as I walked out. Nicholas looked over at me and smiled. He couldn't have dressed better for his appearance. He looked gorgeous in an Armani suit with a crisp white silk shirt and crimson tie. "And there she is," he said. He walked up to me and kissed me on the cheek. "I hope it's okay I came by early."

"It's fine," I said.

"Great. I was hoping you'd have time for me to take you to lunch. The owner of the New Yorker is a friend of mine, and he has a special table waiting for us. If you have time, that is."

Just then Cathy walked out of her office. She stopped when she saw Nicholas. She didn't have to say what she was thinking. "Hi."

Nicholas stepped forward, offering his hand. "Hi, I'm Nicholas."

"Cathy," she said, sounding unsure of herself. "It's nice to meet you."

"Likewise," he said. He turned back to me. "So the New Yorker is okay?"

"Of course," I said, doing my best to sound magnanimous. "Let me get my coat."

As I returned to my office I heard Nicholas say, "The table I can get with a phone call, but Elise, I have to pray she can fit me in."

I walked back into the room, and he reached out his hand to me. "Come on, gorgeous."

"Bye," I said to Zoey. "I might be a few minutes late."

"Take your time," she said meekly.

As we walked out into the hallway, I just looked at him. He was smiling.

"Thank you," I said.

"Is that what you wanted?"

"That was perfect. Are we really going to the New Yorker for lunch?"

"Of course. I told you I'd broaden your culinary horizons."

The New Yorker was just a few blocks from the mall. The restaurant didn't have a formal dress code, but everyone inside was professionally attired. It was the kind of place where movers and shakers met and business deals were made. Needless to say, I had never been there before.

After the hostess had seated us at a table for two, Nicholas leaned forward. "So tell me what that was all about."

"The girls in the office have been intrigued by the gifts you've been sending. I overheard them talking this morning. Zoey said, and I quote, 'the amount of money a guy spends on a woman is in inverse ratio to his looks. He's probably some fat, bald guy with ear hair.' "

"Did I dispel any of that?"

"I think you left them speechless."

"Good," he said. "Fortunately I plucked my ear hairs this morning."

"That's just wrong." I laughed. "Can I tell you something honest?"

"Of course."

"I didn't want you to meet Zoey."

"Why is that?"

"I was afraid you might want to trade up."

"No disrespect, but that would be like trading champagne for Kool-Aid."

I grinned. "That's *totally* disrespectful."

"Not to you," he said.

"And thank you again for the mirror. It's beautiful. As is the thought behind it."

"Did I impress you with the cleaning tips?"

"I was *very* impressed."

He smiled. "I thought you would be. So are you ready to order?"

"No." I looked through the menu. "What do you recommend?"

"The tomato soup is always good," he said.

"Why don't you just order for me?"

"I'd be happy to. Something to drink?"

"I'd like a glass of wine."

"Okay," he said. He ordered a glass of Chianti for me, a cranberry juice for himself, and our meal. That was the first time I realized that I had never seen him drink. I wondered if he did.

As the waiter walked away I asked, "So what's next on our agenda?"

"It's your call. You were going to come up with something for our weekend."

"I have an idea," I said. "There's something I've always wanted to do."

"Name it," he said.

"Do you sing?"

"In the shower."

I nodded slowly. "That will do."

CHAPTER

The Golden Rule is a two-edged sword. If some of us treated others as we treat ourselves, we would be jailed.

Elise Dutton's Diary

I had always looked forward to Fridays, but now even the weekdays were better. The whole office anticipated Nicholas's daily gifts. The FedEx man delivered my Friday gift around eleven.

"What is it?" Cathy asked as I opened the box.

"It's New York cheesecake. It's really from New York."

Cathy read the label. "S&S cheesecake from New York. Zagat rated number one."

"I'll get some plates," I said.

"Really?" Cathy said. "You're going to share?"

"If I ate that much cheesecake by myself, I would look like our Christmas tree."

"Bless you, child," Cathy said.

Mark walked out of his office. "Did someone say cheesecake?"

"Elise is sharing the cheesecake her friend sent her."

He walked over and looked at the box. "S&S cheesecake," he said. "I've heard of that. It's the best. And pricey. They sell it by the ounce. Like gold."

I cut the cheesecake up with a plastic knife, and work stopped while everyone ate. Mark closed his eyes as he savored a bite. "Incredible," he said. "If you don't marry that guy, I will."

"Your wife might have something to say about that," Cathy said.

"It doesn't matter," Zoey said. "I've got first dibs."

Nicholas and I didn't have lunch that day because he was in court, but that evening he picked me up at my apartment at six.

"How was your day?" I asked, as we walked to his car.

"Good. We won."

"Do you always win?"

"No. But more than I lose." He opened the car door for me then walked around and got in. "How was your day?"

"Good," I said. "The cheesecake was a hit."

"It doesn't get better than S&S."

"How did you know about them?"

"I'm not as provincial as you might think."

"Believe me, I've never thought of you as provincial. You're the most cosmopolitan person I know."

"Well, I'm definitely not that either. I just love cheesecake, and I discovered S&S from a client who sent me one last Christmas. That's one of the advantages of having rich clients."

The holiday traffic was heavy as we made our way downtown to Abravanel Hall, Salt Lake City's main concert hall and home to the Utah Symphony. The hall was designed by the same acoustical consultant who had designed the Avery Fisher Hall renovation in New York and the Kennedy Center in Washington, D.C. In the gold-leafed lobby was a thirty-foot-tall red blown-glass sculpture designed by renowned glass artist Dale Chihuly.

The event I had chosen for us was a *Messiah* sing-in with the Utah Symphony, which basically meant that we were part of a three-thousand-member choir. To make sure we sounded good, the singing organizers brought in a few ringers, peppering the audience with about a hundred voices from the University of Utah and the Mormon Tabernacle Choir. We were handed paper scores as we walked into the concert hall.

"I thought we were going to hear a choir sing the *Messiah*," Nicholas said to me as we found our seats. "I didn't realize we *were* the choir."

"It's more fun this way," I said. "I asked if you sing."

"I just thought you were curious."

We sounded better than I thought we would. After the concert we drove over to Ruth's Chris Steak House. I had the petite filet while Nicholas ordered the Cowboy Ribeye. He also ordered a tomato and onion salad to share, a seared ahi tuna appetizer (something I'd never had before), and a sweet potato casserole, which I could have eaten for dessert.

"How do you eat like this and stay thin?" I asked.

"Simple," he replied. "I don't always eat like this."

"I think I've gained a few pounds since I signed the contract. You're spoiling me," I said. "I'm not sure all this spoiling is a good thing."

"Why would spoiling you not be a good thing?"

"Because in five weeks our contract is going to expire, and then where am I?"

"I don't know," he replied. "Where are you?"

I shrugged. "Certainly not eating here."

He looked at me for a moment, then said, "Do you know what I like most about you?"

"I have no idea," I said.

"How grateful you are. In a world growing increasingly entitled, you are truly grateful. It makes me want to do more for you."

"You already do too much," I said.

"My point exactly," he replied. "You're a beautiful soul."

"Fortunately for me, you don't really know me."

"No, you told me everything there was to know about you last week."

"Not everything."

He was quiet for a moment, then said, "I probably know you better than you think."

The statement struck me as peculiar. "What do you mean by that?"

He paused for another moment before he said, "I'm just a very good judge of character."

"That may be," I said. "But the thing is, you don't know what you don't know. No one's perfect. Some of us aren't even that good."

Looking at me seriously, he said, "What I do know is that everyone makes mistakes. That's why forgiveness is so important. Unfortunately, so many of us are bad at it." He let his words settle before continuing. "When I worked for the prosecutor's office, one of my first cases was a man who had shot to death a clerk at a convenience store. We had video of the crime, and I thought it was an open-and-shut case. But because of a technicality we lost. As we were leaving the courthouse, the man slapped me on the back and said, 'Thank you, Counselor.' I said, 'For what?' And he said 'For screwing up the case. Of course I killed him. But there's nothing you can do now.' "

"He confessed?" I asked.

"Right there on the courthouse steps."

"Why didn't you just go back in and tell the judge?"

"It wouldn't have done any good. It's called double jeopardy. He can't be tried again for the same offense. It's in the Fifth Amendment to the Constitution. 'Nor shall any person be subject for the same offence to be twice put in jeopardy of life or limb.' The concept was of such importance to the founding fathers that they actually made an amendment to the Constitution for it. But that's in a court of law. In our hearts, there's no such thing. People punish others over and over for the same mistake. We do it to ourselves. It's not right, but still we do it."

I felt like he was reading my mind. He watched me silently. "Elise, you're not as bad as you think you are. Remember that."

When I could speak I said, "So the man was never punished."

"Actually, his case turned out a little differently. Unfortunately for him, he couldn't leave well enough alone. He wrote a letter to the prosecutor's office, bragging that he'd gotten away with murder and stating very specific details of his crime. We reopened the case based on new evidence, and he was found guilty."

"Fool," I said.

"Yes, he was." Nicholas changed the subject. "So the Hitesmans are very excited that you will be joining us for Thanksgiving. Do you still want to bake those pies?"

"Yes," I said. "Except the mincemeat."

"I've already ordered it. When will you bake the others?"

"Wednesday night after work."

"Would you like some help?" he asked.

"Making pies?"

"I don't know how much help I'll be, but I'll keep you company."

"I would love your help," I said. "And your company."

"Great. I'll be there. I'll bring dinner."

That night as I lay in bed remembering our date, I had a frightening realization. My feelings for Nicholas were growing bigger than the contract I'd signed. I wondered if he felt the same way. Not that it mattered. In spite of everything Nicholas had said about forgiveness and redemption, I knew there was no chance we could ever be more than friends. Not if he knew the truth about me. Not if he knew what I'd done. Not if he knew my darkness.

CHAPTER

Eleven

Oftentimes, the hottest fires of hell are fueled from within.

Elise Dutton's Diary

FIVE YEARS EARLIER

June 2007 was hot. The whole world was hot. Greece reported their worst heat wave in history with eleven heat-related deaths, and the entire European power grid nearly collapsed beneath unprecedented demand for air-conditioning.

It was equally hot in the western part of the United States. In Salt Lake City temperatures which normally would have been in the high eighties exceeded a hundred degrees. Our apartment's swamp cooler struggled to keep things tolerable, and the first thing I did on waking was turn it on to full before getting ready for work.

Dan never helped in the mornings. He said it wasn't his "thing," whatever that meant. I resented him for that. In spite of the fact that I worked longer days than he did, I would get up at least an hour before him to get ready, make breakfast, then get our little girl, Hannah, fed and ready for the day. The one thing Dan did that was helpful was drop Hannah off at day care, since it was only three blocks from his office.

However even that had now changed. I had wearied of

Dan's constant complaints about the cost of Hannah's day care, so a week earlier I had found another place at nearly half the price. Since it was on my way to work, now I would have to leave even earlier to drop her off. I didn't like the place as much as the day care where we'd been taking her, but since Dan's commissions were always down during the summer, I decided it was at least worth giving it a try. I wasn't used to the new routine, and one day I'd forgotten to drop her off and had had to turn around just a block from my work and take her to the new place.

On this morning, Hannah was unusually quiet as I got her out of bed. "Are you tired, sweetie?" I asked.

"Yes, Mama," she replied.

"I'm sorry you had to get up so early. I made you Mickey Mouse pancakes."

She smiled. I fed both of us at the same time. Dan stumbled out of bed as I was finishing up.

"Pancakes," he said dully. Dan was taciturn by nature, at least with me, and before nine o'clock getting more from him than a string of three words was rare.

"What's wrong with pancakes?" I asked.

"Had them yesterday."

"No. I made crepes yesterday because you said you wanted them."

"Same diff," he said, sitting down at the table.

I shook my head as I carried our plates over to the sink. I filled the sink with soapy water, then looked down at my watch. "I'm going to be late. I need to grab Hannah's bag, will you please put her in her car seat?"

"Can't you? I'm eating."

"Come on," I said.

"Whatever," he said, standing.

I quickly brushed my teeth, grabbed Hannah's bag, and ran out to the car. "See you," I said to Dan.

"Bye," he said, waving behind his back.

I threw Hannah's bag into the backseat of my Toyota. I looked back. She was asleep. "Sorry, sweetie," I said softly.

I had just pulled out of our subdivision when my cell phone rang. I checked the number. It was work.

"Hello."

"Elise, it's Shirlee," my boss said. "We've got a problem."

"With who?"

"The Tremonton group. Did you book the Smithsonian for today?"

"No, they're tomorrow."

"No, we changed it, remember?"

I groaned. "That's right."

"They're standing outside the Smithsonian. They're telling them that our vouchers aren't good."

"Just call the office of direct sales. Natalie will let them in."

"Where's the number?"

"It's in my Rolodex on my desk. Look under Smithsonian."

"Just a minute." There was a long pause. "You don't have Smithsonian here."

"Of course I do."

"I looked through all the *S*'s, Elise. It's not here."

I was puzzled. "I don't know where it would be. It's got to be there."

"Do you have it in your phone?"

"No."

Shirlee groaned. "There's the driver on the other line. He's got to go. He's got another pickup."

"Just tell him to wait a second, I'll be right there."

I sped into the office. I pulled into a parking place and ran inside. I had accidentally filed the Smithsonian card under *N* for Natalie. But that's not the only mistake I made. I left my three-year-old Hannah in the car on the hottest day of the year.

I've heard it said that there's no greater pain than losing a child. But there is. It's being responsible for your child's death. The day it happened to me is indelibly etched into my mind. People have questioned the existence of hell, but I can tell you it's real. I've been there. Seeing my beautiful little girl's lifeless body in the backseat of my car was hell.

I don't know how long it took for the switch to connect, but after work when I got to my car I just looked at her, the sight incomprehensible. Why was Hannah in the car? Why wasn't she moving? Then reality poured in like a river of fire. I pulled her out, screaming at the top of my lungs. A crowd gathered around me. I tried CPR, I tried mouth-to-mouth, I prayed with everything I had for a miracle, for a heartbeat, for a single breath, but she had been gone for hours. The world swirled around me like a tide pool, spinning me out of control. The paramedics arrived. The police arrived. There was talk of heatstroke and core temperatures and hyperthermia. I fell to the ground unable to walk, unable to do anything but scream and babble, to plead for my baby's life.

A police officer tried to get information from me, but it was like I wasn't there. My little girl's body was taken. I screamed as they took her away even though she was already gone. My Hannah. My reason for living, was gone.

A woman came and put her arm around me. I don't know who she was. I never saw her again. I wouldn't recognize her if I did. She said little, but she was there. Like an angel. Somehow I could talk to her. "I want to die," I said.

"I know, honey," she said. "I'm so sorry."

Then she was gone. Had I imagined her?

The press arrived with cameras and video cameras. Dan arrived after them. "What have you done?" he shouted at me. *"What have you done?"* I couldn't answer. I couldn't even speak. I was catatonic.

There were discussions on whether I should be tried for murder or manslaughter. There would be an investigation. It had already begun. People were talking to Dan. To Shirlee. To my co-workers. To people who didn't know me well enough to speak about me. *What kind of person was I? What kind of mother was I?* No one asked me. I could have answered the latter. I was the worst kind. The kind who killed her own child.

They put me in a police car and drove me downtown to the station. I waited alone in a room for more than an hour. It seemed like no one knew what to do with me. A few police officers came in and asked me questions. Inane questions. *Did I know she was in the car? Had I left her in the car on purpose? When did I realize she was in the car?* "Probably when I started screaming hysterically and collapsed," I wanted to say.

Then a man about my age came and talked to me. He wasn't with the police. He wore a suit. His voice was calm. Sympathetic. He asked me questions, and I mostly just blinked at him. He told me that he was from the prosecutor's office or someplace official. He finished with his questions and spoke with the police. There was a discussion on whether or not I should be arrested and fingerprinted, but the man intervened. The talk of court and jail scared me, but nothing they could do could match the pain I already felt. Someone asked if I wanted a sedative. I turned it down. I deserved to feel the pain. I deserved to feel every barb, every hurt, then, God willing, to die.

And the barbs came. My Hannah's death set off a firestorm of media. The television covered it, reducing my tragedy to four minutes of entertainment followed by a commercial for tires. Both newspapers, the *Deseret News* and *The Salt Lake Tribune,* weighed in. There were columns of letters to the editor about me. Some said I deserved life in prison for what I'd done. Some said I should be locked in a car with the windows rolled up. I agreed with the latter. The cruelest thing said was that I had killed my Hannah on purpose.

Most confusing to me was how deeply people I didn't know hated me. The attacks lasted for months. I don't know why strangers went so far out of their way to hate me. Maybe it made them feel like better people. Or better parents. Maybe it convinced them that they would never do such a thing. Maybe it masked their fears that they were flawed like me.

I noticed stories like mine everywhere. One British lawyer called it forgotten baby syndrome. *It's not a syndrome,* I thought. *It's an accident. A horrible, exquisite accident. A failure of humanity.*

Once a psychiatrist on TV spoke out for me. He said, "Our conscious mind prioritizes things by importance, but our memory does not. If you've ever left your cell phone in your car, you are capable of forgetting your child." He pointed out that this was an epidemic and there were scores of stories like mine. In one state three children died in one day. He said that this was a new phenomenon, that ten years ago it rarely happened because parents kept their babies near them in the front seat. Then airbags came, and our babies were put out of the way, where we couldn't see them.

He explained that there were two main reasons that people left babies in cars: change of routine and distraction. I'd had both. He said, rightly, that no punishment society could give could match what I was already feeling. I don't know how he knew. I guess it's his job to know.

Through it all, Dan's moods were as volatile as the Utah weather. He was supportive and sympathetic, then, sometimes in the same hour, angry and brooding. He was always moody. He was gone a lot. I didn't know where he went. I didn't really care. It was easier being alone. I was fired from my job, not that I could have worked. I stayed in bed most of the time, hiding from the world, wishing that I could hide from myself.

Then, one night, I got sick with appendicitis. If I had known that my appendix had already burst, I might not have gone to the hospital. If I had stayed home for just another hour or two, I could have ended it all. I had been given a way out. I don't know why I didn't take it. Perhaps, in spite of my self-loathing and pain, some part of me still longed to live.

As I lay in bed wracked with fever, I thought about my life. It was then that I had an epiphany. It came to me that one day I might see my sweet little girl again. *What if she asked me what I had done with my life?* I was not honoring her by retreating from the world—from life. At that moment I resolved that things might be different. That *I* might be different. That I might be *better*.

Then my husband divorced me.

CHAPTER *Twelve*

Even in the darkest of days there are oases of joy. And there's usually pie.

Elise Dutton's Diary

As a rare gesture of magnanimity, Mark closed the office two hours early on the Wednesday before Thanksgiving. On the way home from work I stopped at the grocery store for pie ingredients. It had been years since I'd made pies. I unearthed the old cookbook my mother had written her pie secrets in; that cookbook was one of the few possessions I got after my mother's death.

Before settling in to bake I put the Mitch Miller *Holiday Sing Along* CD on my stereo to set the mood. The truth was, I was already in a good mood. It seemed that I always was when I was about to see Nicholas.

Nicholas arrived at my apartment a little before six. I had finished making all the crusts, and the cherry and apple pies were in the oven, along with a baking sheet spread with pecan halves.

"I got here as soon as I could," he said apologetically. He carried a paper coffee cup in each hand, and a large white plastic bag hung from the crux of his arm. He breathed in. "It smells heavenly." He handed me a cup. "I got you a salted caramel mocha."

"How do you always know what I want?"

"It's easy. I find the sweetest thing on the menu and order it."

"You've pretty much got me figured out," I said.

"It's probably sacrilege, but I brought us Chinese for dinner. I got wonton soup, sweet and sour pork, walnut shrimp, and pot stickers."

"Which will all go nicely with pumpkin pie," I said. We walked into the kitchen. Nicholas set the bag of Chinese down on the table.

"So, I'm making apple, cherry, pumpkin, and pecan," I said. "The apple and cherry are already in the oven. They're just about done."

Nicholas examined the latticework on my apple and cherry pies through the oven window. "Those are works of art," he said. "Where did you learn to make pies?"

"My mother. She was famous for her pies. Well, about as famous as you can get in Montezuma Creek. She won a blue ribbon for her cherry pie at the San Juan County fair. It was the only prize she ever won. She hung it in the living room next to my father's bowling trophies." I opened the oven and took out the pies, setting them on the counter to cool. "I don't have a lot of happy memories from my childhood, but when she made pie, life was good. Everyone was happy. Even my father."

"My mother always made pies at special times," Nicholas said, "like the holidays or special family get-togethers. But my favorite part of pie making was after she was done and she would take the leftover dough, sprinkle it with cinnamon and sugar, then bake it."

"I know, right!" I said, clapping my hands. "Piecrust cookies. They're the best. Which is why I made extra dough."

"You're going to make some tonight?" Nicholas asked.

"Absolutely," I said. "When the pies are done."

"So, what fat do you use for your crust? Butter, shortening, or lard?"

"My mother was old school. She said that lard made the flakiest piecrust. She thought butter was lazy and shortening was a sin. She was religious about it."

"People get a little fanatic about pies," Nicholas said.

"I'm just getting ready to mix the pecan pie filling. Would you mind getting the pecans out of the oven? The mitts are right there."

"On it," he said.

While he brought the baking sheet out of the oven, I mixed the other ingredients.

"Where do you want the pecans?" he asked.

"Go ahead and pour them in here," I said.

"The pecans rise to the top?"

"Like magic."

In the end I made four regular-size pies for Thanksgiving as well as two tart-size pies—one pecan, one pumpkin—for us to eat with our dinner.

After the last of the pies were in the oven, we sat on the floor in the living room and ate our Chinese food with chopsticks. This was followed by the small pies for dessert and piecrust cookies as a postdessert with decaf coffee.

As I finished my coffee I lay back on the carpet. "I'm too full for Thanksgiving dinner."

"No, we're just stretching out our stomachs to get ready for Thanksgiving dinner," Nicholas said.

"That's a brilliant excuse for gluttony," I said.

"My father used to say that," he said. "He used to make a big breakfast Thanksgiving morning."

"I bet your mother loved that."

"Oh yeah, a dirty kitchen to start with."

"Thanks for bringing us dinner," I said. "What was the name of that restaurant?"

"Asian Star," he said. "And it was nothing. If I'd known you were such a good cook, I would have added a clause in the contract requiring you to cook for me."

"You didn't have to," I said. "I'm happy to cook for you whenever you want."

"There's an open-ended commitment," he said. "Speaking of commitments, how is the contract going?"

"Our contract?"

"The Mistletoe Promise," he said.

I wondered why he was asking. "I think it's going very well."

"So you're glad you signed?"

"Yes."

"Good," he said.

We decided to watch television as we waited for the last of the pies to bake. I turned the lights out, and we sat next to each other on the couch. I handed Nicholas the remote, and he channel-surfed for a few minutes until we came to *It's a Wonderful Life* on PBS.

"Let's watch this," I said. "I love Jimmy Stewart."

"And that Donna Reed," Nicholas said. "That is one low-maintenance woman."

"Like me," I said.

He smiled. "Just like you."

I must have been exhausted, because I don't remember falling asleep next to him. Actually, on him. I woke with my head on his shoulder. I jumped up.

"You're okay," he said.

"The pies?" I said. "I didn't hear the buzzer."

"I got them out. They look perfect. Marie Callender herself would be proud."

He turned off the television, then walked me to my bedroom. I sat down on the edge of the bed, rubbing my forehead and yawning. "Thank you."

"You're welcome. I'll see you tomorrow. I'll just let myself out."

"Nicholas," I said.

"Yes?"

"Are you glad you signed the contract?"

He smiled, then came up next to me and kissed me on the forehead. "I'd do it again."

CHAPTER

Thirteen

It seems a long time since I remembered all I have to be grateful for. Perhaps that's why it's been such a long time since I've been really happy.

Elise Dutton's Diary

Thanksgiving arrived with a heavy snowfall, and I woke to the sound of plows scraping the road. Around nine the snow stopped, and the roads were clear by the time Nicholas arrived at two. Traversing a slippery sidewalk, we carried the pies out to his car, laid them on lipped cookie sheets on his backseat, and drove off to Thanksgiving dinner.

"Tell me about the Hitesmans," I said as we drove.

"You'll like them. Good people. Scott is one of those small-town boys who made good." He turned to me. "He grew up in Burley, Idaho, working the potato fields. Went to Yale for law. The firm picked him up out of college."

"What's his wife's name?"

"Sharon. You'll love her. She's one of those people who's always baking bread for the neighbors or visiting people in the hospital."

The Hitesmans lived in a medium-size home in the northernmost section of the Avenues. A large pine wreath garnished their front door. Nicholas rang the doorbell, then opened the door before anyone could answer. We were engulfed by the warmth of the home, the smell of baking, and the sound of the Carpenters' Christmas music playing from another room.

A woman walked into the foyer to greet us. She looked to be about my age, pretty with short, spiky auburn hair. Over a red knit shirt she wore a black apron that read:

THE ONLY REASON
I HAVE A KITCHEN
IS BECAUSE IT CAME
WITH THE HOUSE

"Nicholas," she said joyfully. "And this must be Elise. I'm Sharon."

"Hello," I said. "Happy Thanksgiving."

"Happy Thanksgiving to you too," she returned. She looked down at the pies we carried. "Those look delicious, let me take that from you," she said, taking the cookie sheet from my hands. "Boys, come here. Fast."

Two young boys, close in age, appeared at her side.

"Carry these into the kitchen and don't drop them."

"Okay," they said in unison.

"Now we can properly greet," she said, hugging me first then hugging and kissing Nicholas. "It's so good to see you. You haven't been around much lately."

"Work," he said. "And more work."

"You lawyers work too much. But Scott says your absence might have something to do with your new friend," she said, looking at me. "Elise, we're so pleased you've joined us. Nicholas has told us so much about you."

"Good things, I hope."

"All good," she said. Suddenly her brow fell. "Wait, have we met before?"

"I don't think so."

"You look familiar. I have a pretty good memory for faces. You aren't famous, are you?"

"No."

"You haven't been in the newspaper or on TV?"

I froze. It wasn't the first time someone had asked, but I was always caught off guard. "I . . ."

"Sharon," Nicholas said lightly, "stop interrogating her. She just has one of those faces."

Sharon smiled. "She definitely has a pretty one. I'm not often wrong about things like that, but there's always a first."

"Thank you," I said.

"Now come in, come in. We're almost ready to eat. Make yourself at home. I need to check on the rolls, but let me take your coats."

I shrugged off my coat and handed it to her. As she started to turn away, a man, stocky and broad shouldered with blond hair neatly parted to one side, walked up behind her. "St. Nick," he said, extending his hands to Nicholas in greeting.

"Hey, buddy," Nicholas returned. They man-hugged and then, with his arm still across the man's shoulder, Nicholas said to me, "This is Scott."

Scott reached his hand out to me. "So glad you could come. Nick's told us so much about you."

All I could think of was Nicholas's description of Scott as a potato picking Idaho farm boy, which was exactly what he looked like, except without dirt beneath his fingernails. I took his hand. "Thank you. I was glad to be invited."

"I guarantee you won't go away hungry," Scott said. He turned to Nicholas. "I hate to do this today, but can I ask you something about the Avalon case? I've got to get back to them by seven."

"No rest for the wicked," Nicholas said. He turned back to me. "Sorry, I'll be right back. Just . . . mingle."

As they slipped off to Scott's den, I walked into the living room and kitchen area. Adjoining the living room was the dining room, with a long table that was beautifully set with a copper-colored linen tablecloth, gold-trimmed china plates on gold chargers, and crystal stemware. There was a floral centerpiece in autumn colors with two unlit red candles rising from its center.

The two boys were now lying on their stomachs, playing a video game in front of the fireplace. Across from them, on the sofa, was an elderly woman I guessed to be the grandmother. She looked like she was asleep. I drifted toward the kitchen, where Sharon was brushing butter over Parker House rolls.

"May I help?" I asked.

"I could use some help," she said. "Would you mind opening that can of cranberry sauce and putting it on a plate? The can opener is in that drawer right there."

I found the can opener, opened the can, and arranged the sauce.

"Your pies look divine," Sharon said. "Nick usually just picks them up from Marie Callender's."

"Thank you. I like making pies. Except mincemeat. We bought the mincemeat."

"I'm not a mincemeat fan either. It's really just for Grandma."

"That's what Nicholas said."

"He didn't bring it one year. Grandma let him know that she wasn't happy." We both looked over at the old woman. "It's a lot of work making pies. Especially the lattice tops," Sharon remarked.

"I enjoy making them," I said again. "And Nicholas helped."

She looked at me with surprise. "Nicholas helped you make pies?"

"Yes."

"Wow," she said. "You domesticated him. Things must be going well with you two."

I didn't know how to respond. Finally I said, "We're having fun."

"Fun is good. He said you met at work."

"Sort of. We work in the same office building. I'm four floors beneath him."

Sharon donned hot mitts, then opened the oven. "Time to bring out the bird," she said as she pulled a large roaster out and set it on the granite-topped island in the middle of the kitchen. She lifted the lid, exposing a large browned turkey.

At that moment, Nicholas walked in, trailed by Scott. "I see you put her to work," Nicholas said to Sharon.

"I did," Sharon said.

Nicholas said to me, "She comes across as nice, but she's really a heartless taskmaster. Last year she made Scott and me put together the boys' Christmas bikes before we could eat."

"Shhh!" she said. "They're right there. Santa brought those bikes."

Nicholas grinned. "Sorry." He turned to me. "Did you meet Grandma?"

"Not yet," I said. "She's asleep."

"And don't wake her," Sharon said. "Let sleeping dogs lie."

"I heard that," Grandma shouted. "I'm not a dog. I'm old, not deaf."

I glanced furtively at Nicholas, who looked like he might burst out laughing.

"I want a Dr Pepper," she shouted. "No ice."

"Would you mind?" Sharon said to Nicholas. "There's one in the fridge. She likes it in a plastic cup, no ice."

"Sure," he said. He retrieved the soda, poured it into the cup, then took my hand and led me over to the woman. "Here you go, Grandma," he said, offering her the drink.

She snatched it from him, took a long drink, burped, then handed the half full cup back to him without thanks.

"Elise, this is Grandma Wilma," Nicholas said. "Grandma, this is Elise."

"Did you bring the mincemeat?" she said.

"Of course."

"One year he didn't bring it," she said to me.

"That must have been really awful," I said.

Nicholas stifled a laugh. Grandma just looked at me. "Who are you?"

"I'm Elise."

"You his wife?"

"No. We're just friends."

"There's nothing wrong with marriage," she said. "No one gets married these days. Why would they buy the cow when the milk's free?"

"Grandma," Sharon said from the kitchen. "That's enough."

"It's nice to meet you," I said.

"It's time to eat?" she said back.

"She said *meet,*" Nicholas clarified.

"We got a turkey," she said. "That's all the meat we need." She turned to Sharon. "When do we eat? I haven't got all day."

"Nick," Sharon said. "Will you carve the turkey? Then we can eat. Scott, take the rolls in. Boys, stop playing that stupid game."

The boys just continued playing. Nicholas walked over to the bird. "Where's your electric knife?"

"I don't know where it went," Sharon said. "I think Scott ruined it making the boys' pinewood derby cars."

"That's possible," Scott said.

"You're going to have to do it the old-fashioned way," Sharon said.

Nicholas pulled a knife from a wooden block and began carving while I helped Sharon carry the last of the food over to the table.

"I'd have Scott do the carving," she said to me, loud enough for her husband to hear, "but he just makes a mess of it. I end up using most of it for turkey noodle soup. You'd think, being raised on a farm, he'd know how to carve a turkey."

"I know how to raise and *kill* a turkey," Scott said.

"Fortunately, this one came dead," Sharon replied. "Boys, put away the game and help Grandma to the table."

After we had all settled in at the table, Sharon and Scott held hands and Sharon said, "Nick, will you say a prayer over the food."

"I'd be happy to," he said. He took my hand, and we all bowed our heads.

"Dear Father in Heaven, we are grateful for this day to consider our blessings. We are grateful for the abundance of our lives. We are grateful to be together, safe and well. We ask a blessing to be upon this home and Scott and Sharon and their family. Please bless them for their generosity and love. We are grateful that Elise has joined us this year and ask that she might feel as blessed as she makes others feel. We ask this in the name of Jesus Christ. Amen."

I looked over at him. "Thank you. That was sweet."

"He says the best prayers," Sharon said. "That's why we always ask him to pray."

"I want turkey," Wilma said.

"Scott, get her some turkey," Sharon said. "Just white meat."

✦

Scott was right: there was no way we were leaving the table hungry. There was turkey, corn-bread stuffing, pecan-crusted candied yams, mashed potatoes and gravy, sweet corn, Parker House rolls, apple-pineapple salad, and green beans with bacon. By the time we were through eating, I was too full for pie. We all helped with the dishes. Then Nicholas said, "I think I need a walk."

"I'll join you," I said.

We retrieved our coats and went outside. The sun had just fallen below the western mountains, and we walked out into the middle of the vacant, snow-packed street. Nicholas turned to me. "Having fun?"

"Yes. They're nice people. Grandma's a hoot."

"I know. Every year they say this is her last year, but it never is. I think she'll outlive all of us. When death comes for her, she'll slap his face and tell him to get her a Dr Pepper, no ice."

I laughed. "Why do you think old age does that to people?"

"I don't know. Old age seems to make some people meaner and some sweeter. Maybe it's just an amplifier." I slipped on a patch of ice, and Nicholas grabbed my arm. I noticed that he didn't let go. "So how does this compare to your normal Thanksgiving?"

"The food is better. The company is *much* better."

"I'm sure the harem isn't the same without you."

"Dan will survive."

"So what is Dan like? Or have I crossed the line of addendum one."

"We have pretty much obliterated addendum one," I said. "How do I describe Dan?" I thought a moment then said, "His good side, he's not bad-looking and he's ambitious. He has big dreams. Not really practical ones, but big. At least he did when we were dating."

"And the dark side?"

"He's got a nasty temper and he's a narcissist. He's insecure but conceited at the same time. He's a chronic womanizer. On our wedding day he flirted with some of the guests. Probably the best compliment I could give him is that he's not my father."

"That's a short measuring stick," Nicholas said.

"It's the measuring stick life gave me," I replied. "It's funny how different kids can be from their parents."

"Like you," Nicholas said.

"Yes, but I meant Dan. Dan's father is the most humble man you'll ever meet. He's had his same job as a hospital administrator for more than thirty years. He adores his wife and treats her like a queen. Sometimes I wish I had married Dan's father instead of him."

"No you don't," Nicholas said. "He's too old."

I smiled. "You're right." I breathed the cold air in deeply. "Now, may I ask you a deep, probing question?"

"It's only fair," he said.

"Do you ever wish you were married and had children?"

He thought a moment. "Yes. To both."

"Then why don't you? It's not like that would be hard for you. Just in my office I know two women who would be more than happy to oblige you."

"I guess it's just taken me a little while to get to this place."

"So why the contract? Why not just date?"

"Training wheels," he replied.

"Training wheels," I repeated, smiling. "I like that." I slipped again. Again Nicholas caught me.

"It's the shoes," I said. "They don't do snow."

"I think *you* need training wheels."

"I think you're right."

"Let's go back and have some of that pie," he said.

"All right. Just don't let me fall."

By the time we returned from our walk, the boys had disappeared and Grandma Wilma had already eaten her sliver of mincemeat and retired to the guest room to nap. Nicholas and I joined Scott and Sharon at the table for coffee and pie.

"Elise," Sharon said. "Your pies are divine. This pecan pie is amazing."

"Thank you," I said.

"You're definitely on our guest list next year."

"Or at least your pies are," Scott joked. "In case this doesn't work out."

I furtively glanced at Nicholas, who didn't respond.

We sat around and talked for nearly an hour. Eventually our conversation turned to the natural sleep agent properties of tryptophan in turkey, to which Nicholas yawned and said, "I need a nap." He looked at me as if seeking permission.

"Go for it," I said.

He went into the living room, leaving the three of us still at the table.

"The food was really great," I said to Sharon. "Thank you for letting me join you."

"Thank you for coming," Sharon said. "You know, you're good for him."

Scott nodded. "In all the years I've known Nick, I've never seen him this happy."

"We've only known each other for three weeks," I said.

"And the last three weeks he's been a changed man," Scott said.

Sharon nodded. "He's definitely in love."

The word paralyzed me. The L word. I suddenly wished that Nicholas had told them the truth about us.

"I think I'll check on Nicholas," I said. I pushed back from the table and went into the living room. The light was off, and the room was lit by the orange-yellow fire.

Nicholas was asleep on the sofa in front of the fireplace. I sat down next to the couch and just looked at him, the flickering flames reflecting off his face. He was beautiful. More beautiful since I'd gotten to know him. *Do I really make him happy? Why does our relationship feel so real?* I took a deep breath. An inner voice said to me, *You're losing it, Elise. You know it's not real. You're going to get your heart broken.* Then another voice said back, *I don't care.* I lay my head against him and closed my eyes and pretended that we were the couple everyone thought we were.

"And for all I [illegible]"

I went into the living room, leaving the directions still on the table.

"The food was really great," I said to Sharon. "Thank you [illegible] [illegible] to [illegible]"

"Thank you for coming [illegible]" [illegible] [illegible]

[illegible] [illegible] [illegible] [illegible] we [illegible] [illegible] I've never [illegible] [illegible] this [illegible]

"[illegible] [illegible] known [illegible] [illegible] [illegible] were [illegible]," I said.

"A [illegible] [illegible] [illegible] we [illegible] [illegible] [illegible] changed [illegible] [illegible]

[illegible]

[illegible] [illegible] [illegible] [illegible] [illegible]

[illegible] [illegible] [illegible] [illegible] [illegible] [illegible] [illegible] that [illegible] had [illegible] the [illegible] [illegible] [illegible]

"I think [illegible] [illegible] on [illegible]," I said. I [illegible] back from the [illegible] and [illegible] into the living [illegible]. The [illegible] and the [illegible] [illegible] the orange [illegible] [illegible]

[illegible] was [illegible] on the [illegible] [illegible] [illegible] [illegible] [illegible] [illegible] [illegible] [illegible] [illegible] [illegible] the [illegible] [illegible] [illegible] [illegible] [illegible] [illegible] [illegible] [illegible] [illegible] beautiful. [illegible] [illegible] [illegible] [illegible] know him [illegible] [illegible]

[illegible] [illegible] [illegible] [illegible] [illegible] [illegible] [illegible] [illegible] [illegible] [illegible] [illegible] said to [illegible] [illegible] [illegible] [illegible]

[illegible] [illegible]

CHAPTER *Fourteen*

Cars are remarkable machines. A man may devote his life to charity, but put him in a car and take his parking stall and he'll cut your throat.

Elise Dutton's Diary

I woke the next morning to my phone ringing. It was still dark outside.

"Hello?" I said groggily.

"What are you doing?" Nicholas asked.

"I'm sleeping. What time is it?"

"Six. Almost."

"Why are you calling me so early?"

"It's Black Friday," he said. "I need to do some Christmas shopping. Want to come?"

"Is this on our schedule?"

"No, I'm completely ad-libbing here."

"Can I get ready first?"

"Of course. I'll be over in twenty minutes."

"Okay," I said. "Wait, I can't be ready in twenty minutes."

"How long do you need?"

"Give me an hour."

"That's a lot of daylight," he said.

"I need an hour," I said firmly.

"All right. See you in an hour. Bye."

"Bye." I hung up, then climbed out of bed and took a

shower to wake myself up. As usual, Nicholas was right on time.

"Where are we going?" I asked with my eyes closed, reclining the seat in his car.

"City Creek Center."

"It's going to be a zoo."

"I know," he said.

A few minutes later I asked, "Why aren't you tired?"

"It's a day off. Do you really want to sleep through it?"

"Yes," I said.

The shopping center was crazy crowded, and parking was at a premium. We passed two people trying to pull into the same slot in the parking garage, both unwilling to yield. They just kept honking at each other.

"Think we'll find a space?" I asked.

"I'd bet on it," he said. A few minutes later he pulled into a reserved spot with his name on it, and we took the elevator up to the ground level.

The shopping center had only opened the previous year and was clearly the place to go. It was an upscale, open-air shopping center that had a simulated creek running through it. It occupied six acres in downtown Salt Lake City with a sky bridge over Main Street connecting the two blocks.

We were walking out of Godiva Chocolatier, where we had stopped for chocolate-covered strawberries (which was probably the best breakfast I'd had in years), when Nicholas said, "I need to stop at the Coach store to pick up a bag for one of the partners. Do you mind?"

"Of course not." I followed him to the shop.

A professional-looking man, bald with a graying goatee, approached Nicholas. "May I help you, sir?"

"I'm looking for a leather carry-on bag."

"I've got just the thing," said the man. He led us over to a wall display of leather bags. "I've got the Thompson foldover tote, that's been quite popular. And the new Bleecker line. I've got the map bag in leather; it comes in two colors, brass and mahogany, and a leather-trimmed webbing strap."

"No, it looks too much like a man purse," Nicholas said. "How much is this bag?" he asked, lifting one to examine it more closely.

"That's the Bleecker flight bag. It's four hundred and ninety-eight dollars."

That was almost my entire life savings.

"What colors does it come in?" Nicholas asked.

"Just what you see here, black and brass."

"I'll take the brass."

"Very good choice," the man said. "Much more masculine design. Do you need anything else?"

"No, that's all."

"Give me just a moment and I'll ring you up."

"Here's my card," Nicholas said, handing him a black credit card. There was a long line of people making purchases.

"That's a nice bag," I said.

"It's for one of my partners," he said. "He'll like it. He likes luggage."

"It's expensive."

"Not for him," he said.

"Or you," I added. As we waited in line I noticed that there was a Pandora shop across the way. Cathy was a Pandora fanatic, and she always loved getting new charms.

"Nicholas," I said, "I'm going to go over to the Pandora shop."

"No problem. I'll come over after."

I walked over to the store and browsed the display cases until I found a sterling silver clover with green enamel. It was perfect. Cathy was Irish and proud of it.

"May I help you?" a woman asked. I looked up. The woman was about my age, heavy with gold, permed hair.

"I'd like to purchase that charm right there," I said, pointing to the piece.

"The clover?" she asked.

"Yes, please."

She lifted it from the display case. "This also comes in gold with diamonds."

"The silver charm is fine, thank you."

"Anything else?"

"No, that's it."

"This way, please."

I followed her over to the cash register.

"Will that be cash or plastic?"

"Plastic," I said, handing her my Visa card. She ran my card, glanced at the name, then back up at me. "Do I know you?"

"I don't think so."

She glanced once more at my name on the credit card. "Elise Dutton. No, I think I do. What school did you go to?"

"I'm not from around here."

"Hmm," she said, handing me back my card. Then a look of recognition came to her eyes. "I know who you are. I read a story about you a few years back. You . . ." She stopped abruptly.

"Yes?" I said.

"I'm sorry," she said. "I'm mistaken."

She quickly packaged up my purchase and handed me the bag. "Thank you for shopping. Have a good day."

"Happy holidays," I said dully, then quickly left the store.

Nicholas met me as I was walking out. "Sorry that took so long," he said. "That guy was inept with a cash register." He looked at me closely. "Are you okay?"

"I'm not feeling well," I said. "Can we go?"

"Of course." He glanced over at the store, then took my hand. "Come on. It's too crowded here anyway."

CHAPTER

Fifteen

Dan came to see me today. He's about as welcome as a January utility bill.

Elise Dutton's Diary

The next Monday was calmer than usual since we didn't have any tours out that week. The holidays were our slowest time of the year, and most of our efforts then went toward preparing and marketing the next year's tours.

A little before noon I looked up to see Dan standing in the doorway of my office. "Flowers," he said. "Where'd you get those?"

"What do you want?" I asked.

He stepped into my office. "You weren't at Thanksgiving dinner."

"I told your parents I wouldn't be there."

"You didn't tell me."

"What do you want, Dan?"

"I came to see what's up. Why you didn't come."

"I was busy."

"On Thanksgiving?"

"Is that so hard to believe?"

"What, you had work?"

"I had another invitation to dinner," I said, annoyed by his persistence. "I always thought it was weird anyway, going to dinner with you and Kayla."

"An invitation from who?"

"A friend."

"A friend," he said suspiciously. "Male or female?"

"I don't need to report to you."

"A man, huh?" He walked closer to my desk. "Tell you what—I'll take you to lunch, and you can tell me about this guy. I'll pay." He made the offer sound remarkably magnanimous, and, for him, it was.

"I already have lunch plans," I said.

"Since when do you have lunch plans?"

"Since when do you care?" I said. "Where's Kayla? Why don't you take her to lunch?"

"I need to talk to you about her," he said. "Who are you lunching with?"

"A friend," I said.

"The Thanksgiving guy?"

"That's none of your business."

"What's Thanksgiving guy's name?"

"Nicholas," Nicholas said, walking into my office.

Dan turned around. The look on his face was priceless, a mix of surprise and fear.

"Hi, Elise," Nicholas said. He leaned forward and kissed me on the cheek.

Dan glanced back and forth between us, still not sure how to react.

"This is Dan," I said. "My ex-husband."

Nicholas looked at him coolly. "Dan."

"Whassup," Dan said. I knew Dan well enough to know that he was intimidated. Subconsciously, he threw his chest out a little.

Nicholas turned back to me. "Are you ready?"

"Yes." I took his hand. "I'll talk to you later," I said to Dan.

"Yeah, whatever," Dan said.

Nicholas and I walked out of my office, leaving Dan standing there alone. I should have known that he'd never leave my new relationship alone.

CHAPTER

Sixteen

Dan's the kid in the sandbox who always wants the toy someone else has.

Elise Dutton's Diary

Dan was waiting on the landing outside my apartment when I got home from work.

"Whassup?" he said as I approached. "I was just in the area, thought I'd stop by."

"What were you doing in the area?" I asked. I unlocked the door and walked in.

"I came to see you." He followed me inside, took off his coat, and threw it, then himself, on my couch. "So how was your date?"

"What date?"

"The one I caught you on. With what's-his-name."

"You didn't *catch* me," I said. "And don't act childish. You know his name."

"Dick?"

I didn't answer.

"Dickolaus."

I just glared at him.

"Whatever. The Nick-man. So where'd you meet him?"

"In the food court."

"Oh, that's cool."

"*We* met in a Laundromat," I said. "What does that make us?"

"Divorced," Dan said. "So what, he's like your boyfriend now?"

"Something like that. What's it to you?"

"Kayla's gone."

"Gone where?"

"She cheated on me. With some old rich guy."

"Am I supposed to feel bad for you?"

"Would it kill you to show a little sympathy?"

"She's a cheater, what did you expect?"

"I expected she would be loyal."

"Like you?"

"I was loyal to *her*."

For a change, I thought. I breathed out in exasperation. "What do you want, Dan?"

"I want you. I want us to be like we were."

"That ship has sailed," I said.

"You didn't give me a chance. I stuck by you when you screwed up, but I slip up and you're gone."

"*You* didn't stick by me. You divorced *me*."

"Only because you were going to divorce me."

"I never said I was going to divorce you. I should have, but I never did."

"But you were *going* to."

"You don't know that. I don't even know that, which is pathetic, since you were cheating on me with my best friend while I was in the ICU clinging to life."

He looked at me for a moment and his voice softened. "Elise, it's always been us. We understand each other. We've been through the storms together. We should be together. You know it."

"I believed that once," I said. "I don't anymore."

"Why, because some rich lawyer comes knocking at your door? He's probably married."

"No, he's not married. Not everyone cheats like you, Dan."

"A lot more than you think. How long have you known him?"

"A few weeks."

"I don't trust him."

"You don't know him well enough to not trust him."

"Neither do you."

I groaned with exasperation. "I'm not having this conversation. You need to leave."

"Come on, 'Lise. We match. Just admit it. If we didn't, then why did you marry me?"

"I was desperate."

"No, you believed in us. And you were right. Drop the lawyer and I'll move in with you."

"It's not going to happen, Dan. Now you need to go. I have to go grocery shopping."

He grabbed his coat and smiled. "You'll come around," he said. "Like a boomerang. You'll think about it, then you'll see the light. Who else knows everything about you? You know how people are when they learn about . . ."

"About what?"

"You know. Hannah."

"Get out," I said.

He remained undaunted. "See you later, 'Lise." He stepped across the threshold, then said, "Boomerang."

I shut the door after him. As much as I hated hearing it from him, Dan was right. Whenever people made the connection between me and the woman in the newspaper who killed her daughter, they just mysteriously disappeared. I leaned against the door and cried.

CHAPTER
Seventeen

The annual ICE Christmas affair is about as classy as a truck pull, but without the dress code.

Elise Dutton's Diary

The ICE Christmas party was a perennial redux—a potluck affair that was always held at my boss's home in Olympus Cove. He lived in a Tudor-style house decorated with plastic reindeer in the front yard and a fake plastic chimney on the roof with Santa's boots extending straight up as if he were stuck.

Nicholas had picked me up along with my pomegranate-and-poppy-seed-dressed salad. I brought the same salad every year, and took it home every year barely eaten, since most of the office avoided salad like a toxin. Still, Mark insisted that I bring it because his wife, Shelley, once remarked that she liked it. I had since concluded that she was only being polite since she hadn't eaten any of it for the last two years.

Nicholas parked his BMW across the street from the house, and I carried my bowl up to the door.

"Shall I ring the bell?" Nicholas asked.

"No. They won't answer; just walk in."

He opened the door. As I anticipated, there was no one to greet us, and the only sounds came from the television in the family room.

"I'll take your coat," Nicholas said.

I set my salad on the floor, then took off my coat and handed it to him. "They put them in the living room," I said.

Nicholas added our coats to a pile of outerwear already covering the crushed-velvet sofa. Then we walked into the kitchen. No one noticed (or cared) as I lay my salad on the counter.

My boss, Mark Engeman, was notoriously tightfisted, and the party's food was grocery store platters of meat and cheese laid out next to plates of Ritz and saltine crackers dressed with cheese from a can. There were also jalapeño poppers, store-bought rolls to make sandwiches, and a large bowl of carrot-raisin salad, which was always Cathy's contribution.

The one place Mark splurged was on beer. His refrigerator was stocked with all the Budweiser it could hold. There was also a plastic cooler filled with beer. I think he caught on that his guests rated the party by the level of intoxication they achieved, which was just one of many reasons that I was always the first to leave.

Everyone else was already there. Mark and his wife, Shelley; Cathy, who brought Maureen, her snarky sister. And Brent and Margaret, our two group escorts, whom we rarely saw because they were on the road more than two hundred days out of the year, with their spouses.

Closest to the kitchen were Zoey and her date. As usual, Zoey had brought someone none of us had ever seen and would likely never see again, which made introductory conversation pointless. Her boy du jour was tall and muscular, handsome but not especially bright-looking. He wore a sleeveless Utah Jazz jersey, which emphasized his biceps and myriad tattoos but seemed out of place considering the abundance of snow outside.

With the exception of Shelley and Margaret, everyone was sitting around the living room eating nachos and watching the Jazz play the Portland Trail Blazers. They had all gotten an early start on drinking, and empty beer cans littered the coffee table that three of them had their feet on. Cathy was the first to notice us. "Elise. Nicholas," she said. "You made it."

Everyone looked over.

"Hi, everyone," I said.

Nicholas looked as unsure of himself as he had when he first approached me in the food court.

"Hey," Mark said. "Help yourself to a beer. Got Bud in the fridge."

"Thank you," Nicholas said, making no movement to act on the offer.

"Come watch the game," Zoey said.

"Go ahead, sit," I said to Nicholas. "I'll get us some food."

Nicholas sat down on a chair next to the others. Zoey was holding an open beer. She already looked a little buzzed. She almost immediately leaned toward Nicholas, drawn like steel to a magnet. I walked to the kitchen table and began making ham and cheese sandwiches.

"Thanks for all the gifts you've been sending," Zoey said to him. "Especially the cheesecake. It was *dreamy*."

"I'm glad you liked it," Nicholas said casually, politely

glancing at her before looking back at the television. "What quarter are we in?" he asked.

"Just started the third," Mark said. "You ever watch the Jazz play?"

"Sometimes. We've got box seats," he said. "At the firm."

"And you're a partner, right?" Zoey asked rhetorically.

"Yes."

Zoey's date just stared ahead at the screen, sucking on a beer, completely oblivious to her obvious interest in my date.

I walked back over with our food. "Here you go," I said, handing Nicholas a plate with some of my salad and a sandwich. I sat down between Nicholas and Zoey.

"Thank you," Nicholas said, turning all his attention to me. For the next hour we just watched the game, which the Jazz ended up losing by four points.

"They never lose when I wear this shirt," Zoey's date said angrily.

"Are you ready to go?" I asked Nicholas.

"Whatever you want," he said.

"I'm ready."

"Okay," he said. "I'll get the coats." He walked out of the room.

Zoey stood and walked out after him. I also stood up and walked out, stopping in the hall just outside the living room. I could hear Zoey talking. "So where did you and Elise meet?"

"We just bumped into each other. In the building."

"I'm in the building," she said. There was a short pause,

then she added, "I'm sorry we never bumped into each other. I mean, before you two." There was another pause. "Is it serious? You and Elise."

"You mean, would I be interested in exploring other romantic possibilities?"

"You're so smart," she said. "Yes. I mean, hypo"—she struggled with the word—"hypo, hypothetically."

"That's a big word," Nicholas said.

"I'm not dumb," she said. "Maybe a little drunk."

"Hypothetically, no. I wouldn't. And you better get back to your date."

"He's an idiot," she said.

"We'll just keep that to ourselves," Nicholas replied.

I wasn't surprised by Zoey's antics, but I was still angry. I walked into the room glaring at her. "Let's get out of here," I said to Nicholas.

Zoey was either too drunk or too dumb to realize that I'd been listening. "Bye, Elise," she said.

I didn't answer her. I was fuming.

Nicholas took my arm. "Let's go home."

I didn't say much on the way back to my apartment. Nicholas must have known how I was feeling because he didn't pry. It had started snowing, and the BMW's windshield wipers kept beat to the Christmas songs on the radio. The cheerful tunes were completely incongruent with the thoughts running through my head, which were definitely not peace on earth goodwill to men.

Outside my apartment door Nicholas asked, "Are you okay?"

I blew up. "I can't believe she hit on you."

"Yes you can," he said calmly. "She was drunk."

"She would have done it anyway."

"Maybe."

"Why are you defending her?"

"I'm not. But don't go too hard on her. If she was happy with her life, she wouldn't have come after me. *And* she'd been drinking."

I took a deep breath. "I don't have to like her."

"No. But you do have to work with her. So you might as well keep things civil."

"Civil," I said angrily. "I want to pluck her eyelashes."

Nicholas laughed. "Promise me you won't do that. Or anything else. Just let it go."

"But she's a—"

He put a finger to my lips. "This is for your good," he said. "Trust me. Promise me."

Honestly, I liked that he was touching my lips. "All right," I finally said. "Why do you have to be so rational?"

"It's a habit."

After a moment I said, "May I ask you something?"

"Of course."

"If it wasn't for the contract, would you have hooked up with her?"

"No."

"Why not? Everyone else wants to."

"She's not my type."

"What's your type?"

He just smiled. "Let me know when you figure that out." He kissed me on the cheek. "Good night, Elise. I enjoyed being with you." He started to walk away, then stopped and turned back. "Oh, do you know what today is?"

"No."

"It's our midpoint. We're halfway through our contract." He turned and walked away.

I watched him walk out to his car before going inside. His final words hurt my heart even more than Zoey's betrayal.

CHAPTER

Eighteen

Everyone has a dark and light side. How much we see of either is usually less a matter of the moon's position than where we're standing.

Elise Dutton's Diary

In spite of my promise to Nicholas, the next day at work I treated Zoey coldly. I was still angry, hurt, and jealous, a perfect storm of emotion. Even if Nicholas wasn't really mine, Zoey didn't know that. She had scores of men and she went after mine. I'd never forgive her for being so cruel.

A little before noon Zoey brought a package into my office. "Here's your present," she said softly.

I glanced up only for a second, then went back to my work. "Just put it on the chair."

"Okay," she said. She didn't leave my office.

After a minute I said, "Do you need something?"

"Elise, I'm sorry."

"For what?" I asked innocently, forcing her confession.

"I had too much to drink last night and I hit on Nicholas at the party. I feel really bad."

"Why would you do that to me?" I asked, unleashing my anger. "What have I ever done to you?"

"I'm so sorry." Her eyes began welling up with tears. She wiped at them. "I'm an idiot, I know it. And just so you know, Nick didn't go for it for a second. He's completely loyal to you."

I still wasn't in a mood to forgive her, so I didn't say anything. Zoey started crying in earnest. She continued. "When I got home I was really mad at myself. I thought, *What's wrong with me? Why would I do that? Elise is such a good person.*" She grabbed a Kleenex from my desk. "The thing is, I'm just really insecure inside. I have this need to prove myself. It's like . . ." She shook her head. "This isn't coming out right." She took a deep breath, then said, "I'm sorry, okay? I'm just really jealous of you. Because, Nick is really great and he really loves you, and the guys I meet just love my body and the way I look and no one wants to keep me, they just want to use me. But Nick loves all of you. Inside and out. And you deserve that. You deserve a nice guy like him. You really do." I couldn't believe that Zoey was jealous of me. She looked at me, then said, "I'll quit bothering you. But I'm sorry." She turned to go.

"Zoey," I said.

She slowly turned back, wiping her eyes.

"I understand."

"You do?"

"I didn't know you felt that way. I've judged you wrong. I'm sorry."

After a minute she said, "Can I give you a hug?"

"Yes."

I stood while Zoey came around my desk and put her arms around me. "I'll never do that again," she said. "I promise."

"I know you won't."

"If I can do anything to make it up to you, just ask."

I looked at her a moment before asking, "Do you really mean that?"

She nodded.

"I have some parties coming up with Nicholas, and I don't have anything to wear."

"You want to borrow my clothes?"

"Right," I said. "I couldn't fit this body into anything you own. But I'm not good with fashion. I've been out of the game for too long. And everyone he works with is rich and cool."

She suddenly smiled. "You want me to dress you?"

"If you would."

"I'd love to."

"I don't have much money."

"We don't need money," she said. "I have friends. Can I work on your hair too?"

"Yes."

"We'll knock Nicholas off his feet," she said. "I mean, you will. I'll just help you."

"Thank you."

"When's your next party?"

"Saturday night."

"This Saturday?"

I nodded.

"Okay. I hope your Saturday is open, because we've got some work to do."

CHAPTER

Nineteen

Nicholas is like a golden ticket.

Elise Dutton's Diary

December first. Exactly one month since Nicholas had approached me in the food court. Zoey arrived at my apartment Saturday afternoon with a pile of dress bags, two large makeup boxes, a jewelry box, four shoe boxes, and a canvas bag filled with hair supplies. It took us three trips to get everything in from her car.

She had found me four dresses, all on "loan" from Nordstrom, where one of her ex-boyfriends was a manager. There were also several sets of matching jewelry for each dress.

All the dresses Zoey brought were stunning. I tried them all on, and Zoey snapped pictures of me with her phone. It took us an hour to settle on two. The one I would wear that night at the firm party was a black, form-fitting crepe sheath with a sheer top.

The other dress was the most expensive of the four: a one-shoulder nude evening gown with beads. I decided to save it for the partners' party, because we guessed it would be the fanciest of Nicholas's events.

We looked through her boxes of shoes, and for the first dress I chose a simple but elegant pair of black patent leather pumps. For the partners' party I chose a glittery pair of peep-toed high heels. Then we chose earrings and necklaces for both dresses.

With the dresses and accessories selected, we took a break and drove to the nearest Starbucks for a latte. After we got back we discussed my general look, experimenting with different shades of makeup for almost an hour. As Zoey worked on my makeup, she taught me some new techniques.

"You *can* teach an old dog new tricks," I said.

Zoey stepped back to look at me. "You're not *old*, and you're not a *dog*. Never, ever call yourself that."

"I was just joking," I said.

"Especially joking," she said. "Your subconscious mind doesn't know the difference. You need to be your own best cheerleader."

I was impressed by her counsel. There was a lot more to Zoey than I'd given her credit for.

Sitting in my kitchen, Zoey wasn't the same girl I knew in the office. She was much more funny, relaxed, and vulnerable. She was also sweet. She kept telling me that with my natural beauty I didn't need a makeover, just a few enhancements. "You don't make over gorgeous," she said.

I hadn't had a girlfriend since Kayla had betrayed me, and it was wonderful to have female companionship again. I wondered if, in spite of the age difference, Zoey and I might be friends. Nicholas had brought me out of my cave, and I was going to need someone to do things with after our contract expired.

Zoey worked on my hair for over an hour and experimented with several shades of lipstick before finding the right one. Finally, she stepped back and scrutinized me like a sculptor examining her creation. She nodded, then said, "Oh my, Elise. You should look at yourself."

I walked out to the hall mirror. I couldn't believe it. "I look pretty," I said.

"No, you look *hot.* He's in serious trouble."

While I was helping her pack up her things, Zoey said, "You and Nick are such a great couple. If you want, I'll help you with your makeup at your wedding."

I wasn't sure what to say. Finally I said, "I would like that."

Zoey left just a few minutes before Nicholas arrived. He rang the doorbell at seven. "Come in," I shouted, wanting to present myself properly.

He let himself in. "Hi, it's me."

"I'll be out in just a minute. Help yourself to the fridge. I think there's some soda and juice."

A moment later he said, "There's something green in a blender pitcher. Is it supposed to be green?"

"It's not mold," I said. "It just looks like it. That's my kale drink."

"Looks like kale," he said, which sounded like 'Looks like hell,' which I think was his intent. "How was your day?"

"Good."

"What did you do?"

"Not much," I said. "Zoey came over."

"After the other night, I'm surprised that you two are talking."

"She apologized for coming on to you."

I spritzed myself with perfume, took a good look at myself, then walked out into my front room. Nicholas was sitting on my couch. He immediately stood. "Wow."

"What?" I asked innocently.

"You look amazing."

I smiled. "Shall we go?"

Nicholas's office party was held each year at La Caille, an expensive French restaurant tucked away on a twenty-acre reserve at the mouth of Little Cottonwood Canyon. I had been to the restaurant only once before, for a wedding of one of Dan's co-workers, and I had never forgotten it. Housed in a stucco, ivy-covered French château, it had its own three-acre vineyard, and during the warmer months peacocks roamed the yard amid statuary and topiaries, while black and white swans glided in the swan pool. Tonight, the grounds were covered in snow and were extravagantly lit with strings of white lights.

Nicholas pulled his car up the restaurant's tree-lined cobblestone drive to a roundabout near the front door. He handed his keys to the valet, then took my arm and led me inside. The lobby was exquisite, with a large antique chandelier and parquet-tile floor. Harpsichord music softly echoed through the tile and stucco interior.

The young hostess who greeted us looked like a model, and, as I remembered from the wedding, all the waitresses wore low-cut gowns that were presumably all the rage in eighteenth-century France.

"Your firm rents the entire restaurant?" I asked.

"Every year," Nicholas said.

"What does that cost?"

"Enough," he said with a pained smile.

We walked up a circular stairway to the main dining room, which was crowded with several hundred of the firm's staff and guests. Everyone seemed pleased to see Nicholas.

"You're very popular," I said.

"Of course," he said. "I'm a partner. I help decide what they get paid. Would you like something to drink? They have remarkable eggnog."

"I would love an eggnog," I said.

"Coming up."

While I was waiting for Nicholas to return, a stunningly attractive woman in an eggplant-colored strapless evening gown walked up to me. "Hi, I'm Candace," she said.

"Hi. I'm Elise."

"You're Nick's girlfriend."

"I . . ." I smiled. "Yes."

"It's nice to meet you." Something about the way she said it made me doubt her sincerity.

"Are you a legal secretary at the firm?" I asked.

She practically grimaced with disgust. "No, I'm a lawyer," she said. "And what is it that you do?"

"I'm in travel," I said.

"Travel," she repeated lightly. "I avoid it if I can. I'm a diamond-level frequent flier with Delta."

"That's way too much time in the air," I said.

"You're telling me," she replied. "How did you and Nicholas meet?"

"We just started talking in the food court."

"The food court. At the office?"

"I know. Not very romantic."

"I guess I need to start eating more fast food. This Paleo diet certainly isn't doing anything for me."

"I would disagree," I said. "You look gorgeous."

She seemed surprised by the compliment. "Thank you."

Just then Nicholas returned, carrying two glasses. "Hello, Candace," he said.

Both her expression and her body language changed as if someone had flipped a switch. "Hello, Nicholas."

Nicholas handed me my drink. "One eggnog."

"Thank you," I said.

"Candace is one of our more successful litigators," Nicholas said.

"What he really means is that I have more billable hours than most."

"That too," he said, smiling.

She took a step toward him. "I heard about the Bellagio case. That should be interesting."

"I might have to make a few research trips to Las Vegas."

"Oh, that sounds painful. If you need any backup, I'd be happy to help."

"Thanks for the offer," he said.

"Think about it," she said. "Have a good night." She glanced at me once more, then said rather stiffly, "It was nice to meet you, Alicia." She turned and walked off.

I stood there, a little stunned.

"Sorry about that, Alicia," Nicholas said.

"Was that intentional?"

"Probably." He took my arm. "Come on, let me introduce you to some of the others."

I followed Nicholas from one side of the restaurant to the other as he shook hands and introduced me to what seemed like a hundred strangers. Near the center of the room I was glad to see Scott and Sharon Hitesman. While Nicholas and Scott talked, Sharon sidled up to me.

"Elise, you look stunning."

"Thank you. And thank you again for letting me crash your Thanksgiving dinner."

"You have no idea how glad I was to finally see Nicholas with someone. He deserves someone like you."

"Someone like me?" I said.

She smiled at me. "Someone who makes him happy."

A minute later Nicholas returned to my side to resume our tour of the floor. He was definitely well liked. And, with the exception of Candace's snub, everyone was friendly.

"Hungry?" Nicholas asked.

"I'm starving."

"Me too. Enough of this obligatory socializing, let's eat."

Like the surroundings, the fare was extravagant—the opposite of my office party. Actually, everything was the opposite of my office party. Instead of a plastic Tupperware bowl filled with ice and beer, there were silver ice buckets with expensive wines and a large ice sculpture of a swan.

"It's not Cafe Rio," Nicholas said, "but it's edible."

"It may surprise you, but I actually eat more than Cafe Rio."

"Yes, I've seen you eat turkey," he said. "And steak. And Chinese food."

"And Thai," I added.

"I think I'm getting through to you," he said, setting some shrimp on his plate. "I love shrimp."

"I love shrimp, too," I said.

"I'll get enough for both of us." He loaded up his own plate, then pointed at some other things for me to get. Salmon on rice, roast chicken, crab-stuffed mushrooms, quiche, Brie and pâté de foie gras with crackers, chocolate-dipped strawberries, and puff pastries shaped like swans.

We carried our plates up the stairs to a small dining room where there was only one other couple. Nicholas found us a quiet place tucked in the corner behind the servers' station.

"So what do you think of our party?"

"I feel a little out of place," I said. "Everything is so nice."

"You deserve nice," he said. "Thank you for coming with me. Usually I just put in my time, eat a few shrimp, and bolt. It's been really nice having you here."

"I think everyone's fooled," I said.

"What do you mean?"

"They really think we're a couple."

He ate a few more shrimp, then said, "You know what's sad is that we might be one of the most authentic couples here tonight."

"What do you mean?"

"Charles, Blake, and Stephanie are having affairs. Phil and his paralegal Rachel have mysteriously disappeared at the same time every Thursday afternoon for the last three years, and Kurt is waiting for the optimum financial opportunity to divorce his wife. What we have might be more real than much of what we saw out there tonight."

"Are Scott and Sharon happy?"

"Yes. They're the real thing."

"They seem happy," I said.

Nicholas must have tired of the topic because he took a drink of eggnog and said, "I know I said it before, but you really do look beautiful tonight."

"It's the dress."

"That's like saying the *Mona Lisa* is beautiful because of its frame."

We stole off from the party without saying good-bye. Nicholas took the long way back to my place, which I didn't mind. I didn't want the night to end. It was almost midnight when he pulled up in front of my apartment.

"I hope that wasn't too painful," he said.

"No. It was really nice. Actually, I haven't been anywhere

that nice for a long time. They treated me better than my own colleagues."

"You can accuse us lawyers of many things, but we are civil. At least most of the time. Candace could have been nicer."

"I'm afraid I drew first blood."

"How's that?"

"I asked her if she was a legal secretary."

Nicholas grimaced. "Yes, that would definitely pull her chain."

"I'm sorry," I said.

"It's all right. She'll get over it." He leaned over and kissed me on the cheek. "Good night, Elise."

"Good night." I reached for the door handle, then looked back. "May I ask you something?"

"Of course."

"Why are you so nice to me?"

He was quiet a moment, then said, "It makes me sad that you had to ask."

I didn't know what to say to that. "Good night, Nicholas. Thank you for a lovely evening."

"It was my pleasure."

That night as I lay alone in bed thinking about how nice the evening had been, a terrible thought crossed my mind. *Maybe I shouldn't have signed the contract after all.* Sometimes it's just better not to know what you're missing.

CHAPTER *Twenty*

Something is wrong with Nicholas. I wish I knew what to do.

Elise Dutton's Diary

For the first time since I'd started working at ICE, I found myself looking forward to Monday. More specifically, seeing Nicholas. And I loved anticipating his gifts. I don't know how he kept up with them. Though I suspected his secretary helped with them, I was sure that he picked them out himself. Monday I got a candle scented like Christmas sugar cookies, on Tuesday a DVD of *A Christmas Carol* (the George C. Scott version of course), and on Wednesday a CD of a Kenny G Christmas album.

On Thursday the sixth, something changed. There was no gift. And Nicholas was different. He was tense and withdrawn. He wasn't just acting different, he looked different. At lunch he barely ate. He barely spoke. He barely even looked at me. I wondered if I'd done something to upset him.

Finally, I asked, "Is something wrong at work?"

"No," he said darkly. "Same old tricks. People suing each other, divorcing each other, contesting wills, brother against brother, sister against sister, everyone looking out for themselves." He shook his head with disgust. "As if there weren't already enough pain in this godforsaken world."

The tone of his voice frightened me. After a moment I asked, "Are you okay?"

He pushed his salad around a little, then looked up. "I'm fine."

"You're not yourself today."

"It's nothing," he said.

We sat quietly for a moment until I said, "If I did something . . ."

"It's nothing," he repeated sharply.

Emotion rose in my chest. "I'm sorry," I said. I stood. "I better go."

He likewise stood, reaching for my arm. "No, please. I'm sorry. I didn't mean that." He hesitated for a moment, then said, "I'm just under a lot of pressure. I'm really sorry I snapped. Please . . . forgive me."

I looked into his anxious eyes. It was more than stress. There was pain in them. "Okay." We both sat back down. After a moment I said, "It's not your fault. I kept pushing you. I was afraid that maybe I'd done something wrong."

He looked at me for a moment, then said, "It's not you."

"If I can do anything to make you feel better . . ."

He reached across the table and took my hand. "If there were something anyone could do, you would be the one I'd go to. I'll be okay. I promise. I go through this every year around this time. It will pass."

I wondered what he'd meant by that, but I wasn't about to ask. We sat there for a few more minutes eating in awkward silence. I wasn't really hungry anymore, and there didn't seem to be much more to say. "I guess I better let you go," I said.

He looked sad. "I'm sorry I wasn't better company." We both stood. "I'll see you on Monday." He turned to go.

"Nicholas," I said. I walked up to him and put my arms around him. "I don't know what's going on. But I care." I hugged him tighter.

When I stepped back, I noticed that his eyes were slightly red. "Thank you," he said softly. "That means more than you know." He turned and walked away.

The next day I didn't leave my office at lunchtime, which everyone noticed.

"Where's Nick?" Zoey asked.

"He's out of town," I said, not really knowing where he was. It just seemed the best way to explain why I wasn't with him.

"Good. Then you can come to lunch with us," Zoey said. "Cathy and I are going to get sushi."

"Thanks," I said. "But I'm not hungry."

Zoey touched my arm. "Are you okay?"

"Nicholas is just acting a little different."

She nodded. "It will be okay. Sometimes men just need some space. Some cave time."

I forced a smile. "I'm sure you're right." Inside I wasn't sure.

I worried about Nicholas all weekend. I wanted to call him, but never did. Maybe it was just fear, but something told me not to. Our time apart revealed to me just how much I cared about him and needed him. I was beginning to fear Christmas.

CHAPTER Twenty-one

When I signed the contract I knew the relationship was fake. So why doesn't it feel that way anymore?

Elise Dutton's Diary

I was anxious from the moment I woke on Monday. For the first time since I'd signed the contract I was nervous to see Nicholas. My anxiety grew as lunchtime neared.

About a half hour before noon Mark walked into my office. "We've got a problem," he said. "The Marriott you booked in New York for our Dayton group has a gas leak and had to evacuate. We've got sixty kids on a bus and no place to stay for the night."

I groaned. "All right. I'll get on the phone." I pulled up my list of New York hotels and began calling. Nicholas called from the food court at a quarter after noon. I had been so involved in my crisis that I hadn't realized what time it was.

"You're standing me up?" he asked.

"I'm sorry, I didn't realize it was so late."

"Then I'll wait," he said.

"No, I can't come."

"Then you *are* standing me up?"

"No, it's just, I have a problem. One of my hotels shut down, and I need to find someplace for sixty kids to stay. This might take all afternoon."

He was quiet a moment before he said, "Well, you have to eat. I'll bring something up."

"That would be great," I said.

"Pork salad?"

"Anything," I said.

Nicholas arrived about fifteen minutes later carrying a bag of food. As worried as I had been to see him, he looked fine. He set the bag on my desk. "Here you go," he said. "Change of cuisine."

"What did you get?"

"A Chick-fil-A sandwich. I figured you need something you can eat while you talk on the phone." He brought out the sandwich and a drink and laid them on my desk. "And the lemonade is sugar-free. How's it going?"

"Not well. It's hard finding a block of that many rooms last minute."

"Can I help you call?"

"Really?"

"Why not?"

"How much time do you have?"

"Maybe forty-five minutes."

"That would help." I printed off a list of hotels, then tore it in half. "Just tell them it's an emergency and ask if they have a block of thirty-two rooms, double-occupancy, for tonight."

"What if they have availability for twenty?"

"That's not enough."

"I know, but couldn't you use two hotels?"

"If we have to," I said. "But they'd have to be close to each other."

"What phone should I use?"

"There's one out in the reception area. Use line three."

"Line three," he said, walking out with the paper I'd given him. Less than a half hour later he walked back into my office. "I've got one on the line," he said. He laid the list down on my desk. "I circled it," he said. "The Liss Suites in Brooklyn."

He had doodled all over my phone list. There was a cartoon picture of a woman with her hair on fire.

"Is this supposed to be me?"

"No. Maybe."

"It looks like me."

He grinned. "It probably is."

In spite of my stress I laughed. "Okay, so did they give you a rate?"

"No. But the manager said that they'd match your rate if it was reasonable."

"You're a doll," I said. I picked up the phone while Nicholas sat back and watched. The hotel worked out perfectly. It was actually nicer than the one I had originally reserved.

"Sounds like my work here is done," Nicholas said as I hung up.

"Thank you. Thank you."

"You're welcome."

"You're good at this. You might put me out of my job someday."

"I've been looking for something meaningful to do with my life," he said.

"You saved sixty kids from sleeping on the streets of New York."

He stood, "Sorry to save the day and run, but I need to get back to my other job."

"I'll walk you to the elevator," I said.

In the hallway he asked, "How was your weekend?"

I looked him in the eyes. "Awful." We stopped in front of the elevator.

"Why awful?"

"Because all I did was worry about you."

He was quiet a moment then said, "Thank you for worrying." He pushed the up button and said, "I told you I'd be okay."

"I know. You look much better."

"I am."

"So, I'll see you tomorrow?"

"I'm around all week. And we have the partners' party this Friday."

"When do you leave for New York?"

"Monday. Have you ever been to New York at Christmastime?"

"I've never been to New York at any time."

"Not even to check out the hotels?"

"Not even. Either Mark or one of our guides does that."

"That's a shame," he said. "There's no place like New York at Christmas. Rockefeller Center, Fifth Avenue, Radio City Music Hall. It's magical."

"Maybe someday," I said.

"Come with me next week."

"Yeah, right," I said.

He looked at me seriously. "You said we'd see how things were going. I think they're going well, don't you?"

"Yes," I said.

"Then come with me. I'll have meetings during the day, but you can go sightseeing. Then at night, we'll go out on the town. It will be fun."

"I'd have to see if I can take the time off."

"How much vacation time do you have?"

"I don't know."

"When was the last time you took a vacation?"

"I don't know."

"Exactly. Time to cash some in." When I didn't speak, he said, "Look, when are you going to get another offer for an all-expenses-paid trip to New York City?"

"I'll think about it," I said.

"All right. You think about it. But let me know soon so we can book your flight. The flights get pretty full this time of year."

"Okay," I said. "I'll let you know by tomorrow."

Just then the elevator bell rang. Zoey and Cathy stepped out.

"Hi, Nick," Zoey said. "Hi, Elise."

"Hello, ladies," Nicholas said. He leaned forward and kissed me on the cheek. "Think about it." He stepped past them into the elevator. "Have a good day."

After the door shut Zoey said, "Think about what?"

"Did he propose to you?" Cathy asked.

"No," I said. "He wants me to go to New York with him."

"At Christmas?" Zoey said. "New York is amazing at Christmas. What's there to think about?"

I thought for just a moment, then said, "You're right."

I called Nicholas just ten minutes later. "I want to go."

"Excellent," he said. "I'll have Sabrina book the flight."

"How long will we be there?"

"All week," he said.

"I'm so excited."

"Me too," he said. "You're going to love it."

CHAPTER

Twenty-two

Tonight Nicholas took me to his home. I would have liked to stay longer. Much longer. Like forever.

Elise Dutton's Diary

Nicholas and I skipped lunch the next Friday because he had too much to do before leaving town. Instead I spent my lunch break with Zoey, who used the time to fix my hair for Nicholas's partners' party.

"You better take a lot of pictures tonight," she said. "I want to see you in that dress. Do you remember which earrings we picked out?"

"We put them in a Ziploc bag and wrote the date on it with a Sharpie."

She laughed. "Oh, yeah. No margin for error."

"I'm a little nervous," I said. "That first party was so fancy, but I'm afraid this one is going to be more so."

"Just have fun. You're going to be great."

"I just don't want to embarrass Nicholas in front of his partners."

"The only problem you'll have is all their wives will hate you."

"Why would they hate me?"

"Because all their husbands will be ogling you."

I smiled. I was sure Zoey had had more than her share of wife-hate.

"Speaking of ogling," she said, "have you noticed how Mark looks at you these days?"

The comment caught me off guard. "He's married."

"Yes, but he's not blind."

"Why would he suddenly notice me?"

"Probably because someone else did," she replied.

When I got home from work I took a quick shower, then put on *the dress*—the silk masterpiece Zoey and I had chosen for tonight. I had never worn anything so elegant. It hung from one shoulder, and the beads sewn into the fabric shimmered as I moved. Then I put on the jewelry that we had picked out. The earrings were larger than I was used to, but they matched the elegance of the dress. The heels I'd chosen were also taller than I usually wore, but they made a statement as well. I felt gorgeous.

Nicholas shook his head when he saw me. "Wow," he said. "Just wow."

The party was held at the founder's home on Walker Lane. It was only twenty minutes from my apartment but a world away.

The house was a mansion. Or, more accurately, a villa, since it was Italian in design with rock and stucco exterior, a large, pillared portico, and beautiful wrought-iron front doors. Gas lights highlighted the brick-lined arched portals of the four-car garage. The yard was lit like a resort with lush landscaping and statuary.

Nicholas took my arm, and we walked up to the front door. A man standing in the lit portico opened the door for us. As we stepped inside the foyer we were embraced by a rush of light, smells, and music. The floor was polished wood, covered in places with lush area rugs. A brass chandelier, at least eight feet in diameter, hung above us from the high, domed ceiling.

In the sitting room across from the front door, a young woman was playing a harp next to a group I assumed, from the instruments around them, were members of a string quartet taking a break. I had never been inside such a luxurious home. I felt even more out of place than I had at La Caille. As usual, Nicholas was in his element.

"I don't think they'll be serving jalapeño poppers and Budweiser," I said.

"And the party will be the worse for it," he replied.

"May I take your coat?" a young man asked.

"Yes, please," Nicholas said. He helped me off with the stole Zoey had also brought me and handed it to the man.

Just then a mature, silver-haired man wearing a beautiful burgundy suit walked up to us. He was accompanied by an elegant woman I guessed to be his wife. "Nicholas," he said. "You made it."

"And this time you brought someone," the woman said. "And she's lovely."

"Thank you," I said.

"Elise, this is Alan McKay, our senior partner, and his better half, Careen."

"Thank you for having us," I said. "Your home is beautiful."

"Thank you, dear. We enjoy it."

"Food and drink is that way," Alan said, pointing to a side room. "Please, enjoy yourselves."

"Thanks, Alan," Nicholas said. "Careen."

Our hosts flitted away like butterflies.

"They were nice," I said.

"They're good people," Nicholas said. "Alan is the firm's founder and senior partner. He's also the one who brought me over from the prosecutor's office."

The party was considerably smaller than the one at La Caille, with maybe thirty guests in all. As we walked around I recognized some of the lawyers from a couple weeks earlier.

"Will Scott and Sharon be here?" I asked.

"No. Scott's not a partner. At least not yet."

"How many partners are there?"

"Eleven."

"And how many lawyers does your firm have?"

"Ninety-seven."

"How come you're the one with your name on the door?"

"They like me."

There were two food tables in the dining room, one savory, one sweet. At the head of the savory table was a man in a white chef's coat and hat, carving roast beef. There were also various hors d'oeuvres: bacon-wrapped scallops, crab puffs, jumbo prawns, caviar, carpaccio, and sushi.

The sweet table had three chocolate fountains with dark, white, and milk chocolates, the bases of the fountains surrounded by fruit. There were miniature key lime pies and cheesecakes, sweet croissants, puff pastries, baklava, millefoglie, and dipped chocolates.

"This is amazing," I said. "I think I'm going to gain weight."

"I'll help," Nicholas said.

We filled up our plates and sat down near the musicians. A few people came by to talk to Nicholas. They were all very warm and welcoming.

When I had finished my plate, Nicholas said, "Would you like to see the house?"

"I'd love to. Will they mind?"

"No," Nicholas said. "Alan loves to show it off."

"Why wouldn't he?" I said.

Nicholas led me up the circular stairs to a long hallway, both sides of which were lined with doors. The hallway led to another hallway and ended at a loft and another set of stairs.

"I could get lost in here," I said.

"Lots of people do," he said. "Come look at this." We walked into a spacious room lined with bookshelves, many filled with leather books. It had a fireplace with an antique model of a ship on its mantel, and in the center of the room was a beautiful antique desk. The ceiling was high and multifaceted with a wooden beam stretching the length of the room.

"This is Alan's den," Nicholas said.

"It's beautiful."

"Alan likes nice things."

I turned back to him. "Are Alan and Careen happy?"

Nicholas pondered the question. "They've been married almost forty years, so I hope so. Alan's not an especially affectionate man, so their relationship is very partner-like, which isn't necessarily a bad thing."

"But he's not cheating on her."

Nicholas shook his head. "Oh no. He's a man of strong ethics and a very conservative Catholic. He once told one of the lawyers, 'If you're going through a midlife crisis, don't cheat. Buy yourself a Ferrari instead. It's cheaper.' " Nicholas smiled. "Want to see something cool?"

"Yes."

He pushed on one of the shelves, and it opened into a room. I clapped. "That's like in the movies."

"Every man wants a bookshelf that opens into a secret room."

"Where does it go?"

"Come inside," he said.

We stepped into the room. Like the outer room it had bookshelves, though the books weren't legal tomes but novels and personal reading, including a few Grisham, Patterson, and Vince Flynn thrillers. There were also several framed photographs of Alan with famous people, including President Bill Clinton, Bob Hope, and Maureen O'Hara.

"Actually, it's a safe room," Nicholas said. "In case terrorists or someone crazy breaks into his house. They can hide in here until the police arrive."

"Sometimes I'd like a safe room to hide in," I said.

"To hide from what?" Nicholas asked.

"Life."

Nicholas looked at me, then nodded as if he understood. "My father served in Vietnam. When I was young he told me that everyone needs an emotional foxhole. A place to hide when life's storms hit."

"Do you?"

"Of course," he said. "There's a quote widely misattributed to Plato that says, 'Be kind, for everyone you meet is fighting a hard battle.' It's true. Everyone has struggles. Everyone has suffered more than you know. That includes you and me."

I didn't know what to say, so I just nodded.

We walked back downstairs. The string quartet had resumed playing. Nicholas introduced me to a few more people, and then we went back and sat down next to the musicians.

As I looked around the ornately furnished room, I wondered what Nicholas's house must be like. "Where do *you* live?" I asked.

"Not far from here, actually." He suddenly smiled. "Would you like to see my house?"

"Yes."

His smile turned to a conspicuous grin.

"What?" I asked.

"When I first offered the contract you asked if this ended

up back at my place. I bet you didn't think you'd be asking me to go."

I grinned back. "A lot has changed since then," I said.

✦

Nicholas lived less than ten minutes away. His home was new, a Cape Cod–style house with shutters and a large front porch. He pulled his car into the garage. The door from the garage opened into the kitchen, where he flipped on the lights. The room was bright and immaculate, with not even a dish in the sink.

"This is really cute," I said.

"Wasn't really going for *cute,*" he replied.

"It's big," I said.

"For one person it is."

"It's big for a lot of people," I said.

"Hopefully I won't always be living here alone," he replied.

There were pictures on the wall. "Is this your family?" I asked.

He nodded.

"This is you with the long hair?"

"I'm afraid so."

"How old were you?"

He leaned forward for a closer look. "I think I was fifteen in that one." In none of the pictures was Nicholas older than fifteen or sixteen.

"These are your parents?" I asked.

"Yes."

"Have they ever been here?"

"No. My mother died before I built the home. My father wouldn't come."

"You know, you might be the cleanest bachelor in the country. You must have a cleaner."

"Rosa," he said. "She comes once a week. But actually, I'm pretty OCD. I don't like a messy house."

"I would drive you crazy."

I looked over a long row of porcelain figurines he had displayed on a shelf. He had three female nudes with angel wings, a larger piece of a mother breast-feeding her baby, and a glossy figurine of Don Quixote sitting in a chair holding an open book on his lap and a sword in his hand. "Tell me about these," I said.

"I collect Lladró. I just think they're beautiful. There's one piece I'm coveting, but I haven't gotten up the nerve to buy it yet. It's Cinderella in her pumpkin carriage with her horses and groomsmen. It's more than thirty thousand dollars."

"Wow," I said. "I can't imagine spending that much on art. Do you think you'll buy it?"

"I'll buy it someday," he said.

"I hope you let me see it when you do."

"Of course. You like Cinderella?"

"Who doesn't like Cinderella?"

He just looked at me thoughtfully, then changed the subject. "So are you ready for New York?"

"I haven't finished packing, but I'm very excited." I looked at him. "May I ask you a delicate question?"

"Of course."

"Are we sharing a room in New York?"

For a moment he just looked at me, and I had no idea how he was taking the question. Had I embarrassed him by implying that I didn't want to be with him, or had I embarrassed myself by presuming that he would? "I'm sorry," I said. "I didn't know."

"No, we're not," he said. "I booked you a separate room. It's in the contract." The moment settled into silence. Then he said, "It's late. I better get you home."

We were mostly quiet on the drive back to my apartment. He pulled up front and walked me to my door.

"Thank you for coming with me tonight," he said. "I've never enjoyed the partners' party more."

"Best partners' party I've ever been to," I said, smiling. "Thank you for letting me into your world."

We just stood there looking at each other. I suppose that I was still afraid I had offended him with my question about rooms in New York. But even greater than my fear was my desire that he would kiss me—not just on the cheek as he did in public, but really kiss me, passionately. Finally he leaned forward and kissed me on the cheek. "Good night, Elise."

"Good night, Nicholas," I said softly, hiding my disappointment. "I'll see you Monday morning."

He turned and walked away. I walked alone into my dark apartment. *The night had been magical. Why didn't he kiss me? Was I reading this all wrong?*

CHAPTER

Twenty-three

I'm a long way from Montezuma Creek.

Elise Dutton's Diary

Monday morning, Nicholas arrived at my apartment a little after eight-thirty. I came to the door dragging my suitcase, which he looked at in wonder. "That's what you're bringing?"

"Yes."

"Did I tell you we'd be gone for five days or five weeks?"

"A woman needs more things."

"Playing the gender card," he said, smiling. "Let me get that." He lugged my massive bag down the stairs, opened his car trunk by remote, and dropped it inside while I climbed into the passenger seat.

He turned to me and said, "Ready for an adventure?"

"I'm always ready for an adventure," I said.

On the way to the airport Nicholas asked, "When was the last time you flew?"

"It's been a while."

"How long's a while?"

"About eleven years. It was my honeymoon."

"Where did you go?"

"Orange County. We went to Disneyland."

The airport was thick with travelers. I didn't know if it was busier than usual since I hadn't flown for so long.

"I can't believe all the people," I said. "Is it always this crowded?"

"It's the season. The airports are always crazy during the holidays." He looked at me. "Are you afraid of flying?"

"No," I said, shaking my head. "I'm afraid of . . . *not* flying."

"What do you mean?"

"As long as you're in the air there's no problem, right? It's coming back to earth that's the problem."

He grinned. "I think you just said something profound about life."

Our flight was direct from Salt Lake to JFK. Nicholas had booked two first-class tickets, which secretly thrilled me. I had never flown first-class before. We boarded first, before the throng of passengers that surrounded the gate.

"So this is how the other half lives," I said, sitting back in the wide, padded seat.

"When you fly as much as I do, it's more of a necessity than a luxury."

"It's still luxury," I said.

I must have looked a little nervous as the plane took off because he reached over and took my hand. Or maybe he just wanted to hold my hand. I hoped for the latter.

"Is our hotel in the city?" I asked.

"We're staying at the Parker Meridien on Fifty-Sixth," he said. "It's a nice hotel. French. And it's close to things. It's only six blocks from Rockefeller Center."

"That's where the big Christmas tree is," I said.

He nodded. "And we're only one block from Fifth Avenue."

"What's on Fifth Avenue?"

"Shopping," he said.

The flight was just a little over four hours. Nicholas fell asleep shortly after they served us lunch. As hard as he worked, I wasn't surprised. Even though I hadn't slept well the night before, I couldn't sleep on the plane. I was too excited. I felt like a girl on her first school field trip. Nicholas didn't wake until we began our descent. He rubbed his eyes, looked around, then checked his watch. "I slept for two hours. Why didn't you wake me?"

"You needed the sleep," I said.

After we had disembarked, Nicholas stopped in a terminal store for some melatonin, then I followed him through the labyrinth of JFK to get our luggage. Downstairs, next to the baggage carousel, was a man in a black suit and cap holding a sign with my name on it.

ELISE DUTTON

"Is that for me?" I asked, which I realized was a foolish question.

"Of course," Nicholas said.

"I've never had someone holding a sign for me."

The man took our bags, and we followed him out into the cold to a black Lincoln Town Car. The ride took us across the Triborough Bridge into Manhattan, which gave us a clear view of the city's famous skyline. "Is that the Empire

State Building?" I asked, pointing at a tall building lit red and green.

Nicholas nodded. "They light it for the season. The last time I was here it was purple to honor our soldiers with the Purple Heart."

The Parker Meridien was just off Sixth Avenue. The lobby was spacious with modern European design and a wry sense of humor. The elevators had televisions that played old Charlie Chaplin movies or Tom and Jerry cartoons, and the room's Do Not Disturb sign was a long hanger that read FUGGETABOUTIT, congruent with the hotel's slogan, "Uptown. Not Uptight."

After Nicholas checked us in, a bellman brought our bags to our rooms on the eleventh floor, just two doors from each other.

For dinner we ate Thai food at a tiny restaurant near the hotel. We said goodnight to each other outside my hotel room.

"I need to do some prep work for tomorrow," Nicholas said. "So I'll see you in the morning. My meetings begin at nine. If you'd like to have breakfast together, there's Norma's on the main floor. Or, you can sleep in and order room service. Whatever you want."

"I want to be with you," I said.

He looked pleased with my reply. "I'll knock on your door at seven-forty-five. Don't forget to turn your watch ahead two hours. I'll see you in the morning." He kissed me on the cheek.

He started to go, but I stopped him. "Nicholas."

"Yes?"

"Thank you."

"You're welcome, Elise. Sleep tight."

I shut my door and lay down on top of the bed thinking about how happy I was. I had never had so much fun.

There was only one week left on our contract.

I didn't fall asleep until after two, so I was tired when Nicholas knocked on my door at a quarter to eight. He looked sharp in his suit and tie.

"You look nice," I said. "Very professional." I didn't. I had just pulled on some jeans and a sweater.

"Shall we go?"

Norma's was a hip restaurant located in the hotel's lobby. I looked over the orange and black menu. "So many choices. Everything looks good."

"They're famous for their breakfasts."

"Oh my," I said, laughing. "Look at this. The Zillion Dollar Lobster Frittata. It's a thousand dollars."

"That's with ten ounces of sevruga caviar," he said. "Read what it says underneath the price."

"Norma dares you to expense this." I looked up. "What would you do if I ordered that?"

"Cancel tonight's dinner."

"I'll get something else," I said quickly. "Who are you meeting with this morning?"

"It's a software company called Revelar. They're buying

up a competitor, and I'm here to make sure that they cross their *t*'s and dot their *i*'s. What are you going to do today?"

"I'm not sure yet."

"Well, unfortunately, it's New York, so there's not much to do," he said. "Especially at Christmastime."

I grinned. "I thought I'd walk around and see the sights."

"You could take the ferry to the Statue of Liberty and Ellis Island. Or you could take a tour of the Empire State Building. Also, you're not far from Fifth Avenue, where all the good shopping is—Saks, Tiffany's, Cartier, Prada, the good stuff."

"The good expensive stuff," I said.

"I'll be done a little after four. I made reservations for six at Keens Steakhouse. Then I thought we'd take in a show."

"What are we going to see?"

"That's a surprise," he said. He looked down at his watch. "I better go." He downed his coffee, then stood. "I'll see you this afternoon."

"Good luck," I said.

He stopped and turned back. "I almost forgot." He handed me his credit card. "Have fun."

I just looked at it. "What am I supposed to do with it?"

"Use it."

I watched him walk out. Then I put the card in my pocket and ordered another cup of hot chocolate.

I went back to my room to finish getting ready, then I took a taxi down to the Empire State Building and rode the elevator one hundred two floors to the top observation deck. It was amazing to look out over the entire city. Afterward I walked just a few blocks over to Macy's on Thirty-Fourth Street, joining the throngs of sightseers gathered in front of the store to see the famous animated holiday windows. The theme was the Magic of Christmas, which seemed appropriate for me this year.

I got into a taxi to go back to the hotel but, on a whim, asked the driver for a recommendation for a good place to eat lunch. He was from São Paulo and he took me to a café in Little Brazil just a block off Sixth Avenue. The stew my waiter recommended was different but good. To drink I had a sugarcane juice mixed with pineapple juice. I walked the ten blocks back to the hotel, undressed, and took a nap. I woke to my room phone ringing.

"I'm sorry I'm late," Nicholas said. "Our meetings went long."

"What time is it?" I asked, sitting up.

"Did I wake you?"

"Yes."

"It's almost five. We should leave for dinner in a half hour."

"I'll be ready," I yawned. I got out of bed, splashed water on my face, dressed in a nicer outfit, and fixed my hair. I was putting on fresh makeup when he knocked. I opened the door. He was still wearing his suit but with a fresh shirt and his collar open. He looked handsome. He always looked handsome.

✦

Keens Steakhouse was in the Garment District between Fifth and Sixth Avenues, though, at the time of its founding, in 1885, the area was considered the Theater District and was frequented by those on both sides of the curtain.

The restaurant was crowded, and the inside was paneled in dark mahogany, covered with framed black-and-white pictures. The rooms were mostly lit by indirect lighting, creating the ambience of a nineteenth-century gentlemen's club, which, in fact, it was. The tables were close together and skirted with white linen cloths. A large, gilt-framed picture of a nude hung above the bar, reminding me of an old western saloon.

Nicholas ordered a half dozen oysters on the shell, which I tried but didn't care for. Then I had tomatoes and onions with blue Stilton cheese, and we shared a Chateaubriand steak for two. The food was incredible.

"What's that on the ceiling?" I asked.

He looked up. "Pipes."

"Pipes?"

"Clay smoking pipes. Every one of them is numbered. In the old days you would request your pipe, and they would find it by its number and bring it to your table. I'm not sure how many pipes are still up there, but I've heard more than eighty thousand. They belonged to people like Teddy Roosevelt, Babe Ruth, Albert Einstein, Buffalo Bill Cody, pretty much everybody who was famous came here. Except the women. It used to be that women weren't allowed inside. It took a lawsuit from King Edward the Seventh's paramour to open it to women."

"When was that?"

"Turn of the century."

"Just a decade ago?"

He smiled. "No. The previous century."

Our conversation was interrupted by my cell phone ringing. "Sorry, I forgot to turn it off," I said. I glanced at the screen, then quickly pressed the power button.

"Was it important?"

"No. It was Dan."

"Does he call you often?"

"No. More lately since his wife left him."

"His wife," Nicholas said. "The one that was your friend?"

I nodded. "Kayla."

"And he wants a shoulder to cry on?"

"He wants more than a shoulder. He wants to get back together."

"He told you that?"

"Right after he reminded me that it was my fault he divorced me."

"Your fault?"

I nodded. "Because of—" I caught myself. "It doesn't matter," I said. "There's no way I would ever go back to him."

"Did you tell him that?"

"Yes."

Nicholas nodded. "Good," he said. "You deserve better than him. So what did you do today?"

"I went to the top of the Empire State Building. Then I walked over to Macy's and looked at their windows, then

I went to a café in Little Brazil for lunch and had this interesting stew. I don't remember what it's called, but the waiter said it's the Brazilian national dish."

"It's called *feijoada*," Nicholas said.

I looked at him in amazement. "Is there anything you don't know?"

He shook his head. "I don't know."

I laughed. "You are the smartest person I know."

"Then you must not know many people," he replied.

As we were finishing dessert, he reached into his pocket and brought out a piece of paper. "I have something for you. I should have done this for you earlier."

"What is it?"

"During my meetings I made a list of things you should do or where you should eat during the day. Actually, it's mostly eating."

I reviewed the list.

Serendipity 3 (Frozen hot chocolate)
Hamburger in lobby at Parker Meridien
Met Museum
Ellen's Stardust Diner (breakfast)
Carnegie Deli (egg cream)

"All right," I said looking up, "Give me the rundown."

"Serendipity 3 is between Second and Third Avenues. It's famous for celebrity clients like Marilyn Monroe and Andy Warhol, but food-wise, it's famous for the frozen hot chocolate. On their fiftieth anniversary they created the world's most expensive dessert, which was basically a thousand-dollar ice cream sundae."

"A thousand dollars. What's on it, gold?"

"That's exactly what's on it. Twenty-three-karat gold leaf, Madagascar vanilla, the world's most expensive chocolate, and gold caviar."

"I won't be having that."

"Thank you," he said. "Next on the list, if you're craving a burger, the hamburger joint in the lobby of our hotel has one of New York's best."

"There's a hamburger joint in our hotel?"

"I know, strange, right? It's behind the curtain just past the registration counter. You wouldn't know it's there unless someone told you. The menu signs are all handwritten in marker." He looked back down at the list. "Next is the Met, the Metropolitan Museum of Art. But I'm sure you're already familiar with it."

"We send students there."

"Time to send yourself," he said. "Be warned: it will take most of your day. And for breakfast, if you want something different, we're not far from Ellen's Stardust Diner. It's a retro fifties diner that attracts a lot of Broadway actor wannabes as waiters and waitresses, so occasionally they break into song. The challah French toast is especially good.

"Then, just a couple blocks from the hotel is the Carnegie Deli. It's also a good lunch stop. They're known for their pastrami and corned beef, but I'd go there just for the egg cream."

"What's an egg cream?"

"It's a soda, basically. Ironically it has neither eggs nor cream, but you must try it. I always have at least one when I come here. The Reuben sandwiches are definitely more than you can eat at one sitting."

"There's so much to do here," I said.

"So much to eat," he said. He glanced down at his watch. "We better get going."

"Where are we going?"

"Radio City Music Hall."

The cab dropped us off a half block away from Radio City. The sign on the marquee read:

The Radio City Christmas Spectacular
Featuring the Rockettes

We picked up our tickets and found our seats in the fifth row of the middle section. The room buzzed with excitement. Nicholas leaned into me. "I think you'll like this."

"Have you seen it before?"

"No. But I've heard good things about it. Everyone needs to see the Rockettes at least once in their lifetime."

"When I think of the Rockettes, I just think of legs," I said.

He laughed. "Well, that's what they're famous for. And dancing."

There were fourteen musical numbers, concluding with

a living nativity, the Wise Men arriving at the manger on a caravan of real camels. The showstopper was the fifth act, "The Parade of the Wooden Soldiers," when, in the finale, a cannon shot knocked the dancers over like a line of dominoes. As the curtain fell, the crowd joined in singing "Joy to the World."

The temperature outside had dropped to well below freezing, and Nicholas pulled me in close as we walked back to our hotel. I only wished that it was farther away.

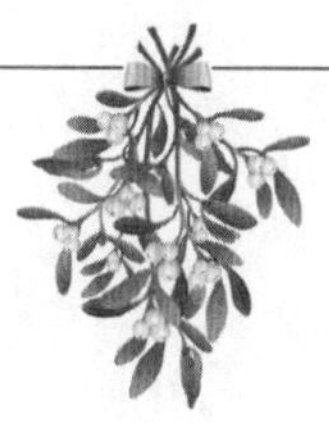

CHAPTER

Twenty-four

I bought Nicholas a present today. Even though it emptied my savings account, it's nothing compared to what he's spent on me. I hope he appreciates the widow's mite.

Elise Dutton's Diary

I slept in the next morning. Nicholas had a breakfast meeting with his client, so he left without waking me. He also said that I needed the rest, which was true. He had left a note under my door asking if I would do him a favor and pick up something for him at Tiffany on Fifth Avenue. I had already planned on shopping. I wanted to get something for Nicholas.

I ordered room service, which was another first for me, then sat in a robe near the window looking out over the city while I ate my oatmeal brûlée. I felt a long way from Montezuma Creek.

After breakfast, I took a cab to the Metropolitan Museum. Since I had started working at ICE I had purchased more than a thousand tickets for the museum, but I had never been there myself. I went into the sales office and met my sales representative, Justin, who was demonstrably excited to meet me after all these years. He was young, flamboyant, chubby, and bald and looked nothing like I expected.

He insisted on taking me on a personal tour of the museum's highlights. The breadth of the collection was stunning. I was amazed to see actual Picassos and Rembrandts, and Van Gogh's sunflowers.

Around two o'clock I thanked Justin and took a cab to the Montblanc store on Madison Avenue. As I looked over a display case of pens, one of the sales personnel approached me. "May I help you?"

"Hi," I said. "I need to buy a gift for a friend. A pen."

"Male or female?" he asked.

"Male. And he's a lawyer."

He smiled a little at my description. "I'm certain I can find you something that will impress him. How much were you thinking of spending?"

I swallowed. Many of the pens were in excess of a thousand dollars. I lightly grimaced. "About five hundred dollars."

The man just nodded. "We'll find him a pen he'll never forget."

Even though the price of the pen was just a fraction of what Nicholas had spent on me, it was nearly all my savings. But it was something I wanted to do for him. It wasn't the amount of money he'd spent on me as much as it was the way he'd done it. Lovingly. He had shown me more love than my own husband and my own father ever had. In our pretend affair, he had opened my eyes to what a real relationship could and should be.

"I recommend this one," the man said, delicately presenting me a pen. "We just got it in. This is our Bohème Marron pen. The rollerball is a bit more practical than the fountain pen, and better priced."

"It's pretty," I said. "Is that a gem?"

"Yes. It's a brown topaz."

"How much is it?"

"It's five hundred and twenty-five dollars, plus tax."

"Okay," I said. "I read that you can engrave something on it."

"Yes, ma'am."

"How long does that take?"

"It usually takes a day or two."

"Is it possible to do it any sooner? I was hoping to give it to him this evening."

He smiled at me. "If you can come back in an hour, I'll walk it over to the engraver myself. What would you like engraved on it?"

I thought for a moment, then said, "Love, Elise."

"Let me get an order form." He wrote down my words, then showed it to me for approval and a signature. I gave him my credit card. "Very well, Ms. Elise, I will have this for you in one hour."

"Thank you."

I left Montblanc and walked a block to the famous Tiffany store. I went up to the first sales counter I saw. "I'm here to pick something up for a friend of mine."

"Were you thinking gold, silver, or diamonds?" she asked.

"I'm sorry, I meant, he already purchased the item. He wanted me to pick it up for him."

"My mistake," she said kindly. "What name would that be under?"

"Nicholas Derr," I said.

"Nicholas Derr," she repeated. "Just a moment." She typed

something into her computer, then walked away from the counter, returning about five minutes later. "Mr. Derr requested that the gift remained wrapped," she said.

"That's fine."

"I will need to see some ID."

"Of course." I brought out my wallet. "There's my license."

She looked at it. "Elise Dutton." She looked at the receipt on the box. "Elise Dutton. Very good." She handed me back my license, then the box. "Let me get you a bag for that." She lifted the famous robin's egg blue bag and set the box inside. "Thank you for visiting us."

I walked back to the Montblanc store and picked up the pen, then walked the four blocks back to the hotel. My feet were getting sore from all my walking. My phone rang on the way. I was excited to talk to Nicholas but disappointed when I saw it was Dan calling.

"What do you want, Dan?"

"We need to talk, Elise."

"No we don't."

"I've discovered some things about your new *friend*. So open your door."

"I'm not home."

Don't lie to me. I can see your car."

"I'm not home, Dan. I'm in New York."

He paused. "What are you doing in New York?"

"Living," I said. I hung up on him. He called back, but I didn't answer. Then he texted me.

We need to talk about your lawyer "friend." Crucial

I shook my head. There wasn't a thing he could tell me that I would consider crucial. Still, his text did make me curious. What could Dan possibly know about Nicholas? Then my phone rang again. I was going to tell Dan to stop calling when I saw it was Nicholas.

"Hi," I said.

"Hi. Are you at the hotel?"

"Not yet. I'm just walking back."

"How was your day?"

"Amazing."

"Good. We have dinner reservations at six. We should leave a half hour before."

"I'll be ready," I said. "What are we having for dinner?"

"How does Italian sound?"

"I love Italian."

"You'll love this place," he said. "See you in a few minutes."

Nicholas knocked on my door at five-thirty. He smiled when I opened. "Hi."

"How was your day?" I asked.

"Challenging. But let's not talk about it."

"Let me grab my coat," I said. "Just a minute."

He held the door open. "Did you get a chance to run by Tiffany's?" he asked.

"Yes. Let me grab that for you." I put on my coat, secretly

put the Montblanc box in my purse, then brought over the Tiffany bag. "Here you go."

"Thanks for picking that up for me."

"No problem."

"I better leave it in my room," he said. "I'll be right back." He walked to his room, then returned empty-handed. "Shall we go?"

We had to wait awhile for a cab, and we arrived a few minutes late for our dinner reservation. The restaurant Nicholas had decided on was called Babbo, and it had a famous chef, Mario Batali, who was sometimes on television. The atmosphere was elegant with, incongruently, loud rock music.

Everything was exquisite. I ordered wine with my meal. Babbo had more than two thousand wines, which they served *quartino*, meaning in a carafe that held about a glass and a half. Our waiter recommended a Calabrian wine called Cirò. Nicholas ordered sparkling water. After the waiter left, I asked, "Do you drink?"

He shook his head and said, "No," but nothing more.

The evening passed quietly between us, but not uncomfortably. Nicholas just seemed a little lost in thought, something I attributed to his "challenging" day.

As we were finishing our meals, Nicholas said, "Did you recognize who's sitting behind me?"

I looked over his shoulder. "Is that really Kevin Bacon?"

He nodded. "And his wife, Kyra Sedgwick." Just then someone walked over to their table to ask them for their autographs. They politely demurred.

"That's one of the things about New York," Nicholas said. "It's a cultural mecca."

"Like Montezuma Creek," I said.

Nicholas laughed. "Just like Montezuma Creek. After all, you did get the Harlem Globetrotters."

"Yes we did. That's my brush with fame."

"Now you can say you've been one degree from Kevin Bacon. Did you enjoy your meal?"

"Immensely. I don't think I'll ever be able to eat store-bought spaghetti sauce again."

"Then I've done you a service," he said. "One can get to be a food snob in New York."

"What was that last dish you had?"

"Lamb's brain Francobolli."

I just looked at him. "I can't tell if you're kidding me or not."

He smiled. "I'm not. They're famous for some interesting fare. But there was a reason I chose this place besides the food."

"And what was that?"

"Just a moment," he said. He stood up and left the table. He returned a couple minutes later and sat down. "I have something for you." He brought from his pocket the Tiffany box I had picked up earlier and set it in front of me.

"That was for me?"

"Of course."

I took the beautiful blue box, untied its ribbon, and lifted the lid. Inside was a velvet jewelry box. "What did you do?" I asked.

"Keep going," he said.

I set the cardboard box down on the table, then pried opened the jewelry box's lid. Inside was an exquisite rose gold pendant. It was conical, about an inch long, with elegant spiraled lines. I gasped.

"Do you like it?"

I looked up at him. "It's beautiful."

"It's from Paloma Picasso's collection," he said. "It was inspired by the hanging lanterns of Venice. That's why I thought it was appropriate we had Italian for dinner."

"This is too much."

"I know," he said. "Try it on."

I lifted the pendant from the box. "Would you help me put it on?"

"I'd love to," he said. He stood and walked around the table. I lifted the back of my hair as he draped the chain around my neck. The pendant fell to the top of my cleavage.

"I've never had anything so nice before," I said.

"Then it's about time," he said. I stood up and hugged him. "Thank you."

"I'm glad you like it."

"I don't like it, I love it."

We finished our desserts, olive oil and rosemary cake with a pistachio gelato, then we took a cab to Rockefeller Center to see the tree. Even though it was cold enough to see our breaths, I left my coat open to reveal my new necklace.

The eighty-foot tree was brilliantly lit, and the plaza was crowded with tourists. Beneath the statue of Prometheus, skaters glided gracefully, and some not so gracefully, across the rink.

We had been there for a while when I said, "I have something for you too."

Nicholas looked at me in surprise. "You do?"

"Remember when we signed the contract, I asked you if you had a pen? You said, 'I'm a lawyer. That's like asking me if I have a lung.' "

He grinned. "And you made a snarky remark about me not having a heart."

"I was wrong," I said. "You're all heart." I took the pen from my purse and handed it to him.

"What's this?"

"It's a present."

He unwrapped the box. "You bought me a Montblanc pen." He looked up at me. "Elise, this is way too expensive."

"It's nothing compared to what you've spent on me."

"You can't . . ."

I touched his lips. "Remember when you got mad at me for complaining you spend too much? Now I'm telling you the same thing. I know it's not much in your world, but it's all I have. Please let me enjoy this."

He just stood there quietly as the world noisily swirled around us. He looked deeply affected. "Thank you."

"I just wanted to give you something that you would use. And maybe when you saw it, you would think of me. And remember this time we've had together."

"I don't need a pen for that," he said softly.

"Thank you for bringing me to New York. Thank you for everything you've done this season. I don't know why you've done all this, but thank you."

"You still don't know why?"

I dared not say what I hoped, that he felt about me the way I did about him. That he loved me. We gazed into each other's eyes, then he put his hand behind my head and gently pulled me into him and we kissed. Then we kissed and kissed. It was the first time I'd kissed anyone in years, but I'd never kissed anyone like that in my entire life. I had never felt more swept away, more lost in someone else, or even my own head. When we parted I said breathlessly, "So much for the platonic clause."

"Men can't have platonic relationships."

We kissed again. In spite of my best efforts, I'd done exactly what I knew I shouldn't. I'd fallen deeply in love with a man who was going to leave me.

We walked back to the hotel holding hands. We stopped outside my room and kissed again.

"Do you want to come inside?" I asked.

"Desperately," he said. He breathed out slowly. "But I better not."

"You're right," I said. "Are you sure?"

"Barely," he replied. We kissed some more, and then I reluctantly pulled back a little, just until our lips were apart, our noses still touching. "I better let you get some sleep."

"Okay."

"Thank you for tonight. For everything. I love my necklace."

"I love *you,*" he said.

The words shocked me. I pulled back and looked at him. As much as I had wanted to hear those words, I hadn't expected to. Emotion welled up inside me. Of course I loved him, but he couldn't love me.

"What's wrong?" he said.

I couldn't speak. I kissed him again, then quickly ducked inside my room, leaving him standing there in the hallway, confused. I fell on my bed and cried. I also felt confused, torn by two equally powerful emotions, joy for being loved and fear of being loved, horrified by the truth that he'd fallen in love with someone he didn't really know and wouldn't love once he did.

CHAPTER

Twenty-five

It's been said that "perfect love casts out all fear,"
but, in my case, it seems to be the source of it.

Elise Dutton's Diary

I woke the next morning crying. I had had a terrible nightmare. Nicholas and I had gotten married. I was in an elegant, beaded ivory wedding dress, he was in tails with a wingtip shirt and red band tie and sash. We ran from the church to a car decorated by our guests, climbed inside, and drove off. Then Nicholas looked in the mirror. "What's that?"

"What's what, dear?" I asked.

"In the backseat. There's a box or something." We both turned around. In the backseat was my daughter's coffin.

I looked in the mirror at my necklace. It was the most beautiful piece of jewelry I had ever owned. Even my wedding ring paled in comparison. But I couldn't keep it. Just like I couldn't keep him.

Nicholas called my room three times the next morning. I didn't answer. I was too afraid. Then he called my cell phone, which I didn't answer either. Finally he knocked on my door. "Elise," he asked through the door. "Are you all right?"

I should have answered the phone, I thought. Now he was going to see me, puffy eyes and all.

"Elise, are you all right?"

I opened the door just enough to see him. "I'm sorry," I said. "I'm okay."

He looked at me anxiously. "What's wrong?"

"It's nothing," I said.

He looked baffled. "Nothing?"

"We can talk later," I said. "After your meetings."

He looked at me for a moment more, then said, "I meant what I said last night. I do love you."

My eyes welled up. "I know."

"I'll be back soon. We'll talk. Everything will be all right."

"Okay," I said.

He walked off down the hall. I went back to bed, but couldn't get back to sleep. After an hour I dressed and went out. I wandered around Central Park. I tried to calm myself, to believe his words that everything would be okay, but the fear didn't leave. It had been with me for so long it didn't take eviction lightly.

Before you judge me too harshly, consider your own deepest fears—real or imagined. Actually, all fear is born of the imagination, which means that the danger we fear doesn't need be rational or even real to be potent. Like my fear of snakes.

When I was eighteen I drove my car off the highway into a ditch because there was a snake on the road. It didn't matter that the snake couldn't have bitten me through the car. It didn't matter that the snake probably wasn't even poisonous or might even have already been dead. It didn't even matter that swerving off the road at fifty miles per hour posed a much greater danger than the snake I was frightened of. Fear doesn't listen to reason. It takes its own counsel.

While my saner self recognized that my fear of snakes was partially irrational, my fear of rejection wasn't. I'd never been bitten by a snake, but I'd been bitten by rejection more times than I could remember. After all the attacks and abandonment I'd endured since Hannah's death, my heart wasn't about to believe that someone might be different. Not even someone as beautiful as Nicholas.

Nicholas came back to the hotel at four, and we went to dinner at a restaurant close by, the Redeye Grill. We started with small talk, which considering where we'd ended the evening before seemed especially peculiar. He waited until we had mostly eaten before he asked, "Elise, what's wrong?"

I didn't answer. I was afraid to answer.

"Was it because I told you that I love you?"

I slowly nodded.

He frowned deeply. "And you don't love me."

"I'm madly in love with you," I said.

His look of sadness gave way to a smile. "Then what's the problem?"

"You can't really love me," I said. "You don't know me."

"I know you," he said. "I know that in spite of a harsh childhood you're kind and giving and sweet. I know that you give more than you take. I know that you're grateful for even the smallest acts of kindness. And I know that I can't live without you. What more do I need to know?"

My eyes welled up with pain. I could no longer keep my secret from him. "There's something you don't know about me. Something I've done. Something horrible."

He looked at me for a moment, then said, "Does it have to do with Hannah?"

CHAPTER

Twenty-six

I had locked from him the deepest chambers of my fear, only to discover that he had his own key.

Elise Dutton's Diary

Every part of me froze. When I could speak I asked, "How do you know about Hannah?"

He didn't answer. I could see my fear reflected in his eyes. I would say that I felt as if I'd been stripped naked, but it was more than that. I felt as if my skin had been flayed, my innermost parts exposed to the world.

"How long have you known this?" I asked. "Did you know before the contract?"

He gazed at me anxiously, then said softly, "I knew long before the contract."

"How?"

He looked down for a moment, then said, "We've met before."

"I've never met you before."

"Yes, we have," he said. "But in the state you were in, I doubt you would remember. I wouldn't have." After a pause he said, "Do you remember that I told you I worked for the prosecutor's office?" He paused again, and I was terrified of what he was going to say. "I had been there about a year when we got a call from the Salt Lake County Sheriff's Office saying a child had been left in a car and died of hyperthermia. They weren't sure whether to arrest the mother. I was sent out to assess the situation."

Suddenly I knew who he was. Tears welled up in my eyes. "You're the man who interviewed me."

He nodded.

I was speechless.

"I knew it was an accident the moment I saw you. And that no punishment the justice system could dish out would be as bad as what you were already experiencing. I went back and convinced them not to prosecute."

His words rushed through me, freezing me like ice. No, broken ice. I felt shattered and pierced.

"You knew the whole time."

He warily gazed into my eyes, then slowly nodded.

"Have you been stalking me for all these years?"

"Of course not. A couple of months ago I saw you in the elevator. I knew I recognized you, I just didn't remember from where. After I got out I remembered."

For several minutes I was speechless. I had never felt so exposed before. "Why did you lie to me?"

"I didn't lie to you."

"You withheld the truth. That's the same as a lie."

"It wasn't important."

I stared at him incredulously. "It wasn't important?"

"No," he said.

"It was to me," I said. "How could you be so cruel?"

He looked stunned. "Elise . . ."

"I need to go," I said.

"Elise, please."

"I need to go," I repeated. "Now."

"All right. We'll go."

"Alone," I said.

He looked at me for a moment, then nodded. "All right."

I retrieved my coat from the coat check and walked alone back to the hotel.

CHAPTER

Twenty-seven

It's been said that the truth will set you free. But the truth can also bury you. It's not the hurricane that breaks your heart, it's the phone call afterward informing you that all is lost.

Elise Dutton's Diary

The night passed in a strange delirium. Nothing was what I thought it was. My Nicholas, my beautiful, safe fantasy man, was an intricate part of my worst nightmare. He was part of my past, and, whether he had intended to or not, he had reengulfed me in it.

The next morning Nicholas called me several times, but I didn't answer. The fourth time he left a message. "Elise, your flight to Salt Lake leaves at two-ten. It's nearly an hour ride to the airport, so you better leave the hotel by noon. I booked a car for you. It will be downstairs at the curb waiting for you at twelve. It will have a sign in the window with your name. If you have any problems, just ask the hotel attendant for help. Don't worry about checking out; I'll take care of everything.

"I won't be going with you. I'm going to stay here for an extra day so you can have time to think. I'm sorry for hurting you. I didn't mean to. I would never intentionally hurt you. I hope you can forgive me." Then he said something I didn't understand. "Please have faith in me. I understand your pain better than you know."

Hearing his voice intensified my emotion, and I felt like

I might have some sort of breakdown. I sat on the floor of the shower crying for nearly an hour, the water pouring over me, mixing with my tears and carrying them to the drain.

I was two people, and it was tearing me apart. Part of me wanted to run to Nicholas for comfort. To be held and loved and protected by him. The other half wanted to deny ever knowing him and everything that had happened since the contract. Mostly, I just wanted to crawl back into the dark, safe cave of my previous world.

As I packed my bag, someone knocked on my door. My heart froze. I didn't want to see him, but I couldn't stop myself either.

I opened the door, but it was only a woman from housekeeping wanting to clean my room. I told her I'd be leaving shortly. A few minutes before twelve I dragged my bag out of the room. I stole a glance at Nicholas's door as if hiding the action from myself. I hoped he would be watching for me, but he wasn't.

The elevator door opened into the lobby, and I walked out to the street. A black town car was waiting at the curb with a sign that read DUTTON. The bellman put my bag in the trunk, and I cried as the car pulled away from the hotel.

"Are you okay, ma'am?" the driver asked.

I shook my head. "No."

He didn't say anything more.

My flight landed in Salt Lake a few minutes before five. I retrieved my bag, then took a cab back to my apartment. As I undressed I realized that I was still wearing the gold necklace Nicholas had given me. I poured myself a glass of wine and drank it. Then another. Then another. It had been a long time since I'd drunk to get drunk, but that's exactly what I was doing. Then I lay down on my bed and cried myself to sleep.

The next day was Saturday. I lay in bed until almost one in the afternoon. I was hungover and my head ached, but that was nothing compared to the pain I felt in losing Nicholas. I didn't have the energy or desire to get out of bed. Most of all I didn't have any reason to. I wondered if Nicholas had made it back to Salt Lake. I craved him. I missed him as much as I feared him. I hoped he would call, but he never did. I kept my phone nearby just in case it rang. It never did.

CHAPTER

Twenty-eight

There is not only more to each soul's journey than we imagine, usually there is more than we can *imagine.*

Elise Dutton's Diary

My doorbell rang twice on Christmas Eve. Both times filled me with intense anticipation. The first time was the UPS man delivering a package from New York. It was from Nicholas. I supposed it was my last gift. I didn't open it. I couldn't bring myself to read his letter.

The second time the doorbell rang was later that afternoon. I was sure it was Nicholas. I hoped it was as much as I hoped it wasn't. I took a deep breath before looking through my door's peephole. Dan was standing outside leaning on one hand against my door. He must have known I was looking through the lens because he suddenly leaned forward and looked through the opposite side of the peephole until his eye filled my field of vision.

I pulled opened the door. "What do you want?"

"Glad you finally decided to come home," he said.

"What do you want?" I repeated.

"I already told you what I want. I want us again. The way it should be."

"And I told you I wasn't interested."

"Why? Because you think you're in love?"

"No," I said. "It's over."

"So things didn't work out with the lawyer in New York."

I didn't answer.

"Well, it's for the better. With a past like his, you didn't want to get mixed up with that guy anyway."

"What are you talking about?" I said.

"Will you let me in? It's freezing out here."

I stepped back from the door, and he walked in. He sat on my sofa. "So, I got the lowdown on your lawyer. He's not who you think he is."

"No one ever is," I said.

"That's where you're wrong," Dan said. "I am. With me, what you see is what you get."

"You mean a narcissistic cheater," I said.

He grinned, looking more impressed by my words than insulted. "Looks like you've finally grown some attitude."

"It's about time I did."

"So let me tell you about your *friend*."

"I don't care," I said.

"Good. Because he's a first-class loser."

Hearing this made me angry. "No, he's nothing like you."

"Then you're not over him."

"He's a good man."

"Then you won't mind me telling you that he's a drunk."

I shook my head. "He doesn't even drink."

"Then maybe he stopped after he killed the family."

I looked at him. "What are you talking about?"

"Your friend has a serious criminal record. Or at least he

should have one. He was driving drunk when he crashed his car into a family crossing a crosswalk. Two parents and two children. He killed three of them."

"You're a liar."

"I thought you might say that, so I brought proof. I printed it off the Internet."

He unfolded a piece of paper from his coat pocket and handed it to me. The headline read,

For Three Deaths Teen Gets Two Years

Nicholas Derr, a 16-year-old Highland High School student, was sentenced to juvenile detention for up to two years after admitting Monday that he killed three and injured one in a DUI accident.

There were shouts of protest in 3rd District Juvenile Court when Judge Anders handed down the sentence.

"He kills three people and he's out in just two years?" said Mark Buhler, a friend of the deceased family. "Where's the justice? Is that all their lives are worth?"

Derr had a blood-alcohol level at 0.10 percent; the Utah legal limit is 0.08. Derr and a friend (name withheld) were driving down 2100 south from a Parley's Canyon party where alcohol was being served when his vehicle struck the Hayes family in a crosswalk just north of Sugar House Park at 8:41 P.M. on December 7.

Vance Hayes (28), Michelle Hayes (27), and their two daughters, Olivia (3) and Victoria (1), were just leaving the park when witnesses say that Derr ran a red light and struck the family. The two young children were in a double stroller. Derr's car was estimated to be traveling nearly twice the speed limit of the 30 mph zone. The father and one-year-old were killed instantly. The mother was DOA at University of Utah Hospital. Only the three-year-old survived the crash. She sustained multiple broken bones and major internal injuries, but doctors believe she will recover. Derr and his friend were uninjured.

Derr, who had just received his driver's license two weeks before the accident, pleaded guilty to three counts of second-degree felony automobile homicide and one count of negligent injury. Derr has no previous DUIs or criminal record.

"He's a good kid," a neighbor, who asked to remain anonymous, said of Derr. "I've known him for years. He comes from a good family. He mows the lawn of one of the widows on our street and shovels her walk in the winter. One time some bullies were picking on my son and Nick protected him. I don't know what happened with this accident. He just made some bad choices, like any kid could."

Earlier this month, Judge Anders decided against ordering Derr to stand trial in adult court, where the teen would have faced up to 30 years at

Utah State Prison. Derr will be eligible for parole in as few as twenty-four months.

I looked at the picture of an upside-down car and an area cordoned off with police tape. Then I looked up at Dan. His dark eyes brimmed with satisfaction. "Looks like the two of you have more in common than you thought."

"Get out of here," I said.

"Don't kill the messenger, honey."

"Get out of here!" I screamed.

He looked at me for a moment, then stood. "I should've figured. Two killers, no jail time. You're perfect for each other."

I slapped him so hard my hand stung. "Don't you ever call me that again!" I shouted. "Do you hear me? Never call me that again!"

Dan was stunned. The imprint of my hand was fresh on his cheek. "I've paid a thousand times over for my mistake. A thousand times a thousand. I have suffered and bled for something that I would give my life to have prevented. I would have gladly traded my life for hers, but I can't. But you will not hold this over my head anymore. I have paid the debt. Do you understand me?"

He didn't answer.

"Do you understand me?"

"Yes 'Lise."

"Now get out of here."

He slowly turned his back on me. He had just walked out the door when I shouted after him, "And you're right.

Nicholas and I *are* perfect for each other." I slammed the door shut after him.

For the first time since the day Hannah died, I felt free. And I fully understood why Nicholas had been so good to me. He understood. He had weathered the same fierce storm.

I grabbed the package he'd sent and tore back the paper to reveal a satin box marked WATERFORD CRYSTAL. I untied its ribbon and lifted the lid. Inside the red-velvet-lined box was a crystal Christmas ornament. A star. Next to the star was a scrolled parchment note tied with ribbon. I untied the ribbon and unrolled the note. It was written in Nicholas's hand.

My dear Elise,

It's been said that the Magi, wise men, gazed up into the night skies, following a star. But they were not looking for a star. They were looking for hope. Hope of a new world. Hope of redemption. Light is not found in dark places, and hope is not found looking down or looking back. May you always look up. It has been my greatest joy spending this holiday season with you. And though things did not end between us as I hoped, whatever the new year brings, I will always hope the best for you and be forever grateful for your love. I will always love you.

Nick

CHAPTER

Twenty-nine

Our contract has expired.

Elise Dutton's Diary

When I arrived at Nicholas's home I knocked on his door, then rang his doorbell, but he didn't answer. There was one set of car tracks in the driveway, and I guessed he had gone somewhere. I sat down on the cold concrete porch to wait. The temperature dropped with the sun until it was well below freezing. Or at least until I was. I shivered with the cold, but I wasn't going to leave. I couldn't make myself leave.

It was after dark when Nicholas's car turned in to his driveway. His garage door opened, but he saw me and stopped before pulling in. He got out and walked up to me.

"What are you doing here?"

My chin was quivering with the cold, making it difficult to speak. "We had a date. Remember?"

He looked down a moment, then said, "That was before you said I was cruel and ran away."

My words pierced me. "I came to apologize."

For a moment he seemed unsure of what to say. "How long have you been waiting here?"

"Three hours."

"You must be freezing."

I nodded, my body involuntarily shuddering with the suggestion.

He put out his hand. "Come in and get warm."

He unlocked the front door, and we stepped into the foyer. His home was warm and dark, illuminated only by a hall light and the colorful blinking strands of his Christmas tree. He led me to a small den, told me to sit on the sofa, and then left the room. I could hear him moving around in the kitchen. It seemed that I sat there for the longest time before he returned without his coat and carrying a porcelain mug. "Drink this. It's hot cider."

"Thank you," I said, taking the cup from him with both hands. I sipped the hot drink while he sat down backward on the piano bench. The warm drink spread through my body. When I could speak I asked, "Do you play?"

He nodded. "Yes."

I didn't know what to say and I'm not sure he did either because the silence was interminable. He looked at me until I couldn't stand it anymore. Finally I took a deep breath and said, "Dan came by to see me this afternoon. He's still trying to get me back. He thought he could scare me away from you with this." I set the newspaper article on the table between us.

Nicholas barely glanced at it. "And he didn't even need it. I scared you away without it." He took a deep breath. "And you think I owe you an explanation?"

"You don't owe me anything," I said.

"Then why are you here?"

The question stung, filling my eyes with tears. I bowed my head, afraid to show my eyes, afraid to look into his. "After reading the article I realized that you really did understand me. And that you might be the only one in the world who could really love me."

He was silent for a moment, then said, "I'd like to explain what happened."

I looked up at him. "You don't have to."

"I want to," he said. "I was barely sixteen years old. I was a sophomore in high school. My girlfriend had broken up with me a couple days before. You know how teenagers are, all drama and hormones. I was depressed and had pretty much taken to my bed, just listening to music all night. A friend of mine came over to cheer me up. He talked me into going to a party some seniors were having up in the canyons.

"They had a keg. Everyone was drunk or getting there. I resisted, at first. My parents were Mormon, so we didn't have alcohol in our house. I had never even drunk alcohol before. But between the peer pressure and my depression and my friend nagging, I gave in. It was the worst mistake of my life. It didn't take much to get me drunk. I had maybe three beers. My friend was completely wasted, so I took his keys and drove us home."

I could see the pain grow in his eyes.

"We were coming down Parley's Canyon onto twenty-first south. I was driving fast, close to sixty miles per hour, when I reached Sugar House Park. Wrong place, wrong time. There was a young family leaving the park. They were in the crosswalk. A mom, dad, a three- and a one-year-old in a double stroller. It was dark, and I was driving so fast I don't know if I would have seen them anyway, but I hit them. The father saw me just before; he tried to push the stroller out of the way. He was killed instantly. I hit him and his wife and clipped the stroller, then rolled the car into a telephone pole.

"The mother was thrown more than eighty feet, but somehow she was still alive when the ambulance arrived. I climbed out of the car and walked around the scene like I was in a nightmare, listening to the mother scream for her children. When I have nightmares, that's what I hear, that mother's screams." He looked into my eyes. "The three-year-old lived. Her name is Olivia. She's seventeen now."

I let the story settle over me. When I could speak I asked, "Have you met her?"

"A year ago," he said softly. "I've taken flowers to the grave every year on the anniversary of their deaths."

"December seventh," I said. "That's where you were."

He nodded. "Last year I was in the cemetery, just kneeling there, praying for forgiveness, like I always do. When I stood, there was a teenage girl behind me. I hadn't heard her come up. She just looked at me for a moment and then she said, 'It's you, isn't it?'

"I said, 'I'm so sorry.' She looked at me for a moment and then she did something I'll never forget. She said, 'I forgive you.' " Nicholas's eyes welled up. "The power of those words. I fell back to my knees and wept. Olivia was almost the same age I was when I took her parents and sister from her. I don't know how she did it. But she knelt down next to me and held me. She said, 'You were just a kid, like me. Sometimes we do dumb things. Sometimes there are consequences.' " Nicholas shook his head. "I don't know how she found the strength to say that to the man who had killed her parents."

"What happened after the accident?" I asked.

"I was arrested. I was put in youth corrections for nineteen months—until my eighteenth birthday. It would have been longer—much longer—but because I was underage and it was my first offense, the judge ruled that I would be tried as an adolescent. A lot of people wanted me tried as an adult. Some of those people were waiting outside the juvie center with placards when I got out. They stood there and jeered at me. One called me a murderer. One had a drawing of a headstone with the word *justice*. I'll never forget a woman shaking a finger at me and saying, 'Rot in hell.' "

"I understand," I said.

He slowly nodded. "I know you do. You also understand that even though the law was done with me, my punishment had just begun. I carried the weight of what I'd done every day of my life. My relationship with my parents changed. My trial and fines had just about bankrupted them.

"My mother was severely depressed. She was very religious and she blamed herself for what had happened. She felt like God was punishing her for being a bad mother. She became addicted to prescription medications. My dad tried to keep things together, but eventually it was too much for him too. My parents divorced. My brother and sister blamed me for destroying the family. I can't blame them; it's true. But since then I've been alone. None of them will talk to me. I'm dead to them. My mother died of an overdose six years ago.

"It's been a long road. It seemed like anytime I started to feel happiness, the memory of the Hayeses' deaths or my mother's death would rise up to smack me back down. Something would say to me, 'How can you be happy when they're in the ground?' I've wondered if God could ever forgive me.

"I don't know why I decided to go into law, maybe it was all the time I'd spent in court and working with lawyers, but I had an aptitude for it. I got the second highest LSAT score in the state of Utah. I focused all my energy on my career. I worked hard, not just to succeed, but because there was nothing else in my life. Deep inside what I was really trying to do was prove that I wasn't worthless.

"But no amount of success in my career could fill that hole inside me. It was always there. I never felt free to find joy until I met Olivia. That's when I decided I would find someone to spend my life with. I dated some, I didn't have any trouble getting women, but I suppose I felt like you did. I didn't think they could comprehend or love the real me.

"When I saw you in that elevator I was speechless. I knew you didn't recognize me, but I recognized you. I felt like, in some way, we were kindred spirits. After that I couldn't get you off my mind. I wanted to know you better."

"That's why you came up with the contract," I said.

He nodded. "It seemed like a safe way to get close without hurting anyone. But then I fell in love." He looked into my eyes. "It wasn't hard. You're very loveable."

I looked at him gratefully but didn't speak.

"I wanted to protect you," he said. "From the world and from your past. But I'm part of that past, so that meant protecting you from me as well. I know I should have told you, but the timing never seemed right. And the stronger my feelings grew, the more afraid I was of losing you. And I had my own secret I didn't know how to share. In a way, I was fighting the same demon you were—deep inside I wondered whether you would reject me too if you knew the real me."

"I'm sorry I left you," I said. "You've had enough abandonment from those you loved." My voice fell with shame. "You didn't need it from me." I looked down for a moment as the emotion of the moment filled me. Then I looked back up into his eyes. "Could you still love me?"

It seemed an eternity that we gazed into each other's eyes, and then Nicholas came over to me and we embraced. Then we kissed. Passionately. Honestly. Completely. For the first time we kissed without masks. When our lips finally parted, I whispered, "I want to renew the contract."

He didn't speak for a moment. Then he said, "It's got to be a different contract."

"Different?"

He leaned back to look into my eyes. "We need to change the expiration date."

"To what?" I asked.

"In perpetuity."

I laughed. "You sound like such a lawyer."

"I am," he replied. "And no more platonic clause. It's definitely not going to be platonic."

A wide smile crossed my lips. "No," I said. "It's definitely not going to be platonic." I looked deep into his eyes. "In perpetuity?"

He nodded. "This time you really are signing your soul away."

I looked at him for a moment before I said, "All right, Mr. Lawyer. Got a pen?"

EPILOGUE

It should not surprise us that, at the end of a journey, our destination looks different than we imagined at the beginning. Everything looks different up close.

Elise Dutton's Diary

Nicholas and I were married the next spring in a small Italian village called Greve, nineteen miles south of Florence, in the Chianti wine district. It was a very small wedding, which was what we wanted. My sister, Cosette, and her husband, Ron, came. From the law firm there were Alan and Careen McKay and Scott and Sharon Hitesman. From ICE, Zoey was there. She financially swung the trip by talking Mark out of some of his frequent-flier miles. Not surprisingly, she's now carrying on a long-distance romance with an Italian guy named Dario.

The biggest surprise of our wedding day was the arrival of Nicholas's sister, Sheridan. She came without telling him. And she came to forgive. I don't think his joy could have been more full. To this day it's one of the few times I've seen Nicholas cry. We still have hopes that his brother might someday forgive him as well. We don't expect it, but we hope.

After our wedding, we honeymooned for two weeks in Rome and Sorrento and on Capri and the Amalfi coast, eventually flying back to the United States from Naples. When we got back to our home in Utah, there was a special wedding gift waiting for me—a Lladró of Cinderella and her pumpkin carriage. It was perfect. Maybe the figurine was really for Nicholas, but it doesn't matter. The story is mine.

I no longer work at ICE. I quit two months after I found out I was pregnant. I'm due next February, coincidentally the same month my Hannah was born.

Life is good. I'd be lying if I said that I had stopped being haunted by ghosts or trying myself in the court of regret. But things are different. The judge and jury are more merciful. After all these years, they are willing to listen to reason. And in court I'm no longer arguing my case alone. I found myself a pretty good lawyer.

✦ ABOUT THE AUTHOR ✦

Richard Paul Evans is the #1 bestselling author of *The Christmas Box*. Each of his more than twenty-five novels has been a *New York Times* bestseller. There are more than 20 million copies of his books in print worldwide, translated into more than twenty-four languages. He is the recipient of numerous awards, including the American Mothers Book Award, the *Romantic Times* Best Women's Novel of the Year Award, the German Audience Gold Award for Romance, three Religion Communicators Council Wilbur Awards, *The Washington Times* Humanitarian of the Century Award, and the Volunteers of America National Empathy Award. He lives in Salt Lake City, Utah, with his wife, Keri, and their five children. You can learn more about Richard on Facebook at www.facebook.com/RPEfans, or visit his website, www.richardpaulevans.com.

ALSO BY RICHARD PAUL EVANS

The Walk Series

The Walk

Miles to Go

The Road to Grace

A Step of Faith

Walking on Water

The Mistletoe Promise

The Four Doors

A Winter Dream

Lost December

Promise Me

The Christmas List

Grace

The Gift

Finding Noel

The Sunflower

A Perfect Day

The Last Promise

The Christmas Box Miracle

The Carousel

The Looking Glass

The Locket

The Letter

Timepiece

The Christmas Box

For Children and Young Adults

The Dance

The Christmas Candle

The Spyglass

The Tower

The Light of Christmas

Michael Vey: The Prisoner of Cell 25

Michael Vey 2: Rise of the Elgen

Michael Vey 3: Battle of the Ampere

Michael Vey 4: Hunt for Jade Dragon

Michael Vey 5: Storm of Lightning

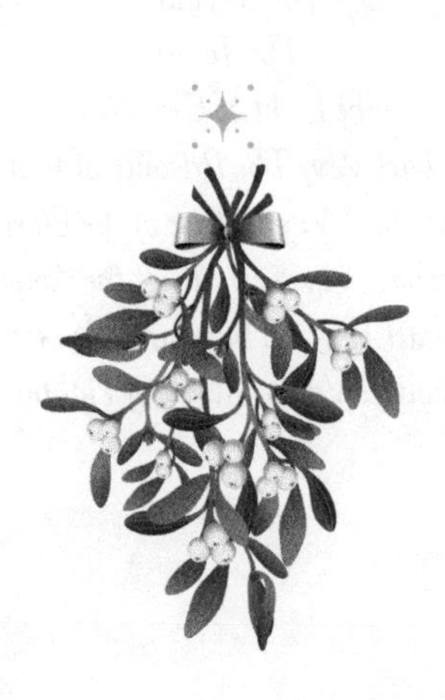

RICHARD PAUL EVANS

The Mistletoe Inn

SIMON & SCHUSTER

NEW YORK LONDON TORONTO SYDNEY NEW DELHI

Simon & Schuster
1230 Avenue of the Americas
New York, NY 10020

This book is a work of fiction. Any references to historical events, real people, or real places are used fictitiously. Other names, characters, places, and events are products of the author's imagination, and any resemblance to actual events or places or persons, living or dead, is entirely coincidental.

First Simon & Schuster hardcover edition November 2015

For information about special discounts for bulk purchases, please contact Simon & Schuster Special Sales at 1-866-506-1949 or business@simonandschuster.com.

The Simon & Schuster Speakers Bureau can bring authors to your live event. For more information or to book an event, contact the Simon & Schuster Speakers Bureau at 1-866-248-3049 or visit our website at www.simonspeakers.com.

Manufactured in the United States of America

3 5 7 9 10 8 6 4

Library of Congress Cataloging-in-Publication Data

Evans, Richard Paul.
The Mistletoe Inn : a novel / Richard Paul Evans. —
First Simon & Schuster hardcover edition.
pages cm.
1. Christmas stories. I. Title.
PS3555.V259M56 2015
813'.54—dc23
2015031357

ISBN 978-1-5011-1979-8
ISBN 978-1-5011-1980-4 (ebook)

In memory of my mother
June Thorup Evans

✦ AUTHOR'S NOTE ✦

A few years ago I decided to write a collection of holiday love stories: The Mistletoe Collection. The first book in that collection was 2014's bestselling *The Mistletoe Promise*. This book, *The Mistletoe Inn*, is the second. The third book (still unnamed, but it will have the word "Mistletoe" in the title) will come out in the fall of 2016. These books are not a trilogy; rather, they are three independent love stories abounding with inspiration, humor, and romance—a Christmas present for my readers.

That's not to say that there's *no* connection between the three books. In this novel, our protagonist, Kim Rossi (named after my third-grade teacher), is an aspiring romance writer working on a book titled *The Mistletoe Promise*. This is a bit of an inside joke. I used the title only for fun, as it has little to no bearing on the actual story or its outcome.

I hope you enjoy this holiday offering and that it fills your home and heart (and those of the people with whom you share this book) with joy, love, and peace.

Blessings,
Richard Paul Evans

PROLOGUE

When I was eleven years old I was walking home from a friend's birthday party when I saw an ambulance parked in the driveway of my house. I dropped my party favors and sprinted home. When I got inside, the house was crowded with people: aunts and uncles, some neighbors, and our pastor. Everyone except my parents.

"What's going on?" I asked.

My aunt crouched down until we were eye level. "Kimmy, your mother tried to take her life."

The words froze my heart. "Is she still alive?"

"I don't know, honey. We're waiting to find out."

I began to cry, wiping my eyes on the sleeve of my blouse. "I need to see her."

"You shouldn't right now," my aunt said, gently taking me by my arms. I pulled free from her grasp and ran to my parents' room. A husky paramedic stopped me outside the bedroom door, grabbing me firmly by my waist. "Hold on there."

"Let go of me!" I shouted, struggling against his powerful grip.

"It's best that you not go in there."

"She's my mother!" I screamed.

"That's why it's best."

My father must have heard me. I stopped struggling when I saw him. He looked weary and in pain. He squatted down and put his arms around me. "She's going to be okay," he said. "Everything will be okay. I need you to wait out here while the paramedics finish up. We need to get Mom to the hospital, okay? We'll talk on the way there."

Someone, I don't remember who, took my hand and led me back to the front room and the somber faces. I could feel everyone's eyes on me. I felt like I was in one of those Tilt-A-Whirl rides at the carnival, the kind that spins you around until you don't know where you are. Or at least until you want to throw up.

Then the bedroom door opened and the room quieted as a processional emerged, a line of men carrying my mother out of the house on a stretcher, a blanket pulled up tightly to her neck, my father at her side, stoic and pale. I remember the heavy clomp of the paramedics' boots.

On the drive to the hospital I asked my dad, "Why did she try to kill herself?"

"Same as before," he said. "Sometimes it just takes her."

"Will she try again?"

He just looked ahead at the road. Even at that age, I knew that he was struggling to decide if he should tell me what I wanted to hear or the truth. "I don't know, sweetie. I hope not. But I don't know."

Twelve weeks later, on Christmas, my mother tried again. This time she didn't fail.

CHAPTER

One

The combined ballast of my life's abandonment is only balanced by the substantial weight of my father's love.

Kimberly Rossi's Diary

My mother attempted suicide four times before she finally succeeded. At least those are the attempts that I know about; there could have been more, as my father often ran interference, hiding things that he thought would hurt me. My mother suffered from major depression. She also had migraines. By most accounts they were unusually severe. She almost always had visual effects, seeing strange lines and flashes of light and sometimes hearing voices. When the migraines came she never left her room.

Doctors tried to help, though it seemed to me like they were bailing out a sinking boat with a paper cup. Most just medicated her with the latest trending mind drug: Valium, Xanax, Prozac, etc. A few told her to "buck up," which was like telling a stage-four cancer patient to just get over it. Then there were the insufferable people who said stupid things like, "I was depressed once. I went for a walk," or, "You have so much to be thankful for, how can you be depressed?" then smugly walked off as if they'd just performed a service to society.

With my mother almost always ill, my father did his best to pick up the slack. It was not unusual for him to come home from a long day of work, make dinner, clean the kitchen (with my help), then put in the laundry. I could never figure out why my father stayed with her.

The Christmas afternoon my mother died was the first time I ever saw my father cry. He also cried at her funeral, which for me was the most upsetting part of the day. I know that sounds weird, but in my young mind, my mother had died long before we buried her.

After the funeral, my aunt took me for a couple of days, until my father came and got me and we went on with our lives. Just like that. Just like nothing had happened.

My father, Robert Dante Rossi, didn't have a degree, but he was smart. He had started but never finished college (even though he insisted that I did). He was hardworking and good with people. I once heard one of his colleagues describe my father as "the kind of guy who could tell you to go to hell and you'd look forward to the trip."

He was a Vietnam vet and had served two years in the air cavalry, which meant he saw a lot of combat. He rarely talked about those experiences, but he didn't seem overly affected by them either, at least not in the way the movies like to paint Vietnam vets: handicapped in mind and spirit. I remember when I was fifteen I asked him if he had ever killed anyone. He was quiet for almost a minute, then looked at me and said, "I served my country."

When he got back from the war he went to college for a year before deciding it wasn't for him. He took a job managing a Maverick convenience store in Henderson. After five years and as many promotions, he was in charge of the entire Las Vegas region for Maverick. I don't suppose that he ever made a lot of money, but I never felt like we were poor. My father was disciplined and frugal, the kind of guy who still mowed his own lawn and drove an old Ford Taurus.

He did his best to raise me alone. He got up early every day, made my lunch, then drove me to school. He took a late lunch break so he could pick me up after school. I usually just stayed with him as he finished his rounds, talking about my day, then doing my homework in the car when he went inside a store. He'd always return with a slushie drink, a chocolate MoonPie, and a couple of fashion or teen magazines—the previous months that they were about to throw out. I liked being with him.

When I was a little older he decided that as long as I was making the rounds with him I should get paid for it, and he hired me as an employee. I would go into the stores he was visiting and wipe down the soda dispensers and clean the glass on the refrigerators. That's pretty much how my life went during my teenage years.

My memories of my mother were vague and hazy, perhaps because they were so heavily wrapped in trauma. Most of them were of her in a dark room lying in bed. I didn't really know her. I suppose my father could have filled in the blanks, but the truth is, I didn't want them filled in. The few times my father started to tell me about her I stopped him. "I don't want to know," I said. Looking back, I think that hurt him, but my intent was the opposite. I was trying to prove to him that I was okay without her. I felt my mother was a failure and a traitor, not just to me but even more to my father. I deserved someone who cared enough about me to stick around and so did he. We both deserved someone better than her.

At least that's how I saw it.

In high school I was one of those girls who always had to have a boyfriend. Starting in the eighth grade, I had a string of boyfriends until my senior year in high school when I started dating Kent Clark. (Yes, people teased him about his name. His friends called him "Steel of Man.") Kent was a popular guy. He was on the high school basketball team and lettered in track and wrestling as well.

Two years after high school, Kent proposed to me and I said yes. My dad, with a neighbor woman's help, went through all the work of reserving the reception center, caterer, flowers—the whole matrimonial shebang.

Then the Steel of Man kryptonited the day of the wedding, running off with a high school girlfriend he'd dated before me. It was the most humiliating experience of my life. Not the worst experience. Just the most humiliating.

Alone, I continued on with college, pursuing my general

education where my father had dropped out—the University of Nevada–Las Vegas. That's where I met Danny, another basketball player. Two years later, I was a fiancée again.

Danny was a walk-on for UNLV's basketball team and quickly moved up to starting forward. I should have known that the odds were against any kind of real relationship with a rising basketball star, but I thought I was in love and was caught up in the thrill of being the future wife of a professional athlete. I soon learned exactly what that meant, which was, to Danny, almost nothing. The more he rose in the public's (and his own) view, the less he regarded *us*. I began hearing that he was not behaving like a betrothed man on road trips. The next year he was drafted by the Orlando Magic and left Vegas, and me, behind.

Twice burned by young athletes, I found Marcus, who was nine years older than me. I also met him at college. He was my history professor, which should have been my first red flag.

My father wasn't thrilled with any of the guys I'd been with, but for the most part kept his silence. For Marcus he made an exception. He said that a professor dating his student was as unethical as a psychiatrist courting a patient. Still, as much as it pained him, he believed in letting me make my choices no matter how stupid they were. I thought it a great accomplishment that Marcus didn't leave me before we reached the altar.

In retrospect, I wish he had. I learned on our honeymoon night the extent of his cruelty. He got drunk at our wedding—drunk enough that I drove to our hotel while he yelled at me about how the wedding had been all about me, how I had neglected him, and how selfish I was. In the pain of the moment I begged his forgiveness, but he still made me sleep on the couch in the guest section of the suite my father had paid for. That was our honeymoon night. I suppose it was a preview of how my life would be with him. Before we were married, Marcus couldn't keep his hands off me. Now he wouldn't touch me. I was embarrassed to undress in front of him since he started calling me chunky and telling me that I needed to lose weight, even though I knew I didn't. He criticized me constantly, not just the way I looked, but the things I said, the things I thought, even the music I liked. He constantly called me stupid or ditzy. Nothing I did met his expectations.

What I didn't realize until later, much later, was that emotional manipulation was his modus operandi. He was a master at it. He should have taught psychology instead of history. He controlled our relationship by keeping me emotionally needy, giving me just enough "love" to not give up, but never enough to feel satisfied. It was like filling a dog's water bowl half-full. I never felt like I was enough, and apparently I wasn't. I should have left him, but I didn't. I suppose that I believed, like my father must have, that marriage was for better or for worse.

Three years after our marriage, Marcus was offered a bigger paycheck at the University of Colorado in Boulder. I hated leaving my father and Las Vegas, but it was a promotion and Marcus was insistent. I didn't fight it. I believed that supporting my husband was the right thing to do. Also,

Marcus frequently complained that I was too close to my father and that it got in the way of our marriage. I thought that the experience of being alone in a strange town would bring us closer together. It didn't.

I filed for divorce two years later when Marcus was exposed in a campus investigation for ethical misconduct, something you may have read about in the *Huffington Post*. I'll never forget the night he told me. In a cruel twist of irony, it was Valentine's Day and I had spent the day making him a romantic candlelit dinner. When I stopped crying I asked, "Why did you cheat on me?"

"You're too clingy," he said stoically. "You were suffocating me. You forced me into it."

"I forced you to cheat on me?" I said.

"Yes, you did," he said. "Besides, monogamy is unnatural. Anyone with half a brain knows that."

That evening when I called my father and told him what had happened, he never once said "I told you so." He just wanted to beat Marcus to a pulp, and likely would have if he'd been there.

The next day the press arrived at our apartment. You wouldn't believe the things they asked me.

> Press: How do you feel about your husband being sexually involved with six university students?
>
> Me: You're really asking me that?
>
> Press: Are you upset?
>
> Me: . . .

After our separation, Marcus ran off with not one but *two* of his female students. Alone again, I moved forty miles south to Denver. My father wanted me to come back to Las Vegas, but shame kept me away. I didn't want to return home a failure, even if that's what I was.

I got a job in Thornton, a suburb of Denver, as a finance officer at a Lexus car dealership, which is where I was the winter this story began.

As I look back at where I was in my life at that time, it wasn't so much that my life wasn't what I *thought* it would be, as that's likely true of all of us. Rather, it's that it wasn't what I wanted it to be. I wanted someone to build a life with, someone who would think about me when they weren't with me. I wanted someone who loved me.

I also wanted to live a life of consequence. I wanted to be someone who mattered, which leads to something else you should know about me. In spite of my catastrophic love life, more than anything I wanted to be a romance writer. I know that sounds strange. Me writing about romance is like a vegan writing about barbecue. Still, I couldn't let the dream go. So when I got a flyer in the mail for a romance writers' retreat at the Mistletoe Inn, a little voice inside told me that it might be my last chance to find what I was looking for. That voice was far more right than I could have imagined—just not in the way I ever imagined it would be.

CHAPTER

They say love is blind, but it's not. Infatuation is blind. Emotional neediness is blind. Love sees the fault—it just sees beyond it as well.

Kimberly Rossi's Diary

Denver was cold. Like arctic cold. It was a late Friday afternoon in November when Rachelle, the other finance manager, came to my office. Rachelle was gorgeous. Before being hired at Lexus she had been a Denver Broncos cheerleader, which also made her the finance manager with whom our male buyers most wanted to process their car purchases. Invariably they flirted with her, which she used to her advantage. She sold more paint protectant than the rest of us. If she wasn't so picky about men, she would have broken up half the marriages in Denver.

"Hey, Kim," she said, leaning through my door. "Could you please take this last customer? I've got an early date tonight with a guy as hot as a solar flare."

"You say that about every guy you date," I said.

"I can't help it if I'm a heat magnet. And you might like this one."

I shook my head. "Go on your date."

"You're a doll," she said, mincing away.

"You're a Barbie doll," I said under my breath.

The man Rachelle had passed on to me was in his late fifties and, in spite of it being winter, wore plaid golf pants, a lemon-yellow sweater, and a pink Polo golf shirt that stretched over his ample belly. He also wore a beret, which failed to cover his bald spot. His forehead was beaded with sweat that he constantly wiped with the handkerchief he carried. I couldn't believe that Rachelle thought this guy was my speed. No, actually I could. She had always treated me as a wallflower.

The man sat down in one of the vinyl chairs in front of my desk while Bart, the salesman who had sold the car, introduced us.

"Kim, this is Mr. Craig, the proud owner of a new GX 460." He turned back to his huffing client. "Kimberly is one of our finance officers. She'll take good care of you."

"I do hope so," the man said in a thin, whiny voice.

"I'll run to service and make sure they've got your car ready to drive home," Bart said to the man, then left my office.

"It's a pleasure to meet you, Mr. Craig," I said. "I'll get your information typed up and get you out of here to enjoy your new vehicle."

I was entering the purchase information when the man suddenly blurted out, "Is it hot in here or is it just . . . *you?*"

I looked up at him. He was gazing at me with an insipid grin.

"It's a little warm," I said. "If you like I can turn down the heat."

"No," he said, a little thrown that I hadn't fallen for his line. "I like it hot." Then he started to hum that song, ". . . *some like it hot, some sweat when the heat is on* . . ." He was definitely sweating.

"Okay," I said. "What's your phone number?"

"My phone number," he repeated. "My phone number." He pretended to look through his pockets. Then he said, "I seem to have misplaced it. Can I have yours?"

"Excuse me?" I said.

He just looked at me.

"Your phone number?" I repeated.

"It's 555-445-3989."

I typed in the number. I hoped that the awkwardness had successfully dissuaded him but it hadn't. A few minutes later he said, "Your name is Kimberly?"

"Yes."

"May I call you Kim?"

"Yes, you may," I said, continuing typing.

A beat later he asked, "What time?"

I looked up. "What time . . . what?"

"What time may I call you, Kim?"

I breathed out slowly. "Okay, Mr. Craig . . ."

"Tim."

"I'm flattered, Tim, but I'm not in the market right now, so you just hang on to those gems for some other lucky gal."

He slightly blushed. "Sorry."

"No need to be sorry," I said. "Now, if you'll just fill out your insurance information."

He silently filled out the paperwork. When he finished he said, "Are you almost off work?"

I looked up from my computer.

"Because, if you are, I'll take you for a ride in my new car. Maybe we could go to dinner. Or *something*."

"Just a minute," I said, standing. "May I get you some water?"

"I'm not thirsty."

"I meant to cool you off."

"No, I'm good," he said.

"All right, I'll be right back."

I walked into the employee break room and grabbed myself a ginger ale. My manager, Steve, was sitting at a table working on his iPad. Steve was a good guy, and one of my few real friends at the dealership.

"Just kill me now," I said. "Please."

"What's going on?"

"Mr. Beret is. He thinks the car should come with a dealer-installed woman."

"That would increase sales," Steve said. "I wonder if it's ever been done."

"You're not being helpful."

"Sorry. Is it the GX?"

"Yes."

"Wasn't that Rachelle's?"

"Was. She asked me to take it for her. She had a hot date."

"Rachelle always has a hot date," he said. "Want me to finish up for you?"

"No. I just needed someone to commiserate with."

"Consider yourself co-commiserated."

"Thanks."

I started to walk back to my office when Steve said, "Just tell him you're not interested in dating."

"Yeah, I did."

"It didn't help?"

"No."

As I walked back to my office I thought, *Is that what everyone thinks about me?*

CHAPTER Three

There have been seasons of my life when rejection rained down. And then there have been typhoons.

Kimberly Rossi's Diary

In spite of the Denver traffic, my commute wasn't too bad. I was glad to get home. For once I had plans for the evening. I had a second date with Collin, a man I had met at the dealership. He wasn't buying a car—he was a vendor who sold tools to our service bay. I had gone to get a bottle of water from the waiting area and he was there drinking a coffee. He struck up a conversation by the coffeemaker, then asked me out.

I stopped by the Java Hut for a coffee, then headed home. I lived in a decent but inexpensive apartment complex in Thornton, about a half hour from the dealership. Walking into my apartment with my hands filled with my coffee, purse, and mail, I heard my phone chirp with a text message.

"You will have to wait," I said to myself. I unlocked my door and went inside. I set down my coffee and mail, then dug through my purse for my phone. I lifted it to read the text message. It was from Collin.

Sorry. Something came up. Rain check? I'll call you.

I'm sure you will, I thought. I sighed. I liked the guy. I felt like a rejection magnet.

I started looking through my mail. There was a letter from the Boulder County Clerk's office. I tore it open.

IN THE DISTRICT COURT OF THE BOULDER JUDICIAL DISTRICT OF THE STATE OF COLORADO, IN AND FOR THE COUNTY OF BOULDER

Kimberly Rossi,
Plaintiff,
vs.
Marcus Y. Stewart,
Defendant.
Case No.: 4453989
DECREE OF DIVORCE

This matter came before the court on the seventh day of October 2012. It appears from the records and files of this action that a Complaint was filed and served upon the Defendant.

The rest of the letter was just typical legal jargon, which basically said over and over that we were over. However, the last line stopped me.

3. Name Change. Wife will retain the last name of Rossi.

Rossi again, I thought. *Back to where I started.*

The paper was dated and signed by the magistrate and judge. The formalities of our divorce had taken longer than I had expected, as Marcus had fought the divorce the whole way. He wasn't trying to keep me, he was trying to keep his money.

I don't know why the letter made our separation feel any more official—I hadn't seen Marcus for more than six months—but it did. He was a liar, a cheater, and he didn't love me. So why was I so sad?

I flipped through the rest of the mail. As a child, I had thought mail was something magical. There were handwritten letters, cards, and thank-you notes. Now it seemed to be nothing but circulars and junk mail—the physical equivalent of spam.

Then I saw a letter from a publisher.

"Please, please, please." I tore open the envelope.

Monday, October 12, 2012

Dear Author,

They didn't use my name. Not a good sign.

Thank you for giving us the opportunity to consider your manuscript. We read it with interest. While there was much to like about your book, we regret we will not be making an offer of publication. We do not feel that we are the right publishing house to successfully publish your book.

Thank you for thinking of us, and we wish you every success in finding a publisher for your work.

Yours sincerely,
Sharlene Drexell

Strike three. I sighed loudly. Actually, it was more of a groan. The universe must have conspired to bring me so much rejection at once. I was almost in a daze as I looked through the rest of the mail, which I did more out of habit than of interest.

That's when I saw the card for a writers' conference at the Mistletoe Inn.

CHAPTER

Four

There are people whom we've never met in person yet feel closer to than those we brush up against in real life.

Kimberly Rossi's Diary

I must be on a wannabe-writer list somewhere. Six years ago I attended a two-day writing seminar in San Francisco and ever since then I've gotten notices every month about the latest writing conference, seminar, retreat, or authors' workshop—a faucet I'd probably turn off if I had any idea where the spigot was. But this one looked interesting.

THE MISTLETOE INN WRITERS' RETREAT

Attention Aspiring Romance Writers—

Bring Your Brand of Love to the Mistletoe Inn!
This Holiday Give Yourself a Once-in-a-Lifetime Christmas Gift.

Writing Workshops • Panel Discussions
Agent Pitch Sessions • Open Mic Readings

Special Keynote Speaker

H. T. Cowell

December 10–17, 2012

$2,199 includes room / breakfast & lunch each day

What especially caught my eye was the name H. T. Cowell—and not just because his name was printed in type twice the size of everything else on the piece. Cowell had earned twenty-point type. You probably remember him, or at least his name. He was once the bestselling romance writer in America.

Actually he was one of the bestselling writers of any genre. He didn't just dominate the genre, he defined it. What Stephen King did for horror, Cowell did for romance. He's also the writer who made *me* want to be a writer. For years I read everything he wrote. And then, like the other men in my life, he was gone. The difference was, no one knew where he went.

Cowell, who was reclusive to begin with—his books didn't even have an author photo—was one of those literary-world enigmas like J. D. Salinger or E. M. Forster who, at the top of their game, disappeared into the shadowy ether of obscurity, like a literary version of Amelia Earhart.

Of course, that just made him more intriguing to his readers. The year he stopped writing was the same year Danny left me. I think, on some level, I had fallen in love with H. T. Cowell. Or at least the idea of him. I couldn't believe that after all this time he was coming out in public.

I looked over the advertisement, then set it apart from the rest of the mail. The event was pricey, at least for me, but it was, as advertised, a once-in-a-lifetime experience. And right now I needed a once-in-a-lifetime experience. I needed something to look forward to. Frankly, I needed something to live for. I looked over the advertisement again.

To book your space, call 555-2127. Or register online.

I made myself some ramen noodles for dinner, then was turning on *The Bachelor* when my phone rang. It was my father.

"Hey, Dad."

"*Ciao, bella*. How are you?"

"I'm okay," I said. "How are you?"

"*Bene, bene*." He sounded tired. "I wanted to make sure you're still coming out for Thanksgiving."

"Of course."

"And Christmas?"

"That too."

"Do you know what day you'll be here?"

"For Thanksgiving, Wednesday afternoon. I'm not sure about Christmas. What day is Christmas this year?"

"It's on a Tuesday."

"I'll probably be out the Sunday before, if that's okay."

"Great, but you might have to take a cab from the airport. There's a chance I might not be back until late Sunday night."

"Where are you going?"

"A group of us are taking a Harley ride over to Albuquerque."

"That sounds fun. Just be careful."

"I always am."

"You know, your Harley has two seats."

"Are you inviting yourself?"

"I meant you might want to take a friend. A female friend."

"Well, don't faint, but I've invited someone. I'm waiting for her to get back to me."

This was a first. "Does this *someone* have a name?"

"Alice. She works down at the VA. We've been spending some time together lately."

"It's about time."

"It's nothing serious," he quickly added. "I'm not really looking for anything but a little companionship."

"That's a good place to start."

"How about you?" he asked. "Any new friends?"

"Nothing special."

"No need to rush into anything. And I'm so glad you're coming out. We'll have a wonderful, relaxing time."

"That sounds nice," I said. "Nothing like the dry desert heat to warm your bones. Especially at Christmas."

"Which reminds me. What do you want for Christmas?"

"I don't need anything," I said.

"I didn't ask what you needed, I asked what you wanted. Besides, I'm just spending your inheritance anyway. You want it now or after I check out and taxes are higher?"

"I'd rather you not talk about 'checking out.' You're going to live forever."

"Ah, denial." He was quiet a moment, then said softly, "We all check out sometime, baby."

"Can we please not talk about this?"

"Sorry. So help me out here. What can I give you for Christmas? My mutual funds did well this year. I'd like to do something meaningful."

I hesitated a moment, then said, "Well, there is something."

"Name it."

"I wouldn't ask for you to do the whole thing, but maybe you could help me with part of it. There's a romance writers' conference in Vermont that I'd like to go to."

"Still holding on to the dream?"

"Barely," I said.

"I'm glad you are," he said. "You're such a talented writer. You hang on to it. Without dreams, life is a desert."

"With a love life like mine I should be writing horror, not romance."

"We're Italians. We invented the word *romance*. So you just hang on to that dream until it happens. That's what gets us up in the morning."

I sighed. "So what do you dream about?"

"My daughter," he said without hesitation. "Mostly. And her next visit. I can't wait to see you."

"I can't wait to see you, Dad. I love you."

"I love you too, girl."

CHAPTER

Like a balloon, a full heart is easier to puncture.

Kimberly Rossi's Diary

The next few weeks passed slowly. We had several major snowstorms, and business at the dealership was slow. There's a predictable psychology of car sales and people don't like to buy new cars in the snow, unless, of course, there's too much snow and they suddenly need a four-wheel-drive vehicle.

I was very glad for Thanksgiving break. I left work early Wednesday afternoon and drove myself out to the airport for my flight to Vegas.

Much can be said about the Denver airport, and much is. There are groups of conspiracy theorists who believe that the Denver airport is the secret headquarters of the Illuminati, New World Order, or the Neo-Nazi party, evidenced by the fact that from the air, the airport purportedly looks like a giant swastika.

My favorite theory is that the airport is an underground base for aliens. However, if the airport *were* run by aliens, you would think they would do a better job of managing things. A technically advanced civilization that can travel at light speed should, for instance, be able to get your luggage to you.

And then there's *Blucifer*, the airport's famous thirty-two-foot, anatomically correct blue horse sculpture. With its blazing red-bulb eyes and crazed expression, the piece is enough to stir fear in the most seasoned flier. What adds to the sculpture's lore is the fact that in a Frankenstein's-monster sort of way, the creation killed its creator. Luis Jiménez, the sculpture's artist, was crushed when a piece of the massive sculpture fell on him.

Not surprisingly, the airport was slammed with pre-Thanksgiving traffic, and the security line at Denver International looked more like the start of the Boston Marathon than any sort of a civilized queue. The insanity didn't ease after the security checkpoint, as every gate was thronged with travelers.

As I was at the gate checking on a possible seat upgrade, a harried young father walked up next to me.

"There's been a mistake," he said to a ticket agent, laying a stack of boarding passes on the counter in front of him. "They've scattered our seats throughout the plane."

The agent, who looked as if he'd had better days, glanced down at the passes, then back up. "I'm sorry," he said gruffly, "the flight's overbooked. There's nothing I can do about it now."

"But we have four children," he said. "Three of them are under four. Our flight's already been delayed three hours. These kids are going crazy."

"You should have thought of that when you booked the tickets."

"I should have thought that you would delay the flight three hours?" the man asked.

"A delayed flight's always a possibility, sir. But I meant you should have booked your seats together."

"They were all booked at the same time six weeks in advance. There was no reason to believe that you would scatter them."

"*I* didn't do anything to your seats," he said defensively. "And it's out of my hands. There's nothing I can do about it."

I looked sympathetically at the frustrated man, wondering what he would do.

"Can I talk to a manager?" he asked, doing his best to remain civil.

"She's not here right now," the agent said. "We're a bit busy." He scooped up the passes and handed them back. "I'll call you up to the counter when she can talk. But, like I said, the flight's overbooked. I doubt there's anything she can do."

The man took his passes and returned to a seat next to his wife, who looked equally stressed—more so after he relayed the information he'd just received.

I was told that all the first-class passengers had checked in, so I took a seat directly across from the man and his family. I watched the exhausted couple become increasingly exasperated as their small children grew more impatient. About forty-five minutes later the man still hadn't been called up so he returned to the counter. The agent spoke loud enough that I could hear him say curtly, "I told you I'd call you up when she had time."

The man again returned to his seat. Busy or not, there was no excuse for the agent's rudeness, I thought.

Another half hour passed when the man stood and walked back up to the counter. The gate agent stiffened as the man approached and I expected an explosive confrontation. Instead, the man said, "Hey, about my request. Don't worry about it."

The agent looked at him with a blank expression. "What?"

"It's cool, really. You're busy, don't worry about it. We're good."

The agent looked even more disturbed than before. "What?"

"Look," the man said calmly. "After four hours in this airport with these kids, we're exhausted. If you're offering free babysitting, we're all over that. They can be someone else's problems." He turned and walked back to his seat, leaving the agent speechless. Less than ten minutes later the agent paged the man over the intercom, then said nothing as he handed the man a pile of boarding passes, presumably all next to each other.

Well played, I thought. *Well played.*

My flight landed in Vegas at around five. Not surprisingly the Las Vegas airport was even more slammed than Denver's. I retrieved my bag from the carousel, then called my father. "I'm here."

"I'm just parked in the cell phone lot," he said. "I'll be right there."

Just a few minutes after I arrived at the curb my father pulled up in his metallic-blue 2004 Ford Taurus. He climbed out to hug me. One of the effects of not seeing my father for such long stretches of time was that he always looked older. But this time he was thinner too. Regardless, it was always good to see him. We embraced and he kissed my face all over until I laughed—just as he had done when I was a little girl.

"It's so good to see you, sweetie."

"It's good to see you, Dad. You lost weight."

"It happens," he said.

"I wish it would happen to me."

"You don't need to lose weight. You look perfect." He grabbed my bag and threw it into the backseat of his car. "Are you hungry?"

"Famished."

"Good. I thought we'd stop by Salvatore's on the way home." When we were on the freeway he asked, "How was your flight?"

"Crowded," I said. "People were grumpy."

"Crowds make people grumpy," he said. "Nothing like holiday travel to foul some people's mood."

"Not you," I said.

He smiled. "No, not me. I get to see my girl."

We stopped at my father's favorite Italian restaurant, Cucina Salvatore. I hadn't been there for years, not since I'd moved to Colorado. The owner, Salvatore, loudly greeted my father as we walked in.

"Roberto, *bello*. It has been too long."

"You say that every time," my father said. "I was here just last week."

"You are *famiglia*. It is always too long. *Sempre troppo tempo*."

"He says that to everyone," my father said to me.

Salvatore gestured toward me. "How is it you are always with beautiful women?"

"Oh really?" I said.

"This is my daughter," my father said.

"*Questa bella donna è la tua figlia? No!*" Salvatore put his hands on my cheeks and kissed me. "They grow too fast."

Salvatore sat us at a small table near the corner of the restaurant. "For family, the best table in the house," he said. "*Buon appetito*."

After he had left, my father smiled, then said, "Always the best table in the house." Then he told me that Salvatore had said that about two other tables.

We ordered bruschetta with baked garlic, sun-dried tomatoes, and goat cheese for an appetizer, then shared a Caprese salad. For our *primi piatti* I ordered a scallop risotto and my father ordered the mushroom gnocchi. For our second plate my father ordered Florentine steak while I had breaded chicken cacciatore.

After we'd been served our meals, my father asked, "So how's work?"

"Living the dream," I said sarcastically.

He nodded understandingly. He took a bite of steak, then said, "Tell me about this writers' conference."

"It's small. Intimate. From what I read, it's more than just a conference, it's a weeklong retreat with daily workshops where I can refine my book. And there will be real agents I can show my book to. But the best part is that my favorite writer of all time is going to be there. H. T. Cowell."

"I don't think I know who that is," my father said. "What has he written?"

"Nothing you would have read. He's a romance writer."

"Did Mom read him?" he asked. "She loved those romance books."

The question bothered me. "No. He came after her."

I think he sensed how uncomfortable I was and changed the subject. "Have you ever shown your book to an agent before?"

"No. I've sent it to a few publishers, but they just sent back rejection letters." I took a drink of wine. "Maybe it's just not good enough. Maybe I'm not good enough."

"Stop that," my father said. "All great artists get rejections. It's part of what defines them. Decca Records turned down the Beatles."

"I'm not the Beatles," I said. "And I'm no great artist."

"Why? Because you know yourself? A prophet is without honor in his own country, but more so in his own mind."

"I'm not a prophet either."

"But you might be a great writer," he said. "Or will be." My dad leaned forward. "Writing and work aside, how are you doing? How are you handling the divorce?"

"I'm fine," I said. "I'm doing really well."

For a moment he looked deep into my eyes, then said,

"Remember when you were a teenager and you told me that you hadn't taken my Buick with your friends?"

I wasn't sure why he chose this moment to bring up that not-so-pleasant memory. "Yes."

"Well, you're no better a liar now than you were then."

My eyes filled with tears. Then I bowed my head and began to cry. My father reached across the table and took my hand. "I'm sorry."

I wiped my eyes with my napkin, then looked back at him. "Why doesn't anybody want me? What's wrong with me?"

My father looked anguished. "Honey, there's nothing wrong with you."

I continued wiping my eyes. "You haven't really liked any of the guys I dated."

"I liked that Briton guy. The med student."

"That lasted only four weeks," I said. "I saw him on Facebook. He's married now, has two children and his own practice. He's doing well."

The moment fell into silence. Our waiter, Mario, came over and refilled our water glasses from a carafe. After he left I said, "You didn't like Marcus."

"No," he said, failing to hide the anger that Marcus's name still provoked. "He was a five-star loser. I saw that train wreck a mile off."

I shook my head slowly. "Why didn't I?"

He looked at me for a long time, then said, "Maybe when you figure that out, you won't be lonely."

I frowned. "Maybe." We both went back to eating. After a few minutes I said, "Well, at least I have you."

My father stopped eating, then looked at me thoughtfully. "That brings up something," he said slowly. His forehead furrowed. "You know when we were on the phone and you said I was going to live forever?" I just looked at him. He looked uncomfortable. "Three weeks ago I had a colonoscopy. They, uh . . ." He hesitated, looking into my fearful eyes. "They found a tumor."

I set down my fork. "But it's benign . . . ?"

He let out a nearly inaudible groan. "I have colon cancer."

I couldn't speak.

"Unfortunately, we didn't catch it early, so it's regionalized. It's what they call stage 3A."

Tears began to well up in my eyes. "I can't believe this."

"Now hold on, it's not as bad as it sounds. I know, stage three sounds like I've already got a foot in the grave, but I don't. There's an almost seventy percent survival rate. I'll take those odds any day of the week. Heck, just taking my Harley out on the road I have worse odds."

"Where are you getting care?"

"At the VA."

"The veterans hospital? You might as well just hang yourself."

"You're being dramatic. It's not that way."

I broke down crying. He took my hand. When I could speak, I said, "Can we go home now?"

He leaned over the table and kissed my forehead, then said, "Whatever you want, sweetheart. Whatever you want."

CHAPTER *Six*

How different life would be if we knew just how little of it we actually possessed.

Kimberly Rossi's Diary

My father's house was simple but beautiful—a typical Las Vegas rambler with a rock-and-white-stucco exterior surrounded by palm trees. It wasn't a large home, and everything was on one floor—three bedrooms, two baths—but there was plenty of room for the two of us.

In spite of my aching heart, or perhaps because of it, I was especially glad to be back. After all this time it still felt like home.

My father gave me his keys to the house, then grabbed my suitcase and followed me in. In the foyer was a large new saltwater fish aquarium filled with beautiful exotic fish, his newest hobby.

"How are your fish?" I asked.

"The fish," he said, sounding a little exasperated. "I had an incident last week. I purchased one of those triggerfish. It started eating the other fish, including my hundred-dollar pygmy angelfish."

"Expensive hobby," I said.

"Too expensive for my budget," he said. "Never should have done it."

He carried my bag to my old bedroom and set it down next to the bed. "I washed the sheets and everything."

"Thanks, Dad." There was an uneasy awkwardness between us, as if he wasn't sure if he should leave me alone or not. Finally I asked, "Are you ready for tomorrow?"

"Just about. I baked the pies this morning."

"*You* baked pies?"

"It's something new I'm trying," he said. "I got the recipes off the Internet. And I had a little help. That woman I told you about from the VA hospital. She came over and helped me cook."

"You mean Alice?" I said.

He grinned. "Alice. As in, Alice's Restaurant."

"Whatever that is," I said.

"So I made a pumpkin pie and a pecan pie. The pecan pie was a little tricky, but it turned out all right."

"I'm glad that she came over," I said. "I don't like you being alone all the time."

"I'm not alone. I've got fish."

"If they don't all eat each other."

I suspect that he guessed I was just making small talk to avoid the cancerous elephant in the room, because he sat down on my bed next to me and put his arm around me. "Let me tell you something. When I was in Nam, there was this guy I served with named Gordie Ewell. He was regular infantry, served four years in combat. That man was indestructible. He was in some of the most intense battles of the war: Hamburger Hill, Khe Sanh, and Cu Chi. He survived a crash in a downed helicopter, had a jeep blown up beneath him from a land mine, was hit by grenade shrapnel in a trench, got bit by a viper and shot twice. But nothing stopped him. The men nicknamed him Boomerang because he always came back.

"When he was finally released, he was awarded three Purple Hearts. He went home to Brooklyn in June of seventy-three, around the time the war started winding down.

"About a month later he went in to get a wisdom tooth pulled. He was given too much anesthetic and died in the dentist chair."

I just looked at my father. "Exactly what part of that was supposed to make me feel better?"

"I'm just saying that when it's your time, it's your time. I know that might sound foreboding, but I take hope in it." He put his hands on my cheeks. "I don't believe it's my time, girl. We've still got plenty of good years ahead of us, you and I." He kissed me on the forehead, then stood. "Now go to bed. We've got a lot to do tomorrow."

"Good night, Dad."

"Good night, sweetheart." He walked to the door, then looked back. "Our best years are still to come. Don't forget that."

"I hope you're right," I said.

"I know I'm right," he said, thumping his fist against his heart. "I know it." He walked out, shutting the door behind him.

I undressed, turned out the light, then crawled under the covers. I cried myself to sleep.

CHAPTER *Seven*

Sometimes the most whole people are those who come from the most broken circumstances.

Kimberly Rossi's Diary

Not surprisingly, I didn't sleep well. Thoughts of my father's cancer played through my mind like a bad song you can't get rid of. I sat bolt upright in the middle of the night after dreaming that I was at his funeral.

In spite of my lack of sleep, I got up early enough to go outside and watch the sun rise over the River Mountains. It was cool outside, probably in the low sixties, but practically sweltering compared to the freeze I'd left back in Denver.

I put on my walking shoes, sweatpants, and a Denver Broncos sweatshirt and walked about six miles, trying to clear my head a little before going back to the house. I was hoping that the walk would make me feel better, but it only made my mind focus more on my father's cancer. I started crying twice, once when I was almost home, so I just kept walking for another mile. I didn't want my dad to see me crying—not that I could have hidden it anymore, as my eyes were already red and puffy. When I walked into the house my father was in the kitchen making breakfast.

"I made you some oatmeal." My father said nothing about my puffy eyes, which I was grateful for. He hugged me, then handed me a bowl. "I made it just the way you like it, with cream, walnuts, raisins, and a lot of brown sugar. Too much brown sugar."

"Thanks, Dad." I sat down to eat.

"How was your walk?"

"It was okay," I said.

My father poured cream over his oatmeal, then sat down across from me. "How did you sleep?"

"It's just good to be back home," I said, ignoring his question.

"It's always good when you're home," he replied. "You don't have to live in Colorado."

"I know," I said.

After we finished eating, my father, as tradition dictated, put on the Carpenters' Christmas album and Karen's rich voice filled our home.

We had a lot of cooking to do, which I was glad for. I needed something to occupy my mind. My tasks were pecan-crusted sweet potato casserole and corn bread stuffing.

I noticed that my father set the table with two extra settings.

"Are we having guests?"

"I invited a couple of men from the hospital. Chuck and Joel. They don't have any family around. Is that all right?"

"Of course. What about Alice?"

"She's in Utah with her children. Her son owns an Internet company up there."

Neither of us spoke for a while. The emotion returned

and I purposely kept turned away from my father, occasionally dabbing my cheeks with a napkin or dish towel. I was chopping pecans for the casserole when he walked up beside me. "What's wrong?"

I kept chopping, avoiding eye contact. "You mean, besides you dying?"

He put his hand on mine to stop me. "I told you I'm not dying."

"Relying on care from the veterans hospital is not exactly filling me with confidence. Las Vegas has one of the best cancer facilities in America. Why don't you go there?"

"Why should I get any better treatment than anyone else?"

"What you should get is the best treatment available."

"I am. The VA is what's available. I can't afford any fancy cancer center."

"But your insurance . . ."

"My Medicare covers the VA."

I shook my head. "There's got to be another way to pay for it."

He didn't say anything.

After a moment I said, "Do you know what makes this even worse, if that were possible? It's that this is happening on Thanksgiving. Now I've lost another holiday since Mom obliterated Christmas and Marcus destroyed Valentine's Day. Now I just need some tragedy on Halloween and Easter."

"I'm sorry," he said. "I shouldn't have told you."

"Of course you should have told me."

"Then you have to believe me that everything is going to be all right."

"What does that even mean? *All right*. Like, dying is *all right*?"

He was quiet a moment, then said, "If it comes to that."

"If it comes to that? Why do you have to be so okay about your death?"

"Why do you have to be so *un*okay about it? Everyone dies."

I looked at him, fighting back tears. "Not you."

"Why not me?"

"Because you're all I have." I broke down crying. "You're all I've ever had."

He put his arms around me and held me close, rubbing his fingers through my hair. Then he said, "You're right. That's not fair of me, is it? You're all I have too."

I sobbed in his arms for several minutes. After I quieted he said, "I meant it when I said I don't think it's my time. But if, God forbid, it is, remember that death is the punctuation at the end of the sentence. It's up to us to decide what kind of punctuation it will be—a period or an exclamation point."

"Or a question mark."

"Sometimes that too," he said. "But if this is the end, and I don't think it is, do we want to leave our sentence unfinished? Or do we make it the best ending possible?" I didn't answer and he leaned forward. "What should we do?"

"We make it the best ending possible."

He smiled. "Good girl. Now have a little faith that things will work out all right. Besides, we have a lot to be thankful for."

At the moment I couldn't think of a single thing. "Like what?"

"Like this moment," he said. "Right now."

As I wiped the tears from my eyes the timer on the oven went off.

"There's the rolls," he said. "And I know you're grateful for those." He donned oven mitts, then opened the oven door. "Just about there." My father made the best Parker House rolls on the planet. He brushed butter on top of the rolls, then shut the oven again.

"How's everything coming on your end?" he asked.

"It's getting there."

"Good. Our friends will be here in a half hour."

My father was carving the turkey with an electric knife when the doorbell rang. "That must be Chuck and Joel. You mind getting that?"

"No problem." I walked to the front door and opened it. The men standing in the doorway didn't look like I thought they would, as I was expecting two of my father's Vietnam buddies. They weren't. One was much older than my father. He was short and had an exaggerated potbelly. He was also blind, which I could tell because his eyes were milky white. The other man was closer to my age, maybe a few years younger. He was cute with thick, curly black hair and the rugged square jaw of a marine. He leaned on a crutch as he was missing his right leg and left forearm.

"Happy Thanksgiving," I said. "Please come in."

"Thanks, ma'am," the younger man said.

"Gentlemen," my father shouted from the kitchen. "Come on in."

"You must be mistaken," the old man said, laughing. "There's no gentlemen here."

My father walked out of the kitchen to greet them. "Sorry, just carving the bird. Come in, come in."

The older man held on to the stump of the younger man's arm as they walked into the house.

"It smells like heaven," the older man said.

"You're not going to leave hungry," I said.

"Who is this lovely young woman answering your door?" the old man asked.

"And all this time I thought you were blind," my father said.

"I can't see," he said. "But I'm not blind." He turned toward me. "I'm Chuck, young lady." He reached out and I gave him my hand. He took it and kissed it. "Thank you for letting an old man crash your party."

"It's our pleasure," I said.

"I'm Joel," the other man said, extending his hand. "I really appreciate the invitation. I'm stuck here in rehab for a little while. It's nice to get out on a holiday."

"Come sit down," I said. "We're just finishing up." I led them over to the table. "Sit wherever you'd like."

"You better show me where," Chuck said.

"Sorry," I said. I pulled out a chair and led his hand to the back of it. "You can sit right here."

"Thank you, little lady."

"Can I get you something to drink?" my father asked the men. "Wine? Beer?"

"I'll have some wine," Joel said.

"None of that fancy stuff for me," Chuck said. "I'll take a Bud if you got one."

My father brought over a can of beer and a glass of white wine. "It's probably sacrilege for an Italian not to serve a Chianti, but I'm supporting the local economy. This vino is called Serenity, it's from the Sanders Winery in Pahrump."

Joel took a sip. "It's good. Thank you."

"It's got a touch of pear and sweet jasmine," my father said, walking back to the kitchen. "I rather like it."

"You talked me into it," Chuck said. "You could be a pitchman for the stuff. I better try some."

"How about you, sweetie?" my father asked. "A little vino?"

"I'll have a glass," I said. *Or maybe the bottle*, I thought.

My father poured two more glasses of wine and carried them over to the table, then retrieved the cloth-lined basket of rolls and brought them over as well. "Hot from the oven. We've got everything but the turkey."

"Don't hold back on the bird," Chuck said. "It's not Thanksgiving without the bird."

As my father brought the platter over, Chuck raised his nose and breathed in the aroma. "Oh, that is heaven," he said. "I'm drooling like one of ol' Pavlov's canines. Let's eat."

"After we say thanks," my father said. He took my hand and Joel's shoulder. The rest of us took the hands of those next to us. "Kim, will you say grace?"

"Thank you," I said. I bowed my head. "Dear Lord, we are thankful for this day to consider all we have to be grateful for. We are grateful for this food and the abundance of it. We are grateful to be together . . ." Suddenly I could feel emotion rise in my throat. "Bless our health. Amen."

"Amen," everyone said.

"Let's get eating," my father said. "White meat is on the side closest to you, Chuck, dark on the other."

"I like them both. You mind dishing up for me, dear?" he asked me.

"Not at all. What would you like?"

"A little of everything," he said. "To begin with."

I dished up his plate and set it in front of him and he again breathed in deeply. "I have died and gone to heaven. Those are real mashed potatoes, aren't they? Not the fake, pearl kind."

"I mashed them myself."

"And the corn. Is it hand shucked?"

"What?"

"It's a line from a Bill Murray movie," Joel said, smiling. "Don't answer him. It will just encourage him."

"And is that divine smell pecan-crusted sweet potatoes?"

"You can smell that?"

"Oh yes. When my eyes went, my nose took over. I can almost read with my nose."

"Chuck's been in the veterans hospital for about three months," my father said. "He's waiting for a liver transplant."

"That's why I got this funny belly," he said, rubbing his stomach. "It's called ascites. It's caused by buildup of fluid in the abdomen. They pump it out, and it comes back a week later." He turned toward my father. "You know, it occurred to me the other day that I might finally be getting old."

"You're only as old as you think you are," my father said.

"I think I'm four hundred years old."

"How long do you have to wait?" I asked.

"Probably a month after I die," he said. "At my age, I'm not exactly a high priority on the donor list. And it is the VA."

His last comment especially bothered me. "Where's your family?" I asked. I immediately regretted the question as a look of pain flashed across his face.

"They can't be bothered with an old man like me."

There was an awkward silence. I took a sip of wine, then said, "My father said you served in the Korean War."

"No," he said. "It wasn't a war. It was a police action. That's what Truman called it."

"But you served in Korea," my father said.

"Yes, sir."

I turned to Joel. "And you served in Iraq?"

"Yes. Iraq and Afghanistan. Afghanistan is where the war ended for me. Our Humvee drove over an IED. I was the lucky one. I lost a few body parts, but everyone else lost their lives."

Lucky hadn't crossed my mind. "You're from Vegas?"

"Originally I'm from Huntsville. But my wife and I lived here with her mother before I left for Iraq." His face fell. "But we're getting divorced." I could see the pain saying this brought him. "She filed for divorce when she found out that all of her husband wasn't coming back."

"I'm so sorry."

"I mean, I can see how it would be hard. I lost more than my limbs." He hesitated. "It's not what she signed up for."

"You're being too kind to her," I said.

He looked me in the eyes. "I've seen a lot of hurt in this world. Can you be too kind?"

I couldn't answer.

Joel took a deep breath. "Anyway, I'm thankful that we didn't have any children before I left. Way things came down, that would have messed them up either way, you know? Half of their father comes home."

"I'm sorry," I said.

He forced a smile. "So your father says you don't live in Vegas."

"I've been living in Denver for the last three and a half years."

"It's too cold in Denver," Chuck said. "That's why they call it the Mile High City."

"They call it the Mile High City because it's a mile above sea level," my father said.

"That too."

"I read that the high in Denver yesterday was six degrees," I said. "There were five-foot snowdrifts."

"That's inhuman," Chuck said. "Like back in fifty in Pusan. The ground was so frozen we had to light flares just to plant tent stakes. Could I have some more of those sweet potatoes? And a little more corn bread stuffing?"

"Of course," I said, taking his plate. As I returned it Joel said, "Your father told us that you're an author."

"I'm an *aspiring* author," I said. "My day job is doing the paperwork at a car dealership."

"What dealership?" Chuck asked.

"Lexus."

"Lexus makes a fine car," he said. "I always wanted one of their little sports cars, but couldn't swing it."

Joel continued. "So have you written some books?"

"One. It still needs to be edited. I'm trying to find a publisher, or an agent, but I keep getting rejections."

"I hear that happens to all writers," Joel said mercifully. "A few weeks ago I saw this author on PBS. He said he had a collection of dozens of rejection letters. After he sold his first million books, he wrote each of the publishers who had rejected him and sent them a copy of the *New York Times* bestseller list with his book at number one and a letter telling them how much money they had lost so far. Then he had all his rejection letters framed."

"I'm still working on my collection," I said.

"What's your book about?"

"It's a holiday romance about this lonely woman who meets a man who is dreading going to all his holiday events alone, so he asks her if she would like to pretend to be a couple."

"Pretend?" Chuck asked.

"Yes. They're the only ones who know their relationship's not real."

"And they fall in love?" Chuck said.

"It's a love story," my father said. "Of course they fall in love. If it was a thriller, they'd shoot each other."

"It sounds interesting," Joel said. "I'd read it."

"You'd read a romance?" I asked. "I see you as more of a Brad Thor or Lee Child reader."

He smiled. "Actually, I do like a good thriller, but I'm open to other genres. If a writer's got a good style."

"She's got a great style," my father said. "She's going to a writers' conference in a couple weeks. She'll get a chance to meet some agents and hopefully sell her book."

"That's really great," Joel said. "I hope things work out."

"I don't know if I'm really going," I said. "I mean, I looked at it, but it was kind of out of my price range."

"She's going," my father said.

I didn't say anything.

"Well, it sounds like a lot of fun," Joel said. "When you have your first book signing, I'll be the first in line."

"You're very sweet," I said.

"The truth is, you could sell books just from your author photo. You're very pretty."

I was a little taken aback. "Thank you."

There was an awkward silence. Joel blushed, then said, "I'm sorry, ma'am. I didn't mean to embarrass you."

"No. That was very sweet."

He still looked embarrassed. "I can't believe I put my foot in my mouth when there's all this delicious food I should be eating instead."

"What can I get you?" I asked.

"Well, I'd give an arm and a leg for some more of that sweet potato casserole."

The whole table went quiet. Then he suddenly laughed. "Wait, I already did."

What a beautiful man, I thought.

"Best Thanksgiving dinner I've ever had," Chuck said, patting his stomach.

"You're being kind," my father replied.

"Since when has anyone accused me of that?" he asked. "You know me, I'm old enough to speak the truth. My first wife was a horrible cook. The second one wouldn't cook. I don't know which was worse."

Joel and I smiled at each other.

"I'll get some coffee," my father said. "Any takers?"

"I'd like some," Joel said. "With a little milk."

"Me too," I said.

While my father made the coffee I brought the pies over to the table.

"What'ya got there?" Chuck asked. "It smells like pies."

"Right again. Pumpkin and pecan."

"I would like both, please."

I turned to Joel. "What would you like, Joel?"

"May I have some pecan, please?"

"Of course. Would you like it à la mode?"

"Yes, ma'am."

"Heated up?"

"No, cold is good. I don't like melted ice cream."

"I'm the same way," I said.

"It's all the same once it hits the stomach," Chuck said.

"I don't know why people say that," my father said.

I served pie to the two men, then took a sliver of both kinds for myself. After coffee, the men watched the Dallas Cowboys and the Washington Redskins football game while I did the dishes. I'm not saying they left me to do them—actually everyone offered to help, especially Joel, whom I practically had to push out of the kitchen. My father was even more difficult to dissuade. I got him out of the kitchen by telling him that he was being rude leaving his guests alone in the living room.

"They're watching the game," my father said. "They don't need me."

"Go," I said. "You always watch football on Thanksgiving. Besides, I don't want anyone in my kitchen."

When he finally realized that I wasn't going to back down, he grabbed a beer and walked out, muttering, "It's my kitchen."

The truth was I wanted to be alone. And I wanted them to enjoy themselves. All three of them were suffering more than I ever had. I guess I had found something to be grateful for after all.

CHAPTER *Eight*

Back to Colorado again. The most certain exiles are those that are self-imposed.

Kimberly Rossi's Diary

The men's shuttle from the hospital came to pick them up a little after seven-thirty. Dad talked the driver into staying for some pie, then sent the pumpkin pie back to the hospital with Chuck. Before leaving, Joel shook my hand.

"Thank you for everything, ma'am. I thought today was going to be miserable, but it wasn't. The food was excellent, and the company was even better. It was a real pleasure meeting you. Maybe we could get a coffee when you're back in town."

"I'd like that," I said. "And thank you."

"For what?"

"For your sacrifice for your country. For us."

"It was my honor, ma'am."

I furtively glanced at his broken body. "God bless," I said.

After they were gone, my father came back to the kitchen and made a turkey sandwich from the rolls and leftover turkey, heating up some gravy in the microwave to dip his sandwich in. Then he sat down at the table next to me.

"Best part of Thanksgiving," he said. "Leftovers."

"I think we have enough to last until Christmas." I looked at him. "Your friends were nice."

"Yeah. Chuck can be a bit cantankerous, but that comes with age and pain. He's a good man. And he's dying. Did you notice his skin was yellow?"

"Yes."

"That's his liver failing."

"But he said he's going to get a transplant?"

My father shook his head. "He says that, but he's too old for a transplant. They wouldn't waste the organ. Besides, he'd never survive the operation."

"How long does he have?"

"A couple of weeks ago I asked his doctor. He said he doesn't have a crystal ball, but he'd be surprised if he makes it to Christmas."

"So this was his last Thanksgiving."

My father nodded. "That's why I invited him."

"And Joel? I can't believe he doesn't hate his wife. I don't even know her, and I hate her."

"Don't be too quick to judge," my father said. "We all mourn loss in different ways. But you're right. Joel's an amazing young man." He looked at me for a moment. "I think he was taken with you."

"I'm sure he's lonely."

"I'm sure he's lonely for female companionship."

"Maybe we'll get a coffee. It's the least I can do."

My father shook his head. "No, don't go out with him out of sympathy. That would be wrong."

"Then how about out of friendship?"

"Friendship is good. If he's attracted to you, he might not be able to handle that. But it's good to let him make that decision. Besides, you never know how these things can go."

"You approve of him?"

"Oh yes. Even with missing parts, he's still more of a man than most of the men I know."

"Or the ones I've been with?"

"He's ten times the man Marcus was. Is. But that's setting the bar low."

"I can't argue with that," I said. "I'm glad you invited them. This morning I couldn't think of a single thing to be thankful for. Now I could make a list."

"Good," he said. "There are bigger problems than ours."

"Cancer is a big problem."

"It can be," he said. "But I'm going to be okay. And I still wouldn't trade my problems with either of theirs."

I nodded slowly. "What you said, about the writers' conference. I'm not going."

"Of course you are."

"No, I'm not. It's too expensive. And I'm not going to take any money from you."

"That's not your decision."

I laughed. "How is it not my decision if I'm going to go or not?"

"It's not your decision whether I give you money or not."

"What, you're going to make me go?"

"No, but I already paid for it. Including meeting with an

agent. I got you two of them in case you don't like one of the agents."

I was stunned. "You signed me up for the conference?"

"You said you wanted to go, so I booked it as your Christmas present."

"How did you even know where to find it?"

"It's not the Holy Grail. I just searched for a writers' retreat at the Mistletoe Inn with H. T. Cowell." He looked somewhat proud of himself. "I gave them a credit card and it's nonrefundable. So no, you don't have to go, but you'll waste a lot of my money if you don't."

"Dad, you've got to get that money back."

"They were very specific about there being no refunds."

I was speechless. "That's not fair."

"What's not fair? It's my money, I can do what I want with it. And what I want is for my girl to pursue her dream."

"Dad . . ." I stopped, overcome with emotion. "I wish you hadn't done that."

"Look, if you really want to make me miserable, stop living. That's when I *will* want to die. Remember, it's about the punctuation."

"You sound like my high school English teacher."

"Whatever works," he said.

I spent the next two days with my father pretending that nothing was wrong. It was a pleasant fiction and I was happy until I flew out Sunday morning and reality returned. I started to tear up on the way to the airport. My father didn't say anything about me crying but reached over and took my hand.

As my father dropped me off he got out of the car and we hugged. "Remember," he said, "the best years of our lives are ahead of us. And it's time that you realized that dream of yours. The world is waiting for you."

"Thanks, Dad." When we parted I said, "Take good care of yourself."

"I always do," he said.

As soon as I got inside the airport I broke down in tears.

CHAPTER *Nine*

Why is it that, so often, those with the least are the most eager to give?

Kimberly Rossi's Diary

For the next few weeks I spent most of my time after work revising my novel, but you can only do that so many times before the words all start to look the same. It's simple psychology. After you've driven the same route a thousand times, you stop noticing the landscape. My father was right, a retreat would be helpful. Still, after he had sacrificed so much, the pressure of going to the conference was heavy. What if it didn't work out? How would I tell him that no one wanted my book?

To add pain to my misery, Rachelle and her new boyfriend were now talking marriage and I was suddenly her confidant. It was like she got some sadistic pleasure out of telling me how happy she was and, twisting the knife, how certain she was that I would someday find someone nice as well, managing to wrap her condescending tone in faux magnanimity.

As the days went on, my father's cancer was always in the back of my mind, lurking in the shadows like a stalker. I was relieved when he finally had his first appointment with an oncologist at the VA a week after I'd flown home. He called me that night after work.

"What did he say?" I asked.

"Actually, it was a cancer care team," he said. "And, generally speaking, they were pretty positive about things. Other than the cancer, I'm quite healthy, so surgery is an option. They're recommending a partial colectomy followed by some chemo."

"When are they going to operate?"

He paused. "Sometime next year. Maybe next February."

"*Maybe* next February? They're making you wait?"

"It's just the way it is. They're backlogged."

"That's too long," I said. "It could spread. There's got to be something we can do. Someone we can talk to."

"There's no need to get so upset. If it was more urgent, I'm sure they would have scheduled me sooner. They're not going to take chances with someone's life."

"You don't know that," I said. "Bureaucracy kills people. This isn't right. I'm going to make some calls. I'm going to talk to your oncologist."

"I talked to my oncologist," he said. "He said this is what they can do."

"But is it what they *should* do?"

"He said that he'll do all he can. He can't break the rules, but sometimes he can bend them. So stop worrying about me; everything will be okay. You've got a writing retreat coming up. You need to be focused."

"How am I supposed to be focused when I'm worried about you?"

"You just focus on knocking them dead at that retreat. That's what I want."

I sighed. "I'll do my best."

"I love you."

"I love you too, Dad." As I hung up the phone, I wished that I had never told him about the retreat.

CHAPTER

Sometimes there's a fine line between trepidation and excitement.

Kimberly Rossi's Diary

The morning of December 10th I parked my car in the long-term parking lot of the Denver Airport and took the shuttle in to the terminal. There wasn't a direct flight from Denver to Burlington, Vermont, so I had a three-hour layover in Detroit, where I ate lunch and wandered through the airport. In a magazine shop I watched people browse through the books. *How would that be?* I wondered. *To have a book on one of those shelves?*

It was dark when my cab drove up a pine-lined lane to the Mistletoe Inn, each of the trees wrapped with white Christmas lights.

"It looks cozy," I said.

"Yeah," the driver said. "It's a real nice place. Kind of fancy."

The inn was decorated for the season with twinkling, draped garlands running the length of the hotel, glowing against the snow-blanketed backdrop of the deep purple night.

As I got out of the taxi, a young man wearing a long blue wool coat with black piping and a black felt top hat walked up to me. "Would you like help with your bag?"

"No, thank you. I just have the one. It's not heavy."

"No problem; let me get the door for you."

He opened the tall wooden doors and as I walked past him I was embraced by the warmth and ambience of the inn's extravagant lobby. "Greensleeves," played on a harpsichord, faintly reverberated throughout the room. All around the lobby were flickering red candles, and the room was filled with a pleasant scent of cinnamon, clove, and pine.

There was a large Christmas tree next to the check-in counter hung with red baubles and silver icicles and tiny white flickering lights. The lobby walls were paneled with dark wood planks, and black metal carriage lamps hung from the high ceiling.

In the center of the room was a large fireplace with a roaring fire inside. The fireplace's mantel was made of polished dark pine with a garland draped over it, tied with red velveteen ribbons.

In front of the fire were two leather sofas and two red-velvet armchairs, arranged beneath a massive light fixture made of deer antlers. The sofas were occupied by an older couple and two young women, all holding wineglasses.

A few yards in from the door, on a gold easel, was a sign that read:

Romance Writers

Conference

Registration

An arrow, which looked like the nib of a fountain pen, pointed to a table to the right of the check-in counter. The table was occupied by a lone fortyish woman with short auburn hair and thick-rimmed glasses. There was a small line at the hotel's check-in counter so I walked to the registration table. The woman smiled as I approached.

"Hello," she said warmly. "Are you here for the conference?"

"Yes," I said, setting down my bag. "I'm Kim Rossi."

"Rossi, let me look that up." She lifted a two-page roster and slid her index finger down the list, stopping about halfway on the second page. "Rossi," she said. "Kimberly."

"That's me."

"You came clear from Colorado. How was your flight in?"

"It was good," I said.

"Good, good. Let's get you checked in." She handed me a manila envelope with my name handwritten in purple marker on the outside. "This is your conference packet; it has your credentials along with a list of panels and lectures and some other information." Then she lifted a white canvas bag from the floor behind her. "And this is a little welcome gift from the Vermont Tourist Association. It has a brochure with some coupons and a list of things to do in the area. There's also some locally produced maple syrup and maple candies in there. I should warn you, the maple walnut fudge is addicting."

"Thank you," I said, taking my things. "I'll be careful with the fudge."

"And don't forget, our conference opening reception is tonight at 7 p.m. in the grand ballroom. You won't want to miss it."

"How many are registered for the conference?"

"We have just over a hundred," she said.

A voice behind me asked, "What's the male-to-female ratio?"

I turned around. Standing behind me was a beautiful woman about my height and maybe a year or two younger. She had long red hair that fell past her shoulders, freckled cheeks, and green eyes that were unusually brilliant.

"Unfortunately, the odds are in favor of the men," the woman said. "There are only seven men enrolled."

"May the odds be ever in your favor," I said to the woman.

She looked at me. "That's from . . . wait, I know this."

"*Hunger Games*," I said.

She clapped. "Yes! Are you Suzanne Collins?"

I looked at her blankly, wondering if she was serious. "I'm sorry, I'm not."

"I'm sorry I'm not her either." She put out her hand. "My name is Samantha."

I took her hand, still not sure what to think of her. "Kim Rossi."

"What kind of name is Rossi?" she asked.

"It's Italian."

"I love Italian," she said.

The woman at the table said, "Let me find your registration, Samantha. What's your last name?"

"McDonald."

"Samantha McDonald." She looked through her papers. "Here you are." She handed her a packet and canvas bag, reciting the same spiel she had for me, ending with, "The opening reception is tonight at seven in the grand ballroom. Enjoy the conference."

I thanked the woman again, then walked over to the line at the check-in counter. The line had shortened and there was just one couple ahead of me. Samantha followed me over. "Is this your first time at one of these writers' conferences?" she asked.

"No. But it's my first time at this one."

"This is my first writers' conference. I'm a little nervous."

"You don't need to be nervous," I said. "It's fun to be with other writers. They're all in the same boat as you."

"Are you from Vermont?"

"No. Colorado."

"Oh, we're neighbors. I'm from Montana."

"Are there many writers in Montana?"

"Tons. It's Montana—what else are you going to do?"

"Next, please," the man at the check-in counter said.

"Excuse me," I said.

I got my room key, then, as I turned to go, Samantha stopped me. "Are you going to the party tonight?"

"I was planning on it."

"Do you want to go together?"

"Sure," I said. "I'll meet you here at seven."

"I'll be here with bells on," she said.

I'm not sure why I had agreed so quickly. She seemed a little crazy. But she also seemed kind of fun. Besides, I hated being alone at parties.

My room was nice—well designed, modern, but quaint. In the center of the room was a tall, king-sized bed with an antique headboard of dark oak and tufted dark-brown leather. The bed had a thick, greenish-tan duvet cover with matching pillow shams, along with several smaller decorative pillows.

On the wall opposite the bed was a large, rectangular mirror in an elaborate wooden frame. The mirror made the room look larger.

I sat down on the foot of the bed and opened up my conference packet. Next to several loose forms and registration papers were stapled pages with a schedule of events. I found a pen next to the telephone, then started down the list, checking or circling some of the classes that interested me.

LIST OF PRESENTATIONS AND EVENTS

MEET AND GREET
Monday evening, 7 p.m., Grand Ballroom. Credentials required.

Check.

OPENING SESSION

Tuesday, 9–9:45 a.m. Presenter: Jill Tanner, Chairperson of the Mistletoe Inn Writers' Conference Committee, and Kathryn Nebeker, this year's Vice Chairperson of content.

Check.

DAILY GROUP WORKSHOPS

Tuesday, 10–10:45 a.m.

Wednesday–Saturday 9–9:45 a.m.

Important Note: You will meet each day with your workshop group. You have been preassigned to a group of 10 writers. Please check your packet for a yellow sheet with your designated group letter.

Check. I found an 8 1/2-by-5 1/2 yellow sheet inside the envelope. Printed on it was a large letter C with the instructions that the group would be meeting in the Maple Room. I went back to the list of events.

TWITTER IN YOUR FACE(BOOK)

Building a community of readers through social media.

Maybe. I made a check by it.

HOW NOT TO GET AN AGENT
Famous New York literary agent Laurie Liss shares the 5 things not to do when pitching an agent.

Absolutely. I circled it.

CLOTHES MAKE THE *RO*-MAN-*CE*
Dressing (and undressing) your characters for success.

Probably not. Maybe. I put a check by it.

THE CHANGING FACE OF ROMANCE
From *Romeo and Juliet* to *Love Story* to *Bridges of Madison County* to *Fifty Shades of Grey*: Where the romance world is going next.

Sounds interesting. Circled it.

PUTTING THE *ROME* BACK IN ROMANCE
Creating the perfect Italian setting for an Italian love story.

No. I'm Italian, but my book's not set in Italy.

THE LIMOUSINE LIFESTYLE OF THE BESTSELLING AUTHOR
(Wednesday only) Mega-Selling Author Catherine McCullin recounts her career as one of the world's most celebrated romance writers.

Of course. Circled it.

AGENT SPEED DATING
Fifteen minutes to pitch your book to a real literary agent. (Additional fee required.) Reservations must be made before 1 p.m. on Tuesday. Sessions held Wednesday, Thursday, Friday only. Reservation form is included in packet. First come, first served.

This was what my father had paid for. Twice. I circled it.

FROM WALMART TO HOLLYWOOD
Bestselling Author Deborah Mackey talks about her rocket-like rise from retail store clerk to international bestselling author (via Skype).

Maybe. Don't like the Skype part. Sounds like she's phoning it in.

WHIPS AND CHAINS
(No, nothing exciting.) How to endure the stress and pressures of a sweatshop publishing house.

Probably not.

BORING PUNCTUATION!
How to use punctuation (and not use it) to strengthen your stories.

Definitely boring.

VAMPS AND VAMPIRES
Tips for writing sizzling paranormal romances.

No interest in vampires whatsoever. Was once married to one.

BARE FEET AND BUGGIES
Writing your Amish love story.

Same as vampires. I wonder if anyone has written a vampire-Amish romance. If not, it will happen.

LIVING THE DREAM
Author David Bready shares his secrets to breaking down the walls to the publishing world.

Sounds good. Never heard of Bready. But he's published . . .

THE EYES HAVE IT
Facial gestures that say more than words.

I could use that.

E-LECTRIC
How to heat up the Internet with your e-book.

Yes.

MAKING A 6-FIGURE SALARY ON 4-FIGURE BOOK SALES
How to make a lucrative living as a midlist author.

Quit the dealership to write? Okay.

CHOPPING THE WRITER'S BLOCK
How to keep writing when the words stop coming.

Definitely need this.

CLOSING KEYNOTE: WHY I STOPPED WRITING
H. T. Cowell.

I circled this a half dozen times. It was the first time that I saw what Cowell was speaking about, which frankly was exactly what I wanted to hear. Maybe what the whole world hoped to hear.

I set the conference material on the night table next to my bed and lifted my suitcase onto a luggage stand. I unzipped my case and took out my manuscript. I looked at it, then put it back in my suitcase. There was a little more than an hour before the reception so I set the alarm on my phone for fifteen minutes, then lay back on the bed. As I closed my eyes my phone rang. It was my father.

"Hi, Dad. How are you feeling?"

"I'm good," he said. "So are you there yet? At the inn?"

"Yes. I'm in my room."

"How is it?"

"It's beautiful. The whole inn is beautiful."

"The whole state is beautiful," he said. "I've always thought of Vermont as one of the most beautiful states. Especially when the leaves turn."

"I didn't know you'd been here."

"Mom and I went there on our honeymoon. We went on one of those fall leaves tours. It was unforgettable."

I hated the idea that my mother had been here. It was like discovering snakes in Eden. "It's all covered in snow now," I said.

"I'm sure that's beautiful too. So is anything going on to-night or do you get time to rest?"

"There's an opening-night reception in about an hour."

"Then I better let you get ready. I just wanted to make sure you had made it safe. Have a good time. And would you bring me back some of that real Vermont maple syrup? I don't know if it's the season, but there are places where you can see them boiling down the sap into syrup."

"I'll bring you some. I think there's some in my welcome bag."

"Thanks, baby. Have a good time. I love you."

"I love you too," I said. "Take care of yourself."

I tossed my phone onto the bed, then turned around and looked at myself in the mirror across from me. I always felt bloated after flying. "You look like roadkill," I said out loud. I undressed, then went in to shower.

I turned on the water and a cloud of steam filled the small room. I sat down in the porcelain claw-foot tub beneath the spray and closed my eyes. As I lay there thinking about my father, I felt a panic attack coming on. "He's going to be okay," I said to myself. "Everything will be okay. Our best years are still ahead of us."

CHAPTER

Eleven

*Is it favor or folly that we don't know
how far we are from our dreams?*

Kimberly Rossi's Diary

The conference's opening reception was held in the inn's grand ballroom, which, according to the program material, was also where the conference's most popular sessions would take place, including the opening session in the morning and the final keynote speech by Mr. Cowell.

I walked into the lobby a few minutes after seven. I looked around for Samantha but didn't see her, so after waiting for a little while, I went inside to see if she was already there. The lights inside the ballroom were partially dimmed and there was music playing from a set of speakers attached to an iPod. The room wasn't particularly crowded. There were about fifty or sixty people, mostly clustered in small, intimate groups.

The woman at the registration desk was correct in her estimated male-to-female ratio, as the vast majority of the attendees were women. I looked around for Samantha but couldn't find her.

In the center of the room were tables with hors d'oeuvres. I hadn't eaten since lunch in Detroit, so I took a plate and began to fill it with food: quiche, deviled eggs, sausage-stuffed mushrooms, bacon-wrapped water chestnuts, and dates with blue cheese centers.

Next to the food was a round table with beverages: sodas, eggnog in a large crystal punchbowl, and prepoured glasses of wine.

As I lifted a glass of red wine, a man, balding with a narrow, ruddy face, walked up to me. He wore denim jeans and an oxford shirt with a herringbone tweed jacket with leather elbow patches, the kind that Marcus used to wear while teaching. He was also holding a glass of wine. I couldn't tell if his face was red because he'd been skiing or because he'd been drinking.

He furtively glanced down at my bare ring finger as he stuck out his hand, his close-set eyes fixed on me. "Hi, I'm John Grisham."

I set down my drink to shake his hand. "No, you're not."

An eager grin crossed his face. "I know, but it gets your attention, doesn't it? I'm David." He gripped my hand a little too firmly and held it longer than was comfortable.

"I'm Kimberly."

"Hi, Kimberly. I'm sure you hear this often, but you're a very attractive woman."

Not as often as I'd like, I thought. "Thank you."

"Are you here for the writing seminar?" he asked. It was a dumb question since this was a reception for the seminar.

"Yes. And you?"

"I'm one of the presenters," he said, his voice taking on a slightly lilting tone. "I'm *published*."

There is a caste system at writers' conferences—a social stratification between the elite and the untouchables, the published and unpublished.

"Congratulations," I said. "That must be nice."

"Yes, it is. What do you do?"

"In real life I'm a finance officer at a car dealership."

"Living the dream," he said sardonically.

"But I'd like to be writing for a living."

"You and everyone else on the planet."

"That's encouraging," I said. "What is your presentation on?"

"It is on exactly what we're talking about—how to get published. Actually my presentation's called *Living the Dream*."

"I saw it on the schedule. You're David . . . Bready." I pronounced his last name like *Breedy*.

"It's pronounced Brady," he said quickly. "Like Tom."

"I'm sure you'll have a very popular session."

"It's always a crowded session," he replied. "I pack them in." He lifted a stuffed mushroom from the table and devoured it in one bite.

"So what books have you written?" I asked.

He finished chewing, then said, "I co-wrote one of the Chicken Soup books. *Chicken Soup for the Romance Writer's Soul*."

"I didn't know there was one for that."

"Oh yeah. It's one of the bigger sellers."

"How many Chicken Soup books are there now?" I asked. "I mean, hasn't it gotten ridiculous? Like, *Chicken Soup for the Bricklayer's Soul*? How many different souls can there be?"

He gazed at me blankly, clearly offended by my question.

"What else do you write?" I asked.

"I'm best known for the Death Slayer series. I'm sure you've heard of it."

I looked at him awkwardly. "Death Slayer?"

"*Cave of the Slave Girls, Slaughter Alley, Planet Blood* . . ."

"I'm sorry, I don't read a lot of the . . . death and gore genre."

"I've got a film option on *Planet Blood*," he said. "My agent says Hollywood's going nuts over it."

"Congratulations."

"Thanks, but you know how it is. The publisher's never satisfied. The minute you've finished one book they want to know when the next one will be finished. Got to feed the beast."

"Actually, I don't know how that is," I said. "I'd like to."

"Which is why you should come to my presentation." His mouth twisted. "But honestly, between us, being published has its downside."

"Such as?"

"Fame. Groupies. Women following me back to my hotel after book signings."

"That sounds pretty miserable," I said, nodding. He either missed my sarcasm or just ignored it.

"Well, believe me, they're not always as lovely as you. So, why don't you come up to my room and I'll show you what I'm working on. I'll even let you read some pages no one else has ever laid eyes on."

I bit my lip. "Thank you, but I think I'll just stay down here and get to know some of the other attendees."

He nodded as if he understood. "I get it. You want to size up the competition."

"I wasn't really thinking of that."

"You should," he said. "Publishing's the most competitive industry on the planet. Breaking into the business today is like safecracking. If you don't know the combination or the bank president, you'll never make it. It's who you know."

"You mean I need to know someone like *you*," I said.

He cocked his head. "Precisely. I know people in the industry. Agents. Editors. People with a say as to what gets published and what doesn't." He leaned forward. "So. Do you want to come up to my room?"

"Tempting, but still no. Thank you."

His jaw tightened. "Suit yourself. Good luck." The last two words sounded more like a threat than a wish. He huffed off. A few minutes later I heard him say to another woman, "Hi, I'm John Grisham . . ."

I took my wine and food over to a vacant table near the side of the room and sat down. As I looked around it seemed like most of the people already knew each other. I felt like a leper. To my relief, it was only a few minutes before Samantha walked into the room. I waved to her and her face lit when she saw me. She walked over to the table. "Oh, I'm so glad you're here. Sorry I'm late. I couldn't get off the phone."

"It's okay," I said. "I just got here too."

"How's the party?"

"It's good." I tilted my head toward David, who was already well into his next pitch. "Stay clear of that guy."

"I know," she said. "His name is David, but he tells everyone he's John Grisham. It's the most pathetic pickup line I've ever heard."

"So you've met him."

"I met him in the hall after I checked in. He's one of the presenters. He's published."

"Yes, he told me."

"He asked me up to his room."

"He asked me too," I said. "What did you say?"

"I said I thought he was kind of old to be hitting on someone my age."

I laughed. "I bet you bruised his ego."

"Crushed it," she said, smiling.

Just then two other women walked over to our table carrying plates of food, a tall redhead and a shorter brunette with heavy makeup. "Excuse me," the redhead said. "Are these seats taken?"

"No. Go ahead."

The women sat across from us. "I'm LuAnne," the redhead said.

"And I'm Heather," said the other.

"I'm Kim," I replied. "And this is Samantha."

"Hi," Samantha said, looking unhappy that the two women had crashed our table.

LuAnne smiled at me. "Is this your first time here?"

"Yes. Is it yours?"

"No. It's my sixth."

"It's my fifth," Heather said. "You could say we're regulars. We noticed that you were talking to David."

"Actually, he was talking to me," I said.

"He was hitting on her," Samantha said.

"Did he invite you up to his room?" LuAnne asked.

"Yes."

"No surprise there," she said. "He always works the pretty new ones."

"The regulars know better," Heather said.

"David's a regular too?" I asked.

"Pretty much," Heather said. "He's one of the few published authors who will consistently come. I think it's getting harder to get published authors. They only found four this year."

"They got Mr. Cowell," I said.

"If he shows," LuAnne said.

I looked at her quizzically. "What do you mean?"

"He has a reputation for booking events and not showing up."

"Like *never* showing up," Heather said. "If he comes, it will be a first."

"He's the reason I came," I said. "Mostly."

"Well, he could surprise us," LuAnne said doubtfully. "So what kind of romance do you write?"

"Kind?"

"Yes. What's your niche? Paranormal? Erotica? Nicholas Sparks wannabe?"

I wasn't sure how to answer. "Just, the usual," I finally said, not sure what that meant.

"How long have you been writing?" Heather asked.

"About six years," I said.

"Same as me," she said.

"How many books have you written?" Samantha asked.

"Counting the one I'm working on, fourteen," LuAnne said.

"Fourteen?"

"I've written twenty-two," Heather said. "But, technically, two of them were novellas."

"And not one of them published," LuAnne said.

Heather glared at her. "I'm published. I've sold almost two thousand copies."

"*Self*-published," LuAnne said dismissively. "Ninety-nine-cent e-books. The book world has radically changed in the last decade. There are no such things as unpublished authors these days."

"That's true," Samantha said. "Amazon has like a billion books."

"I'm still unpublished," I said. I hadn't even considered self-publishing. I wouldn't know where to begin.

LuAnne said, "A few years ago at the Maui Writers Conference, Sue Grafton said, 'You shouldn't even submit a book to an agent until you've written at least five.'"

"I guess that counts me out," I said.

"How many books have you written?" LuAnne asked.

I felt embarrassed. "One."

Both women looked surprised.

"Just one?" Heather asked.

"Yes," I said. "I guess I've had a lot of distractions."

"The truth is," LuAnne said, "writing the book is the easy part. Getting someone to read it is the real trick. There's so much competition and it gets worse every year. The problem is, everyone thinks they have a book in them."

"Which is precisely where it should stay," Heather said. "*In* them."

"I mean, you walk into a bookstore and you think, each one of these books probably sells a few hundred copies, right?" LuAnne said. "Do you know what the average book sells in a bookstore?"

I shook my head. "No."

"One point eight copies. Not even two."

"How do you sell eighty percent of a book?" Samantha asked.

"It's in the aggregate," LuAnne said.

"It's a doggy-dog world out there," Heather said.

"You mean dog-eat-dog world," LuAnne said.

"That's what I said," Heather said.

LuAnne turned to me. "Have you sent your book out to anyone yet?"

"I've sent it to a few publishers, but they just sent back rejection slips."

"You're lucky you even got an acknowledgment," LuAnne said. "Sending directly to publishers is a waste of time. They get more books than they can read just from the agents. They don't have time to look at the nonagented books. It's the weeding process."

"Have you tried sending out to agents?" Heather asked.

"No. I signed up for the speed-dating thing. I hope I can find one here."

"Good luck," she said. "It's brutal out there."

It's brutal in here, I thought.

"There are two kinds of agents who come to these things," Heather said. "The first is the kind who comes for a junket and doesn't really believe they'll find anything. They're the dream killers. They just love shredding your heart into a million tiny pieces.

"Then there are the passive-aggressive agents who realize that no one wants to hear anything bad about their writing, so they just say nice things to everyone, then never call them back. I've had both and I don't know which is worse."

"It depends if you like the bandage pulled off quickly or slowly," LuAnne said.

"There's a third kind, right?" I said.

"A third?" Heather said.

"An agent who is actually looking for a book to sell."

They were both quiet for a moment, then LuAnne said, "It could happen."

Heather nodded. "Could happen."

I felt like a naive child being told that there is no Santa Claus.

The conversation with the two women pretty much crushed any remaining vestige of hope I still had in getting published. I knew there was a lot of competition out there—anyone who's ever walked through a bookstore knows that—but it was soul crushing to realize that for every one of those published authors on the shelf, there were at least a thousand more like me who wanted their job. *How could I have been so naive? How could I have wasted my father's money?*

I downed the rest of my wine, excused myself, and walked out to the lobby. Samantha followed me.

"I don't like those women," she said.

"I didn't like what they had to say," I said.

"What do they know, anyway? It's not like they're famous authors."

I looked at her. "You're right."

She glanced around the mostly vacant lobby. "The night's still young. Want to talk?"

"Sure," I said. The lobby's sofas were unoccupied, so we sat down in front of the fire. That's when I noticed the massive diamond on Samantha's finger. "Are you married?"

"No," she said, looking a little embarrassed. "Chronically engaged."

"What does that mean?"

"It means that I've been engaged for six years."

I nodded, thinking I understood. "You found a man with a commitment problem?"

"It's not him. We'd be on our fifth anniversary if he had his way."

"What's holding you back?"

"The BBD."

"The what?"

"You know, the bigger better deal. I'm waiting for something better to come along. I mean, at some level, we all eventually settle, right? But wouldn't it be awful to belong to someone else when the right one comes along?"

"That's a song by England Dan and John Ford Coley."

"Exactly my point," she said. "It's so common that someone, like this Dan Ford Coleslaw guy, wrote a song about it. It happens all the time. The minute you take a job, you get offered your dream job. The second you commit to a line at the supermarket, the other line speeds up. It's nature's cruel sense of irony. So, I'm waiting."

"That's kind of awful," I said.

"I know, right?"

"I meant for him."

"I'm nice to him," she said. "Believe me, it's not like he's complaining. And on the looks side, I'm like a nine, or, on a bad hair day, an eight point five, and he's barely a six point five, so he knows he's dating up." She nodded. "I'm good to him."

"You are gorgeous," I said.

"Thank you." She sat back. "How about you? Are you married?"

"I was."

"Divorced?"

"Yes."

"How long have you been divorced?"

"We've been separated for almost eight months, but the divorce just went through a couple of months ago."

"Why did it take so long?"

"He was dragging his feet."

"He didn't want the divorce?"

"No, he wanted the divorce. He just didn't want the settlement."

"What a jerk. What happened?"

I sighed. "He was a professor and he fooled around with a few of his students. It was like a big news thing. Nothing like being publicly humiliated and having your broken heart dragged through the media."

"He really is a jerk," Samantha said. "But there is a bright side."

I looked at her incredulously. "How could there possibly be a bright side to that?"

"Fodder," she said. "Think of all the great stuff you could write about it. You could use your loser ex as fodder for all the villains in your books."

"Why would anyone want to read about that? I lived through it and it was miserable."

"That's *exactly* what people *want* to read. Trashy romance is like an emotional garage sale; people get to rummage through other people's junk. Reading how horrible someone else's life is makes them feel better about their own. Why do you think people gossip? That's all romance writers are, the neighborhood gossip in print."

"That's a horrible way to look at writing."

"Horrible or not, you can't fight human nature," she said. "I've written three books. The first one was based on my sister and her ex-husband. I always thought my sister had the perfect marriage. They seemed so happy together. He sent her flowers and Godiva chocolates every week, dream vacations, nice house, the whole grand illusion. He was a successful salesman for some medical appliance company, so he made a lot of money and traveled a lot. Turns out he had a second wife and family in Tulsa."

"You're kidding."

"God-honest truth."

"That's awful."

"My story gets even better. So when the news comes out, the state Attorney General's office brings loser-husband up on bigamy charges. The prosecuting attorney, this really hot guy, is working with my sister on the case. Get this, they fall in love. Now they have this great marriage and he's like so much better looking than Felon."

"Felon?"

"That's what my sister calls her ex."

"Did they have children?"

"With my sister? No. Felon just kept telling her that he wasn't ready. The truth was, he just couldn't afford two families. I mean, he bought braces for Tulsa wife's kids."

"At least they'll have straight teeth when they go to their counseling sessions," I said.

Samantha laughed. "So what's your book about?"

"It takes place during the holidays."

"Smart. Holiday romances are hot. And that's when people are buying books. Go on."

"It's about this woman who has had a string of bad relationships. She works at a downtown travel agency. It's the day after Halloween and she's dreading going through another Christmas alone, when this guy in the mall food court approaches her. She's seen him before, like in the elevator and around the building. He tells her that he hates the holidays because he's alone and has all these parties to go to. He proposes that they pretend to be a couple until Christmas."

"And they fall in love," Samantha said.

"Of course."

"I like the premise," she said. "Is the guy, like, secretly a serial killer or married?"

"No."

"I'm just saying, it would add a lot of drama, if you, like, had this backstory going and you're wondering if she's going to get killed or run into the guy's wife at a Christmas party."

For a moment I was speechless. "No. He's not going to kill her. It's a love story."

"That's good too," Samantha said, standing. "Would you like some more wine?"

I was glad for the reprieve. "Yes. Red, please."

"I'll be right back," she said, walking back into the reception. She returned a moment later carrying two glasses of red wine and handed me one of them. "The party goes on," she said, sitting down. "John Grisham is still at it, going after lucky contestant number three. Someone should tell him he needs a mint."

I grinned. "What's your fiancé's name?"

She grimaced slightly. "Walt. Walt *Berger*. Who wants the last name of *Berger*?"

"Samantha Berger. It's a little unusual, but it's not . . . bad."

"Oh yeah, well, what if I wanted to hyphenate my

last name? Or just think of our wedding announcements. McDonald-Berger. That's reason enough not to get married."

I couldn't help but laugh. "I'm sorry. That is unfortunate."

"Yeah, someone will put our announcement on the Internet and mock us."

"So what does Walt do?"

"He's a businessman. He owns a chain of hamburger joints."

For a moment I thought she was joking, but she didn't laugh. "Really?"

"Really," she said. "Berger's Burgers."

"It's a catchy name . . ."

"He says that after we're married he'll name a burger after me." She rolled her eyes. "Now that's an honor."

"McDonald Burger? I think there might be some legal problems with that."

"The Sam Burger," she said. "With special Sam sauce. Whatever that is." She sighed. "I don't know. He's not much to look at. He looks like that Willard Scott guy who used to do the weather on the *Today* show, which is ironic, since Willard Scott was McDonald's first Ronald McDonald clown. But he's a good guy. And I can't say he's not patient."

"Not after six years."

"I keep telling him that Jacob in the Bible had to wait seven years for Rachel."

"Technically, I think it was fourteen years, because he got tricked into marrying the oldest daughter first," I said.

"That's good news," she said. "Not for Jacob, but, I mean, maybe I'll use that."

"You would really make him wait fourteen years?"

"No. After seven years I think the universe is telling me that it's time to settle."

I hoped that she'd never say anything that crass to her fiancé, but I wouldn't be surprised if she already had. She didn't seem to have much of a filter. The massive grandfather clock near the check-in counter chimed.

I glanced at my watch, then said, "I think I'll go to bed."

"All right," Samantha said. "See you at breakfast?"

"I'll be there. Good night."

I walked down the hallway back to my room. Even though I was still on mountain time, it seemed late to me and I felt tired. I undressed, laid my clothes over the back of a chair, then turned out the light and got into bed. As I lay thinking about what the two women had told us, I wanted to cry. I didn't want to be here. I had wasted my father's money on an unrealistic dream. Money better spent on saving his life. *Why did he make me come?*

CHAPTER

Twelve

I call it Rossi's Law: the likelihood of having something stuck in your teeth is directly proportionate to the attractiveness of the person you're meeting.

Kimberly Rossi's Diary

The next morning I got up at sunrise and went to the hotel's fitness center. The room was small, with one wall that was all mirrors, presumably to make the space seem less claustrophobic.

There wasn't a lot to work with; a set of barbells, an elliptical, a treadmill, and a stair climber. In the corner of the room a television hung from the ceiling. It was on, tuned to a sports channel.

I draped a hand towel around my neck, then got on the treadmill. I put in my earbuds, turned Josh Groban on my iPod, then turned the treadmill on to a slow jog.

About twenty minutes into my run a man walked in. He was maybe a decade older than me, handsome with short, dark hair and bright blue eyes partially obscured by tortoiseshell-framed glasses. He looked fit, not especially muscular, but nicely proportioned.

He smiled at me as he walked over to the elliptical. Before he got on the machine he turned back to me and said something I couldn't hear. I took out an earbud. "Excuse me?"

"Would you mind if I changed the channel on the television?"

"No, go ahead. I'm not watching."

"Thank you."

I put my earbud back in while he changed the channel from sports to a cooking show, which, I suppose, wasn't what I expected. I would have pegged him as a sports or politics guy.

As he worked out I glanced over at him several times. Once I caught him looking at me. He didn't immediately turn away but smiled pleasantly.

About five minutes before I ended my workout, my towel slipped off my neck, falling to the track. Without thinking I reached for it and, with the machine's momentum, fell to my knees and was promptly ejected off the back of the track, leaving me sprawling on the floor. My iPod flipped across the room.

The man quickly came to my aid.

"Are you hurt?"

My face was crimson as I got up on my knees. "Just my pride."

He offered me his hand. "That can be painful too." He helped me up.

"Thank you."

"You're welcome." He stooped over and picked up my iPod. "I believe this is yours."

"Thanks. Again."

"Don't mention it." He returned to his elliptical.

I was too embarrassed to finish my workout, so I threw my towel into a woven basket and walked back to my room. *Smooth, Kim. Real smooth,* I thought. *Way to impress the cute guy.* Not that it mattered. Chances were that I wouldn't see him again.

I got back to my room at a quarter to eight, which gave me just enough time to shower and dress before breakfast. This time, before I left my room, I put on my wedding ring, just in case I encountered John Grisham again. In the dining room, Samantha was already sitting at a table with a plate of food. She looked pretty.

"Morning, sunshine," she said as I walked over.

"Good morning. What's good?"

"Everything I've tried so far. It's buffet-style. Personally, I'm into the French toast sticks." Her plate was loaded with French toast covered in powdered sugar. "There's also a guy making omelets. Pretty tasty."

"The omelets or the guy making them?"

"Both. I think he's Cuban. He's got a cute accent."

I walked over to the food tables. She was right; everything did look good, including the omelet guy. I took an orange, a small bowl of oatmeal—which I loaded with walnuts, brown sugar, and raisins—grabbed a coffee and creamer, and carried everything back to the table. Samantha had powdered sugar on her lips.

"So after you went back to your room last night," she

said, "I went back into the party to do some reconnaissance. A lot of these people are like writers' conference junkies. They all go to the same conferences and hang out."

"That explains why they all seem to know each other."

"The good thing is that everyone agreed that this is their favorite conference. And there's a betting pool on whether your boyfriend is going to show up or not. They're giving two-to-one odds that he's a no-show."

"My boyfriend?"

"Cowell."

"Oh," I said, feeling awful to be reminded of that possibility. I took a bite of oatmeal, then said, "I can't believe that he might not come."

"If he doesn't, we've definitely got grounds for a lawsuit," Samantha said. "Walt's got a good lawyer."

We ate for a while longer, then Samantha glanced down at her watch. "It's almost time. We need to go if we want good seats."

I quickly downed my coffee, then stood. "Let's go."

"Did you bring the manuscript you plan to work on?"

"No. Do I need it?"

"Well, yeah," she said. "It was in the instructions. Go get your manuscript and I'll save us some seats."

With that she took off and I walked back to my room to get my book. My one pathetic, measly book.

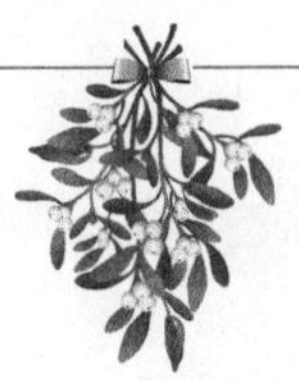

CHAPTER

Thirteen

The conference has begun.

Kimberly Rossi's Diary

The grand ballroom was now brightly lit and filled with chairs. Perry Como Christmas music was playing over the sound system as I walked in, and a crowd of conference attendees, probably double what had been at the evening's reception, milled about visiting or hunting for seats. I spotted Samantha standing near the middle of the third row waving at me. I had to slide past a long line of knees to reach her.

"Good thing I came when I did," she said. "These people are serious about saving places. I sat in one chair and a woman yelled at me. These were the last good seats left."

"Thank you for saving them," I said, taking my seat.

"No worries," she said.

We still had ten minutes before the presentation, so I opened my packet and rooted through it. "Have you looked through all this stuff?" I asked.

"Yes."

"Do you know anything about these workshops?"

"Just what I read in the packet." She lifted her own program. "'You will meet daily with the same designated group of writers, where you will share, discuss, and critique your works.'"

"That sounds painful," I said.

"All artists must suffer," Samantha said. "It is the artist's blood that lubricates the rails of artistic expression."

"Where did you hear that?"

"I just made it up."

"That's pretty good."

"Thank you," she replied. "What group are you in?"

"C."

She frowned. "I'm in F. As in *failure*."

"They're groups, not grades."

"I want to be in the same group as you. Do you think they'd let me switch?"

"It doesn't hurt to ask." I glanced around. "If you can find someone to ask."

Samantha looked around the room for a moment, then said, "That woman up there looks important. Hold my seat." She made her way out of our row and walked up to a woman who was standing next to the stage. They spoke only briefly before Samantha turned and walked back. She looked distraught. "That hurt to ask," she said, sitting.

"What did she say?"

"She said they positively don't allow changes."

"It's just one class a day," I said.

"Which roughly equates to one-quarter of the conference," Samantha said.

"Maybe the F group is the place to be."

"Yeah, right."

Suddenly the music stopped and the room lights dimmed, leaving just the stage bathed in light. The crowd quieted in anticipation as a middle-aged woman in a satin periwinkle business suit walked out to a lectern in the center of the stage.

She tapped the microphone, then leaned forward. "Good morning, writers, and welcome to the Mistletoe Inn Writers' Conference. My name is Jill Tanner and I am this year's conference chairperson. We've spent an entire year putting together what we think is the finest schedule of classes and presentations in the country, with one sole objective, to help you reach your goal of becoming a successful published author."

The audience broke out in applause. She waited for the room to quiet before she continued.

"Never degrade yourself by saying you're *just* a romance writer, for nothing is out of the realm of a romance writer. Romance can take place in mystery, politics, science fiction, fantasy, and horror. Indeed, it's the core of nearly all writing. It is the genre of some of the greatest writers of all time: Shakespeare, Austen, and Hemingway. If the public does not take the genre seriously it's only because too many romance writers don't take it seriously. There are good romance writers and bad romance writers and fifty shades of gray between them."

The audience chuckled at the allusion.

The woman smiled. "A little aside: I met a writer—I swear I'm not making this up—who was writing a spicy Amish romance called *Fifty Shades of Hay*. God is my witness, I couldn't make that one up."

The audience laughed again.

"But as I was saying, there are good romance writers and there are bad romance writers. A good romance writer is one who opens up our hearts to the possibility of love. Every year more than two billion dollars' worth of romance novels are sold worldwide. In America alone, more than sixty-four million people will read at least one romance this year. That number has risen steadily each year since we began holding this conference sixteen years ago.

"What this tells me is that we live in a world hungry for love. You, the world's future romance authors, are the providers of the nourishment this world needs. On behalf of the Mistletoe Inn Writers' Conference Committee, we wish you well with your writing and the best of luck on your publishing journey. Now go forth and change the world."

The crowd broke out in wild applause. As she left the stage another woman walked out. It was the same woman whom Samantha had approached.

"Good morning. I'm Kathryn Nebeker, this year's vice chairperson of content. Hopefully you all have your registration packets with you. If you do, please hold them in the air."

We all held up our packets.

"Good. I see most of you have them. One of the things that makes the Mistletoe Inn Writers' Conference such a success is our unique format. We've been told that there is a writers' conference in California that is now trying to *copy* our format. You know what they say about imitation being the sincerest form of flattery, but we writers have another name for it: plagiarism."

Everyone laughed.

"At any rate, part of what makes our conference unique is our daily workshops. These workshops allow one-on-one time with our experienced facilitators and your fellow writers, giving you the chance to improve and develop your work right here at the conference.

"If you look inside your packets you will find a yellow half sheet of paper that looks like this." She held up a yellow page with a large letter *A* printed on it in black. "Your page will have a letter that indicates which workshop you will be attending each day with the location of where you will meet. I cannot overemphasize that it is vital that you attend the workshop to which you have been assigned. Just this morning I had someone come to me to request a change of workshops. This late in the game we cannot accommodate changes."

I glanced over at Samantha, who was staring at the woman hatefully. "Witch," she whispered.

"If for some reason you do not have your card in your packet, we have posted your name with your group letter on papers right outside these doors.

"Again, we are very happy to have you here and I echo the words of Jill, our president, and say, writers, go forth and change the world. Best of luck and enjoy the conference."

The crowd again applauded. As she walked away, the room lights went up and the Christmas music came back on. We all stood and began filing out to our workshops.

"I hate that woman," Samantha said.

"She's just trying to keep things running smoothly," I said.

"She doesn't have to be such a witch about it."

"Where does your group meet?" I asked.

"Probably in the men's room."

"Give it a chance," I said. "After the workshop I'm going to the presentation on How Not to Get an Agent. How about you?"

"I wrote that down too," Samantha said. "Want to get lunch after?"

"Sure."

"All right. Wish me luck."

"Good luck," I said.

"I'm going to need it," she grumbled as she walked away.

CHAPTER

Fourteen

It turns out that the ship I passed in the night was headed to the same port. Actually, the same harbor.

Kimberly Rossi's Diary

My workshop was in a small conference room near the grand ballroom. There were a dozen chairs arranged in an oval, and one was occupied by a pleasant-looking woman with gray hair. She wore a name badge with a gold presenter's ribbon. I guessed her to be our group's facilitator.

"Welcome," she said with a slight southern accent as several of us walked in. "This is group C. C as in Calhoun, Carlyle, Carroll, and Collodi. C as in cash cow. If you're in the right place, please take a seat in the circle."

I sat down next to the facilitator, and she began checking our name tags against a list on a clipboard. The only person in the room whom I recognized was Heather, one of the two women I had talked to at the opening reception. She glanced at me and sort of waved. I sort of waved back.

After nearly all the chairs were filled, a man, the only man in our group so far, stepped into the room. To my embarrassment, he was the same man I had seen in the exercise room that morning—the one who had helped me up after my fall.

"Excuse me, is this group C?" he asked from the doorway.

Our facilitator nodded. "Yes, this is C. And what's your name?" she asked, checking her clipboard.

"Zeke," he said. "But I'm not on your list. Jill just told me to come here."

She looked back up. "Jill's the boss. Would you mind shutting the door behind you?"

"Not at all," he said. He pulled the door shut, then came over to the circle. As he took the last vacant chair, I noticed several other women checking him out—some, like Heather, more obviously than others. He didn't seem to notice.

"All right," our facilitator said. "My name is Karen Mitchell, and I will be facilitating this workshop every morning of the retreat. First, a little about me. I worked as an editor for Simon & Schuster Adult Division for about five years before I left to work for Avon, an imprint of HarperCollins, where I work today. What I plan to do with you in this workshop is similar to what I do for my published authors every day."

As she spoke I noticed that an older woman seated across from me kept leaning forward, as if she was having trouble hearing. Then I saw that she wore hearing aids in both ears.

"Before we begin, we're going to be together for a few days, so I think we should get to know each other a little better."

"Excuse me," I said to Karen.

Karen turned to me, looking slightly annoyed by my interruption. "Yes?"

"I'm sorry," I said. "I think this woman might be having trouble hearing." I turned to the woman. "Would you like to change seats?"

The woman nodded emphatically. "Yes," she said, her speech slightly impaired. "I have difficulty hearing."

We both stood and as we exchanged seats the woman touched my arm. "Thank you."

"You're welcome," I said.

As I sat down I noticed the man looking at me. He smiled approvingly.

"Okay, writers, onward. As I was saying, I'd like to begin by getting to know all of you a little better. I know how writers like to talk, especially about themselves, so you can do that on your own time. Right now you have two minutes to tell us your name, how long you've been writing, what you're working on now, and what you're most proud of. And be aware," she said, lifting her phone, "I will be timing you. Let's begin with you, darlin'." She nodded to the young woman at her left who wore granny glasses and a peach-colored dress that could have doubled as a tent. I pegged her as one of those sweet timid gals who wrote Amish love stories. She looked terrified.

"Me?"

"Yes, darlin'. Go right ahead."

Still nothing.

"Is this your first writers' retreat?" Karen prodded.

She nodded. "Yes, ma'am."

"Let's begin with your name."

For a moment I thought the woman might faint from fright. "I'm Marci," she squeaked. "I've been writing for about fourteen years, ever since I was fifteen. I'm currently writing a book called *Gone with the Sin*. It's kind of a naughty love story set during Civil War times."

Didn't see that coming.

"I don't know if I'll ever publish it. My father's the pastor at the First Methodist Church of the Lamb in High Point, North Carolina. He wouldn't be very happy with me if he read it."

"We'll address that later," Karen said. "And what are you most proud of?"

"I don't mean to boast, but I won a writing contest last year sponsored by the Lions Club."

"Very good," Karen said. "Next . . ."

Honestly I didn't hear many of the other introductions as my mind was elsewhere. Actually it was mostly on elliptical guy who, unlike me, seemed very much interested in what everyone else had to say. When it was his turn to speak he looked around the group. It seemed to me that his gaze lingered a bit on me.

"Okay, this feels like an AA meeting. Hi, my name is Zeke. I'm a writing addict."

The women to both sides of me giggled.

"First, I have some advice for Marci. Daddy doesn't need to know—that's what noms de plume are for. As for my writing, all I really know about the book I'm working on right now is the price: twenty-four ninety-five in hardcover."

Everyone laughed again.

"Oh . . . and what I'm most proud of is my eight years of sobriety."

Everyone clapped.

"Thank you," Karen said. "Hopefully by the end of our retreat you'll have more of your book to share than a price."

"That would be remarkable," he said.

He glanced over at me and I smiled.

The next two women to speak, Adele and Maureen, were friends who had come to the conference together. They were co-writing a paranormal romance about shark vampires who were, to quote Adele, "stud-muffin surfers by day, and toothy good-guy sharks by night who keep the waves safe."

When it was my turn to speak, my mouth went dry. "My name is Kim," I said. "I've written just one book. I mean I've almost written it. It's not completely finished, but I've already amassed an impressive collection of rejection letters."

A few people laughed.

"It's a Christmas romance called *The Mistletoe Promise.*"

"Provocative title," Karen said. "Tell us about it."

"It's about a lonely woman who is recently divorced and has had a string of bad relationships. Then during the holidays, she's approached by a man with a proposition: he doesn't want to spend the holidays alone, so he proposes that they pretend to be a couple until December twenty-fourth. Since he's a lawyer, he writes up a contract."

"Interesting premise," Karen said. "I'll be curious to see where you go with that."

"Me too," I said.

This time almost everyone laughed, even though I hadn't meant to be funny. I glanced over at Zeke. He was looking at me, but I couldn't read his expression.

After we finished going around the circle Karen said, "Okay, we're just about out of time. When we meet tomorrow I'm going to have you read a passage from your writing, so pick something that you feel comfortable sharing, hopefully something from the book you're currently working on.

"Also, here at the Mistletoe retreat, we believe in the buddy system. So before we break today I want each of you to find a writing buddy, someone from this group, to work with for the next six days. This buddy is someone you will share your writing with and get a little constructive criticism from before sharing with the rest of us.

"There's an odd number of people in the room, so one of the groups will need to be a threesome, in a strictly nonromantic sense. Since Adele and Maureen are working on the same book, I suggest that the two of you find someone to join you. We have five minutes before we dismiss, so please don't leave until you've found a buddy. I'll see you tomorrow."

We all stood, looking around at each other. Adele and Maureen quickly cornered Marci and I noticed Heather moving in on Zeke when he walked up to me. "It's Kim, right?"

He didn't really need to ask, as I was wearing a name tag.

I always get a little tongue-tied around handsome men. "Yes. I'm Kim."

"Zeke," he said. "I'm the guy from the gym . . ." When I didn't say anything he said, "I helped you when you fell . . ."

"I remember."

"You're okay, right?"

"Yeah. I probably won't need surgery."

He smiled. "Good. Would you like to be my writing buddy?" Before I could answer he added, "If you had someone else in mind, it's all right. No pressure."

I brushed a strand of hair back from my face. "No. I'd like that. Thank you for asking."

"Very good," he said. "I thought the premise of your book sounded really interesting."

"Thank you," I said. "And I thought the *price* of your book sounded very . . . reasonable."

He laughed. "I hope so. So I guess our next step is we should plan a time to get together."

"I was just going to my next seminar, but we could meet for lunch." Then I remembered that I had already committed to lunch with Samantha. "Oh wait. I already promised a friend that I'd meet her."

"Later, then?"

"No, why don't you join us? I'm sure she won't mind. We'll be in the dining room."

"Great," he said. "Then I'll see you around noon. I'm looking forward to working together."

As he turned and walked off I noticed a few of the women looking at me. Heather looked utterly dejected.

Lucky me, I thought.

CHAPTER

Fifteen

The gorgeous man asked to be my writing partner.
What critic is it within me that automatically
questions his motives or judgment?

Kimberly Rossi's Diary

The next presentation on my schedule was titled How Not to Get an Agent. The presenter was Laurie Liss, one of the principals of Sterling Lord Literistic, a New York literary agency. Liss's claim to fame, among other things, was discovering an unknown, first-time author named Robert James Waller, who wrote a book called *The Bridges of Madison County*, which not only made Waller a kajillion dollars but helped catapult Liss to the big time and earn her a coronation from the *New York Times* as The Queen of Schmaltz.

The truth was I hadn't sent my book to an agent out of ignorance. An agent, I thought, was just another hurdle I could bypass by going directly to the publisher, not realizing that I was in effect dooming my chances, as publishers rarely look at unsolicited manuscripts.

There were about forty other people at the presentation and Samantha and I took our seats near the front of the room. Liss revealed what she called Liss's List, a list of don'ts when trying to find an agent. I scrawled down the five things that drove Ms. Liss "insane."

1. Don't tell me that your husband/wife/mother/etc. thinks your book is fantastic. Big surprise: they're either biased or don't want to hurt your feelings and probably both.
2. Don't offer me a bribe, especially a portion of the enormous amount of money you're going to make off your book. I'll just hang up on you. I take a percentage anyway.
3. Don't send me a photo. I don't care what you look like. The other agents in the firm will hang it up on our bulletin board and draw on it with a Sharpie.
4. Don't ever slip pages under a bathroom stall. I will be so offended that you disregarded my privacy that I will use your pages as toilet paper, or at least send them down the toilet and probably clog it, making a huge mess of the bathroom. And yes, this really happened.
5. Don't ever claim to be the "next big thing." You don't know that. I don't know that. No one knows that. It's presumptuous and embarrassing for you.

As we walked out of the session Samantha said, "I wonder if she'd be my agent."

"I thought she was kind of snarky."

"A good agent needs to be snarky," Samantha said. "The snarkier the better. In the publishing world you swim with the snarks."

"At least you know what *not to do* to get her," I said. "Don't follow her into the bathroom."

"How much do you want to bet that someone will still do that at this conference?"

"I wouldn't be surprised," I said. "We are a desperate lot."

"I just wish she had told us the five things we *should* do."

"Number one should be *write a good book*," I said. "I'm hungry, let's get some lunch."

We returned to the same dining room where we'd had breakfast. I recognized several people from my workshop.

"There's John Grisham," I said.

"He's not really Grisham," Samantha said.

"Yeah, I know that," I said. "I'm just not so sure that he does."

We found an empty table near one of the windows and put our bags on it, then went over to the buffet table. The day's main courses were chicken cordon bleu, sausage lasagna, and vegetarian lasagna. I opted for the chicken and Caesar salad.

I gave the woman at the cash register one of my conference meal vouchers and went back to our table. Samantha was already eating.

"How was your workshop group?" I asked. "As bad as you thought?"

"I've decided the *F* stands for freaks," she said. "Just about everyone but me is into paranormal romance. But it was okay. They gave us playing cards to pair us up with writing buddies." She took a bite of food and I waited for her to finish chewing to continue. "I drew the queen of hearts, which I figured was a good omen. How about you? Did they pair you up with someone?"

"Yes. But we picked our own buddies."

"Did you have any men in your group?"

"Just one," I said.

"We didn't have any. He wasn't that one guy, was he?"

"Which guy?"

"You know, the hot one who's got the whole Clooney thing going? Handsome, cool glasses, a little older."

"You mean Zeke?" I said.

"You know his name?"

"He's in my group. And I met him earlier in the gym."

"I want to meet Zeke."

I cut into my chicken. "You will."

Samantha looked impressed. "I love your optimism. It's quantum physics—you make your own reality. Just throw it out to the universe and it's going to materialize."

"In this case it's going to materialize sooner than you think. He's going to be joining us for lunch. He's my workshop buddy."

Samantha looked at me incredulously. "Clooney's your workshop buddy."

"He's not Clooney, but yes."

"I told you I was in the wrong group. The closest thing to a man in our group was this one chick who writes werewolf love stories. She looked like one of them."

"Like a man or a werewolf?"

"Both."

"That's mean," I said. "And here's Zeke now. Watch your tongue."

Zeke walked directly up to our table, his hands in his pockets. "Hi."

"Hi," I returned. "Zeke, this is my friend Samantha. Samantha, this is Zeke."

Samantha just stared at him. "You can call me Sam," she said.

"But Samantha is prettier," he replied.

"Samantha's good," she said.

Zeke turned back to me. "Still all right if I join you?"

Before I could answer Samantha said, "Please."

"Thank you." He pulled out a chair and sat down.

"Did you want to get some food?" I asked.

"What are we eating?"

"I'm having the chicken cordon bleu. It's good."

"It looks good. I'll be right back." He stood and walked toward the buffet tables. Samantha's eyes were glued to him the whole way.

"He's better looking than Clooney," she said.

"No one's better looking than Clooney. Why do you say that?"

"Clooney's not real. Who knows how much of what you see is Photoshop."

"He's a movie star. You can't Photoshop movies."

"Of course you can. It's called special effects."

"Clooney isn't a special effect."

"He has a special effect on me."

I grinned. "You're insane."

Zeke returned a few minutes later with a plate of lasagna and vegetables. As he sat down I said, "You changed your mind about the chicken."

"You didn't tell me there was lasagna. I love Italian."

"Kim's Italian," Samantha said.

I wanted to slap her. Zeke just smiled. As he raised a fork to his mouth, Samantha asked, "Where are you from?"

He put his fork down. "I'm originally from Alexandria, Virginia. But more recently I live in Florida."

"Florida," Samantha said. "Beautiful beaches, beautiful weather."

"If you don't mind an occasional hurricane," Zeke said.

"Where in Florida?" I asked.

"Jupiter Island."

"Isn't that where all the movie stars live?" Samantha asked.

"Some," he said. "Burt Reynolds lives there. Tiger Woods lived there. I'm not sure if he still does."

"You must be rich," Samantha said.

I was now positive that Samantha had no filter.

"Not everyone who lives on Jupiter Island is rich," Zeke said. "Someone's got to mow the lawns and work the 7-Elevens, right?"

Samantha seemed vexed by the concept. "You mow lawns?"

"From time to time," he said.

I moved to change the topic. "Have you been to many writers' conferences?"

"A few," he said. "But this is the first one I've been to in a while."

"How long's a while?"

"A few years. I let my writing go for a while." He took a bite of lasagna.

"Life happens," I said.

"Yes it does," he said.

"What's your last name?" Samantha asked.

I realized that I didn't know what his last name was either.

He finished chewing, then said, "It's Faulkner."

"Faulkner," I said. "Like the author William Faulkner."

"Unfortunately, yes."

"Why unfortunately?"

"Because sharing the same name of a famous author invites comparison, and trust me, I'm no Faulkner. Think of it this way: if your name was Streisand, people would ask you two things—if you're related to Barbra and if you can sing."

"I can see that," I said.

"You could be like that David guy telling everyone he's Grisham," Samantha said.

"I don't know who you're talking about, but Faulkner is really my name."

"It's still a great name," I said.

"What about you?" he asked. "Do you go to many of these things?"

"I've only been to two others. One in San Francisco, the other local, in Colorado."

"You're from Colorado?"

"Yes."

"I'm from Montana," Samantha said.

He glanced at her. "Montana's beautiful. Big Sky Country."

"That's what they say. I mean, we're not really a country, we're a state. Just like the other fifty. But we have a lot of country." She hesitated. "It's kind of confusing."

Zeke looked at her as if trying to figure out whether or not she was being serious. Then he turned back to me. "Where in Colorado are you from?"

"Denver. I used to live in Boulder, but I moved after I got divorced."

"You're divorced," he said. He casually glanced at the diamond on my ring finger. "And the ring is . . ."

"Garlic."

"Garlic?"

"It keeps vampires away."

"Does it work?"

"We'll see," I said.

"So this is your first time at the Mistletoe Inn."

"It's my first time in Vermont."

"Why did you choose *this* writers' conference?"

"It sounded like a good one. But, honestly, mostly because H. T. Cowell is going to be here. I wanted to hear him speak."

"That's a lot of money to hear someone speak."

"He's worth it," I said. "He's the reason I decided to be a writer. I can't believe that he's really going to be here in person."

"Isn't he a bit of a recluse?" Samantha asked.

"That's putting it mildly," I said. "He makes J. D. Salinger look like an extrovert. The funny thing is, how do we really even know that the person who speaks is Cowell? I mean, who really knows what he looks like? They could bring in an imposter and no one would even know."

"Maybe the whole Cowell thing was a fraud from the

beginning," Samantha said. "And the organizers are just betting that Cowell's too reclusive to ever find out."

Zeke looked amused by our ramblings. "So Cowell's your inspiration?"

I nodded. "He's amazing. I've read some of his books five or six times. How about you?"

"I've read his books," Zeke said. "Not five or six times, but I mostly liked them."

"I just want to know why he stopped writing," I said. "His disappearance from the writing world is one of those great mysteries, like, whatever happened to the Mayans or who was Carly Simon really singing about in 'You're So Vain.'"

"Mick Jagger," Samantha said. "Everyone knows it's Jagger." She looked at me. "It was Jagger, right?"

"I have no idea," I said.

"Maybe the words just stopped coming," Zeke said. "Or maybe he was just old. It's like you said, no one knows much about him. For all we know he's ninety years old."

The idea of him being an old man made me a little sad. "Maybe."

"I don't think it's such a mystery," Samantha said. "I mean, why wouldn't he quit? He sold tens of millions of books, which means he made tens of millions of dollars. If I had his money, I wouldn't keep writing. I'd take the money and move to Bali or the south of France and enjoy life." She looked at Zeke. "Or Florida."

"Maybe it wasn't the money," I said, ignoring her flirtation, "but the pressure to keep succeeding. Like Margaret

Mitchell. She hit the top, then just stopped. I mean, after *Gone With the Wind*, where do you go but down?"

"Actually," Zeke said, "Margaret Mitchell claimed that she stopped writing because she was too busy answering fan mail. But it was probably more likely that she just hated the fame and was annoyed by all the people who wouldn't leave her alone. Once she got so mad at a fan who came to her house that she swore that she'd never write another word." Zeke frowned. "Then she was hit by a drunk driver."

"Margaret Mitchell was hit by a drunk driver?" I said.

"That's how she died," Zeke said. "The drunk was a taxi driver with twenty-three previous traffic violations."

"Wasn't Stephen King also hit by a drunk driver?" Samantha asked.

"He was hit by a car, but the driver wasn't drunk. But he did have a lot of traffic violations."

"I heard that the guy who hit him died on Stephen King's birthday," Samantha said.

"That may be true," Zeke said.

"That's creepy," Samantha replied. "Like his books."

"I don't know why Cowell stopped writing," I said. "And maybe we'll never *really* know. But what I do know is that he may be the only man on the planet who understands how a woman feels. I couldn't believe that a man could write like that. For a while I wondered if his books were really written by a woman using a man's name."

"Wait," Samantha said. "That would explain why he hides from the press—or should I say why *she* hides from the press. And why she uses her initials instead of a name that would reveal her true gender, the way Nora Roberts does when she writes her thrillers. H. T. could stand for Helen Taylor. Or maybe it's not just one woman but a group of women."

Zeke nodded. "I used to think that about R. L. Stine, the guy who wrote the Goosebumps books."

"That he was a woman?" Samantha said.

"No, that he was really a group of writers. I mean, he was releasing a new book just about every month and his name is Stine, like Frankenstein. It sounds like a brand, right? Just like Betty Crocker."

Samantha looked confused. "Betty Crocker's not a real person?"

Zeke and I glanced at each other.

"No, Betty Crocker is a fabrication," Zeke said. "Like the Easter bunny. Or the queen of England."

I forced myself not to laugh. Zeke was clearly having fun with her now. Samantha just looked confused.

"And R. L. Stine isn't a real person either," she said.

"No, actually he is," Zeke said. "I met him."

"You met R. L. Stine?" I asked.

"Robert Lawrence Stine," Zeke said. "He goes by Bob. He's a great guy. He started writing humor books for kids under the pen name Jovial Bob Stine, then moved on to kids' horror. He's the man who got millions of boys to read."

"None of this explains why Cowell is such a recluse," Samantha said.

"Maybe he's just so ugly that his publisher decided to

hide him from the public so he didn't ruin women's romantic fantasies."

I shook my head. "You're brutal. And if he does end up coming, I hope you don't meet him. You'll probably just offend him."

"What do you mean, *if* he ends up coming?"

"Last night these women were telling us that he has a habit of missing events he's scheduled for."

Zeke shook his head. "That's the first I've heard of that. What a cad."

I looked at him. "Did you just call him a *cad*?"

"No."

"Yes you did."

"Is that even a word?" Samantha asked.

"It's a word," Zeke said. "Archaic, but still wieldable."

"No one says *cad* anymore," I said.

"You're wrong, because I just did."

"So you admit it."

"I admit it," he said. "Anyone, no matter how famous, who commits to an important event, then, barring some major emergency, doesn't show up, is a *cad*."

"Yeah, you probably shouldn't meet him," Samantha said. "He probably won't like being called a cad, whatever that is."

"It would never happen," Zeke said. "Because if he does show up, he's not a cad."

"He has a point," Samantha said.

"I think you're just jealous," I said.

Zeke thought for a moment, then said, "You're right, of course. We always throw stones upward, don't we?" He turned to me. "It's easy to see why I *wouldn't* like him; men are always jealous of the other rooster in the coop. But the real question is, why do you like him so much? You were a loyal reader and he deserted you, along with millions of others."

"It's his life," I said. "It's not like he owed me anything. And his books helped me during a difficult time of my life." I nodded slowly. "I look forward to seeing him. I just hope I'm not too disappointed."

"I hope not too," Zeke said. "I'd hate to see you waste all that money."

"That would stink," Samantha said.

"I'm also hoping that I might get the chance of getting him to sign something for me."

"What is that?" Zeke asked.

"A first-edition copy of *The Tuscan Promise*."

"You have one of those?"

I nodded. "I was one of the early readers. There were only five thousand of the first editions printed. I bought it for, like, fifteen dollars at the bookstore, but I saw a copy on eBay going for around nine thousand."

"Nine thousand!" he said. "That's insane."

"That's what it was going for."

"You should sell it," he said.

"I'm not going to sell it. To me it's worth more than the money."

"You are a true fan," Zeke said. "And for that reason alone I hope he shows." He turned to Samantha. "What about you, Samantha? What brought you here?"

"A little of everything. Romance, Vermont in the winter, the energy of a writers' conference. But, mostly, Walt was driving me crazy. Frankly I would have gone to a basket-weaving class in Chernobyl to get away from him."

"Who's Walt?" Zeke asked.

"No one," she said, unconsciously leaning toward Zeke.

"He's her fiancé," I said.

Samantha frowned at me.

"How is a fiancé 'no one'?" Zeke asked.

"It's complicated," Samantha said.

"Not really," I said.

"No, not really," she agreed.

Zeke smiled as he poked a fork into his lasagna, which I'm sure was cold by then. He took a bite, then asked me, "What's the rest of your day like?"

"Right after lunch I need to turn in my papers for the agent sessions on Thursday. The sign-up sheet in our packet said our introduction forms and manuscripts are due before one if we want the agents to review them."

"I already turned mine in," Samantha said.

"Did you sign up for an agent?" I asked Zeke.

"No. Not this time," he said. "After you sign up, are you going to any more sessions?"

"I'm going to the Living the Dream presentation."

Samantha said, "Isn't that the one by the guy who was calling himself John Grisham and hitting on us?"

"Yes, unfortunately."

"Why are you going to that? He's a creep."

"Yes, but he's a *published* creep," I said. "So, as far as the afternoon sessions, it's either Faux Grisham, Writing Paranormal Romance, or Exciting Punctuation, and I don't want to spend an hour learning about periods."

"I hate periods," Samantha said.

Zeke squinted. "What?"

"That's not what—" I stopped, too exasperated to explain. "Okay. Punctuation's out. And I don't care for the vampire-love-triangle stuff, so we're back to creepy John Grisham wannabe."

"Well, I better come with you," Samantha said.

I looked at Zeke. "Do you want to come? I don't think he'll hit on you."

"Thank you, but no. I've got some phone calls to catch up on. When should we talk about your book?"

"What about *your* book?" I said.

"I'm not sure it can be saved," he said. "How about we meet for dinner in the dining room at . . . seven."

"Seven is perfect," I said.

He turned to Samantha. "Should I make reservations for three?"

"No," Samantha said, looking disappointed. "I promised my freaky writing buddy that I'd have dinner with her."

"Then it's dinner for two at seven," Zeke said to me. "Don't forget your manuscript. I'll meet you in the lobby."

"I'll see you then."

He got up and left. After he was gone, Samantha said, "Wow, you're totally into him."

"What makes you think that?"

Samantha shook her head. "Because if your smile was any bigger, the top of your head would fall off."

"Okay, I think he's gorgeous and very nice." I frowned. "I hope I'm not that obvious."

"You are," she said. "It's a good thing he likes you too."

"Why do you say that?"

"He was here, right? And he just asked you to dinner? Really, do you need a weatherman to tell you which way the wind blows?"

"Bob Dylan," I said. "You really think he's interested in me?"

Samantha shook her head. "You think? How can a romance writer be so blind to romance?"

"I don't know. I do better in fiction than in real life." I sighed. "All right, let's go. We don't want to keep John Grisham waiting."

CHAPTER

Sixteen

Some people thrill ride on the road of others' failed journeys.

Kimberly Rossi's Diary

Bready's talk should have been titled: *Narcissism: How So Little Success Can Swell a Head*.

Like everyone else at the retreat, I was hoping to hear an inspirational talk about how someone like me could break into the publishing world. Instead Bready basically made it sound like I'd be better off buying a lottery ticket and praying for success. Actually, he almost used those exact words. He said, "To keep your expectations in perspective, submit your manuscript to a publisher, then buy a lottery ticket. Your chances of winning the lottery are better."

He then went on to attribute his own immeasurable success not to luck but to perseverance, hard work, and remarkable talent. (Surprisingly he left off charm and humility.) Seriously, it was like he was using the same message he had used flirting with me, except this time with a room of eighty people, many of whom were growing visibly annoyed with his hubris. A few walked out before he was done.

A useful, but discouraging, thing I learned from his presentation was that finding a publisher was only the beginning of the process. "Getting published is like qualifying for the Olympics," he said. "You still need to compete, and only a handful of the competitors bring home medals."

Halfway through his speech he rediscovered Samantha and me in the audience and began focusing his remarks almost exclusively on us. It was agonizing. I've never been happier to see an hour pass, and as soon as he finished we hurried out of the session before he could trap us.

After we were outside the room, Samantha said, "If ego were money, that guy could pay off third-world debt."

I laughed. "I'm sorry I dragged you to that. We should have gone to the punctuation class."

"I'm not," she said. "It was informative. I learned a lot."

I looked at her doubtfully. "Really? What did you learn?"

"How some people live to sap the hope out of dreamers. It's like once they reach the top, they cut the rope."

"You may be right," I said. "Though I wouldn't say he's reached the top."

"As high as he's going to get," Samantha said. "So where to now?"

"You choose the next session," I said. I took out my conference schedule. "We have three choices. *E-lectric: How to Heat Up the Internet with Your e-Book.*"

"That sounds important."

"*Making a Six-Figure Salary on Four-Figure Book Sales: How to Make a Lucrative Living as a Midlist Author.*"

"That sounds boring."

"And *Chopping the Writer's Block: How to Keep Writing When the Words Stop Coming*."

"That sounds like something I need," Samantha said.

"I was thinking the same thing. Let's go learn how to chop some writer's block."

CHAPTER

Seventeen

Zeke and I had dinner tonight. I swear I know him from somewhere.

Kimberly Rossi's Diary

The main message of the writer's block lecture was that there is no universal cure for writer's block and you have to figure out for yourself what works for you—which made me think there was no reason to go to the class.

I did learn one thing of value. Walking sometimes helps. Thoreau believed that our legs are connected to our brains. I vowed to walk more.

After the conference I went back to my room to rest a little before dinner. I lay on my bed for a few minutes, then rolled over and looked at my manuscript. "*The Mistletoe Promise,*" I said. "By Kimberly Rossi. *New York Times* bestselling author." I groaned. *Right.* I wondered if Zeke would hate my book.

A few minutes before seven I freshened up my hair and makeup, grabbed my manuscript, and walked out to the lobby. Zeke was waiting for me, sitting on one of the crushed-velvet chairs, somehow looking even more beautiful than he had at noon. He stood as I entered. "Hi."

"Hi," I said, walking up to him.

"How were the rest of your sessions? Did you learn anything?"

"I learned that Bready guy is a *cad*."

Zeke smiled. "See, it's a useful word that bears repetition."

The dining room was crowded with a long line of people waiting for a table. The hostess smiled at us as we walked in. "Good evening, Mr. Faulkner. Right this way."

Zeke had reserved a small table for us by a window near the back of the room. The table was set with crystal and a flickering candle. He pulled my chair back for me, which, sadly, threw me a little. Apart from my father, I wasn't used to being with a gentleman.

"I hear the tourtière is very good." He looked up at me. "You're not vegetarian, are you?"

"No. What's tourtière?"

"It's a Canadian meat pie that's made with diced pork, veal, or beef. The chef here told me that he adds venison to it to enhance the flavor."

"That sounds interesting," I said. "Not interesting enough to actually order, but interesting."

He smiled. "Vermont has some interesting food. Bonne Bouche cheese, Dilly beans, fiddlehead ferns, Anadama bread."

"I have no idea what any of those things are."

"Neither do I, and I've eaten all of them. But you can't go wrong with Vermont dairy products. Especially their cheese."

"I love cheese," I said.

We shared some cheese with a duck sausage and cornmeal polenta appetizer, then Zeke ordered a bottle of wine. For my entrée I ordered the goat's milk gnocchi with tomato and pine nuts, while Zeke had the Gloucester cod. After we ordered, Zeke said, "Tell me about yourself."

"What would you like to know?"

"Let's start from the beginning. Have you always lived in Colorado?"

"No, I was raised in Las Vegas."

"Vegas. So you're good with cards?"

"No. I don't gamble." Then I added, "At least not with money."

"What took you to Colorado?"

"My ex, Marcus. He got a job offer in Boulder."

"What did Marcus do?"

"He was a history professor. Now he's just history."

Zeke smiled. "That sounds like a country song. So things didn't work out."

"The *Titanic* didn't work out. My marriage was a disaster."

He chuckled.

"You want the story?"

"I love a good anecdote," he said. "If you're willing to share."

"Why not?" I said. "Marcus and I had been not-so-happily married for about three years when he got the job offer in Colorado. I thought it would be good for our relationship, but two years after we moved, he was caught in a campus sting operation. Apparently he was 'romantically' involved with several of his students, trading grades for . . . *favors*."

"Adds a whole new meaning to *extracurricular activity*," Zeke said with a bemused expression. Then he said, "I'm sorry, I shouldn't joke about that. It's pretty horrific."

"It was horrific."

His brow furrowed. "Did that story make national news?"

"I'm afraid so."

"I think I read about it. I'm sorry."

"And, to add insult to painful injury, after everything hit, he left me for one of his students. Actually, two of his students. So I'm the one who ended up alone."

Zeke shook his head. "That's truly horrific."

"Samantha thinks it's good fodder for a romance."

"More like fodder for a horror story," Zeke said.

"That's what I said. Especially when you add the prologue about my two unsuccessful engagements before Marcus. One left me at the altar, the other got signed by the Orlando Magic and ended our engagement with a text message."

"Classy," Zeke said. "Would I know the player?"

I remembered that Zeke lived in Florida. "You might. Danny Iverson."

Zeke shook his head. "Sorry."

"It was a while back," I said. "He only lasted two seasons before his career fizzled."

"That's karma," Zeke said.

I looked at him for a moment. "With my record, it probably seems weird to you that I want to be a romance writer."

"Not at all. It makes perfect sense."

"It does?"

"Absolutely. It's like this. I have two brothers, Matthias and Dominic. When they were young they both wanted to play the piano. Even though Matthias was older, Dominic was naturally gifted and could play by ear.

"Once we were sitting around listening to the radio when a new Billy Joel song came on. It was 'Vienna' from the *Stranger* album. After it played Matthias said, 'I wonder if they have sheet music for that.'

"Dominic walked over to the piano and played the song flawlessly. I've never once heard him practice. He never had to.

"Matthias was the opposite. He'd get up an hour before the rest of us every morning to practice piano. Most of the time it was agonizing listening to him, since he usually couldn't go more than thirty seconds without hitting the wrong key. But he never gave up. He'd sit there day after day pounding away like he was chiseling a statue.

"Even though he never got as good as Dominic, Dominic eventually lost interest and stopped playing. Matthias is now teaching music at a university and plays for a large Methodist church on Sundays." Zeke looked intensely into my eyes. "I understand why you want to write. We don't appreciate the things that come easy to us as much as we do the things we have to work for. I think that's true for love as well."

No one, including me, had ever understood my dream. I was at a loss for words. After a moment I asked, "What about you? Have you ever been married?"

His expression fell. "I was. For seven years."

"*Was*," I said. "That sounds ominous. What happened?"

"She left me."

"Why?"

"Now there's a question," he said.

"You'd take her back if you could?"

"That's not an option, but yes, I would."

I sensed that he didn't want to talk about it. "I'm sorry."

"Life happens," he said. He took a deep breath, then looked back at me. "So, back to you. Do you have siblings?"

"No. I was an only child."

"And your parents are still in Vegas?"

"My father is. My mother died when I was young."

"How did she die?"

I lied. "She had breast cancer."

"I'm sorry," he said. "How old were you when she died?"

"I was eleven."

"I'm really sorry," he said. "Are you close to your father?"

"He's my best friend." To my surprise, my eyes began to well up. "I'm sorry. He has cancer."

"I'm sorry he has cancer," Zeke said. "That must be especially hard since you already lost your mother to it."

I didn't reply.

"What kind of cancer does he have?"

"Colon cancer."

"What stage is it in?"

"Three A."

He nodded slightly. "Then his odds are still good."

I was surprised that he knew that. "That's what he said."

"Does he have good care?"

I shook my head. "It's been an issue between us. He's a Vietnam veteran, so he goes to the VA hospital. I don't think the care is that good. He needs surgery and chemo, but they won't even get him in until next February."

"Why are they waiting so long?"

"That's what I asked him, but he just shrugged it off with 'it's just how it is.' What makes it worse is that Las Vegas has one of the top cancer institutes in the country."

"The Henderson Clinic," Zeke said.

I looked at him. "How did you know that?"

"Years ago I did some business with them," he said. "It's a state-of-the-art facility. They have one of the highest recovery rates in the world."

I nodded. "That's what I heard. I wish he'd go there. But he never would."

"Why not?"

"He'd never spend the money. He'd rather die and leave what money he has to me." I suddenly felt angry. "He's so stubborn. He paid for this whole conference up front, then told me I had to go. He said he'd be disappointed in me if I didn't go."

"And his disappointment matters to you?"

"Yes, it matters. He's lived his whole life for me. He's my hero."

To my surprise, Zeke suddenly looked moved as well. "Why was it so important to him that you came?"

"He knows it's my dream to be a writer, so he wants that for me. But now I think I want it more for him."

"I can see why he's your hero," Zeke said. He thoughtfully took a sip of wine. After he set his glass back down he asked, "Does he think he's going to die?"

I thought it a peculiar question. "No."

"Then he probably won't."

"Why do you say that?"

"It's just a theory, but I think we know our time. Maybe it's more cause than effect, but I think we have a sense of when we're going to die. Not always, of course. But sometimes. I've heard at least a dozen stories of people who spontaneously put their affairs in order before dying unexpectedly, like in a car accident."

I pondered the assertion. "With him, I don't know," I said. "He's a war vet. He thinks he's indestructible."

Zeke shook his head. "None of the war vets I know think they're indestructible. Not after what they've seen."

Again I was filled with emotion and I dabbed my eyes with my napkin. "May we talk about something else?"

"Of course," he said. "I'm sorry."

"It's okay. Thank you for asking about him."

For a moment we sat in silence. Then he asked, "When did you know you wanted to be a writer?"

"I was barely twenty. I wasn't exaggerating when I said it was Cowell who made me want to write. It was one of those really hard times in my life. My first engagement had fallen through a month earlier when I came across *The Tuscan Promise*. It was the first book of Cowell's I read. It was also the first time a book really made me feel loved. I didn't know how that was possible. I thought, this is like spiritual alchemy, turning ink into emotion. It was the closest thing I could imagine to magic. I wanted to be a magician like that."

Zeke looked at me thoughtfully. "That was the most

beautiful reason I've ever heard for someone wanting to be a writer. You have a poet's heart."

"Thank you," I said. "Have you read that book?"

He nodded. "It was a long time ago. Honestly, I don't remember much about it."

"I mostly remember how I felt when I read it." I breathed out. "What about you? When did you know you wanted to be a writer?"

"I was fourteen and the book was *The Hobbit*. It was the first time that a book had transported me to a different world. More than anything I wanted to write fantasy, so I started writing every day. Today we'd call it fan fiction, but I wrote about the world Tolkien had created with orcs and hobbits and trolls. I was a total nerd. Then, two years later, I fell in love for the first time and that changed everything." He grinned. "It was like a child's first taste of sugar. I've had a sweet tooth ever since."

Just then the waiter brought out our meals. After we had both started eating I said, "What was her name? Your first love."

He smiled shyly and I thought he looked cute. "Linda Nash," he said almost reverently. "She had long blond hair, Windex-blue eyes, and go-go boots."

"Go-go boots?"

"Go-go boots." He laughed and shook his head. "Man, I was smitten. I had never felt that kind of angst before, like pain and ecstasy in the same breath. She'd look at me and my mind would go blank."

"Did she like you back?"

He shook his head. "I have no idea. I was a kid. I never even told her how I felt. Her father was a salesman and her family moved away the next year. But the damage was done. Falling in love was transformative, because that's when I realized that all stories, at their core, are love stories. Whether you're talking about *Star Wars* or *East of Eden*.

"At first I went a little overboard and just wrote love letters, sonnets, poems, syrupy stuff—things that would never be published, but I wrote for the joy of writing. And I fell in love with falling in love."

"Most men aren't like that."

"Probably more than you think," he said. "They just don't use women's language to express it."

"I've never thought of it that way," I said. "So that's why you wanted to write romance?"

"Maybe," he said.

"Maybe?"

"At one of these conferences an author told me that when he was sixteen he was walking through a mall when he saw a man signing books for a long line of women and it occurred to him that if you want to get a girl, there was no better way than being a writer of romance. Smart man, I thought. Where else would women looking for romance line up to meet you? Of course musicians figured this out millennia ago."

"So is that really why you want to be a writer? To meet women?"

He looked at me with a hint of a smile. "On some deep, primal level—much deeper than I'd be willing to admit—

that's probably true. I think Freud would argue that's true of all male endeavors."

"Men are pathetic," I said.

"And women wear high heels, why?"

"To play off men's pathetic nature."

"So who's more pathetic, the junkie or the dealer?"

"That's the question, isn't it?" I said.

"Indeed," he replied. He looked me in the eyes. "I will admit that I'm very glad that I met you."

"I'm glad I met you too."

After a moment he said, "So back to your original question, why do I want to be a writer? Primal urges aside, I started writing because I'm not cutthroat enough to run a Fortune 500 company, I'm not handsome enough to be an actor or model, I can't sing, and I'm not coordinated enough to be a professional athlete. But I did win a tenth-grade creative-writing contest, so I went with my strength."

"I disagree with you on the handsome part. You're definitely handsome enough to be an actor or a model."

"You're being kind."

"I'm being honest. The first time I saw you I thought, That guy is gorgeous."

"Was that before or after you fell off the treadmill and hit your head?"

"I didn't hit my head, and it was before that. And thank you for reminding me that your first impression of me was that I'm a klutz."

"I just thought you were flirting with me."

"By almost killing myself? Really?"

"Any romance writer knows that showing vulnerability is a powerful lure. In the old days a woman would drop her handkerchief. You dropped a towel."

"I dropped my whole body."

"Even better," he said. "It's the whole politically incorrect damsel-in-distress thing."

I just laughed. "So after you decided to be a writer, then what?"

"I got an English degree and taught high school English for six years before I got into real estate."

"And you like real estate?"

He shrugged. "It pays the bills better than teaching did."

We ate awhile in silence, then he said, "So, moment of truth. May I see your book?"

I had actually forgotten that I had brought my manuscript with me. I leaned over and picked it up from the floor. "I can't believe I'm sharing it. When do I get to read yours?"

"Soon," he said. He took the manuscript and immediately started reading.

"Don't read it now," I said. "I'll be embarrassed."

He looked up. "Has anyone read this yet?"

"Other than my father and the publishers that rejected it, you're the first one."

"It's an honor," he said. "I promise that I'll be gentle with my critique and effusive with my praise."

"I just want to know if it's any good," I said. "Or if I should stop writing."

"Those two things have nothing to do with each other," he said. "If you enjoy writing, you should write, whether anyone else likes it or not." He looked back down at the manuscript. "*The Mistletoe Promise*. Did you name it after this conference?"

"No. It's a coincidence. I named it that more than two years ago. What do you think of it?"

"I think it's an intriguing title." He set my manuscript aside. "Would you care for dessert?"

"Not tonight," I said.

He took a sip of wine, then said, "I'm eager to start reading your book. Shall we go?"

Zeke paid the bill, then we walked out to the lobby. "What floor is your room on?"

"This floor. It's right down that hall."

"May I walk you to your room?"

"Yes, thank you."

We walked down the short hallway, stopping at my doorway. "You're really in room 101?"

"Yes. Why?"

"It's Orwellian," he said. "And strangely ironic. In Orwell's book *1984*, Room 101 is the torture room in the Ministry of Love, where people face their greatest fear."

"They're tortured in the Ministry of Love?"

"It's newspeak," he said. "Kind of like American society today. Did you read the book?"

"In middle school, but apparently I've forgotten it." As I took out my card key I said, "And I am facing one of my greatest fears. I just hope you don't hate my book."

"I'm not going to hate your book," he said.

"How do you know?"

"I read the first paragraph."

"You can tell if a book's good by the first paragraph?"

"No. But I can tell if a writer's good by the first paragraph."

I cocked my head. "You're acting very confident for an unpublished author."

He smiled. "You don't have to be a chef to know if the food's good."

"Touché," I said.

"I'll make you two promises. First, I promise that I will withhold all judgment until I've read the entire book. Second, I promise that I will be completely honest with you."

"Thank you," I said. "I think." I pondered what he'd said a moment, then added, "I'm not sure that I want that."

"Trust me, you do," he said. "And remember, I also promised to be gentle."

"I'll hold you to that."

He looked into my eyes, then said softly, "Thank you for having dinner with me. You're very lovely."

I suddenly felt a little flustered. "Thank you. So did you."

A large smile spread across his face. "I better go. I might be up all night reading." There was an awkward pause, and I hoped that he would kiss me. Instead he put out his hand. "Good night."

I took his hand trying not to show my disappointment. "Good night. I'll see you tomorrow."

With my manuscript in his hands, he turned and walked

away. I went inside my room and lay down on my bed. *You're very lovely. Thank you. So did you? That doesn't make any sense.* Then I said out loud, "Please like me anyway." I couldn't believe that I had only met him that morning. I remembered a line I had read in one of Cowell's books: *Love takes shortcuts.* It certainly had. Then I had a strange thought. *Is there really such a thing as a soul mate? If not, why do I feel like I've met him before?*

CHAPTER

Eighteen

I feel like I've stepped over the edge of a cliff.

Kimberly Rossi's Diary

The next morning Zeke wasn't in the fitness center and I wondered if he had really stayed up reading my book. My fears started in on me. What if he hated my book and was now avoiding me? I shook my head. *Why do I always torture myself with the worst possible outcome?*

Coming back from the fitness center, I stopped in the dining room. I was running late and Samantha wasn't there, so I grabbed a banana and yogurt and took it back to my room to get ready for the day. An hour later I walked into the workshop anticipating seeing Zeke, but he wasn't there either. He still hadn't arrived when our facilitator started the meeting.

"Let's see, who are we missing?" Karen asked, looking at her list. "Zeke is AWOL. Who is Zeke's writing buddy?"

Almost everyone looked at me.

"I am," I said, slightly raising my hand. "But I haven't seen him this morning."

"Today we're sharing, so you'll need to pair up with another group," she said.

"You can come with us," Heather said.

I tried to look grateful for the invitation. "Thanks."

I had nothing to share. I had only brought three copies of my book, two for the agents and now Zeke had my third, so I spent the entire workshop listening to Heather and her writing buddy, an eighty-year-old woman, read chapter after chapter of the most cloying love stories ever penned and feigning interest. I was glad when the workshop was over.

As I walked out of the room Samantha was waiting for me, her face twisted with disgust. "I can't even begin to tell you how much I hate my workshop group. I swear they're all freaks."

"And why is this?"

"They spent the whole session arguing over who kisses better, a vampire or a werewolf. What they finally decided was that a vampire is good with its mouth and sucking, where the werewolf is in touch with its inner animal." She breathed out. "What do you think?"

I tried not to smile. "I think it comes down to whether you like hairy men or smooth ones."

"Good point," she said. "I should have said that. Walter isn't hairy at all. Like, my writing buddy is hairier than he is."

"Isn't your writing buddy a woman?"

"That's my point," she said. "I missed you at breakfast this morning."

"Sorry. I was running late so I just grabbed something and took it to my room."

"I thought maybe you'd run off with Clooney."

"No. I don't even know where he is today. He skipped the workshop."

"He wasn't in your workshop?"

"No."

"But you did have dinner last night?"

"Yes."

"And how did that go?"

"It was nice."

"By 'nice' do you mean Walmart greeter nice or Brad Pitt nice?"

"What are you asking?"

"I'll spell it out. Are. You. In. Love?"

I stared at her. "I just met him yesterday."

"And your point is . . ."

"My point is, I just met him yesterday."

She shook her head. "Seriously, you're a romance writer. If you don't believe in love at first sight, you might as well turn in your pen. Did you give him your book?"

"Yes."

She smiled triumphantly. "I knew it."

"You knew what? He's my workshop partner. I was supposed to give it to him."

"Giving him your book is like standing naked in front of him."

"I didn't stand naked in front of him."

"That's your problem."

I shook my head. "You're going to drive me crazy," I said. "Let's go. There's a session on the roles of men and women in modern romance."

"Yeah, you should definitely go to that one," she said.

In spite of my denial, Samantha was right on two accounts. First, she'd detected that giddy, butterflies-in-the-stomach feeling I couldn't shake. Second, what Samantha had said about sharing my book was true. I felt naked and vulnerable and afraid. I wished I hadn't given it to him. I wasn't looking forward to his critique.

CHAPTER

Nineteen

Today's lecture on gender roles reminded me of a quote from Camille Paglia: "Woman is the dominant sex. Men have to do all sorts of stuff to prove that they are worthy of woman's attention." I wish I found that more true in my life.

Kimberly Rossi's Diary

The session on gender roles in modern romance was more interesting than I thought it would be. The presenter challenged the notion that a romance novel should be about helpless women and dominating men. Instead she proposed that in the true romance, it is the female who subjugates and tames the male by exposing his vulnerabilities. She quoted romance novelist Jayne Ann Krentz as saying, "the woman always wins. With courage, intelligence, and gentleness she brings the most dangerous creature on earth, the human male, to his knees."

I wished that had happened in my real life. It seemed like I was always the one who ended up broken.

Samantha and I had lunch together, then I went back to my room to rest a little before the next session. I noticed that the message light on my phone was flashing.

"Kim, it's Zeke. Sorry I missed you. If you don't have plans, I'd love to get together again for dinner. You can call my room, it's number . . ." He hesitated. "Actually, I don't know if this room has a number. Just call the hotel operator and ask for me. Bye."

I pushed zero on the phone. The operator answered. "How may I help you, Ms. Rossi?"

"Could you please connect me with Mr. Zeke Faulkner?"

"Do you know what room number that is?"

"No, sorry."

"Just a moment, please." There was a long pause. "Here you go. Have a good day."

Zeke answered on the third ring. "Hello."

"Zeke? It's Kim."

"Good, you got my message. Thank you for calling."

"Of course," I said. "I'd love to go to dinner again."

"Excellent," he replied.

"I missed you in workshop today. Busy with work?"

"No, I was in my room reading your book."

"Really?"

"I told you that I would. I'm just about finished. So what are you doing before dinner?"

"Samantha and I are going to the Catherine McCullin speech."

"I saw that she's here. Mind if I tag along?"

"Of course not. I'll meet you in the lobby."

Catherine McCullin's presentation was the final session of the afternoon. I met Samantha standing outside the ballroom. "I saved us seats," she said.

"Zeke's joining us," I said. "So we'll need one extra."

"You found Clooney?"

"He called," I said.

"Good, and no problem with the seats. I already saved us three."

"Why did you save three?"

"I didn't want anyone sitting next to me," she replied. "But I'm okay with Clooney."

"Why don't you go ahead and sit down and I'll wait for Zeke," I said.

"All right. We're in the front row, left of center."

"How do you get such good seats?"

"I'm aggressive," she said, walking to the ballroom.

Less than a minute later, Zeke walked out of the elevator. He smiled when he saw me. "Hey, beautiful." He kissed me on the cheek. "Thank you for letting me join you."

"I'm glad you are. Samantha's already inside with our seats." I desperately wanted to ask him if he'd finished my book but decided to wait for him to bring it up.

As we walked together into the ballroom I asked, "Have you ever read one of McCullin's books?"

Zeke shook his head. "No. Fictionalized Hollywood gossip isn't really my thing. I'm not interested in the real stuff, why would I want a fictionalized version? How about you?"

"I'm the same. I've only read one of her books. It was my first and last."

We found Samantha in the front of the room and sat down.

"Did you know McCullin has sold more than a hundred million books?" Samantha said to us. "I want to be her."

"Be careful of what you wish for," Zeke said softly.

Everyone went wild when McCullin came out onstage. Her speech was titled *The Limousine Lifestyle of the Bestselling Author* and consisted mostly of name-dropping and celebrity gossip until the end of her talk, when she focused on personal spending sprees that included a $10,000 laser haircut, a $218,000 pair of high heels shoes with thirty carats of diamonds, and a very long story about the time she made her pool boy fill her hot tub with Perrier because she liked the feel of its "effervescence on her skin."

"It took more than two thousand of those quart bottles," she said. "He drained every 7-Eleven, Safeway, and Walmart between Beverly Hills and Burbank."

Everyone in the audience seemed amused by McCullin's anecdotes. I was bothered by them. Successful or not, she wasted more than six thousand dollars on soaking in tingly water while my father, who had worked hard his whole life, couldn't get the health care he needed. The more she went on with her stories the more I wanted to walk out of the session. I glanced over at Zeke. He didn't look happy either.

After her speech was over the house lights went up while McCullin was still on the stage, thronged by the local press as well as conference attendees wanting her autograph.

"That was something," Zeke said dully. I nodded in agreement.

As we were crossing in front of the stage, McCullin suddenly turned toward us and shouted, "Zeke, baby. Call me."

Zeke gave her a short wave but continued on with the

flow of the crowd. I looked at him with amazement. When we got outside I said, "You know her?"

"The impressive thing," Samantha said, "is that *she* knows *him*."

Zeke looked uncomfortable. "Not really; we met at a writers' conference a while back." He looked at me. "It's nothing."

I was still a bit stunned. "You met at a writers' conference and she remembers you?"

"So, I'm unforgettable."

"Did you see her diamond ring?" Samantha asked. "It covered like three knuckles. I don't know how she could lift her hand with that rock on." She turned to Zeke. "Would you introduce me to her?"

"I'd rather not," he replied. "She's not exactly . . . cordial."

"She seemed cordial to you," Samantha said.

"He means to the little people," I said.

Samantha frowned.

"So, what did Mr. Unforgettable think of her presentation?" I asked.

Zeke scratched his head. "She's an entertaining speaker, but I'm not a fan of conscienceless excess. There are millions of people in this world who can't find healthy drinking water, and she's joking about bathing in Perrier."

I was glad that he felt the same way that I did. "I know, right? And $200,000 shoes? I'd pay my father's hospital bills. And others'."

"I know you would," he said.

"Do you think she really did those things?" Samantha asked.

Zeke nodded. "Yes. I'm sure she did."

I excused myself and went back to my room to freshen up, then met Zeke in the waiting area of the hotel's dining room. Again we didn't have to wait to get a table. In fact, we sat at the exact same table as the night before.

"Why don't we have to wait like everyone else?" I asked.

"I tipped the hostess," he said. "They must not get paid much."

"I'm not complaining," I said.

As he pulled out my chair for me, I said, "I'm still a little shocked that Catherine McCullin knows you."

"I'm sure she knows a lot of people."

"But she asked you to call her, which means she thinks you have her phone number." I looked at him. "Do you?"

"You're not going to let up on this, are you?" he asked.

I shook my head.

"We had dinner once. But, like you said about her books, first and last time."

"I'm impressed. There's a lot more to you than meets the eye."

"That's true of everyone," he said. "There's always more to the book than the cover. Even a bad book."

"Are you a bad book?" I asked flippantly.

To my surprise he turned serious. "There are better books on the shelf." He lifted his menu. "Now what will you be having?"

A few minutes later, the waiter came and took our orders. I ordered a salmon salad and Zeke ordered the prime rib with sweet potatoes.

After the waiter left I leaned forward in my seat. "So what do you think of my book?"

"I'm still reading it."

"But what do you think of it so far?"

"I'm not going to tell you until I read the final word. You wouldn't judge *A Farewell to Arms* until the last page, would you?"

"If Hemingway asked me what I thought of the first chapter, I'd tell him. Just tell me if you like what you've read so far."

"I'll tell you this. You can definitely write. That's all I'll say for now."

I took a deep breath. "Fair enough." I took a drink of wine. "I had this thought today. There's more than a hundred writers here. There's probably a hundred more of these conferences around the country. I'm guessing that less than one in ten thousand will ever make a living writing, which means our odds are better in Vegas."

"That's not hopeful," Zeke said.

"I'm just being realistic," I said. "So what if what we write is never published?"

Zeke's expression took on an exaggerated gravity. "If an author writes a book and it's never published, did the book exist?"

"I'm being serious," I said. "Sometimes I wonder why we bother to write at all."

Zeke looked suddenly thoughtful. "John Updike said, 'We're past the age of heroes and hero kings. . . . Most of our lives are basically mundane and dull, and it's up to the writer to find ways to make them interesting.'" He looked into my eyes. "Writing is life. Sometimes it's all that remains of civilizations.

"Do you know where the oldest writings were found? On tortoise shells. The Chinese carved histories into tortoise shells, then broke them for divination. We know of their wars and strivings from tortoise shells. From their writings. We write, therefore we are."

"I like your brain," I said.

He leaned forward and smiled. "Me too."

A few minutes later our waiter brought out our food, which was again delicious. We ate for a while, then I said, "There's something I've been wondering."

He looked up from his meal. "Yes?"

"Why did you pick me as your partner?"

"I told you. I thought your book sounded interesting."

I was hoping for more. "That's the only reason?"

He looked at me for a moment, then said, "No. When I first saw you in the fitness center I hoped that you were with the romance writers. I wanted to get to know you better. Call it chemistry."

"In school I was good at chemistry."

"Clearly."

"And then we ended up in the same workshop," I said. "That was a nice coincidence."

"It wasn't a coincidence," he said.

"What do you mean?"

"I wasn't supposed to be in group C. I changed because that's where you were."

"But they said that they didn't allow changes."

"I'm sure they don't."

"You mean you lied about Jill sending you to group C?"

"Not really," he said. "I figured that Jill, being the head of the romance writers, was a staunch proponent of romance, so when I said Jill wanted me in group C, I was telling the truth, in a matter of speaking."

I laughed. "I can't believe you did that."

"Are you glad I did?"

"I'm very glad." I picked at my meal, then said, "So is that what this is? A romance?"

He just smiled.

An hour later we shared an apple crisp dessert. As we finished eating he said, "We better go."

"It's still early."

"I know," he said. "But I need to finish your book."

"I'm flattered that you're really reading it."

"It's an easy read."

I frowned. "Do you mean it's too simple?"

"Good writing *is* simple. Hemingway once wrote, 'If I had more time, I'd write a shorter book.'"

"Then you're saying it's not *too* simple."

"No," he said. "It's not. The scientist who can explain complex theories to the layman is brilliant. Accessibility is true genius."

"I'm definitely accessible," I said.

A large smile crossed his face. "I hope so."

CHAPTER Twenty

I suppose, like most people, I don't really want to hear truth; I want to hear good things. If they happen to be true, so much the better.

Kimberly Rossi's Diary

The next morning I had breakfast with Samantha. Outside it was snowing hard—hard enough that some of the hotel guests were stranded and the lobby was crowded with disgruntled travelers and their mounds of luggage.

I didn't see Zeke until our workshop. When I walked in he was sitting next to Karen, talking to her. He smiled when he saw me and motioned to the seat next to him.

"I finished your book," he said. "Every word."

He had a perfect poker face, and I couldn't tell whether he liked or hated it. "And?"

"Let's talk about it tonight."

"You hated it."

"Don't go there," he said. "Are you up for another dinner?"

"I'm always up for dinner."

"If the weather improves, I thought we could go into town. I'm starting to feel a little caged. It would be nice to escape the property for the evening."

"I was thinking the same thing," I said.

I left the last session early. Actually, everyone did. It was titled *From Walmart to Hollywood*, with bestselling author Deborah Mackey. The session was Skyped in, and probably due to the weather, the reception was poor. Finally the facilitator just disconnected the call and apologized for the technical difficulties.

I didn't really care. I was glad for the extra time to get ready for our date. As I entered the lobby, Zeke was already standing near the front door. He again kissed me on the cheek. "You look gorgeous."

"So do you."

"Are you ready to go?" he asked.

"Yes, I'm starving. Where are we going?"

"The concierge recommended a little Italian restaurant in Burlington called L'Amante. Does that sound all right?"

"Sounds perfect," I said.

"Good. My car's outside."

It was still snowing as we walked out of the hotel, though not nearly as hard as it had been earlier. The car Zeke had rented was a Mercedes-Benz four-wheel drive. He opened my door for me and I got in, then he came around and climbed into the driver's seat. "Buckle up," he said. "The roads are still a little slick."

I pulled the seat belt over my chest as he drove off into the winter night.

The restaurant, L'Amante, was about a thirty-five-minute drive from the inn. It reminded me a little of Salvatore's in Vegas.

After we were seated I asked Zeke, "How did you know I liked Italian?"

"You ordered the gnocchi the other night," he said. "And you are Italian. Rossi is an Italian name, right?"

"Yes, it means red."

"I knew that," he said. "I studied Italian when I spent a summer in Florence. I was thinking about moving there permanently. It was right after my wife left me and I needed a clean break. Have you ever been to Italy?"

"No. My father and I have talked about going, but it always seems like something comes up." I looked down at the menu. "What are you getting?"

"The concierge at the hotel recommended the orecchiette if you like eggplant."

"I hate eggplant."

"Avoid the orecchiette," he said.

To start our meal, Zeke ordered an expensive bottle of Chianti, a cheese and salami plate, and an arugula salad with shavings of pecorino cheese, roasted beets, pine nuts, and balsamic vinegar. The moment the waiter left our table I pounced.

"So what did you think of my book?"

"Have some wine," he said.

"It's that bad?"

"I didn't say that." He filled my glass with wine and waited until I took a drink. "All right, my critique. The bottom line is, I've got good news, good news, good news, and a little bad news."

"Let's start with the bad news," I said.

"Why would you want to start with the bad news?"

"It's the way I roll," I said. "Eat the bad stuff first, save dessert for last."

He nodded. "All right. The bad news is, your book's not publishable."

His words hit me like a fist in the stomach. When I could speak I said, "You call that a *little* bad news?"

"It is," he said. "Because the good news is, you've got an ear for dialogue, a great sense of pacing, and you can definitely turn a sentence. In other words, you can write. And that's really good news, because, in the end, you either hear the music or you don't. You hear the music."

I think he expected this to compensate for his rejection, but I was still reeling. He continued.

"The second piece of good news is, you've got a great concept for a book, which is much harder to come by than most people realize. And third, your book is fixable."

I just looked at him, my heart and mind aching.

"Let's go back to the not-publishable part," I said. "What's wrong with it?"

"Okay," he said, looking disappointed that I'd focused on the negative. "There are two problems. First, it's not romance you're writing, it's fantasy."

"You said fantasy *is* romance."

"But I didn't say that romance is fantasy."

"What does that mean?"

"Your people aren't credible."

"What's wrong with my characters?"

"Precisely that," he said. "You're not writing characters.

You're writing people. And in the real world, even the best of people are flawed. Your people aren't. And neither is their relationship. Love is full of pain and mistakes. That's what makes it interesting and that's why we explore relationships in literature. That whole 'love is never having to say you're sorry' crap is just that, crap. Love is learning *how* to say you're sorry. It's the trial and error and correction that makes it worthwhile."

I just looked at him.

"Let me put it this way. Love is like learning how to dance. When you first hear the music, you're full of passion and you don't care who's watching because you just want to fling yourself around like an idiot. It's clumsy and it's full of missteps and falls and sometimes you're not even dancing to the same tune, but you don't notice because you're so carried away by the music.

"But then the music begins to wane, and you start stepping on each other's toes. Some think that's the truth of the relationship and run. But the truth is, that's where true love begins. That's when you start to learn each other's rhythm and how to move together. And if you stick with it long enough, you might even learn to be graceful."

After a moment I said, "I guess none of my dance partners stuck around long enough for me to learn that."

"There's that too," he said. "You need to have a partner who cares about the dance. Without that, you won't get far."

I took a deep breath, considering his words. I wasn't even sure how to fix what he'd already suggested. Finally I said, "You said there were two problems."

"The second is tougher," he said.

As if the first wasn't painful enough. My heart already hurt. I dreaded hearing what he had to say.

He looked into my eyes. "Actually, it's a symptom of the same problem. The reason your people aren't believable is because you're not bleeding through them."

"What do you mean?"

"I once heard a writer say, 'It's easy to write a novel; you just slit your wrist and let it bleed on the pages.' She was right. There's not enough of your own blood on these pages. You're not vulnerable enough and you can't hide that. You have pain in your life; let it out in your words. It's like you're writing with gloves on. Take them off. Let the reader really see you. Let them know your fears and hurts. Sophocles and Freud believed that we are defined by our fears. There's a lot of truth to that. When you share your greatest fears, your vulnerability, we bond in that honesty. We connect with each other and we don't feel so alone. And that's what books are really about. Connecting."

Tears began to well up in my eyes. "What if I don't want to share that part of me?"

"Then don't write."

I don't know why hearing this from him hurt so much but it did. I felt humiliated and dumb. I wiped my eyes. "If you know so much, why aren't you published? Why should I listen to you?"

"That's a good question," he said calmly. "Why should you listen to me? Don't. Listen to yourself. You're a writer. So ask yourself if what I'm saying is true. You'll know the answer."

I wiped my eyes with my napkin, avoiding his gaze.

"Kim, when I took your manuscript I promised you that I would be honest. But truthfully, I lied. Because if I thought your writing was beyond saving, I wouldn't have been so direct. I would have told you what you wanted to hear, not what you should hear. But you are a very good writer—good enough to be published. And I believe you have the potential to someday be a great writer. An Amy Tan or a Nora Roberts. But you can't do that halfway."

I took another breath, then quickly dabbed my eyes with my napkin. "May I have some more wine?"

"Of course," he said. He poured my glass nearly to the brim and I took a sip, then a bigger one, hoping to dull some of the pain I felt.

"We can fix this," he said, holding up my manuscript. "I can help you get this right."

I set down my glass. "We?"

"If you want my help."

"You have your own book to work on," I said.

"It can wait," he replied. "I've waited years for this one, what's another few months?"

I knew that he had meant the offer kindly, but all I could feel was the pain of rejection. After a moment I said, "I don't want your help. May I have my book back, please?"

My response hurt him. "Of course," he said softly, handing me the manuscript. "I'm sorry if what I said came out harsh. I would never intentionally hurt you."

"You have your opinion," I said.

The rest of the evening was miserable. We barely spoke,

and I regretted leaving the hotel, since all I wanted was to go back to my room. I barely ate my food, then asked to leave before dessert or coffee.

We didn't speak the whole way back to the Mistletoe Inn. Zeke looked like he was feeling as awful as I did. When we got back to the hotel he pulled up to the front door and I immediately reached for the door handle.

"Kim," he said. "I didn't mean to hurt your feelings. I was only trying to help."

I opened the door, climbed out of the car, then turned back to him. "Thank you for your help." I turned and walked away. When I got to my room I threw my manuscript against the wall, scattering it in a mess of pages. Then I fell on the bed and cried.

CHAPTER Twenty-one

Too many times we lose today's battles because we're still engaged in fighting yesterday's.

Kimberly Rossi's Diary

I didn't sleep well, and I didn't exercise the next morning. I didn't want to take the chance I'd see Zeke. I was embarrassed about how I had handled things. The worst part was that I wasn't even sure why it hurt so much. I knew that he hadn't wanted to hurt me. For that matter, why did I even care? Who's to say that he knew any more than anyone else? What I did know was that being with him had been the best part of the conference so far. Why had I ruined it?

I ordered breakfast from room service, then, after eating, climbed into the tub, where I stayed until the water started to turn cold. I got out and went back to bed, purposely missing the workshop. Today we were supposed to share our partners' critiques of our books, and the thought of that was about as welcome as a kidney stone.

Also, today was my day to meet with the agents, and I didn't want to face them already bloodied. Besides, maybe they'd disagree with Zeke and the whole thing would be moot.

I finally got out of bed around eleven. I dressed and did my hair, then went down to find Samantha. As I walked out into the lobby Zeke was sitting on one of the sofas. He immediately stood. "Kim."

I started to turn away from him.

"Kim, please, talk to me."

In spite of my regret, seeing him brought back the pain. Again my feelings overcame me. "Why? You found more things wrong with my book?"

He put his hand on my arm. "Look, I know how much it hurts to be criticized. Trust me, I've had more than my share. But all criticism isn't the same. Some criticism is mean-spirited and some is shared because someone cares. It's like . . . telling a friend they have something in their teeth."

"In this scenario I'm your slob friend with something in her teeth?"

He raised his hands as if in surrender. "I'm sorry, bad example. I know last night shook you up, but it should have encouraged you."

My eyes welled up. "Encouraged me to do what? Quit? Trust me, don't get a job as an inspirational speaker, because you suck at it."

His brow furrowed. "You're not going to let me apologize, are you?"

Even though I could see how much he was hurting, I said nothing. Finally he breathed out slowly. "All right, I'll leave you alone. Good luck. I hope things go well for you when you meet with the agents today. I hope they're kinder than I am." He turned and walked away.

As I watched him go a tear fell down my cheek. I felt sick inside. The moment I let myself be vulnerable, I got hurt. When would I learn?

As I sat there, Samantha walked up to me. "You'll never

believe what the brilliant workshop group F talked about today. Love and *wormholes*, and would it be ethically wrong to be in love with two different people if they lived in different dimensions. Honestly, I wanted to puncture my eardrums." She stopped. "Are you okay? You look like you've been crying."

I looked down so she couldn't see my eyes.

"Honey, what's wrong?"

After a moment I shook my head. "Nothing. Let's just go to lunch."

At the table Samantha just stared at me. "Talk to me. What's going on?"

I took a deep breath. "You know I let Zeke read my book."

"And?"

"He didn't like it."

She blinked slowly. "And he told you that? I knew I didn't like him. For the record, he doesn't really look like George Clooney, I was just being nice. He looks more like George Costanza on *Seinfeld*."

"No he doesn't," I said, suddenly feeling protective of him. "He's beautiful. And he's sweet. He was just being honest."

Samantha frowned. "How can he tell you your book stinks and still be sweet?"

"He didn't say it stinks. He had constructive criticism."

"Now you're defending him? This is like that Stockholm syndrome."

"This is nothing like Stockholm syndrome."

"It's some kind of syndrome," she said. "So what do you do now?"

"I don't know. He tried to apologize, twice, but I . . ." I took a deep breath. "I'll probably never see him again."

"I'm sorry," she said. "But cheer up. Don't you have your agents this afternoon?"

"Yes."

"Good. Let me tell you what's going to happen. You're going to knock their socks off. And Zeke is going to be eating his words with catsup and French-fried potatoes."

I just looked at her. She was the strangest and sweetest person I'd ever met.

"I love you," I said.

She smiled. "I love you too," she said, then added, "in a totally non-romantic way."

"Thanks for the disclaimer."

She kissed me on the cheek. "Anytime, sweetie. Anytime."

CHAPTER

Twenty-two

There's no point in switching course after you've hit the iceberg.

Kimberly Rossi's Diary

The way the agent meetings worked was fairly standard for these kinds of conferences. I paid—actually my father had paid—a hundred dollars to meet with each agent. I gave the agent a copy of my manuscript, which he or she was obligated to read for fifteen minutes and then write a brief assessment.

The first agent I met with was Timothy Ryan, a twenty-seven-year veteran of the publishing industry. We met in a room with five other agents and authors.

As I settled nervously into my chair, Timothy looked down at his appointment list, then back at me. "You're Kimberly Rossi."

"Yes, sir."

"Just a moment." He fanned through a pile of papers, then stopped on one. He looked over the paper, presumably his notes on my book, then back up at me with a stern, tense expression. "Your book is *The Mistletoe Promise?*"

"Yes, sir."

"Is this the first book you've written?"

"Yes, sir. Can you tell?"

He just nodded slowly as he looked back down at his

summary. He hesitated a moment, then said, "Obviously with our time constraints, I'm prohibited from giving you a complete evaluation of your work, but let me say this—I love the concept of your book, but there are two things that would keep it from selling to a publisher.

"First, your character development needs improvement. Specifically, your characters are too perfect. No one's going to relate to someone that Pollyannaish. They need some skeletons in their closets, if you know what I mean." He gazed at me, waiting for a response.

"I think so."

"Second, I'm just not feeling *it*."

I just looked at him for a moment, then said, "You're not feeling . . . what?"

"The passion," he said, gesturing with his hand. "The 'it.' I think you're holding back, and you need to dig deeper. No one wants to read about a perfect life. There's no interest in the mundane. The masses of readers buy romances because they want to see flawed people healed by love, you know what I mean?" Again he skewered me with his gaze.

"Someone told me that last night."

"Well, you should listen to her. My feeling is, you can write, but I think you can do better than this. This novel almost feels like you're faking the emotion. You need to take it up a few notches." He took a business card out of his pocket and handed it to me. "I'm going to do something I rarely do. Here's my contact information. Do not share this with anyone at this conference. You can send me your manuscript after you've fixed it, and I'll give it another read. Like I said,

I think you've got a great concept, and I think you have talent. If you're able to make the changes I recommended, I might be able to do something with it." He glanced down at his watch. "We're out of time."

I put the card in my purse, then slowly stood. "Thank you," I said.

"Don't mention it. Good luck."

My next agent meeting was less encouraging but not dissimilar in tone. The agent was a woman named Rachel Bestor. She was a former editor for Hay House turned romance agent.

"It's not doing anything for me," she said bluntly. "Your protagonist, this Elise woman, she's like a Girl Scout. Throw some dirt on her. Or show us her dirt. You're not a bad writer, but this book doesn't prove it."

I walked away from the meetings more upset that I had wasted my father's money than bothered by what the agents had to say. They had, essentially, told me the exact same things that Zeke had, yet I hadn't blown up at them. And Zeke was much nicer about it.

I guess, in my heart, I knew that what Zeke was saying was true. Suddenly I understood why I had been so hurt by him. Deep inside I wasn't listening for his critique of my book, I was listening for his critique of me. I never should have confused the two.

After meeting with the agents I felt obligated to call my father, which, as much as I dreaded it, I did the moment I got back to my room.

"How's the conference?" he asked.

"Good," I said. "I met with the agents today."

"How did it go?"

"It wasn't what I hoped. They weren't interested in representing my book. I'm sorry I wasted your money."

"Did they give you any hope of being published?"

"They both said I was a good writer. I mean, maybe they say that to everyone, but they seemed sincere."

"How are you handling it?"

"You know how badly I handle rejection. How are you doing?"

"Hanging in there," he said. "I've been feeling pretty tired. I had to cancel the motorcycle ride."

"I'm sorry," I said.

"It's just for now. I'll get that surgery and be back in the saddle. And that's what I expect of you. Get back in the saddle. I didn't raise a quitter."

I suddenly felt like a little girl again. "All right, Dad."

"Other than this speed bump, have you had a good time? Have you learned anything?"

"It's been a good conference. It's been fun."

"Have you made any new friends?"

"A few."

"That's good. You could use some new friends." After a moment of silence he said, "You know I believe in you."

"I know. Thanks, Dad. I'll talk to you soon. I love you."

"I love you more," he said. Before hanging up he threw out once more, "Get back in the saddle."

The moment I hung up I dialed the hotel operator.

"Hello, Ms. Rossi. How may I help you?"

"Could you connect me with one of your guests, please?"

"Of course, which room?"

"I don't know his room number. It's Zeke Faulkner."

"Faulkner," she repeated. "Just a moment, please."

The phone rang at least half a dozen times before Zeke answered. "Hello." He sounded a little groggy, as if he'd been napping.

"Zeke, it's Kim."

"Hi," he said cautiously.

"Did I wake you?"

"Yes."

"I met with the agents today."

He was quiet for a moment, then obligingly asked, "How did it go?"

"They said what you did."

He said nothing, which was even worse than an "I told you so."

I took a deep breath and pressed on. "I called to say I'm sorry about how I acted last night. And today. I know I don't deserve it, but if you're willing . . . may we go to dinner tonight? I'll pay . . . Or maybe we could just talk."

He still said nothing.

I sat there for a moment in silence, then said, "All right. I know you want to punish me, and I deserve it. But please don't. Please?"

I heard him breathe out.

"Okay, I'll say it. I'm an idiot and I'm not as smart as you. And I'm overly emotional. Is that what you want to hear?"

He exhaled. "No. That's not what I wanted to hear. I would never say those things. Good night, Kim."

"Good night," I said weakly.

I slowly hung up the phone, hating myself. A dark little voice inside of me said, *You sabotage everything. No wonder nobody wants you. You deserve to be alone for the rest of your life.*

CHAPTER

Twenty-three

The problem with the past is that too often yesterday's lessons were meant for yesterday's problems.

Kimberly Rossi's Diary

I tried to read but instead I mostly just lay on the bed and cried for the next half hour until my phone rang. I crawled over and answered it.

"Hello."

"All right," Zeke said softly. "Let's talk."

I wiped back my tears. "Okay. Where?"

"I'll meet you in the lobby in five minutes. Bring your coat."

I stood waiting in the lobby for what seemed a long time, wondering if he'd changed his mind. Then he came out of the elevator. He walked up to me, looking solemn but not angry. "Come," he said. He took my hand and led me toward the front doors. "Let's go for a walk."

We walked away from the inn down the long, rutted drive, lit by the sparkling yellow-white lights of wrapped evergreens. The stars were bright above us and the night air was freezing and moist. We had walked maybe fifty yards when I said, "I'm really sorry."

"Why are you sorry?" he asked.

I didn't know if he was really asking or if he was making me own up to my bad behavior. "I was mean to you. You were only trying to help."

He nodded. "I was trying to help."

"The agents said the exact same thing you did. Only you were kinder." I looked at him. "How did you know what they'd say?"

"It's always easier to critique from the outside," he said. "You would have seen it if it wasn't your own book." His voice seemed lighter. Forgiving.

"I feel so embarrassed."

"No one wants to hear criticism. I don't."

I swallowed. "I don't think I was really angry about the book."

"I know."

I looked at him quizzically. "How did you know?"

"Because every book is about its author. You felt attacked by me, even though I wasn't attacking you. You were fighting shadows."

I looked into his eyes. "What does my book say about me?"

"You're writing about a fake romance, one in which the characters draw up a contract to define the relationship." He looked into my eyes. "You've been hurt and you want a guarantee that you won't be hurt again."

I just nodded.

"It's understandable," he continued. "You're afraid to put your hand back on the stove. That's not weakness, that's intelligence. But wisdom is knowing that we need love and knowing when it's safe and whom to trust."

"It seems like it's never safe," I said.

"I know," he said softly. "But it's an illusion. The thing is, we use past relationships like maps to navigate new ones. But it doesn't work that way, because every human, every relationship is different. It's like trying to use a map of Las Vegas to get around Vermont. It won't work. That's why so many people get lost." He looked at me. "I don't know everything that's happened to you in your life, but I think there's more to your hurts than your divorce and failed engagements. I think there's something deeper you're afraid of."

I stopped walking and looked at him. "What's that?"

He looked deeply into my eyes, then said, "I think you doubt that you're worthy of love."

For a while I couldn't speak. I was afraid to look at him. When I finally did he was looking at me lovingly. "Let me tell you something I want you to never forget." He leaned forward until our faces were inches apart, then I closed my eyes as he pulled me into him and kissed me. When we finally parted I was breathless. He said to me, "No matter what anyone says or does, you are worthy of love. You always have been. You always will be. And I'm safe for you. You can trust me."

Then he pulled me back into him. As we kissed, tears rolled down my cheeks. I had never felt so loved.

CHAPTER

Twenty-four

My life has been filled with surprises.
Far too few of them were welcome.

Kimberly Rossi's Diary

The next morning Zeke knocked on my door around nine. I opened it wearing an oversized T-shirt and my sexiest pink sweatpants.

"Good morning," I said, the smile from the night before still lingering.

He leaned forward and we kissed. "What are you doing today?" he asked.

"More of this, I hope."

He smiled. "I meant the conference. Is there anything you can't miss?"

"That depends on the offer."

"I thought we'd spend the day together. I want to take you somewhere."

"Somewhere?"

He nodded. "Somewhere."

"I have to get dressed."

"Okay. But hurry."

"Why do I need to hurry?"

"Because we have a very tight schedule to keep."

"Can I have a half hour?"

"I can give you twenty minutes," he said. "I'll be in the lobby. And dress warm."

"I'll hurry," I said.

Fifteen minutes later I walked out into the lobby. Zeke was standing next to the front doors checking his phone messages. He looked up at me and smiled. "That was fast."

"Where are you taking me?" I asked, offering him my hand.

"Someplace Christmasy," he said.

"I don't like Christmas."

"I know."

"Is *Christmasy* even a word?"

"If you understood it, it's a word."

"Really, where are we going?"

"Remember what I said last night about trust?"

"Yes."

"This is where you show that you trust me."

"Okay," I said. "I'm all yours."

Outside, a pristine, crystalline blanket of snow lay snugly across the grounds of the resort, shimmering beneath the morning sun. Zeke's car was waiting for us just a few yards from the front doors. He retrieved the key from the valet, opened my door for me, then we sped away.

A half hour into our drive I asked, "Are we going back to Burlington?"

"Sort of."

"What does that mean?"

"It means we're going to Burlington so we can leave Burlington."

"Now I'm more confused."

"We're flying out."

"Really?"

"You'll enjoy this," he said.

"I should have called Samantha," I said. "She thinks we're having lunch."

He smiled.

We parked the car in the airport's covered parking lot, then hurried through the terminal. As we approached the check-in counter, I said, "May I ask where we're going besides someplace 'Christmasy'?"

"Bethlehem."

"Israel?"

"Bethlehem, Pennsylvania. Christmas City, USA."

A half hour later we boarded the first-class section of the plane. We flew from Burlington into Newark, then took a smaller plane into ABE, the Lehigh Valley International Airport in Allentown, Pennsylvania. In all, our flights were less than three hours and we arrived at our destination around four in the afternoon.

"Let me tell you about Bethlehem," Zeke said. "It was named Bethlehem on Christmas Eve 1741 before America was even a country. They have one of the most famous Christmas markets in America called the Christkindlmarkt.

There's music and shops, artisans, and really great food. I think you're going to love it."

We took a cab from Allentown and it was already starting to get dark as we pulled into the Christmas village in the center of the Bethlehem Historic District. The streets were beautifully lit for the season and crowded with tourists. In the center of the town we passed a massive Christmas tree.

As I got out of the taxi, my senses were assaulted by the sweet-smelling wares of the outdoor vendors—candied nuts, kettle corn, caramel-dipped fruits and chocolate—all sharing the crisp air with the sounds of school and church choirs and street musicians.

We stopped on one corner to listen to an elderly man dressed in army fatigues and a thick army jacket play "Winter Wonderland" on a saxophone. Zeke tipped him a twenty-dollar bill and the man was so pleased that he asked Zeke if he could play a request for his "lovely lady." I asked him to play "Silver Bells," which he did beautifully. Zeke gave him another twenty.

For dinner we stopped at a little German shop and had a meal of bratwurst with sauerkraut and cheese-beer soup, and to drink we had Glühwein, a delicious hot red wine seasoned with mulling spices and raisins.

I don't know if it was more the wine or my heart, but I was intoxicated. The mood around the city matched the music inside of me and I felt jovial and festive and free. I hadn't had that much fun for as long as I could remember. Especially not at Christmas.

For several hours we wandered among the booths of artisans, admiring their creations. We spent time watching a glassblower and Zeke bought me a glass ornament to commemorate the evening.

As the night waned it occurred to me that we wouldn't be going back to Vermont. "Where are we staying tonight?"

"The Waldorf Astoria."

"There's a Waldorf Astoria in Bethlehem?"

"No. It's in New York."

"We're spending the night in New York?"

"Have you ever been there?"

"No. I've always wanted to. When are we going back to the conference?"

"Tomorrow night," he said. He smiled. "Don't worry, you'll be back in time to hear your beloved author and get your book signed."

"You didn't tell me we were spending the night. I don't have anything to change into."

"I think you might be able to find something to wear in New York," he said. "I'll take you to Saks Fifth Avenue as soon as they open."

I looked at him. "Why are we going to New York?"

"It's Christmasy," he replied.

"Christmasy," I repeated.

"You wrote about New York in your book. I thought you ought to at least go there and take some notes. It's always better to see what you're writing about. Otherwise you miss the details that really make a book. Like where we are now. Smell the air. What do you smell?"

I took in a deep breath. "Cinnamon and sugar, from the man over there making candied almonds. And I smell wassail."

He smiled. "Details, details. Books are like life. It's all in the details."

Zeke had booked a sedan, a white-pearl Lincoln Town Car, to drive us to New York. I hated to leave Bethlehem, but I was excited to finally see Manhattan. The ride was about two hours but it didn't seem that long. I wished it would have been longer. Much longer. The steel-gray leather-upholstered seat of the car was soft and spacious, and Zeke held me the entire way.

About forty minutes out of Manhattan we began to kiss and we didn't stop until the car stopped on Park Avenue at the front doors of the Waldorf a little after midnight. The driver had to clear his throat to announce that we'd reached our destination. Zeke had the most delicious kisses.

I had wondered if Zeke had planned for us to share the same room, but I should have known better. He was a gentleman. Still, I have to admit that I was a little disappointed. We kissed some more, then said good night. After I closed the door to my room I thought of calling my father to tell him where I was, but I quickly decided against it. Based on my history with men, he'd want to know all about Zeke and he would probably hate him before he even knew him. I didn't want my father to hate him.

As I lay in my luxurious bed surrounded by the opulence of the hotel and the sounds of a city that never slept, I took in a deep breath and smiled. My face was slightly warm and stubble burned from all our kissing and I liked the feel of it. This may have been the best day of my life. And there was still tomorrow. It wasn't often that I looked forward to tomorrow.

CHAPTER

Twenty-five

To be in love is something. To be loved is everything.

Kimberly Rossi's Diary

New York during the holidays is like a Christmas show with a million extras. Zeke woke me early and, wearing our hotel robes, we ate breakfast together in my room. Then I showered and put my only clothes back on and we walked to Saks Fifth Avenue. Zeke bought me more than just an outfit for the day. He spent more than a thousand dollars.

Then he took me to Tiffany and bought me a beautiful rose-gold "Return to Tiffany" heart tag pendant with a gold chain. He wanted to spend more on a different necklace, but I had always wanted a simple Tiffany heart, so against my protests, he bought me a matching heart bracelet to go with it instead.

As we were riding the elevator down from the second floor, Zeke asked, "Have you ever seen a Broadway show?"

"I've seen *Jersey Boys*," I said. "In Vegas."

"I liked *Jersey Boys*," he said. "Who doesn't like Frankie Valli? Is there anything else you've wanted to see?"

"Hypothetically speaking?"

"Yes."

"I've always wanted to see *Wicked*. Have you seen it?"

"A few times. I got to see it with the original cast." He took his phone out of his pocket. "Just look around for a minute. I need to make a call."

I browsed through the first floor's glass jewelry cases for about ten minutes before Zeke returned. "I've got us matinee tickets to *Wicked*," he announced.

"How did you do that? Aren't they sold out months in advance?"

"I know people," he said.

Two hours later we were sitting in the second row in the middle section of the Gershwin Theatre.

The show was as good as I hoped it would be. Afterward, Zeke bought me a "Defy Gravity" T-shirt and took me to dinner at a wonderful historic restaurant called Keens Steakhouse.

"You should put this place in your book," Zeke said. "It's got great history. Do you know who's dined here?" Before I could guess he said, "Teddy Roosevelt, Babe Ruth, Will Rogers, Albert Einstein, General Douglas MacArthur, 'Buffalo Bill' Cody, pretty much the who's who of humanity." He smiled. "And Kimberly Rossi. Someday they'll boast about you. One of America's great writers."

I couldn't help but smile.

For dinner I ordered a petite filet mignon and a crab cocktail and Zeke ordered prime rib. As we ate Zeke asked, "Did you enjoy the show?"

"I loved the show."

"I know Gregory Maguire."

"Who?"

"Gregory Maguire. He's the author of *Wicked*. Did you know how he came up with the name of Elphaba?"

"No."

"It comes from L. F. B., the initials of L. Frank Baum, the author of *The Wizard of Oz*. And, for the record, Gregory has a beautiful singing voice."

"Okay, you're blowing my mind," I said. "First it's Catherine McCullin and R. L. Stine, now Gregory Maguire. How do you know these people?"

"Writers' conferences," he said. "I used to go to them all the time."

"I went to a writers' conference with Mary Higgins Clark, but we're not best friends."

"I never said we're best friends. I'm just good at making acquaintances."

"Like me?" I asked.

His expression immediately turned. "No. Not like you. Do you think I'm just playing around with you?"

"Honestly, I don't know what you're doing with me," I said softly.

He was quiet for a moment, then his expression relaxed. "I'm sorry. Of course you don't. You don't even know me." He took a deep breath. "I don't often get close to people, especially women. But this time I have." He looked into my eyes. "I'm afraid I've fallen in love."

CHAPTER

Twenty-six

The reason we cage the past is sometimes only understood after we un-cage it.

Kimberly Rossi's Diary

It was a short flight back to Vermont. We flew out of LaGuardia at nine and our plane landed in Burlington just a little after ten-thirty. We retrieved Zeke's car and headed back to the inn. It wasn't quite midnight when we arrived and Zeke parked his rental car just short of the portico, leaving it running to keep the heater on.

After leaning over and kissing him I said, "I'm curious, how hard was it to plan all that?"

"It was simple."

"That was *simple?*" I said doubtfully. "We flew to Bethlehem, drove to New York, spent the night in the Waldorf Astoria, shopped Fifth Avenue, took in a Broadway show, had a fabulous dinner, then flew back to Vermont, and you call that simple?"

"Very simple," he said. "I'm a simple guy."

"*You* really think you're simple?"

"I *know* I'm simple," he said. "What you see is what you get."

"You're a lot of things, but you're definitely not simple. You're an enigma wrapped in a mystery, or whatever Churchill said."

"Really. What's enigmatic about me?"

"The mind reels," I said.

"Go on," he said. "What makes me enigmatic?"

"Okay, to begin with, why are you single? Why would any woman in her right mind leave you? It would be like driving a Rolls-Royce over a cliff. You're the whole package. You're kind, you're fun, you're smart, and you kiss like a Hoover vacuum cleaner . . ."

One brow rose. "Is that a good thing?"

"That's a good thing," I said. "You're very, very good-looking . . ."

"Thank you."

"I'm not done," I said. "You must have a lot of money, but you're not obsessed with it. And you know more about books than anyone I've met, but you aren't published. So no, you're not as simple as you think you are. In fact, you're so complex it's scary."

"Scary?" he said. "In one minute I went from 'not simple' to 'enigmatic' to 'scary.' Explain scary."

"They say if it's too good to be true, it is. You should have that yellow caution tape wrapped all around you, because you're way too good to be true."

"I'll take that as a compliment."

"I don't know if it is one," I said. "Because *too good to be true* leaves a lot of questions unanswered."

"Such as?"

"The big one?"

He just gazed at me with an amused smile. "If you have a question, just ask. I'll give you a simple answer."

"Okay, here's the big one." I took a deep breath as he looked at me in anticipation.

"Go on," he said.

"I'm building up to it. It's a big question."

He grinned.

"Here goes. Why do you like me?"

He looked at me. "That's it? That's all you got?"

"Yes."

"Simple. Pretty much for every reason you just said about me. You're kind, smart, funny, fun, grateful, and beautiful.

"And to answer your question, why am I single? Because until now, I've chosen to be. There have been other women in my life and many of them have been smart and stunningly beautiful and yes, at my age, chemistry is still important. But something about my chemistry has changed. I've found that when someone is beautiful on the outside but spiritually dark inside, all that outer beauty is just lipstick on a pig."

I smiled at the metaphor.

His tone turned more serious. "When I was younger and more full of myself, I wanted to be with the cool people—the clever, arrogant ones with the snarky comebacks and designer clothes. And then life went on and I saw how they treated others. And me. Eventually, I got sick of their pretense and their fraudulent personalities. Frankly, I didn't want to be with someone who was that much work.

"And I didn't want to entrust my heart to women who were so full of themselves that they could hardly see me through their Gucci sunglasses. I wanted someone real. Someone who would laugh at the same stupid things I laugh at and think it's fun to stop in a little café and eat bratwurst and beer-cheese soup. I wanted someone who would worry if she had hurt someone's feelings or would help a complete stranger."

I thought about what he was saying. "You mean like the hearing-impaired woman in our workshop."

"Exactly," he said. "That's when I knew you were more than a pretty face. You were the only one who noticed that she was struggling. But you didn't just notice, you spoke up and changed seats with her. You showed compassion." He looked down for a moment, then back up. "That's what my wife would have done."

I looked at him softly. "You speak almost reverently of your wife," I said. "But she left you. Why did she leave?"

He was quiet for a moment, then said, "It wasn't her choice to leave. She was five months pregnant when she had a hemorrhage in the night and died. I wasn't with her. I should have been, but I wasn't. I was away on a business trip. I wasn't there when she needed me." His eyes welled up. "Now you know my simple truth."

As I looked at him my eyes filled with tears too. I pulled him in to me and, for a moment, just held him against my breast. Then I said, "There's something I need to tell you too."

Sensing the gravity of my tone he sat back up.

"When you said the other night that you felt I was hiding something, you were right." I took a deep breath and leaned back to look into his eyes. "My mother didn't die of cancer. She committed suicide."

Zeke frowned. "I'm sorry."

"You're the first person I've ever told that to. Ever. I didn't even tell my husband."

"He didn't know how your mother died?"

"No. But he wouldn't have cared anyway."

He continued to look at me sympathetically.

"As long as I knew her she struggled with depression. By the time she killed herself, it was her fifth attempt. The first time she tried I blamed myself. I wasn't even ten years old and I was certain that it was my fault.

"By her third attempt, I was eleven, and my feelings had changed. I was scared and confused, but more than that, I was angry. I wondered how I could mean so little to her that she could just leave me. What does that say about me?" I looked at him. "I've carried the shame of her abandonment my entire life.

"Since then I've looked for validation of myself in every relationship and ended up holding so tight that I squeezed the life out of them. I just wanted someone to prove to me that I was worth sticking around for. I wanted to know that I was worth loving. But the more I chased it, the faster it fled. Knowing your self-worth isn't something others can validate. You either believe it or you don't. I never have."

"Faith," he said softly. "Having a sense of self-worth is an act of faith." He looked at me for a moment, then said, "Kim, your mother wasn't running from you. She was running from herself. When someone's depressed, it's like they're trapped in a burning high-rise. No one wants to jump out of a sixteenth-floor window, but if it's that or be burned alive, they don't feel like they have a choice. I know."

"How do you know?"

"I'm not as far removed from it as you might think."

Something about what he'd said filled me with fear. "What do you mean?"

"I read somewhere that authors are twice as likely to commit suicide than the average person." He looked into my eyes. "They're right."

Fear's grip tightened. "What are you saying?"

He hesitated for a moment, then said, "It was right after my wife died when I tried to kill myself."

"What?"

"I tried to kill myself by overdosing on painkillers. I was revived at the hospital. I'm alive today because I botched my suicide attempt."

At that moment something happened to me. Something I couldn't explain and couldn't resist. An evil slithered from the darkest recesses of my mind, a fear I hadn't felt since childhood, a thick black serpent that wrapped around my chest, cinching tighter and tighter until I couldn't breathe. I couldn't speak. I couldn't think.

At that moment I wasn't in Vermont. I was a little girl standing in the doorway of her mother's bedroom looking at the blood running down her mother's arms, screaming at her to put down the knife. Everything around me turned to white. I began shaking uncontrollably. "No."

Zeke reached out for me. "Kim . . . what's going on?"

"No," I said, suddenly drawing away from him. "No. I can't do this. I can't go through that again."

"Kim, I'm not suicidal. Listen to me. It was a really hard time."

"Life is always hard. It's always hard. I can't do it. I can't." Tears ran down my cheeks in a steady current. I felt like the world was spinning. I felt nauseous. "I'm so sorry, I can't."

"Things are different now. It was a phase. A dark phase."

My body was shaking and I began rocking back and forth. "I'm so sorry. I'm so sorry. I'm so sorry. I'm so sorry."

"Kim, I won't leave you. Ever. I promise."

I covered my eyes with my hand. "I'm sorry. I can't believe you. There are no promises in hell." Leaving my bags of presents, I opened the car door and ran into the hotel.

The night was a blank. I don't remember going back to my room. I don't remember getting undressed or hiding under the covers. All I remember was darkness.

CHAPTER Twenty-seven

*Why must I prove to myself over and over
that I am my own worst enemy?*

Kimberly Rossi's Diary

The conference was over. Everything was over. I woke to someone knocking on my door. "Kim? Honey?"

I lay in bed with the lights out, the closed shutters glowing from the morning sun. I felt as if I had an emotional hangover. I didn't want to see anyone. I wanted the outside world to just go away. I wanted to go away.

"Kim, it's Samantha. Are you there? I'm going to call security."

"Hold on," I said, groaning. I got up, pulled on a robe, then walked to the door, opening it just enough to peer out.

Samantha looked at me with a concerned expression. I'm sure I looked awful. "Honey, where have you been?"

"I went away with Zeke."

"Did he do something to you?"

"No. I left him."

"May I come in?"

I moved back from the door. Samantha stepped into the room and put her arms around me. "I'm so sorry."

After a minute I asked, "Do you know what day it is?"

"It's Monday," she said.

"What time is it?"

"It's almost nine. Hotel check-out time is eleven. And I have news. Cowell's confirmed. He's speaking at noon. What time is your flight home?"

My mind was so jumbled that it took me a moment to remember. "Three, three ten. Something like that." I sat down on the corner of the bed. Samantha sat next to me. She took my hand and held it in her lap.

"I don't even care if I see him," I said.

"Zeke?"

"Cowell," I said.

"Of course you do," Samantha said. "You've waited years for this. You're not going to miss it. I won't let you."

"I just can't go out."

"No," she said. "You're going through with this. No excuses, no regrets. You'll be angry at yourself if you miss it."

After a minute I took a deep breath. "All right."

"All right you'll go with me to his speech?"

I nodded. "I still need to get ready and pack."

"Okay. I'll go save us some seats."

"It's not until noon."

"There's already a line. This is going to be huge. So don't you dare stand me up. I'll be inside the ballroom waiting for you with a seat."

"I'll be there."

"Promise?"

"I promise."

She hugged me. "I'm sorry things didn't work out." She kissed me on the cheek, then walked out of the room.

I lay back for almost twenty minutes, then undressed and went in to shower. I sat under the hot water for a long time, trying to avoid a panic attack. My mind was a labyrinth of thoughts. I had waited years to meet H. T. Cowell. So why was my mind fixated on another man?

CHAPTER

Twenty-eight

Ironically, what makes an author popular is not shouting to the masses but rather quiet, solitary whispers.

Kimberly Rossi's Diary

More than two hours before Cowell's speech the room was already filled to capacity. There were at least quadruple the number of people in the room than had even attended the conference. I knew that Cowell's return was a big deal to me, but I had failed to realize that it was a big deal to millions of people—like *finding Jimmy Hoffa's body* big. There were television cameras lining both walls of the ballroom and at least a couple dozen photographers sitting on the floor in front of the dais.

I looked around for Samantha for nearly ten minutes, finally finding her in the front row. "How did you get front-row seats?" I asked.

"When I left your room they had the ballroom doors locked and there was already a long line to get in, so I sneaked in through the employee service entrance."

"You were serious about getting a good seat," I said.

"I did it for you," she said. "After the man bomb I thought you needed it."

"Thank you."

"My pleasure," she said. "How are you feeling now?"

I couldn't answer. My eyes immediately started to well up.

"Still bad," she said. "I'm sorry. Love's a mess."

"Then why are we romance writers?"

"Someone needs to clean it up."

People continued to crowd into the ballroom, and still there were long lines outside the ballroom doors. Then a fire marshal walked into the room, and security began turning people away.

The excitement in the room was palpable. At noon the lights went down and the room fell into a hush. A single spotlight cast a broad light on the podium. Then there was a slight ripple of light on the curtain and I could see that someone was walking behind it, looking for the opening. Then a single hand reached out.

I once spoke to someone who had been to a Beatles concert at the height of Beatlemania. She said as the curtain lifted just enough to reveal the Beatles' feet and ankles, girls began fainting around her. That's what it felt like. Even with my heart aching, I could feel the collective energy in the room just waiting to explode. Suddenly the curtain parted.

"There he is," Samantha said.

The entire room fell into total silence as the curtain was pulled back and a man emerged from the darkness. For a moment I was speechless. It was him.

CHAPTER Twenty-nine

The difference between fiction and nonfiction is that fiction must follow rules of legitimacy. Reality doesn't.

Kimberly Rossi's Diary

H. T. Cowell looked the way I envisioned Tolstoy would look. He wasn't tall but he was dignified and straight and, as Zeke had ventured, old. He wore round wire-rimmed glasses and his hair and the beard that covered his entire chin were almost white. He walked slowly to the podium. For just a moment the audience was silent as the sound of his footsteps echoed in the room. Then the assault of the paparazzi began. The electric clicking and whirring of cameras was accompanied by bright, staccato flashes.

"You were right," Samantha said. "He's old."

"He's ancient," I said. "But he looks . . . right."

He was immaculately dressed in clothes that appeared custom tailored: dark wool slacks, a cashmere jacket, and an oxford shirt, which he wore open without a tie. As he stepped up to the microphone it seemed that the world around me disappeared. But it wasn't just me who had fallen into a trance; everyone seemed similarly hypnotized. The experience was like waiting for a monk who had taken a lifetime vow of silence to speak his first word. We waited in breathless anticipation.

He took a square piece of paper from his breast pocket,

unfolded it, and set it on the lectern. Then he lightly tapped the microphone, cleared his throat, and leaned forward until his lips were nearly on the appliance.

"Is this working?" he asked gruffly into the microphone. There were a few audible responses from the back of the room and he nodded. "Thank you."

He stood rigid as a signpost as he slowly surveyed the room with an unmistakable confidence, as if he were still deciding whether or not the congregation was worthy of him. Then he leaned forward again.

"Books are important things."

The simple words reverberated with authority throughout the darkened room. It was like God had spoken.

"Books are more than paper and glue and ink. They are more than digital imprints. They are sparks. Sparks that ignite fires. Sparks that ignite revolutions. Every major revolution began with a book." He looked around the room again as if ensuring that every eye was on him. They were.

"Every major religious revolution started with a book. The Bible, the Talmud, the Koran, the Tipitaka, the Tao Te Ching, the Book of Mormon, *Dianetics*—all these faiths have books at their foundations. Billions of people have followed a specific life path because of a book.

"Every political revolution began with a book. From John Stuart Mill's *On Liberty* to Karl Marx's *Communist Manifesto* to Hitler's *Mein Kampf*.

"Every cultural and societal revolution began with a book. Harriet Beecher Stowe's *Uncle Tom's Cabin*, the book that Abraham Lincoln said started a very big war, not only ignited the Civil War but led to the ongoing war for civil rights, not just for blacks in America, but for all races. Then there's Rachel Carson's *Silent Spring*, which began the green movement.

"These powerful, world-changing books did not spontaneously appear. They were not conceived by committee or board. They were created in one mind, by one author. Many of you are here today because you desire to be an author. You may not have understood the power or implications of your desire, but you have desired well.

"But greater than the desire to be an author is the desire to write something of consequence. To write truth. Such an author is rare." He again cleared his throat. "Perhaps it is a good thing, though. The world can only handle so much revolution." He stopped and took several gulps from a bottle of water. "When such writers come along, we should revere them. We should understand that we are in the presence of greatness.

"That is why I'm especially honored today to introduce an author who has written truths that have captured the world's imagination. I am honored to introduce Mr. H. T. Cowell."

A discernible gasp rose from the audience. Someone behind me said out loud what I was thinking, likely what we were all thinking. *That's not Cowell?*

Samantha leaned into me. "It's not him. That's not Cowell."

The man continued. "H. T. Cowell is one of those rare breeds of authors who has made a difference in this world. His first book, *The Tuscan Promise,* defined a genre and launched a thousand writers and ten thousand imitations.

"A lesser mind might attempt to discount the influence of Cowell's works by saying he only wrote romance. *Only*. As if romance were of no consequence. Romance is the thing that dreams are made of and all great human endeavors are borne of dreams."

He paused, and again his gaze panned the audience. "Ladies and gentlemen, it is my profound honor to give you H. T. Cowell."

The entire audience rose to their feet, including me. For a moment there was no one. Then the curtain parted. Zeke walked out onto the stage.

CHAPTER

Thirty

Sometimes we think we know the author from his book, only to learn that we didn't even know his book.

Kimberly Rossi's Diary

Zeke hugged the speaker, who turned and walked back to the curtain. Zeke followed the man with his gaze, then turned back to the audience, which was still applauding wildly. Except for me. I couldn't move.

"Thank you," he said, raising his hand. "Thank you. You're too kind. Please sit down." The applause only slightly diminished. "Please."

It took several minutes before everyone sat.

"I'd like to thank my agent, Mr. Harvey Yospe, for that eloquent, not-so-modest introduction." His eyes scanned the audience as if he were looking for someone. Then his eyes met mine. I was frozen. He held my gaze for a moment, then turned away.

"It's been a while since I've stood before an audience. A long while. I've missed this.

"I don't title my speeches like I do my books, but I noticed that the hosts of this noble event have saved me the trouble. They appropriately named my talk *Why I Stopped Writing*. So that is what I will talk about.

"I will never forget the day that Mr. Yospe called me at my home in Bethlehem, Pennsylvania. Rarely in life does our reality exceed our dreams. For me, that was the first of many such days. At the time I was a high school English teacher with a very modest salary. To celebrate our good fortune my wife, Emma, and I splurged. I took her to Pizza Hut."

The audience laughed.

"The book he was interested in was *The Tuscan Promise*. Three weeks after I hired Mr. Yospe as my agent, the roller coaster began. My book went into a publisher's auction, selling for more than two million dollars. Overnight I was a multimillionaire. Then the movie rights sold. Big directors and big actors signed on. I was asked, or at least allowed, to co-write and co-produce the movie's screenplay. Truly, my life changed overnight.

"Some of you are here, presumably, because you want to be me. Or, at least, to be *like* me. You want to experience the Limousine Lifestyle of the Bestselling Author that my esteemed colleague Ms. McCullin talked about earlier from this very stage.

"I realize that, to a hopeful author, I am the dream. I know this. Five years after I began writing, Scott Simon on National Public Radio asked me, 'What does it feel like to have the life that thousands of aspiring writers covet?' I replied, 'Blessed.'" Zeke nodded slowly. "*Blessed*, I said." Then his expression changed. "Blessed," he repeated more softly. "Just six months later I would have changed that word to *cursed*.

"My wife, Emma, the love of my life, was a very private person. Private and shy. Almost pathologically shy. She was that way when I met her, dated her, and married her. She was also sweet and loving and content with the simple life we had when I was a teacher. I suppose we were poorly paired in this regard because I was not content. I wanted more. And I went headlong after it.

"After things took off in my career, she was quite uncomfortable with the invasion of our privacy. I thought I could temper the differences in our personalities by appearing camera shy. No pictures of me were put on my books. I rarely did television appearances, and newspaper interviewers were required to display a picture of my latest book instead of me.

"Once *People* magazine wanted to do a photo spread of the Cowell family. I knew it was a privilege. My publisher had pushed hard for the publicity, but Emma was mortified. We considered alternate ways of making the shoot happen until the photographer insisted on coming to our home and taking pictures of Emma and me cooking together. If you haven't noticed, *People* is big on kitchen shots. That doomed the photo shoot. While every author on the planet was begging for media attention, I did my best to shun it.

"But being mysterious only fueled the public's interest and curiosity. Book sales continued to grow. And, with each book, each movie, each multimillion-dollar advance, the quiet life Emma and I had together faded a little bit more. My love slowly became a stranger to me—part of a former life I sometimes barely recognized anymore.

"I was gone almost all the time, on tour or speaking. Even touring I still maintained some anonymity. Photographs were not allowed. I grew a beard and wore dark glasses indoors even before Bono made it cool. Yes, the pay was good." He shook his head. "Actually, it was obscene—thirty thousand to fifty thousand dollars for a forty-minute speech. That was more than my entire annual salary just a few years earlier.

"And as the books kept coming, the powers that be pressured me for more. Two a year. Then three. I learned to write in airplanes and airports and in private suites in luxury hotels in cities that I never really got to see. I simultaneously went everywhere and nowhere.

"When I wasn't touring in the U.S., there was Europe, Canada, South America, then Asia. And with each flight I put more miles between Emma and me, figuratively as well as literally. It was ironic, I suppose. Emma was the love of my life. I wrote my first book and dedicated it to her because she was my inspiration." His eyes turned dark. "She inspired me right out of her life.

"I knew we were going the wrong way. But I kept telling her it was only going to be a little while longer." He scratched his head. "I was right. Just not the way I meant.

"I didn't know the full extent of her pain; she wasn't a complainer, but she did become more withdrawn. She once said to me, 'Things are different with us.' I said, 'Yes, they're better. We have a beautiful home, nice cars, nice vacations, everything we always wanted.' She looked at me sadly, then said, 'I already had everything I wanted.' Then she said, 'But now I've lost you.'

"I was in Chicago on a book tour when it occurred to me that a child might be the solution to our marital rift. We had planned to have children one day. Maybe, I reasoned, if we had a baby, Emma wouldn't feel so alone. Maybe she wouldn't be so sad. Two months later she got pregnant. And I was gone when she found out. I was gone when she had her first doctor appointment. I was gone when she learned it was going to be a little girl.

"For the most part, the pregnancy went well, nothing unusual. Then one time, this one time . . ." His voice cracked. "Emma was five months pregnant. I was packing to leave for another event when she said to me, 'I need you to stay.' I can't explain it, but her voice was different this time. There was something unusual about the way she asked. I looked in her eyes and I saw someone reaching out for me. Someone desperate. Someone I used to know.

"Something told me that it was a turning point in our marriage. I knew I needed to stay. I knew the former me, the man who married her, would have stayed." His voice fell with shame. "But Emma was right. I wasn't that man anymore. And I didn't stay. There were ten thousand strangers in an auditorium in Dallas who had shelled out thirty-seven bucks apiece to see me. Strangers. I chose them over my love."

At this moment he paused and I could see him change with emotion. I could feel his pain. "I was still in Dallas when the phone call came. Emma had hemorrhaged in the night. She bled to death."

Someone behind me gasped. The entire audience was still. Many were weeping. Zeke took off his glasses and wiped his eyes.

"She bled to death because I wasn't there. I don't know if she somehow knew—if perhaps she had had a premonition—but whether she knew or not doesn't matter. She was hanging over a cliff and she cried out to me to save her, and I . . ." He paused. "I let her go. Somewhere along the line I had traded in my heart for a check and a temporary seat on a bestseller list."

People around me were sniffing and rubbing their eyes with tissues. I couldn't keep the tears from rolling down my face.

"Coming home to an empty house—there was no home anymore. Only then did I fully understand that *she* was my home.

"I disappeared. I drank to take the edge off my pain. Then I kept drinking to stop my heart. But that wasn't working, so I tried to overdose on painkillers. My housecleaner found me unconscious and called 911. She saved my life." He paused and looked out over the audience. "Why did I stop writing? I stopped writing because I was a fraud. I had betrayed love, so I was no longer worthy to write about it."

I could hear Samantha's stilted breathing. It matched my own. Zeke took a deep breath.

"So, my dear aspiring writers, here's a nickel's worth of advice from a man who's reached the pinnacle of success and thrown himself off. You have this beautiful dream before you and some of you are waiting for it to happen for your life to begin. I'm not here to take away your dreams. We need dreams. But you're in the middle of life right now. Never trade what you love for what's behind curtain B. Never. I would give everything I have, everything I've experienced, to see my love sitting in the front row right now." He took a deep breath. "I would give anything to be you—anonymous and hopeful you." His voice cracked with emotion. "I would give anything to be a poor English teacher in Bethlehem, Pennsylvania."

He turned and walked away. For a moment all four hundred–plus of us sat in stunned silence. Then the audience burst into thunderous applause and a standing ovation. Zeke never returned to accept it.

CHAPTER

Thirty-one

The times we most want to forget are likely the ones we never will.

Kimberly Rossi's Diary

When the house lights rose, I sat there, paralyzed with emotion. My face was streaked with tears. The people around me began to rise, moving out of the room slowly, as if in a daze. I just sat there wiping my eyes.

"Did you know any of that?" Samantha asked.

"I didn't know it was him."

"You need to talk to him."

Tears filled my eyes. "It's too late," I said. "I already ruined it. He'll just think I want H. T. Cowell." I breathed out slowly. "It's time for me to go home."

With the crowds milling about it took us nearly half an hour to get a taxi. Samantha's flight was thirty minutes before mine, and I was a little nervous that she might miss it, but she wasn't. "Stop worrying about other people's worries," she said. "You have enough of your own. Besides, I've slept in airports before. It's no big deal."

"I'm going to miss you," I said.

"No you're not," she said. She kissed my cheek. "We're going to keep in touch."

We got to the airport with a few minutes to spare. Samantha was on a different airline and we stopped at her terminal first. I got out with her.

"I'm so glad I met you," she said.

"Me too. You saved me."

"No, you saved me. You have my number. You need to come see me in Montana. I'll take you horseback riding after the snow's gone."

"Next summer," I said.

"Next summer is perfect," she said. "I'm holding you to it." We hugged. As we embraced she whispered into my ear, "I'm sorry things didn't work out with Zeke. But you wouldn't trade it, would you? I mean, how many people get to break H. T. Cowell's heart?"

I smiled sadly. "Just two of us, I guess."

"You watch, you'll probably end up in one of his books. I can see it now: *The Mistletoe Inn*."

"I hope not."

"And I hope so." She kissed me, then reached down and grabbed her bag. "Next summer," she said. "Au revoir."

"Good-bye," I said. She turned and walked into the terminal. I got back into the taxi. "Delta, please."

"Headed home?" the driver asked.

"Yes."

"Just in time for Christmas. Did you have a good stay in Vermont?"

"I don't know," I said.

The driver said nothing.

CHAPTER

Thirty-two

We cannot run fast enough to escape some failures.

Kimberly Rossi's Diary

On the flight back to Denver my mind kept changing channels. *If only I had known the whole story,* I thought. But that's the point of love, isn't it? We never know the whole story. The true test of our hearts is how we respond with what we have. Zeke had put himself out there, and I had rejected him. I had failed miserably. I had failed him. He was a beautiful soul, more than I deserved. I hoped he was okay, then I thought, *Don't flatter yourself. He's H. T. Cowell. I'm sure there are already a thousand women lined up for the chance you just blew. Especially after his real love story hits the press. It's better than any of the love stories he's ever written.*

The flight home was direct and, with the time change, I landed just before sunset at around 5 p.m. In my absence the city had been hit by several large snowstorms and from the air Denver looked like a ruffled, white linen sheet.

I picked up my bag and took the shuttle out to my car, which wasn't easy to find since it looked like an igloo covered with more than a foot of snow. I got my snow brush from the backseat, dug out my car, then drove home to Thornton.

My apartment was as dark and cold as I felt inside. I had

forgotten how quiet it was. I switched on the lights, turned up the heat, undressed, and took a warm shower. A half hour later, as my water heater began to run out of hot water, I got out and dressed, then went to make myself some dinner. My refrigerator was pretty much bare, so I made some ramen noodles, then drove to the grocery store to pick up some food.

As the cashier rang up the woman in front of me, I examined her purchases. Along with her groceries she had a mass-market paperback romance, the kind usually referred to as a "bodice ripper," with a long-haired, bare-chested hunk on the cover.

"We don't sell as many of those as we used to," the checker said to the woman. "These days, people just download them from the Internet."

"I'm old-fashioned," the woman said. "I still like the feel of paper. And I like to read in the bath. I'd probably just drop an e-book in the water."

"I know what you mean. If I really like an author, sometimes I'll buy the e-book and the paper book." She finished ringing the woman up. "That'll be forty-nine-oh-five. You can scan your card right there."

As the woman ran her credit card through the reader, the cashier said, "I heard on the news that H. T. Cowell is coming out with another book."

The woman looked up with interest. "I thought he was dead."

"No. He just stopped writing for a while. But he's come out of retirement."

"I loved his books," she said.

"Don't we all? I've already ordered it online."

"Thanks for the tip."

"No problem. Have a good day." The cashier turned to me. "Evening, darling. Paper or plastic?"

"Plastic, please."

She began ringing up my items. "That's a good deal on those red peppers. Do you have a customer discount card?"

"Yes. Right here." I handed her my card.

She scanned it, then handed it back. "That will save you a little."

As she bagged my purchases, I said, "I overheard some of your conversation. I've met H. T. Cowell."

"Is that right? What was he like?"

Unexpectedly my eyes filled up with tears. "He was . . ." A tear fell down my cheek. I suddenly wished I hadn't said anything. "Sorry," I said, wiping my eyes with my sleeve.

The woman smiled a little. "I used to get the same way whenever I'd read one of his books. The man makes women cry for a living." She finished ringing up my groceries. "Have a good evening."

"You too."

As I walked to my car I realized that I would never be able to escape him.

CHAPTER Thirty-three

Routine is the refuge of cowards, failures, and the wise.

Kimberly Rossi's Diary

I was glad to be back at work on Monday morning. I needed something to get my mind off my pain. I had only been in my office for ten minutes before Steve came in.

"I'm so glad you're back. Rachelle's so distracted with her upcoming nuptials that she keeps making mistakes. How was your book conference?"

"It was a writers' conference," I said. "It was good."

"Good," he echoed. "Well, if you hit it big with your book, that doesn't mean you can just leave us all behind."

"I wouldn't be looking for my replacement anytime soon."

His smile fell. "I shouldn't be sorry to hear that, but I am. You deserve a break."

"Thanks, Steve."

"Welcome home," he said.

The day was busy. Car sales are always big right before Christmas. Our clientele were the kind of people who would call on Christmas Eve and say, "I want a new car for my husband delivered on Christmas Eve with a ribbon on it" and we'd move heaven and earth to make it happen. All morning long I had a steady flow of clients in my office. I finally got a short lunch break at one.

As I walked into the break room, Rachelle was eating lunch with Charlene, one of our newer salespeople. Rachelle looked up at me as I entered. "Hey, Kim, didn't you just meet H. T. Cowell at some conference?"

Now Zeke has followed me to work. I nodded. "Yeah. He was the keynote speaker." I walked over and took a can of Diet Coke from the refrigerator.

"That's so cool," Rachelle said. "There was an article about him in *USA Today* this morning. And you know how no one knows what he looks like? There was almost a full-page picture of him. He's gorgeous."

"What did the article say?" I asked.

"It said he's coming out with a new book and the movie rights have already been sold. And he finally told why he stopped writing. It was because his wife died. I mean, is that romantic or what? After all his success, she committed suicide."

"Why would she do that?" Charlene said. "People die for that kind of life, not because they got it."

"She didn't kill herself," I said. "It was an accident."

Rachelle shook her head. "No, she killed herself. I just read it in the paper."

"Then whoever wrote the article got it wrong," I said. "His wife was pregnant and died of a hemorrhage. It was an accident."

Rachelle didn't back down. "And you know this because . . . ?"

"Because he told me," I snapped. The sound of my voice fairly echoed, leaving me embarrassed. The two women just looked at me.

"H. T. Cowell told you how his wife died?" Rachelle said.

"You talked to H. T. Cowell?" Charlene asked.

"Yes."

Rachelle looked at me skeptically. "You mean, like, not in a crowd, but one-on-one."

I felt like I was talking to six-year-olds. Obnoxious six-year-olds. "Yes, I talked to him like we're talking now."

Rachelle looked like it was all she could do not to laugh. "So you and H. T. Cowell are now BFFs."

"I didn't say that."

"But you're talking about really personal things . . ."

I breathed out slowly to relieve my annoyance with her. "Yes. We went on a few dates."

Rachelle looked so incredulous I thought she was going to burst out laughing. "You dated H. T. Cowell?" she said.

"Yes, I dated H. T. Cowell. Why is that so hard to believe?"

The two women just grinned like they were sharing an inside joke.

"I don't know," Rachelle said. "Why wouldn't we believe that you're secretly dating one of the most famous writers in the world?"

Both women continued to gape at me. After a moment I said, "You're right. I wouldn't believe it either. Why would he date someone like me?"

I took my drink back to my office, shut my door, and cried.

CHAPTER Thirty-four

I'm not sure where home is anymore, but I want to be there.

Kimberly Rossi's Diary

My father called that night on the way home from work. "You didn't call."

"Sorry. I wasn't feeling well last night. How are you feeling?"

"I'm fine," he said dismissively. "How was the rest of the retreat?"

"It was fine."

"For as much as it cost, I expected more than *fine*."

"Sorry, it was great. It was much better than the San Francisco one."

"How was Cowell? Was he worth the money?"

I hesitated. "I'd rather not talk about it."

"So the conference was good, but Cowell was a disappointment."

"I didn't say that. It's just . . ." There was a long pause. "It's just complicated."

I'm sure my father knew that there was more; he could read me like a Times Square billboard, but he also knew when not to press. "You're still coming out for Christmas, aren't you?"

"Yes. I'll be there Sunday night if that's okay."

"Of course."

"I'd come sooner if I could, but work's crazy and I was gone all last week."

"I understand."

I sighed. "I've got to get out of here."

"Maybe it's time you moved back, girl."

For the first time ever I didn't launch into a defense. After a moment I said, "Maybe it is."

To my surprise my father didn't jump on my concession. Either he was too surprised or he heard the defeat in my voice. Probably the latter. He finally said, "I'm just glad you're coming when you can. You're Christmas to me."

"Thank you, Dad. I'll see you Sunday night."

As I hung up the phone I pushed out the thought that this might be the last Christmas we'd ever have together.

CHAPTER Thirty-five

Finally, good news. Finally.

Kimberly Rossi's Diary

The Las Vegas casinos do a large advertising push outside the United States during the holidays, so the airport is always crowded around Christmas with international tourists. My plane landed at nine-thirty, and after fighting the crowds for almost an hour, I retrieved my bag and met my father at the curb.

As usual he got out of his car to greet me. I was stunned when I saw him. As thin as he already was at Thanksgiving, he'd probably lost another ten or more pounds. Also, his eyes looked hollow and ringed as if he hadn't slept well for a while. It took effort not to show my concern. In spite of his condition his face beamed with joy. "How was your flight, sweetie?"

"You know, the usual holiday insanity."

As he put his arms around me I could feel how different his body was. The cancer was taking its toll. I still couldn't believe that they were making him wait until February to operate. It was obvious to me that at the rate he was deteriorating, February might be too late.

"It's so good to see you," he said, kissing my cheek. He opened my door and took my bag and set it in the backseat.

I sadly noticed that he had a little trouble lifting my bag. He'd lost muscle as well.

As we were driving away from the airport he turned off the radio, then said to me, "I have some good news."

I looked over at him. "You're getting married."

"I said *good* news."

"Tell me."

"I have a new oncologist."

"At the VA?"

He smiled, excited to answer. "No, at the Henderson Clinic. And they're going to operate this coming Friday."

My heart leapt. "What?"

"It gets better. The doctor's name is Lance Bangerter. He's ranked as one of the top-five colon cancer experts in the country."

Even though my father was merging onto the freeway I leaned over and hugged him. "Thank you, thank you, thank you!" My eyes welled up. "You have no idea how much this means to me."

"I think I do," he replied. "And thank God. He's the one who arranged it."

"I thought your insurance didn't cover the institute."

"It doesn't," he said.

"I don't care," I said. "Whatever it takes. I'll give you every penny I have."

He looked at me lovingly. "I know you would, sweetheart. But you don't have to. Things have worked out. Fate has smiled on me."

"It couldn't smile on a more deserving man."

"I don't know about that," he said. "But the longer I live the more certain I am that God is in the details."

We pulled into the driveway. My father wouldn't let me carry in my bag, and even though it pained me to see him struggle with my suitcase, I knew it would be demoralizing to him if I didn't let him take it. As we walked into the house I noticed the fish tank was gone.

"Where are your fish?"

"They died," he said, shaking his head. "So I sold everything. I guess I chose the wrong hobby."

I looked around the house. As usual, my father had put up his Christmas tree in the front room to the side of the television. It was one of those expensive fake PVC ones that looked real. It had red and silver baubles and strings of flashing colored lights and a lit star on top. There were presents under the tree, which I knew were for me. I was dismayed that in addition to the conference he'd bought me more gifts.

"Those had better not be for me," I said.

"Who else would they be for?" he said.

"You already gave me the writers' retreat."

"Let an old man have his fun."

"You're not old," I said. Then I smiled. "But you are fun."

After we were in my room, my father said, "I guess I'll turn in. I'm sure you're exhausted; it's almost midnight in Denver."

I knew that he was much more tired than I was, but I said, "Good night, Dad. I'll see you in the morning."

As he started out of my room I said, "Dad."

He turned back.

"Thank you for changing your mind about that clinic."

He smiled. "Remember, sweetheart. Our best years are still to come."

After he left I undressed, turned out the light, and climbed under the covers. As I lay in bed I actually smiled. Things hadn't been going my way lately, but now the most important thing had. My father was getting the care he needed. I didn't know how we'd pay for the treatment, but at the moment, I didn't care. All that mattered was that he had a chance. I knew that in spite of all my pain I was still a very lucky woman. It made me sad that I wanted to call Zeke and tell him.

CHAPTER Thirty-six

Change is coming. I don't know how I know this, but I can feel it.

Kimberly Rossi's Diary

I got up early Christmas Eve morning, put on my sweats, and went for a walk. The temperature was in the high sixties, again a veritable heat wave compared to Denver. *Why do I live in Denver?*

There was already heavy traffic on the main roads, and I guessed that the procrastinators were out in force frantically pursuing those last-minute Christmas purchases.

Looking out over the horizon I breathed in the luxurious dry desert air. It was time for a change in my life. A new year was coming. A new year, a new life. Denver is a nice city but Las Vegas was home. I was finally ready to come home. I needed to be home. My father would need help through his recovery. I owed him that. More than that, I wanted to help him. He was the one person who had never let me down. It was about time I returned the favor.

The more I thought about moving back the more it made sense. There were dozens of car dealerships in Las Vegas and at least three Lexus dealerships. With my experience and references I wouldn't have trouble finding a job. I would miss Steve. But not anyone else. Not Rachelle. Definitely not Rachelle.

The idea of moving home filled me with joy. I wasn't scheduled to be back at work until January 2. That gave me the entire week after Christmas to find employment and get things in order. I just needed to make it through Christmas.

CHAPTER *Thirty-seven*

For individuals, as for nations, there are days that live in infamy.

Kimberly Rossi's Diary

The power of Christmas is its capacity to evoke memories. For most, the familiar songs and decorations bring back cherished feelings of Christmas past—fond memories of shared experiences with family and loved ones.

For my father and me, that power was turned against us and Christmas brought out the worst of memories. Crippling memories. Christmas Day 1995 was the day we found my mother dead.

For me 1995 carried its own special horror. It was still morning. I had opened my presents with my father, as my mother was in bed with a migraine.

I still remember what I got that year. Trauma has a way of indelibly linking the incidentals to the profound. I received boxes of Swedish Fish and Lemonheads, some clothes, the album *Pieces of You* by Jewel, and my big present, a Sony Discman CD player.

I had just opened the last of my gifts when my father got up to check on my mother. It seemed that he was gone a long time and I put on my earphones and started listening to "Who Will Save Your Soul" on my new CD player. Even with the music playing I heard him cry out. I ran into the bedroom to find my father on his knees bent over my mother's still body. He was sobbing.

CHAPTER

Thirty-eight

The truth will set us free not only from external shackles but, more often than not, our own.

Kimberly Rossi's Diary

When I got back to the house, my father was in the kitchen making breakfast. Christmas music was playing.

"Good morning," he said.

"What are we doing today?" I asked.

"We've got cooking to do," he said. "And, of course, dinner at the Jade Dragon."

"Of course," I said. Every Christmas Eve, except during the years I was married to Marcus, my father and I had gone out to dinner for Chinese at the Jade Dragon Restaurant, a Christmas Eve tradition we'd loosely borrowed from our perennial Christmas favorite, *A Christmas Story*—the movie with Ralphie and his Red Ryder BB gun. "I have a little shopping to do."

"Just take the car," he said.

I had already purchased my father's Christmas presents; I just wanted to get out, hoping to keep ahead of my panic attacks. I also wanted to scout out some car dealerships. They were open, of course, and there were people inside. As I said, there are always those last-minute Christmas purchases.

If I was trying to outrun my anxiety, I was failing. You can't outrun fog. As the evening fell my anxiety grew worse. My father recognized it, of course. I'm sure he was expecting it. We went to dinner at six. My father told jokes and funny stories about the VA, but I just grew more somber. We finished our meal and drove home, my father growing increasingly uncomfortable with my moodiness.

As we walked into the house he asked, "What's wrong?"

"You know what's wrong," I said. "I hate Christmas."

"I know," he said. "You always have. At least since . . ."

"Since my mother annihilated it?" I said, saying what he wouldn't.

He paused, and for a moment there was just silence. Then my father said, "Honey, I need to tell you something about your mother."

"I don't want to talk about her."

"I know. And for years I've honored your feelings. But this time, you're going to listen to me. Let's go in the family room."

I was stunned by the gravity of his voice. My father had never before spoken to me this way about my mother. I followed him into the family room and sat down on the couch across from his chair. He took a deep breath and looked at me with a somber expression.

"Kim, it wasn't easy raising you alone, especially after all you went through. But I did my best. I'm sorry I wasn't a better father."

I looked at him incredulously. "Don't say that. You're the best father I could ever have."

"I don't know," he said. "I've always believed in letting you be you and make your own decisions. But sometimes I think that might have been a mistake. There've been times in my life when I've remained silent when I should have spoken up. Like when you married Marcus. I knew he was rotten. I should have told you no. I don't know if you would have listened to me, but I regret not doing more to stop that.

"But there's one thing that I feel even worse about than Marcus and that's your mother. There's something you need to know about her—something that I don't think you fully understand—and you need to understand. You need to listen to me carefully." He leaned forward, and even though he looked old and tired, his eyes were strong and clear. "Kim, you need to know that I not only loved your mother, I still do. And knowing what I know now, I would marry her all over again."

I couldn't believe what he was saying. "Why?"

"I knew your mother at her best. You don't know that side of her, but she was sunshine. She was my one true love. She healed me from the pain of war. She was there in my hardest times. She was there in my nightmares.

"When you were little, you thought your mother's name was Tessa. That's because you heard me call her by my nickname for her, Tesoro. That's Italian for *treasure*. That's what she was to me. My treasure.

"The first years of our marriage were beautiful. She struggled a little with depression, it ran in her family, but she fought it and she always came back.

"It wasn't until after she gave birth to you that she went into the deepest depression I had ever seen in her. It was something chemical. She fought it for years. She did everything every doctor, every counselor, told her to do.

"One time, at a holistic counselor's advice, she went off

all of her medications cold turkey. I sat with her through the night as she went through withdrawal. She sweated out her clothing and shook and wept, but she didn't give up. She did whatever she thought she had to do. Not for herself, but for you and me. But it didn't get better; it got worse. It began to overcome her.

"Depression is a horrible thing. It overtakes a person like a parasite, feeding off their hope and self-esteem until there's nothing left. Mom wasn't trying to run away from you or me, she was trying to run away from the monster that was eating her from the inside out.

"What happened when she took her life was unimaginably painful for you. And for me. But you need to know how hard she fought to be with us. In the end, she lost the battle, but she fought as courageously as anyone I've ever seen." He looked into my eyes. "Now answer me honestly. If cancer overtook me now, would you think that I had abandoned you?"

I began to cry. "Of course not."

"No. You wouldn't. And you shouldn't with your mother. People make judgments about suicide and depression based on their own experience, but that's like me describing the surface of Mars. I've never been there. I can only guess what it's like.

"Depression alters the mind's ability to think rationally. Things that would horrify someone in their right mind suddenly seem like a good idea. Like ending their life. They might even believe that they're doing the right thing for those they love." A tear fell down my father's cheek. "Before her death, she left a letter. In it, she said that she had finally set me and you free to be happy. She thought it was the right thing."

I was quiet for a moment, then said softly, "You want me to forgive her?"

To my surprise he shook his head. "Forgiving her won't help her. She's gone. What I want is for you to forgive yourself."

"Forgive myself for what?"

"One thing I know is that somewhere deep inside, in spite of what we tell ourselves, part of all survivors believe that they could have changed the outcome by doing something different.

"Then we try to ease our pain with anger. But anger isn't strength. It only masks itself as strength. It's weakness. At its core, it's fear. Fear of facing what might be the truth."

I bowed my head. My mind felt as if it were spinning.

"I should have talked to you about this much, much sooner. But for so many years I didn't understand all this myself. I was struggling with my own paradox. You see, Mom's depression changed after she gave birth to you. If she had never given birth . . ."

I looked up. "You're saying it's my fault?"

"Absolutely not," he said firmly. "You had no say in the matter. But I did. And I've wondered so many times . . ." He looked down. When he looked back up there were tears in his eyes. "She knew. In her last letter, she wrote, 'I would do it again for my Kimberly. She is the one beautiful light to shine from my darkness. Even if I cannot be the mother I want to be, the mother she deserves, I have never regretted my decision to have her.'"

My father began to openly cry. Then, at that moment, a dam of emotion broke, flooding through my entire being. I began sobbing. My father came over and put his arms around me as my body heaved.

It took me a while to realize what was happening. After all these years I was finally mourning my mother.

My father held me for a long while. After I finally began to calm, he said, "Let's go to bed." He helped me up and went into the bathroom. He came out holding a warm, wet washcloth, which he handed to me.

"You've been through something traumatic tonight. I want you to not think about it anymore but put this on your face and relax. Your mind needs to rest. An army psychiatrist told me that helps."

"Thank you," I said.

"Kim," he said. "Remember, our best years are ahead of us."

We hugged and I went to my room. I turned out the lights, lay back in bed, and put the hot cloth on my face. I did my best to clear my mind. For the first Christmas Eve in years I felt peace. "Merry Christmas," I said to myself. "And a happy New Year." I quickly fell asleep.

CHAPTER *Thirty-nine*

Nothing done with joy is done in vain.

Kimberly Rossi's Diary

My father woke me the next morning with his Bible in hand and a cheerful "Merry Christmas." It had always been our tradition to read from the second chapter of Luke on Christmas morning. Afterward we went out to the tree and opened presents. I had bought him a big bag of turkey jerky, socks, a plush bathrobe, and a book on raising saltwater fish. "You can take that back," I said.

He had bought me a new laptop computer. "This is too much," I said.

"It's for your writing," he said. "And here." He handed me another present to unwrap. Inside was a describer's dictionary. "I read online that that really helps."

I didn't know what to say. "Dad, no one's going to publish me."

"Who cares?" he said. "I'm not going to get signed by a record label but it doesn't stop me from singing in the shower."

"It should," I said, laughing.

He also laughed. "It should, but it won't. So you write because you love to write. It's how you sing. Remember that."

I couldn't help but smile. "Thanks, Dad."

✦

After we opened our presents we had our traditional Christmas morning breakfast of crepes with apricot jam and whipped cream. My father made the world's best crepes.

"It was a profound night last night," he said as we ate. "How'd you sleep?"

"I slept really well. The best I have in years." I smiled. "At least until I woke with a cold, wet washcloth on my face."

He smiled.

I took another bite of crepe, then said, "I've been doing a lot of thinking. And I think it's time for some change in my life. So I've made a decision. I'm moving back home." I looked into his eyes. "If that's okay."

A smile spread across his face. "That's wonderful."

"That way I can be here if you need any help and just be with you. I miss it here."

"That makes me so happy," he said. "That's the best Christmas present ever."

"Good. So I'll start looking for a job tomorrow." I ate a little more, then I said, "You know, it's strange, but I have a feeling that you're right. Maybe our best years are still to come."

My father, who hadn't stopped smiling since my announcement, said, "Oh, they are, honey. More than you know. Now hurry up and eat. We've got cooking to do."

✦

As we got ready for Christmas dinner I noticed that my father had placed an extra setting at the table. "Will Chuck or Joel be joining us?" I asked.

He shook his head. "No. I'm sorry, I didn't tell you, Chuck passed away."

I stopped washing the potatoes. "When?"

"While you were at the conference. I was with him when he went. I'm grateful for that. No one should die alone."

"How's Joel doing?" I asked. "I was thinking of looking him up while I was here."

"That might not be a good idea," my father said.

"Why is that?"

"His wife came back."

"Really?" I said. "That's a surprise."

"It was for Joel too. He called me two weeks ago and told me that she came to see him. She asked him if he would forgive her and take her back."

"And he took her back?"

"Oh yes. Sometimes, when you least expect it, people do the right thing. And the best news, they're going to start trying to have children."

"He can do that? I mean, physically . . . ?"

"No. They'll have to use insemination. But that's not what makes a man a father."

"Then Alice is coming?"

"No," he said. "Prying her away from her grandchildren will take a lot stronger man than I am."

"Her loss," I said.

"She's perfectly happy with the situation. Something

about grandchildren is magical. I hope to discover that myself someday."

"Pressure," I said. "Then who's coming?"

"Just a business associate of mine. I've been helping him with a project. He lives back east and was here alone on business, so I invited him over. He'll be here in a few minutes."

"What kind of project?" I asked.

"Nothing too exciting. Personnel stuff. He ran into one of my old employees from Maverick. She told him about me and he was looking for someone in Vegas.

"But here's the remarkable part—he's friends with Dr. Bangerter. He's the one who arranged for him to see me. In fact, he has so much clout, Dr. Bangerter actually came to the house to meet with me."

"One of the top oncologists in the country made a house call?"

"I know, you could have knocked me over with a feather. I guess it helps to have the right friends."

"I'm so happy, Dad."

As I went back to the potatoes, the doorbell rang.

"Unless you're expecting someone," my father said, "that's probably our guest. Would you mind getting the door?"

"Sure." I started walking toward the foyer. "What's his name?"

"You'll know," he said.

"Why would I know?"

"Just trust me."

I opened the door. Zeke was standing on our front porch.

CHAPTER

A new song has begun.

Kimberly Rossi's Diary

I just stood there. The moment was like something out of a dream and I was frozen in it, unsure of what to do next.

Zeke smiled. "I take it your father didn't tell you I was coming."

"No."

My father walked up behind me. "Kim, show some manners. Invite Zeke in."

"Sorry," I said, still in shock. I stepped back as Zeke walked into our house. My father and Zeke shook hands.

"How are you, Rob?" Zeke asked.

"Well, thank you. And very grateful. Dr. Bangerter has been very helpful. Thank you for making this possible."

"It's my pleasure," he said.

I stood there, my eyes darting back and forth between the two of them. "How do you know each other?"

"He called," my father said, as if it were just the most natural thing in the world. "He asked for my permission to date my daughter and I said yes. You know, he's the first man you've dated who had the class to call me." He turned back to Zeke. "We're still getting ready to eat. I'll give you two a moment to catch up."

"Thank you," Zeke said.

As my father walked out of the room Zeke turned back to me. "Merry Christmas," he said.

I was still in shock. "Thank you for helping my father."

"I can see why you idolize him. He's a good man."

I stood there still unsure of what to say.

"I'm guessing that you were surprised to learn that Zeke Faulkner and H. T. Cowell are the same man."

"Why didn't you tell me you were H. T. Cowell?"

"You never asked."

"That's not something I usually go around asking people."

He grinned. "That's understandable."

"Why did you say your name was Zeke?"

"I've gone by Zeke my whole life. H. T. stands for Hezekiah Tobias," he said. "Hezekiah. Who names a child Hezekiah? Tell me you wouldn't go by Zeke too."

In spite of my emotion I almost smiled. "Why did you go to the writers' conference?"

"I was invited to speak," he said. "My publisher decided that it would be the perfect timing for my 'coming out,' which is why there was so much national press. But I went to the conference early to be with the unpublished writers. That was for me. I wanted to feel their passion. I wanted to remember why it was I started writing to begin with. If I had told them who I was they would have acted different."

He was right about that. I wouldn't have been able to talk to him.

"I wanted to talk to you after your speech," I said. "But I didn't know what to say after behaving so badly. Twice." I looked into his eyes. "I didn't think you would want to see me."

He looked at me for a moment, then said, "I told you in New York that I had fallen in love with you. I had. After the retreat I couldn't get you off my mind. I wasn't going to give up on love. I did that once before. I wasn't going to do it again."

"How did you find us?"

"That part was easy. You told me that your father had paid for the retreat, so I called the organizers and asked for his contact information. I called your father and introduced myself. I told him that you and I had met at the conference and that I would like his permission to court his daughter and that my intentions were honorable."

"Honorable," I repeated. "He must have loved that."

Zeke smiled. "He seemed impressed. But trust me, he wasn't easy on me. So I thought it best that I flew out to meet him. I told him that we had had a difficult parting and I asked his advice on how best to approach you. He thought that the best time for me to see you would be now. So I made arrangements to return."

"And the doctor?"

"I knew how upset you were about the treatment your father was receiving. I've raised millions of dollars for the Henderson Institute, and Dr. Bangerter once said that if he could ever do anything for me to just ask. So I asked. It was a token of my appreciation to your father for his help. And maybe a little bribe."

"A bribe?"

"It's the law of reciprocity. I knew that if I made some magnanimous gesture you would at least have to give me a chance to win back your love."

"You never lost it," I said.

For a moment we looked at each other, then we kissed.

After several minutes of kissing, Zeke leaned back and said excitedly, "I have a Christmas present for you." He took an envelope from his jacket and handed it to me.

"What is it?"

"Open it."

Inside the envelope was a letter from Trish Todd, an editor at the Simon & Schuster Adult Publishing Group. "What's this?"

"I took your book to my editor and she liked it. The letter says if you're willing to make a few revisions, which I would be happy to help you with, they would like to offer you a contract."

I was speechless. I looked up from the letter. "You mean they're really going to publish my book?"

He smiled. "Yes they are. I also let them know that I would be helping to promote your book with my readers. If I still have any."

"The whole world is waiting for your next book," I said. "Everyone is talking about it." After looking at him for a moment, I said, "Why are you being so good to me?"

He looked at me intensely, then said, "I thought you might ask that. And I am prepared with three answers. First,

I'm a romance writer. I love happy endings. Second, because you are immensely loveable. And third, most of all, I heard the music and I wanted to dance with you."

I looked at him for a moment, then said, "And when the music stops?"

A broad smile slowly crossed his face and he again took me in his arms and we kissed. When we finally parted he said, "When, and if, the music ever stops there's no need to worry."

"Why not?"

"Because when the music stops, that's when we make our own."

EPILOGUE

Zeke stayed with me the week after Christmas. I never went looking for a job; Zeke kept me too busy working on my book. Imagine being tutored by one of the world's greatest authors. He taught me how to be vulnerable in print. He taught me to love my readers. He taught me how to write with honesty.

It was an amazing experience to see how he coaxed words from thin air—like a magician. It seemed to me that his process was more like discovering a book than creating it. William Faulkner once said, "If I had not existed, someone else would have written me, Hemingway, Dostoyevsky, all of us." Zeke believed that. He taught me to believe that as well.

My life is new. On New Year's Eve I went alone to my mother's grave and took her a flower. An anthurium. Somewhere in a recently unlocked room of my mind I remembered that she loved anthuriums. I knelt down and kissed her stone and apologized to her. I thanked her for giving me life at the expense of her own. For the first time in my life I saw her not as a traitor or a failure but as a real person just doing her best. For the first time since I was a child I loved her again. And, not coincidentally, I felt her love.

I tried to get my father to join Zeke and me for dinner that night at a fancy restaurant at the Bellagio. He wouldn't budge. "I'm too old for all that New Year's hoopla," he said. "I just want to go to bed." Later I learned why he had refused. At 12:01 on January 1, 2013, Zeke asked me to marry him. My father was awake when we got home. This time he was happy with my choice.

The ring Zeke had given me that night was on loan from a jewelry store as he wanted to pick out our rings together. (It had a diamond that would have made Catherine McCullin salivate.) The next day we went ring shopping at Tiffany, and as we looked at settings fit for a princess I realized what I really wanted. That evening I asked my father if I could have my mother's tiny half-carat rose-gold engagement ring. Nothing could have made my father happier. It made Zeke happy too.

After our engagement Zeke went back with me to Denver to help move me out of my apartment. He also went with me to the dealership to get my things. I think he especially wanted to go after I told him the story of how Rachelle and Charlene had mocked me when I told them that I had dated H. T. Cowell. As I introduced Zeke to Rachelle and Charlene, he referred to himself as H. T. Cowell. It was the only time I've ever heard him do that. You should have seen their faces. We laughed about it all through dinner.

Zeke had no problem with the idea of moving to Las Vegas, especially while my father was dealing with his cancer. He said that he had always wanted to live in the West. At first I thought he was just being kind, but I learned otherwise. He secretly wanted to be a cowboy, which he ended up writing a book about. (What woman doesn't love a cowboy?) That summer he went with me to Montana to see Samantha and ride horses. He bought a ranch.

My father's surgery and post treatment were successful. Today he is three years in remission. We bought a home just ten minutes away from his. He's still volunteering at the VA, but he's also spending more time with Alice, who it turns out is a rabid H. T. Cowell fan. It's kind of annoying.

As you probably remember, Zeke's return to writing rocked the publishing world, and I traveled all around the world with him on a book tour. London, Paris, Tokyo, Sydney, and Warsaw. He arranged the release of his third book to coincide with the release of mine, *The Mistletoe Promise*. Not surprisingly, both of our books hit the *New York Times* bestseller list—though of course his was number one and mine was eight. Still, I'm now a *New York Times* bestselling author. When we got the advance copy of the bestseller list I think Zeke was happier for me than for himself. Actually, I know he was. Yes, I know I hit the list because of his help—both with his help writing and his legion of fans—but it still feels wonderful. I feel like I've done something that matters. I actually get fan mail.

On May 3, 2014, Zeke and I were married in San Gimignano, Italy, the birthplace of my father's parents. Samantha was my maid of honor. She brought her new husband, Walter. He's a great guy. For the record, I don't think she settled. I'm now thinking of writing a love story that takes place in Italy, and I keep wishing that I had gone to that session at the Mistletoe Inn Writers' Conference. You know the one—*Putting The* Rome *Back in Romance*. Our wedding made all the magazines, which was much better than the last time I got press.

Speaking of which, two months after our wedding I got a call from Marcus. He knew about Zeke and my writing. He wanted to know if I would write a reference letter for him for a high school teaching position. I almost agreed until I thought about those young girls he would be around and declined.

The most important thing Zeke has taught me about love has nothing to do with books. Romance novels are all about desire and happily-ever-after, but happily-ever-after doesn't come from desire—at least not the kind portrayed in pulp romances. Real love is not to desire a person but to desire their happiness—sometimes even at the expense of our own happiness. Real love is to expand our own capacity for tolerance and caring, to actively seek another's well-being. All else is simply a charade of self-interest.

Zeke taught me that. Not through words but by example. He's taught me how to dance. And we're getting good at making our own music.

My father was right all along. The best years of our lives are ahead of us.

✦ ABOUT THE AUTHOR ✦

Richard Paul Evans is the #1 bestselling author of *The Christmas Box*. Each of his more than thirty novels has been a *New York Times* bestseller. There are more than 20 million copies of his books in print worldwide, translated into more than twenty-four languages. He is the recipient of numerous awards, including the American Mothers Book Award, the *Romantic Times* Best Women's Novel of the Year Award, the German Audience Gold Award for Romance, four Religion Communicators Council Wilbur Awards, *The Washington Times* Humanitarian of the Century Award, and the Volunteers of America National Empathy Award. He lives in Salt Lake City, Utah, with his wife, Keri, and their five children. You can learn more about Richard on Facebook at www.facebook.com/RPEfans, or visit his website (and read his weekly blog) at www.richardpaulevans.com.

ABOUT THE AUTHOR

[illegible]

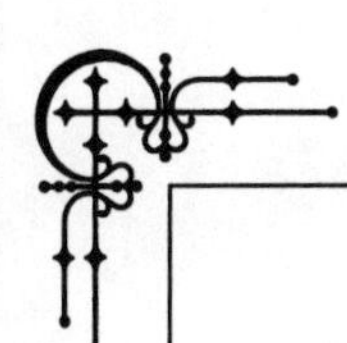
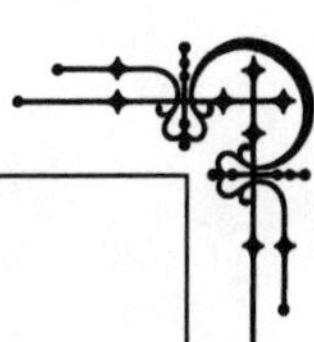

WHAT CHRISTMAS TREATS WOULD YOU SERVE AT THE MISTLETOE INN?

Submit your most beloved recipes at

MISTLETOEINNRECIPES.COM

and Richard will share his favorites!

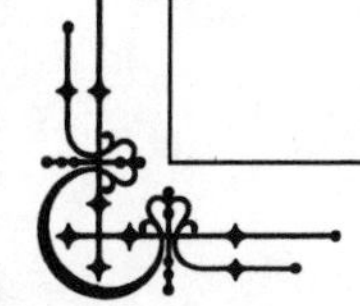